Family Secrets

Book Two
The Annie Velasquez Mystery Series

EJ Kindred

Launch Point Press
Portland, Oregon

Published by Launch Point Press
Portland, Oregon
www.LaunchPointPress.com

The Annie Velasquez Mystery Series
In Harm's Way

Synopsis

Annie Velasquez has been the person of interest in a murder, but one day, she runs into Nicky, the woman she allegedly killed. Unsure if the police believe her, she looks for Nicky herself.

Annie and her brother Joe rebuild their father's bike shop, but thefts and vandalism repeatedly set the project back. A woman drives a truck into the shop, injuring Joe. She is identified as Annie's mother, long believed to be dead. Is she the person responsible for sabotaging Annie's efforts to open the bike shop? Will these family secrets destroy what Annie has fought so hard to build?

Dedication

To Mom (1936 – 2017)

When I was in the second grade, she bought me sets of books that she thought were too advanced for my reading level, but she promised to read them to me. She never did, so I read them myself, and I've never looked back. Thanks, Mom, for my first steps into independence. Sometimes unintended consequences are good ones.

"A woman is like a teabag—you never know how strong
she is until she gets in hot water."
~Eleanor Roosevelt

Chapter One

My Monday went well until I locked eyes with a dead woman.

After picking up materials for the new Velasquez Cycles shop my brother and I decided to build, I stopped at a nearby coffee shop to wait out the warm July rain that started to fall while I was driving. I also figured since I was a diligent worker bee, I deserved a treat for my drive back to the construction site. A steaming hot mocha would fit the bill perfectly.

A cloudburst erupted right when I parked, so I sprinted from my car up the concrete steps to the coffee shop door, hood pulled low against the downpour. As I reached the door, through the water-streaked glass I saw a customer on her way out. I opened the door and found myself face-to-face with an impossibility.

"Nicky?" Electric shock jolted my body and I gasped.

The other woman's hood was up, obscuring much of her face. She held a paper cup with a corrugated shield around it to protect her fingers from the heat of the beverage. At the sound of my voice, she stopped, startled. Her face became pale, and her eyes wide. She turned away and tried to pull her hood further over her face.

"Sorry, you've confused me with someone else," she mumbled.

Without thinking, I reached for her, but she pushed past me and ran to a silver minivan parked at the far end of the lot, throwing her cup to the ground. The plastic lid popped off, and the contents spewed in a steaming arc as the cup rolled.

"Nicky, is that you?" My heart was pounding. I ran after her, my hood falling off. Rain pelted my face. "Nicky! Stop!"

She ignored me and jumped into the van, slamming the door. She backed out of her parking spot in a rush, coming close enough to a couple walking through the lot to force them to run several steps to avoid being hit. The man swore loudly and slapped the van's rear window. She didn't slow at all. She sped out of the coffee shop parking lot, nearly colliding with two cars in the street. Horns blared and tires protested as they slid on the wet pavement. She looked back at me before rounding the corner.

And then she was gone.

I stood in the parking lot, dumbfounded, until the couple approached me. They were angry and upset.

"Are you okay?"

"Yes." The woman's voice was shaky. "That was close." The man put his arm around her shoulders and held her against his chest to comfort her.

After they went inside, I stood outside the door, oblivious to the pounding rain, and stared down the street. Surely I was imagining things. Nicky Fleming, the woman I'd loved and intended to marry, who was killed over a year and a half earlier after causing the death of my beloved father, and whose murder had made me the center of police attention, could not have emerged from this coffee shop.

Could she?

"Earth to Annie."

I blinked and tried to focus. Grandma Natalie and Joe were eyeing me with concern. "I'm sorry. Did you say something?"

"You've been staring off into space for the last five minutes," Joe said. "I don't think you've heard a word we said. Are you okay?"

I got up from my chair to refresh my glass of iced tea. "I called Patrick on my way home and asked him to come over as soon as he could. I was hoping he'd be here by now."

I resumed my seat at the round kitchen table, again the focus of their worried faces. My grandmother's Swedish blue eyes and blonde hair, not yet threaded with gray, and Joe's dark brown eyes and even darker skin comforted me in a way I couldn't describe. My family.

I heard the front door close, and Patrick Wyatt rushed into the kitchen. As always, his hair was perfectly coiffed, and his suit was impeccable. He inherited his dark hair and brown eyes from his Italian forbears. We'd been close friends since elementary school, and I considered him a brother every bit as much as I did Joe. He was also an attorney, and as far as I was concerned, a lifesaver, given my current legal peril.

He dropped into the last unoccupied chair. "I got here as soon as I could. Are you okay? You sounded, well, I'm not sure how to describe it. Jangled? Upset for sure. What happened? Why didn't you tell me on the phone?"

I had to smile. "Nobody has ever described me as jangled, but I'll go with it." I sat back in my chair and inhaled deeply, trying to center myself. "You're all going to think I'm nuts. And I'm not sure you'll be wrong. But I need to see your faces when I tell you what happened."

They waited. I did, too, for as long as I could, still questioning myself. Before I spoke again, I tried to anticipate their reactions.

"I saw Nicky this afternoon."

After a moment of stunned silence, they all started talking at once.

"What do you mean?"

"No, she's dead."

"It's not possible."

"You must be wrong."

"It had to be someone else."

They babbled until they ran out of steam. Then Grandma Natalie, in the way of all grandmothers, got up from the table, came around, and gave me a tight hug. She had tears in her eyes when she let me go. She went to the cupboard and came back with a plate piled high with homemade cookies. If chocolate chips and snickerdoodles could cure a person's woes, maybe they'd banish hallucinations about dead girlfriends.

When she was seated, she spoke carefully. "Tell us."

As I described what happened, I again felt the pounding of my heart, the same as I'd felt standing at the coffee shop door and seeing a woman I'd allegedly murdered drive away in a panic. I took another deep breath. "Maybe I'm losing my mind."

They all demurred, as family members do, but they must have had doubts about what I'd seen. I certainly did.

Finally, Patrick, always the pragmatic one, spoke. "She had a hood pulled over her face?"

"Yes."

"She could've been someone who resembles Nicky."

"If that were the case, why did she go pale as if she'd seen a ghost and nearly run over two people getting out the parking lot? Hell, she even threw her coffee on the ground before getting into her van. She was obviously panicked."

He thought about it for a moment. "Identical twin sister? Look-alike cousin?"

"Not possible. We were together for years. I was with her family many times, saw the family photos. I even went to one of their family reunions."

"Doppelgänger," Joe said. "Created by plastic surgery. Or maybe I've read too many spy novels."

I reached over and squeezed his arm. I could always count on Joe's flights of fancy. He put his hand over mine and held it for a moment.

They were reaching, trying to find a logical explanation, but I understood. I'd been trying—and failing—to find one myself ever since the encounter.

"I've been mulling it over ever since I saw her, and the only explanation I can come to is Nicky is alive. Nothing else makes sense, except thinking she's alive also doesn't make sense. I mean, they found her body. Right?

"Do you have any other ideas?" I prompted them. "Because I have to tell you, I'm open to anything other than thinking I'm losing my mind. Well, I'm also not too fond of finding out she's alive and she left me with no explanation for a year and a half. And on top of it all, I've been a murder suspect for the whole time." I felt anger rising at the thought and tried to squelch it.

"Person of interest," Patrick said absently.

"Tomato, to-*mah*-to. Either way, far too much attention paid by the Portland police." I paused, unsure whether I wanted the answer to what I was about to ask. "Patrick?"

He waited with an inquiring expression.

"You saw the crime scene photos, right? And you have the reports?"

"Yes. I know you haven't wanted to see any of it."

"And I won't if I can avoid it. Is there any way the person in those pictures wasn't Nicky?"

He pondered my question before answering. "I don't know how. Her parents identified her at the morgue."

"Look, I came face to face with a ghost today. I don't want to see those pictures and I won't read the medical examiner's report if I don't have to, but you can tell me what's in them. I need to know. Even more, I deserve to know."

He took a breath and sat forward in his chair, elbows on the table. "Annie, sometimes I have to be your friend first and lawyer second, and this is one of those times. I'll call the detective and set up a time to meet. We need to talk with her in any event to tell her what you just told us. She can be more objective than I can."

I thought for a few moments. "Sounds good."

He took his phone from the inside pocket of his suitcoat and pressed a few buttons. While he waited for an answer, I thought about Detective Beth O'Brien, the Portland homicide detective who was in charge of investigating Nicky's murder. She was smart and driven, an excellent detective by all accounts, and damn it, one of the most beautiful women I'd ever met. When Patrick introduced us, he thought it was funny she also "played for my team," as he put it. He never let me forget how I'd totally botched trying to play it cool when I met her.

"Beth, Patrick Wyatt here." He'd shifted into lawyer mode. He could be a goofball of the first order, so hearing him sound professional was as amusing as it was reassuring. "Annie and I need to meet with you as soon as you have time. She might have new information on the case." He listened for a few seconds. "Is he up to speed yet?" More waiting. He turned to me with his phone to his ear. "Tomorrow at ten?" When I nodded, he spoke into the phone. "That works. See you then." He ended the call.

"Is who up to speed yet?"

"Beth has a new partner, someone who joined from another department. She says he's an experienced investigator. She's showing him the ropes here in Portland, and he'll be at our meeting."

I said, "I hope the new guy doesn't throw a monkey wrench into the works."

"I know what you mean. We have a solid working relationship with Beth, and I don't want it disrupted."

"You don't suppose hallucinations are enough to get me off a murder charge, do you?"

"Not funny," Patrick said.

"You know what's really not funny?"

He raised an eyebrow and waited.

"I'll meet the detective's new partner tomorrow morning, and his first impression of me will be that I'm seeing dead people, which I think could put me fairly low on the credibility scale, especially if he's some kind of macho hardliner."

"He could be a good guy, willing to listen. Beth wouldn't partner with someone who wasn't professional to the core."

"If she had a choice." I leaned back in my chair. "It'll be interesting to see what they think. I mean, if Nicky is alive, I can finally be free of the police. It'd be a massive relief to have my life back."

I paused before the glass door and read the black and gold embossing. Portland Police Bureau Homicide Division. I glanced at Patrick.

"Into the belly of the beast?" I tried to make a joke, but since I could barely breathe, it fell flat.

"It'll be fine." He patted my shoulder. "She won't think you're crazy."

"I don't know why not. I do."

We pushed through the doors into the reception area and were directed to chairs along the wall to wait. I tried to sit still, but not until Patrick put his hand on my knee did I realize how much I was fidgeting.

In what felt like an hour but was less than five minutes, Beth O'Brien emerged from the depths of the department, accompanied by her new partner. Any other time, my attention would have focused on Beth. Her heart-shaped face, deep brown eyes, and blonde hair made my pulse quicken, no matter how many times I saw her. This time, the man who accompanied her drew my eye. He was about six feet tall, with a severe crewcut and the broadest shoulders I'd ever seen. Maybe he thought his expression showed he was a serious professional, but from my perspective, he was forbidding. My nervousness ramped up to eleven on a scale of ten.

"Hi, Annie. Patrick." Beth greeted us with quick handshakes. "How have you been? Let me introduce you to Ted Winston. He's new to the Portland Bureau, and he's joining our team."

We all shook hands before she led us to her office, where we settled into the two chairs positioned for guests in front of her desk. Winston settled into a chair at the side of Beth's desk, leaned back, and propped one ankle onto the opposite knee.

"Before we get started," Beth said, "I want you to know Ted has as much experience investigating homicides as I do, but I'm still the lead on your case. You can have the same confidence in him I hope you have in me. Do you have any questions?"

"No." Patrick spoke for both of us.

"Okay then. What did you want to talk with me about? Patrick, when you called, you mentioned you might have new information about the case. As far as I know, there's nothing new to report."

I took a deep breath and let it out. "That," I said slowly, "might not be entirely true."

"Oh?" Seeming intrigued, she took a pad of yellow paper and a pen from the desk drawer, ready to take notes. Winston pulled a notepad and pen from his jacket pocket.

I'd given a lot of thought to how I would tell my story, whether to lead with the surprising—or was it shocking—detail, or build up to it. In the moment, and putting aside my concern about making an unfavorable first impression with the new detective, I decided on the latter.

"As you know, my brother, Joe, and I decided to reopen my dad's bicycle shop."

She waited, pen poised.

"My brother is good friends with the builder, so we agreed to pick up supplies and do some other work for the construction crew. Yesterday afternoon, I went up to north Portland, to one of the building supply places." I gave them the name of the company, which both detectives jotted down. "After I was done, I stopped for coffee at a place they recommended, Jolene's Java Joint."

"Oh, I've had their lattes," Beth said. "Excellent coffee." She added its name to her notes.

I studied my hands, which I had clenched tightly together. I deliberately relaxed them, flexing my fingers while trying to breathe and hoping for the best. Before I spoke to the waiting detectives, I glanced at Patrick, and he gave me a reassuring nod.

Beth didn't speak, letting me take my time. Winston was also still.

"Okay," I finally said. "I don't know what you'll think about this. Hell, I don't know what to think of it myself." I paused again, not for effect, but to steel myself against their reactions. "I saw Nicky Fleming at the coffee shop. She's alive."

If I'd never fully understood the phrase "so quiet you could hear a pin drop," now I did. Beth didn't move, didn't speak, didn't blink, and I wasn't sure she was even breathing until she said, "Tell me more."

I did. I told her about the rain, about opening the door and coming face to face with someone I'd long believed was dead. I described how her eyes went wide, how she lost all color in her face, and how she tried to say I had her confused with someone else. I recounted watching the woman run to her van in an apparent panic, even discarding her coffee on the way, and leaving in a rush.

"She almost ran over two people in the parking lot. And she looked back in my direction before she turned the corner."

While both detectives made notes, I tried to quell my pounding heartbeat. What if they didn't believe me? What if they thought I was making it all up to get out from under the investigation? What if Winston wrote me off as a crackpot in our first meeting? What if I'd truly cracked under the pressure from the past year and a half?

After an eternity, probably far less than a minute, Beth looked up from her notes, and her next words surprised me.

"What was she driving?"

I wasn't sure my jaw didn't drop slightly in surprise. "Silver minivan."

"Do you know the make or model?" She was writing again.

"No. They're all identical as far as I can tell. I think it had tinted windows, if it matters."

"What was she wearing?"

"I'm not sure. Jacket with a hood for sure. Blue, I think. Jeans, maybe?" I waited while she wrote. "Wait, do you believe me?"

She set her pen alongside the pad of paper and sat back in her chair. Her gaze was direct. She was calm and didn't seem at all skeptical. "Our first responsibility is to hear you out and try not to make judgments. What matters is the evidence, not what we may or may not believe. But I understand your question. A woman's body was found and identified as Nicole Fleming. Her family mentioned your name when officers requested the names of her friends and acquaintances, which led to our awareness of the fire at your dad's bike shop, and from there to the shed. And now you're saying you saw her alive yesterday."

"Yes, exactly." I was feeling a bit more confident.

Winston finally spoke, his voice as calm and even as Beth's. "Who else have you told?"

"Patrick, obviously, and my grandmother and brother."

"Did you get the names of the people you say she almost hit?"

I glanced at Patrick, startled by Winston's question. He appeared concerned, but said, "Go ahead."

"No. We spoke for a moment about the close call they'd had, and they went into the coffee shop." A knot started to form in my chest.

"You claim to have had witnesses," Winston said. "We would want to talk with them."

I opened my mouth to object, but Patrick's hand on my arm reined me in.

"Detective Winston, would you expect her to ask those people for contact information in such circumstances? It was a passing incident.

She checked to make sure they were unharmed, which is what any decent person would do. What are you implying?"

"She wants us to believe her, doesn't she?" Winston's eyes narrowed.

"We're getting off track here," Beth said. She gave her partner a sharp glance and an almost imperceptible shake of her head before turning back to me. "Other than the people you mentioned, you haven't told anyone else? Reached out to her family?"

"Not yet," I tried to shake off the anger Winston's veiled accusation had generated. "I'm having dinner with two friends tonight, and I'll tell them."

"Annie, I know it's hard," she said, "but you shouldn't tell anyone else."

"Why the hell not?" I pulled away from Patrick's restraining hand. "They knew Nicky almost as well as I did. We were all close."

"But the more people who know will complicate—"

"Fuck that." My voice was harsher than I intended, so I took a breath and dialed it back. "Sorry, but you have to understand, they're my dearest friends. The four of us were as close as friends could be, all the way through college and ever since. And they loved my dad almost as much as I did. They've seen the hell my life has been since he died."

"I understand, but—" She tried again, but I cut her off.

"Do you now? Do you understand? Have you ever walked into a burned-out building and found the body of the person you loved most in the world?"

"No, I haven't." The detective looked chastened.

"Annie." Patrick's voice was calming. "Please."

I sat back in my chair and took a deep breath, letting it out slowly. "I'm glad you haven't, and I hope you never do. But I have. It's an image I will carry with me for the rest of my life. Then I was told my girlfriend was responsible for the fire that killed my father, which was impossible to believe, and then she was found murdered, which piled grief upon grief. And on top of it all, after losing my father and the woman I loved, having my life under a microscope has been an ongoing nightmare. My family and my friends have been the only reason I'm still upright and functioning. Rachel and Sally are family, no more, no less." Beth started to speak, but I kept talking. "I understand your concern, so I'll ask them to keep it to themselves, but I will tell them. They're the best friends a woman could have, and they'll understand. I hope you do as well." I paused for a moment. "And I apologize for how I spoke to you just now,

Detective. I was out of line, and I'm sorry." I took another deep breath and clasped my hands together to stop them from shaking.

"Thank you, Annie. I understand your perspective, and I do trust your judgment. One more thing. If you remember, I met your friends briefly at the party you had when your grandmother was released from the hospital, but I know little about them. For our records, may I have their names and contact information?"

"Of course. Rachel Simmons. She's a veterinarian and owns a clinic in southwest Portland. Sally Price is a firefighter and EMT." I recited their home addresses and phone numbers, as well as Rachel's clinic address. "Sally recently transferred to a new station. I'm not sure which one yet."

"Thank you. All I ask is you let me know if any of your friends or family talk about Nicky to anyone else. It's important to keep some boundaries around what you've told me."

"I understand, and thank you for seeing my perspective."

She put her pen down and sat back in her chair. "Do you have any questions for us?"

"Since the woman in the alleyway wasn't Nicky, how could there have been such an incorrect identification?"

"She was found with a handbag holding Nicole Fleming's wallet, which had her driver's license and credit cards in it. The bag also held her phone, some makeup, a comb, the usual things most women carry."

"You know the one, Annie," Patrick said. "A leather monstrosity almost as big as she was."

I remembered Nicky's ridiculous bag. I'd called it her suitcase and joked she was always ready to flee the country at a moment's notice. Maybe she had.

"And she was wearing a god-awful orange and black striped hoodie. The one you gave her for her birthday or something."

"Christmas. She loved it, wore it all the time."

"She fit the rest of Nicky's description, height, weight, hair color, and so on," Beth said. "Her parents agreed to identify the body, but with the wound she had, it was difficult. She was shot in the head, and as happens sometimes, her face was severely injured. I heard they tried to cover the worst of the damage so her parents could see the other side of the face, and they identified the woman as their daughter."

I tried not to visualize what she described. "How awful for them. They're good people. But there was an autopsy, right?"

"Yes, as is routine for homicides."

"Fingerprints? DNA?" I was getting frustrated. "I know I'm fishing, but there has to be an explanation for what I saw. She didn't have any sisters or relatives who resembled her enough for anyone to confuse them. Certainly not me, and especially not her parents. I can't make sense of this. I hope you can."

"Hold on a sec." Beth rose from her chair and stepped to a side table holding a stack of boxes prominently labelled "evidence," along with what appeared to be a case number. She opened two of them before she found what she wanted. Back at her desk, she opened the thick file folder she'd extracted from the second box.

"Okay, let's see here. It's been a while since I've looked at these files." She paged through the stack of papers. "Yeah, that's what I thought." She turned to me. "You mentioned fingerprints. Locally, we have no fingerprint records for either Nicky or the dead woman. As far as we can tell, neither of them ever had their fingerprints taken anywhere else. Either that, or they were never uploaded to the national database. It happens sometimes. Anyway, fingerprints were a bust. So were dental records, and trust me when I say you don't want to know why."

She turned several more pages before turning back to Patrick and me again.

"This is interesting. DNA wasn't tested."

"Why not?" I couldn't stay quiet any longer. "It's not routine?"

"Yes, it is." She exchanged puzzled glances with Winston. "But Nicky's parents declined a DNA test, because Nicky was adopted and it wouldn't help."

"Wait. What? That doesn't make sense. There's no way she was adopted. I can show you family photos and you'll see the resemblance. She looks a lot like her mom."

Beth looked doubtful. "It's right here in the investigator's notes."

"There has to be a mistake."

Beth closed the file and sat back in her chair. "Ted and I will re-examine the evidence with what you've told us in mind. We'll talk with the officers who managed the scene and conducted the initial investigation, including the one who requested DNA samples from the Flemings. We'll review all of it. I can't promise what we'll find, but while we work through it, we'll take your information at face value." She turned to her new partner. "Check with the coffee shop. I'll be surprised if they don't have security cameras inside and in the parking lot. If we're lucky, there will be a recording we can review. And see if there are any cameras along the street. Maybe we can get a license plate number for the van."

He wrote in his notebook.

"Thank you." A ton of tension left my body. "I was worried you'd think I'd lost my mind. I've certainly thought so a few times."

Beth stood up behind her desk and extended her hand for me to shake. "Understandable. I can't imagine what a shock it must have been. It makes sense you'd be mulling it over. If you're right, then it raises a lot of questions."

"Here's one. Since it wasn't Nicky's body found in the alleyway, who was the poor woman who was killed?"

Chapter Two

An hour later, I drove into the Velasquez Cycles parking lot and unloaded a tote bag and a cooler from my car. I'd stopped on my way to the shop to stock up on snacks and cold drinks. Brad Baumeister and his crew always welcomed a break from their work, and with the day's temperature reaching ninety, they'd be even happier to delve into the bounty I brought.

Brad, who owned a construction company, was Joe's closest friend and a member of their cycling team, dubbed Team Three and a Half to acknowledge that each of the team members had lost limbs in service to their country. Someone in the group with a quirky sense of humor—most likely Joe—had suggested the team's name since it was about how many complete bodies they had. The math wasn't right, but the name stuck.

Until I stepped from my car, I'd been mentally rehashing my meeting with Beth and her new partner. Seeing the building under construction helped me take my mind off the morning's events, but it was still bittersweet. My dad had died in a fire at the old shop, so the hope I felt for the new shop was tinged by sadness.

The investigators had concluded the fire was caused by a methamphetamine lab constructed by my girlfriend in a shed attached to the bike shop. News of her subsequent murder—or was it alleged murder?—had added to my grief. Not only was I mired in the police investigation, but my beloved dad was gone, leaving me adrift and with no recourse. Discovering Nicky alive added confusion to my overburdened spirit.

I put the treats I'd brought onto an improvised table, a sheet of plywood lying across two sawhorses. Seconds later, shouts of glee erupted when the men saw me and descended en masse. Joe was there, too, hard at work with the crew. Within seconds, they decimated the cold drinks and snacks. Locusts would have envied their efficiency.

"Annie!" Joe swept me up in a hug and spun me around before putting me back on my feet. His dark brown skin shone with the sweat he'd worked up in the mid-July heat. He pulled me aside and lowered his voice. "How did it go with the lady cop?"

"Mostly better than I expected. She seemed to take what I said seriously and asked a few good questions. She told me they'd examine the evidence again. No promises made, but her new partner seems to be a hard-ass."

"Oh? Why?"

"He came within a hairsbreadth of accusing me of making it all up. I think we have to be careful around him."

"What did Grandma Natalie say?"

"I haven't told her yet. She wasn't home when I stopped by to change clothes. I'll tell her tonight."

Joe gave me a long hug before turning me around. "What do you think? Isn't it beautiful?"

We stood side by side, his arm across my shoulders, and considered the sight before us.

"I'm not complaining, but I was hoping more would be done by now. It's just the frame so far."

"You're right, but it's a beautiful frame."

Leave it to Joe to be upbeat about almost anything. Even losing a leg in Iraq didn't slow him down. He was definitely Mister Silver Lining.

"Since Brad agreed to do the work pretty much for free, he fits it in when he's not working somewhere else. So, yeah, it'll take longer, but he does good work."

I had to admit it looked great, even though it was still a skeleton of a building. We'd decided to make the new shop larger than the original so we could have bicycle maintenance classes and a coffee and snack bar. We hoped to make it a gathering place for cycling enthusiasts. Joe was already talking about offering riding groups and sponsoring some of the rides organized by other Oregon businesses. Dad would have loved it. Despite its spare appearance, I could already visualize the centrally placed door with windows, ten feet square, on either side. I felt a pang at the memory of my dad teasing me when, at eight, I told him the shop looked like a face with people walking in through the nose. I felt the start of a tear at the memory.

"He'd have loved this, Joe." My throat ached with repressed grief.

He didn't speak at first. "Oh, I keep forgetting to tell you. People from all over the neighborhood have been coming by to check on our progress. A lot of them knew Dad, and they've told me they're glad we're rebuilding. They already want to know when we'll be open. How cool is that?"

"It's great. I'm glad they remember him, but I also hope they'll buy something."

Joe threw his head back and laughed, which raised my spirits. "They will. They will. Well, not Brad. I promised him free bikes for life, considering he's not charging us for labor. He's saving us a fortune."

"He's a good friend. He can have whatever he wants from the shop. Now let's go check it out."

Joe and I took a quick walk through the building, doing our best to stay out of the way and not trip over anything. Each of the men took a moment to call his thanks to me for the treats I'd brought.

"We have another site to get to today," Brad said, "but we always appreciate the snacks and especially the drinks. We're all sweating like mules in this heat. You keep it up, and we'll get very spoiled. We don't get fed at our other projects."

We went back outside while the men put their tools away and started to leave. I pushed a wheelbarrow toward the debris they'd left strewn about the property.

"Are you staying?" Joe stood with his bicycle, also ready to go.

"You don't have to do it right now, Annie." Brad joined him on his way to his truck. "It's damned hot out here."

"I want to. It's part of our deal, remember? And today, I need to work off some stress anyway."

Brad gave me a quick hug. "Thanks. You save us a lot of time and make it easier for us to work, and I appreciate it."

After he and Joe left, I turned my attention to the task at hand. Brad called it sweat equity, which I found amusing. For myself, I got time at the shop where I could think about my dad and try to envision our new business opening up. The work was physical, which felt good, and I enjoyed seeing the results of my labors.

Today, picking up discarded bits of plywood and loose nails became something to do while I pondered what it meant if Nicky was alive. Where had she been for a year and a half? How could she have left me with nothing but a cryptically worded note? I'd long since memorized it.

"Annie, I know you can never forgive me, but I had no choice. I never would have hurt Dad. I hope you know that. I'm so sorry. I love you. Nicky."

No choice? What did she mean? And how could I believe she loved me when she disappeared with no explanation? I frowned and tried to concentrate on my work. I wouldn't know what she meant by the note unless I could ask her.

Realization hit me, making me stand up straight and stare into the distance, my heart racing. I knew what I had to do.

I'd have to find her.

That evening, I waited for Rachel and Sally in our favorite deeply padded booth in the quietest corner of Doug's Café and studied the menu. Doug's Café was owned by Fujio Tanaka, who made the most exquisite sushi I'd ever eaten. He bought the little eatery, formerly a burger joint, and hadn't changed its name. He also didn't advertise, but word of mouth ensured getting a table wasn't always easy. His menu was intimidating. Narrowing the choices down to enough for one reasonably sized meal was a serious undertaking, and I always took leftovers home. Not exactly a hardship, as far as I was concerned.

I'd almost wrangled the menu into submission when Rachel settled into the booth across from me and dropped her keys onto the table. Sally slid in next to her.

"I hope you're hungry," I said. "You know it's nearly impossible not to eat too much here."

"But it's worth every calorie. Rachel reached for her own menu, but instead of reading it, she said, "Okay, what's the big news? Keeping your friends in suspense isn't nice."

"I do have something important to tell you, but let's order first. I wouldn't be a good friend if I distracted you from such excellent sushi."

They reluctantly agreed and went back to their menus, trading concerned glances.

"Stop it," I said. "I'm not dying, Grandma Natalie is fine, Joe is fine, the bike shop is fine. Now pay attention to your dinner." I tried giving them a stern glare, but they weren't impressed.

"Never become a cop," Sally said. "You're terrible at telling people what to do. And you shouldn't ever try to be intimidating. You suck at it." She returned to perusing the menu.

"Have you decided?"

I started, since I hadn't heard the server arrive at our table. Her name tag read "Mandy," which immediately gave me an ear worm. One of my favorite old songs. We gave our orders, and she left as quietly as she'd arrived.

"Wow," Rachel said. "Did you see her?"

"Yeah, she walks without making a sound. How does she do it? Oh wait, I know. She's a vampire."

"No, you moron. I mean how she was staring at you. I felt the heat from here."

"Oh, please." I narrowed my eyes at her. "She asked for my order, and I gave it to her. It's hardly a prelude to romance."

"She is bringing you sushi," Sally said. "You go starry-eyed over it every time we're here. Maybe if you associate it with your new friend, Mandy, you'll change your tune."

I threw a wadded-up napkin at her. "Don't even start. The last thing I need right now is a girlfriend, or even a fantasy vampire girlfriend." My attempt at a bad joke reminded me of the ghostly Nicky I'd seen, if she was in fact an apparition. I tried to shake it off and took a drink of the ice water Mandy had delivered. "Which reminds me, you're both fired."

Rachel's expression went from puzzled to comprehension to dismay in a matter of seconds.

"Didn't go well?" She grimaced in an "I was afraid of that" sort of way.

"Let's put it like this. Jill and I have been on two dates, and she has now told me the same story both times." I turned to Sally. "You'll love this. At a family potluck, all the women showed up with radicchio salads. Isn't that high-larious?" I rolled my eyes.

Sally decided to weigh in. "What about Megan? You thought she was cute, and she told me she had a good time with you."

"Megan, the one who says 'like' almost every other word?" At Rachel's questioning eyebrow, I adopted what I hoped was a sufficiently vapid tone. "Like, we wanted broccoli for dinner, but like, we were all out, so like, we went to the store, and like, when we got there—"

By then, both of my friends were laughing, making a couple of nearby diners glare at us briefly.

"What were you thinking? You should know me well enough to realize I wouldn't be interested in dating someone who talks like she's twelve and trying too hard. You're both terrible matchmakers. Find someone else to torment."

"What about the detective?" Rachel said slyly. "You've told us she's intelligent and capable of holding an actual conversation. I saw her at your party. She's a hottie and a half. If she asked me out, I sure wouldn't say no."

I tried to ignore the flutter in my chest at the mention of Beth O'Brien. My friends had only seen her once, at the welcome home party Grandma Natalie threw when I got out of the hospital after I was kidnapped by a murderer. She'd attended for a short time, but since then, neither of my friends had stopped teasing me about the beautiful lesbian detective, whether I was attracted to her, whether she'd asked me out or vice versa. With friends like these…

"Look, even if I asked her, which I will not, and even if she'd go out with me, which she wouldn't, I'm not sure dating the woman who could arrest me for murder is a very good idea. Some people might think handcuffs are a turn on, but I'm not one of them." I took a drink of my ice water. "And face it, neither of you has any more dates than I do. Unless, Rachel my dear, Patrick's cousin is in town." I gave her an evil grin.

Rachel blushed.

"Yeah, Rachel," Sally said, "how is Patrick these days?"

Rachel's face got even redder. "I wouldn't know. Annie, how is Patrick doing?" She tried to sound lofty, but her expression told me she wished we'd give it a rest.

"He's fine." I decided to play along. "He's moved on nicely since you ditched him for his cousin."

Rachel's crush on Patrick had long been a source of friendly amusement in our group. He was oblivious, which made it all the more fun to tease her.

But it all changed when our group of friends took Patrick's cousin, Stacy, who was visiting from Los Angeles, out for dinner at an upscale steakhouse. She was attempting to build an acting career, and in the meantime, worked as a model and dancer. She was every bit the stereotypical California blonde, tall, tanned, and slender. And to top it all off, she seemed to be an unassuming and intelligent person.

I said, "For a—shall we say—straight woman, you sure spent a lot of time trying not to stare at Stacy."

"And you didn't? Admit it, you thought she was stunning. We all did."

"True," I said. "Not my type, but gorgeous and funny and nice to talk with. Except we never would have thought she was *your* type."

Rachel tried covering her reddened face with a napkin, but Sally took it from her. "Yeah, Rachel, are you ever going to tell us about it?"

Rachel conceded defeat. "Okay, fine. I got up to go to the restroom, and Stacy also needed to go. She took my arm and whispered in my ear how she saw me looking at her. I was embarrassed she noticed, but damn, her silk top was almost transparent, and I know you remember as well as I do she had nothing on under it. When we got into the restroom, I apologized for staring, but she told me she liked it. She locked the door and then she slid her blouse right off her shoulders."

"Damn." Remembering Stacy and hearing Rachel's story raised my pulse rate.

"I know. And then she kissed me." Rachel's cheeks turned red again. "And, you know, some other stuff."

"You missed dessert," I said.

"No. No, I didn't," Rachel said with a contented expression. "I had a lovely dessert."

"And not just that night, either, I bet," Sally said.

"Well, she was in town for two weeks." Rachel gave her a broad smile. "Happy now?"

As we voiced our agreement, our stealthy server arrived with a bounty of beautiful sushi. Mercifully distracted from images of blouseless blondes, I watched her leave the table as quietly as she'd arrived.

"I've changed my mind," I said. "She's not a vampire. She's a ghost who serves food. A culinary poltergeist."

We filled our plates from the serving platter. I added a generous dollop of wasabi and a few ginger slices to my plate and sat back with satisfaction.

Rachel said, "I don't know how you can eat so much wasabi."

"It adds an amazing flavor and clears the sinuses. How many foods can you say that about?" I selected a salmon roll, touching it to the soy sauce and wasabi mixture I'd made.

Rachel reached for a slice of tuna sashimi, picking it up expertly with her chopsticks. "Okay, Velasquez, you've stalled long enough. Spill it."

While we ate, I recounted my visit to the building supply the previous day. I was apparently telling the story too slowly because Sally, usually the patient one, made a circular motion in the air with her chopsticks, as if to say, "Move it along." I did as she wanted.

"So I stopped at a coffee shop—"

Again with the chopsticks.

"And I saw Nicky."

The chopsticks clattered to the table. "What did you say?"

"I was going in, and she was coming out. She took one look at me and hightailed it out of there as if she'd been set on fire."

Speechless, both of my friends stared at me with expressions of wide-eyed disbelief.

"Oh, trust me, I understand what you're thinking. She's dead, right? Has been for a year and a half. But I *saw* her. Or I was hallucinating, but if you ask the people she almost ran over in the parking lot, I think they'd agree she was real enough."

My friends sat in stunned silence for several minutes, clearly trying to think of what to say. I had no answers for them, so I waited.

"Have you told the detective?" Sally took the first shot. "What does she think?"

"Patrick and I met with her this morning. She took me seriously enough to ask a few questions. I couldn't tell if she believed me. Hell, I'm not sure I believe it myself."

"And Grandma Natalie and Joe?" She retrieved her abandoned chopsticks.

"They were as stunned as you are—and as I was. We talked about it for a long time and came up with nothing logical." I selected a tuna roll from the platter. "At least they didn't call the men with the butterfly net and those jackets with the extra-long sleeves."

Rachel nodded. "There's still plenty of time."

I laughed out loud. "Thanks, pal."

"I hope they can sort it out." Sally picked up a piece of sushi. "I can't believe you'd mistake anyone for Nicky, since you were together for so long. It does sound as if the detective was taking you seriously, which is good."

"I was a bit surprised, to be honest," I said. "I guess now it's a matter of waiting to see what she comes up with."

"In the meantime, you need a distraction," Rachel said. "What you need is a date." She stuffed an entire piece of sushi into her mouth.

I should have known she hadn't given up.

She reached for her next piece of sushi. "I know what's really going on here."

"Do you?" I fixed her with my best steely eyed stare, which fooled her not at all.

As I took a long drink of water, she said, "You have the hots for the lady detective."

Caught off guard, I almost inhaled the water I was drinking, and had to cough a few times. "Don't say stuff like that when I have a mouthful of water." I wiped my chin with a paper napkin.

"Tell me I'm wrong," she said with a puckish expression.

"You're wrong. Not only that, but you're wrong again. You keep bringing her up, and I keep telling you how wrong you are." I couldn't admit to myself I was attracted to Beth O'Brien, so I sure wasn't about to admit it to anyone else. "Picture this. We're at dinner, having a pleasant conversation, and when it's time to order dessert, she says, 'Oh, by the way, you're under arrest.' Yeah, there's the beginning of a fine romance."

"What's the line? I think she protests too much?"

"Now you're bastardizing Shakespeare. You should be ashamed of yourself."

"Point made anyway." She looked unconcerned. "Otherwise, you wouldn't be as red as a beet and have water all down the front of your shirt."

"Drowning will do that for a person."

As if by magic, Mandy appeared with a towel.

"Thank you. Some days, I shouldn't be allowed out in public." I dried my damp shirt as much as I could and wiped up water droplets from the table. Mandy accepted the towel with my thanks and left, walking as quietly as ever. "I still don't know how she does it."

We finished our meal without more talk of dating. Sally asked how the shop was coming along, and we chatted about a couple of friends we had in common and about Grandma Natalie's recovery after her motorcycle crash.

After we'd finished eating, Mandy cleared the table off and left the bill behind. We'd finished calculating who owed what for the dinner when Mandy reappeared. This time, instead of whisking our credit cards away, she stood looking uncertain, even fidgeting.

Her changed demeanor caught my attention. "Is there a problem?"

She bit her lip for a moment before holding a well-worn newspaper clipping out to me. "Is this you?"

I felt my stomach drop. I hoped the dread I felt didn't show on my face.

I took the paper and sure enough, it was the story about how I'd solved the murder of Doctor Carlton Wentworth in Charbonneau, a former timber town in the mountains west of Portland. The story was a sensationalized version of the actual events, making it sound as if I, a housekeeper on a mission, had single-handedly brought a vicious killer to justice. It made no mention of how the killer had almost made my good friend, Mo, his second victim, and me his third. The photograph accompanying the puff piece was grainy but still recognizable.

"Yes, it's me." I handed it back to her. "But—"

She slid into the booth next to me with an eager expression on her face. Startled, I slid over to give her room.

"Did you really find the man who killed the doctor?" Her tone, normally low and pleasant, was tinged with excitement.

"More like he found me, but—"

"But you know how to find people?"

I took a deep breath and reminded myself to be patient. This wasn't the first time I'd been approached after the article was published. At first, I was flattered when people recognized me, and I tried to correct the story when I could, but mostly I hoped people would forget about it.

"You don't understand. Yes, I found the man who killed the doctor, but—"

"Could you find someone for me?" Her expression was so hopeful, it made my heart ache for her.

"Mandy, you have to understand something. I'm not a detective. I worked as a housekeeper for the doctor in that story, and I got carried away thinking I knew who killed him. And you know what? I was wrong. I followed the wrong person, and the actual murderer kidnapped me. He drugged me, and I almost died."

She looked crestfallen, so I put my hand on her arm to comfort her.

"I'm not a detective," I repeated with emphasis. "I'm a caretaker for my grandmother these days, and sometimes I clean houses. I'm sorry, but I can't help you."

"But the article…" She held it up again.

"I know. The reporter got a lot wrong and left out important details. Most of that article is fiction."

She had the beginnings of tears in her eyes. "But my girlfriend has been missing for months. The police say she's an adult, and adults can leave if they want to. She wouldn't have left without saying goodbye. I know something's wrong. I can feel it."

From the corner of my eye, I saw Rachel trying to look encouraging. Not that I didn't feel bad for Mandy or didn't want to help. I knew all too well what it felt like to have a loved one go missing, as I'd felt when Nicky disappeared, and even more so when I learned she had died. Allegedly died, I corrected. I resigned myself to the inevitable, even though I suspected I'd regret it later. "Okay, I can search online, but that's all I can do."

"Really?" She was elated. "You would do that for me?"

"I'm not making any promises, okay?"

"Yes, of course," she said enthusiastically.

I turned to Rachel, who was teary-eyed. She always was the sentimental one. "Do you have a pen and paper?" She retrieved both from her bag and slid them across the table. I wrote for a few seconds and handed the slip of paper to Mandy. "Here's my email address. When you have time, send me her name, date of birth, parents' names, how long she's been gone, any details you can, and I'll see what I can find."

She grasped the paper as if it might save her life, gratitude all over her face. "I'll do it tonight. Thank you so much." She slid out of the booth, collected our credit cards, and with the biggest smile I'd ever seen on her face, she left.

"You're a good person, Annie," Rachel said, and Sally murmured her agreement.

"I'm an idiot. I'll do some searching, and I probably won't find anything useful." I already wished I hadn't agreed to do it. "Best case, I'll find some information for her. Worse case, I'll waste my time, find nothing, and she'll be unhappy again. At least it's the worst that could happen."

Chapter Three

After a nearly sleepless night, I made my way downstairs to the kitchen. The welcome aroma of fresh coffee and toasted bread greeted me, as did my grandmother. She made me sit at the table and brought me a huge mug filled with steaming hot liquid ambrosia, a small plate holding two pieces of buttered toast, and a jar of extra crunchy peanut butter. After I'd added sugar and creamer to the coffee, I took a sip, wincing at the heat. I put a smear of peanut butter on one slice of toast and took a bite. The perfect breakfast.

"You look dreadful." Grandma Natalie took her own chair across from me.

"Thanks for your support." I spoke through a mouthful of peanut butter toast. "I couldn't sleep. Kept thinking about Nicky, trying to make sense of it."

"Completely understandable." She held her coffee mug between her hands. "What's on your agenda today? Resting, I hope."

"Being busy would be better. I need to find something to take my mind off Nicky, so I'll work on Joe's 'honey do' list first, and then I'll go to the shop. Those guys make the place look as if a tornado blew through." At her inquiring eyebrow, I clarified. "Joe gave me a To Do list—calling distributors, opening bank accounts, all the fun stuff." I took a drink of coffee. "Then I'm meeting Rachel at her clinic this afternoon. The regular receptionist is going on vacation and Rachel asked me to fill in while she's away. I'll spend some time with her so she can show me the ropes. If I can stay awake, that is. How about you?"

"Liz is coming by later, and we're going out for Thai." She gave me another seemingly innocent smile, which probably meant she and her friend would exhaust the patience of yet another Harley Davidson salesman before dinner. It was becoming a hobby with those two.

Liz Kirby came into our lives when Grandma Natalie was hospitalized following a motorcycle crash a few months earlier. Some careless idiot had made an illegal turn and hit my grandmother's Harley broadside. She was giving her friend, Ada Brownlee, a ride, and they both ended up in the hospital. Ada's worst injury was a broken leg, but my grandmother suffered head and internal injuries and spent several days sedated in the intensive care unit. The doctors warned us she might have brain damage, but when her first words on awakening were to ask after her beloved Harley, we knew she would be fine.

And she was, but the healing process was taking more time than she liked. Broken bones and damaged internal organs don't knit back together in the best of circumstances, and my irrepressible grandmother was in her mid-sixties. Trying to explain it to her was an exercise in futility, so I gave up and pretended not to watch every step she took. The physical therapist she saw twice a week was able to be more direct with her than I could, not that he got through to her much better than I did.

Liz also kept an eye on her. She'd been Grandma Natalie's roommate in the hospital. I was fairly certain Liz was a sedate sixty-eight-year-old grandmother until Natalie, the thrill seeker, corrupted her. Now they cruised motorcycle dealerships and stayed out until all hours doing who knew what. I'd always thought that, as the youngest person in the family, I'd be the one saying, "Don't wait up," but there was no accounting for Natalie.

After breakfast, I took a mug of hot coffee up to my room. Before I dove into the tasks Joe had given me, I checked my email. Mandy had been true to her word. I scanned the note she'd sent, surprised and somewhat dismayed at how little information she'd provided. She'd called the missing woman her girlfriend, but she didn't know her birth date and wasn't sure of her age. She'd never met the girlfriend's parents, but she thought their names were James and maybe Louise or Lois. In the end, all I had was a name, a guess at the names of the woman's parents, and the period of time since Mandy had last heard from her.

I couldn't see any way to help Mandy find her missing friend. After all, I thought with some sarcasm, how many women could there be named Sandra Smith who might be about twenty-eight years old? She was a needle in a bushel of needles.

I sent her a quick reply saying I'd start searching within a day or two because I had a busy week coming up. As I closed the email, I blew out a frustrated breath. I never should have agreed to Mandy's request, but I'd do what I could. Which wouldn't be much.

Happy to have something concrete to work on, I turned to the morning's tasks. Fortunately, Dad had been a meticulous recordkeeper. His most recent records were lost in the fire, but I'd found several boxes of older documents stashed in Grandma Natalie's garage. She'd always called him a packrat, but having his paperwork made identifying sources for the shop's products a breeze. As I spoke with each supplier, I wasn't at all surprised to learn how well Dad had treated them, so they were happy to work with us.

Making the calls and taking notes for Joe gave me something to concentrate on, but even then, I thought about Nicky. I didn't know where or how to begin, but I had to try to find her. I couldn't sit back and hope Beth and her new partner would do it. For all I knew, they were humoring me.

My phone rang. "Hi, Brad. What's up?"

"You're coming to the shop today, right? Can you pick up an order for us at the building supply first?"

"Sure, no problem."

"Here's what's on the list."

His voice faded into the background when I realized his request meant I could visit the coffee shop where I'd seen Nicky two days previously. While he droned on, I opened my desk drawer and fished around in the clutter until I found what I wanted.

I turned my attention back to the phone as he said, "Got it?"

"Got it." I fibbed, but it didn't matter. The guys at the building supply would have the information. "I'll probably leave in half an hour or so."

"Sounds good. See you when you get here. And thanks." He ended the call.

I picked up what I'd found in the drawer. It was my favorite photo of Nicky. I'd taken it a week before the fire at my dad's shop, when we'd gone out to Cannon Beach for the day. The sun shone on her face, and the wind off the ocean blew her long blonde hair in all directions. She was laughing at her vain attempts to keep her hair off her face. I tucked the picture into my bag, and with renewed energy, I headed downstairs.

Apparently, my car knew the way to the building supply because my mind wasn't on my driving. While I was driving, all I could think about was finding Nicky. I had no idea how to go about it, beyond some kind of online search. I certainly couldn't knock on the doors of her old friends and say, "Remember Nicky? Who died a year and a half ago? Have you seen her recently?" That would either get the police called on me or earn me a stay in a psych ward somewhere. Or both.

What I could do was ask at the coffee shop. Once Brad's supplies were loaded into my Outback, I headed over there.

I scanned the parking lot before I went in, despite knowing full well how futile it was. She'd been driving a silver minivan. I hadn't realized before how many minivans were on the road, and even worse, it seemed ninety percent of them were silver.

Inside, I ordered a vanilla soy latte, and while I waited, I pulled Nicky's photo from my bag.

"Do you recognize this woman?"

The barista who took my order peered at the photo. "Sorry, no, but we get hundreds of people through here every day." She held out her hand. "Let me show the others." She made the rounds of her coworkers and returned the photo to me. "Sorry, no luck. Friend of yours?"

"Yes. I saw her here on Monday, but now I can't find her."

"How about I make a copy of it? We can put it on the message board, and maybe she'll see it."

Several minutes later, the barista delivered my latte and a copy of the photograph of Nicky. She'd written "Have you seen this woman?" across the top in bold letters. I penned my phone number several times vertically across the bottom, and cut tabs into the paper with the barista's scissors. She pinned it to the board next to ads for housecleaning services and pictures of lost dogs. Even though I doubted it would help, it felt good to have taken the first step. And how was I to know she wouldn't see it and call me?

Fortified by hope and excellent coffee, I drove to the bike shop site with Brad's load of building supplies, stopping on my way long enough to get cold drinks and snacks for the construction crew. July gave us midday temperatures in the low nineties, so I was happy to give the guys something cold to drink while they worked.

As Brad's crew unloaded my car, I did a quick cleanup around the construction site. They still had a few hours to work, but I figured I might as well make myself useful.

After a quick lunch of fries and Diet Coke, I drove to Rachel's clinic and stepped up to the reception desk.

"Hi, Becky. Ready for your vacation?"

The young woman behind the desk gave me a tired smile. "And how. Though driving from Portland to Denver with three kids and a dog doesn't sound very restful, does it?"

"I hope you can relax while you're there."

"Trust me, I'm handing my darling little hoodlums off to their grandparents the moment we arrive. I plan to spend the entire time in the hot tub."

"And this guy?" Becky's dog, a massive Newfoundland, had plopped his drool-laden chin onto my shoe while we talked. I couldn't imagine such a huge dog in a car with three kids. "You can't board him here or hire a pet sitter?"

"Percy has worse separation anxiety than my two-year-old son. It's either take him along or have him sedated the entire time we're away. It's why I bring him to work. He's also why we're renting an RV for the trip." She shook her head slowly, as if wondering how her life had turned out this way. "Come around the desk, and let me show you how it all works."

I sat with her for the rest of the afternoon as she showed me the ropes. The appointments were all on the computer, as was the payment system, which I hoped would make the job easier. While she instructed me, she also expertly answered multiple phone calls and questions of clients who appeared at the desk. She scheduled appointments, took payments, and kept up a flow of conversation without pausing. She seemed to know all of the clients, and most of them wished her a wonderful vacation.

"I'm impressed," I said. "I don't know how you do everything all at the same time."

"You will. Really, the hardest part is knowing what to ask people who want appointments, especially if they say their pet is sick. But I wrote a bunch of stuff down for you, and you can always ask Emily or Danielle."

I knew both of the vet techs since my cat, Shadow, was a clinic patient, so I figured I'd be fine.

Rachel appeared at the desk without warning. "Is she trainable?"

"I don't know," Becky said. "You're in for a rough time."

"Oh, I knew that going in." Rachel turned to me. "You ready?"

"As much as I can be."

"Good. See you Monday." She picked up a file from the desk and left to see her next client.

After Becky and I closed the clinic, I slid into my car and buckled the belt. It had been a full day after a sleepless night, and I was tired. I started the car and headed home.

As I drove, I realized the busy afternoon had given my mind a respite from thinking about Nicky. Maybe taking on the job at Rachel's clinic would be good for me. But now that I wasn't trying to absorb the ins and outs of unfamiliar tasks, my thoughts went back to my apparently not dead former girlfriend.

Where had she been all this time? Why hadn't she contacted me? Why did she let me believe she was dead? Or did she even know many people believed she'd been murdered? I'd never know unless I could ask her.

I suddenly realized I was nowhere near home. My sleep-deprived brain had been so preoccupied with unanswerable questions I'd driven to Nicky's neighborhood on some kind of demented autopilot. I didn't realize what I'd done until I turned onto Nicky's street.

"Second time today," I muttered. "Good thing my brain knows how to drive."

Her parents' home appeared the same as it always had. The pale yellow paint still gleamed, and the red brick was clean. Nicky's mom loved to garden, and the front yard was full of rose bushes, and low-growing evergreens framed the yard. The total effect was one of a warm, welcoming place, which had always been true.

I drove by slowly, not sure what I expected. Would Nicky burst out through the door and run to me, calling my name? I tried to quell my overwrought imagination. Nicky's parents thought she was dead. It wasn't for me to tell them otherwise.

When I arrived at the bike shop late the next afternoon, carrying a cooler in one hand and a canvas bag over my shoulder, Joe was hard at work with Brad and three of the men on his crew. They were taking advantage of the long July days, enclosing the building for the first time by nailing sheets of plywood to the outside of the frame. The sharp report of the nail guns, the buzz of the table saw, and the raised voices of men hard at work were music to my ears. I took a deep breath, savoring the scent of the new wood.

Brad and Joe waited for me to join them.

"Brad, this is amazing. You're making a lot of progress." I handed both men cold soft drinks. "There's string cheese and fruit in the cooler and chips and cookies in the bag, if you're hungry."

Brad called to his crew, and they deserted their work in favor of drinks and snacks. The hard-working construction crew appreciated a break and something cold.

Shards of plywood, remnants of cardboard boxes, and discarded straps that had held the stacks of plywood together were scattered on the ground and on the floor inside the new building. Despite the cleanup work I'd have to do in the heat, I couldn't have been happier.

"It's really coming together, isn't it?" I said to Joe. "Now that they're getting some walls up, it's easier to visualize the end result." As frequently happened, I got a tight feeling in my throat, thinking again of my father, who had put so much of his life toward building his bicycle shop and taking care of his family.

Brad held his cold drink and an open bag of chips against his body with his arm prosthesis and dug into his jeans pocket with his free hand. He pulled a key out and offered it to Joe. "I didn't want to forget to return this."

"Keep it," Joe said. "I have another one."

"What's the key for?" I was clearly out of the loop.

Brad put the key back into his pocket. "Stuff has been going missing here, and Joe's been letting us lock some of it in your storage unit."

He gestured toward the sixteen-by-eight-foot portable storage container we'd had delivered to the site when we were cleaning out the original building.

"I'm sorry to hear it," I said. "I hope it's nothing too valuable."

"I've already replaced two tape measures, a few box cutters, and a carton of nails." He was frustrated. "None of it is expensive, but it adds up fast. At first, I thought the guys were being careless or leaving stuff at other work sites, but that's not it. I mean, it's nice when people stop by to check on our progress, but it also means people are here who shouldn't be. We can't watch everyone."

I turned to Joe. "Should we get a temporary fence? It is a construction site, after all. Don't want anyone getting hurt, as well as pilfering stuff."

"Good idea. I'll check into it tomorrow."

I left them to their snacks and got to work collecting wood scraps and cardboard. After another hour of work, Brad told his crew to call it a day. They all thanked me for the food and drinks, and one by one, they drove their trucks off the lot. Joe and I spent some time walking through the new building and talking about getting the shop up and running it before he retrieved his bike from behind the nearby construction dumpster.

"I'd stay and help, Annie, but I have an early meeting tomorrow at the office. I'll be glad when I can quit and spend my days here instead. Accounting isn't nearly as much fun as helping people pick the perfect bike or showing them how to fix a flat tire." He gave me a smooch on the cheek and, in one smooth movement that belied the prosthetic leg visible below his riding shorts, stepped onto his bike and rode away, shouting over his shoulder, "Don't stay too late."

After he'd gone, I went to work cleaning up after the construction crew. I was pulling on my gloves when two people came toward me, the woman pushing a stroller. Joe was right. People did visit.

"Hello," the man called out. "How are you today?"

I met them halfway, took my right glove off, and shook their hands. "I'm good. Something I can help you with?"

"No, not yet," he said pleasantly. "Just keeping an eye on your progress. We miss the old shop." He paused. "I was sorry to hear about your dad. He was your father, right? Manny?"

"Yes, he was. And thank you. We miss him a lot."

"Will this also be a bike shop?"

"Yes, it will. It'll be bigger, but still Velasquez Cycles."

"Oh," the woman said. She fixed her husband with steely eyes. "I suppose you think you need another bike."

He looked sheepish for a moment. "Jen, you know, N plus one."

She and I were both puzzled. "N plus one?"

"You know, how many bikes a person needs. N plus one, where N is the number you have now." He smiled, but his wife wasn't amused.

"You don't ride?" I asked her.

"I used to, but I haven't in a long time. My bike has turned into a coat hanger out in the garage. It's hard to ride anyway. It's old, and I think it's too tall for me. And besides, he's ridiculously fast, and I can't keep up."

"I know how that is. My brother does the same thing to me. He tries not to, but he almost can't help it. Most of the time, I refuse to ride with him."

"And it's been harder since the baby was born. Finding a sitter isn't always easy."

"Well," I said, drawing the word out, "not taking sides here, but we will carry kiddy trailers you can attach to your bikes."

She appeared to think about it, but before her husband could ruin it with his apparent enthusiasm for all things bicycle, I said "N plus one, huh? I like it. Tell you what, when we open, maybe we'll have an N Plus One sale. If you come in, and if you want, we'll fix you up with a new bike and make sure it fits you perfectly, and we'll get you a trailer for your baby."

"Yes," he said, jumping in. "And we can attach it to my bike so I'll pull the little nugget myself, and we can all go together. And I promise not to leave you behind."

She smiled for the first time. They thanked me for the information, and as they turned to leave, I heard her say, "We'll have to come back when they're open."

My spirits buoyed by my visitors, I turned back to my work. I welcomed the distraction from my encounter with Nicky. Allegedly Nicky? I still didn't know what to think. Mulling it over constantly was exhausting, but I couldn't help trying to make sense of seeing her.

And then there was Mandy and her request, which I was sure I'd be unable to fulfill. Sandra Smith. Could someone have a more generic name?

I went back to work picking up bits of discarded plywood and bent nails while trying to relax and not think about the questions whirling in my mind. Despite my efforts to decompress, I thought again about Mandy and groaned. As I dumped a bucket of wood slivers and dust-covered tape into my wheelbarrow, I thought about how I had no idea how I could possibly help her, and I heartily wished I'd refused to try.

🚲

"Are you tired, hon?" Grandma Natalie greeted me with a hug and a tall glass of iced tea with a slice of lemon. We sat at the kitchen table, and I held the damp glass between my hands. After working for two hours in the heat, I particularly appreciated the cold drink and our air-conditioned home.

"I am. After I made more calls from Joe's list, I went to the shop and cleaned up after the construction guys. I'll be happy to crawl into the recliner with Shadow, find something mindless to watch on TV, and refuse to move." I stirred my tea, trying to mash the lemon against the side of the glass with my spoon. "How was your day? And what smells so good?"

"Spaghetti sauce. Garlic bread in the oven. Are you hungry?"

"Famished, and spaghetti sounds like perfection." I set the table and before long, I was savoring my grandmother's famous sauce and pasta. "I think you could bring about world peace with this stuff."

She put her fork down and looked pensive for a moment. Then she got up from the table and left the kitchen. When she returned, she held a folder I recognized from her many forays into Harley Davidson dealerships. I waited.

"I think I found the right one," she said triumphantly. "As soon as the doctors let me, I'm taking a test ride, but I'm pretty sure this is it."

I stifled a sigh. I'd been hoping my grandmother would come to her senses—or at least what I thought should be her senses—and give up buying another Harley. I should have known better.

"When's your next appointment?"

"Tomorrow. The physical therapist says I'm doing really well. I almost don't need the cane at all. Isn't that great?"

"Of course it is, but you know I worry about you riding again."

She reached over and gave me a comforting pat on the shoulder. "I am who am I am, little one. I'll ride until I ride off into the sunset. You know that already."

"Yeah, but you came far too close to riding off into the sunset not too long ago. I might not be able to keep you from buying another motorcycle, but you can't keep me from worrying."

"You get that from me," she said with a mischievous grin.

I got up from the table and retrieved the paper bag I'd left on a table by the front door. "Here." I handed it to her.

She opened the bag and removed its contents, a photograph of my mother and me, taken when I was a toddler. It usually sat on the end table in the living room. Grandma Natalie had accidentally knocked the photo off the table with her cane and cracked the glass, so I'd gotten it replaced.

"Aren't you a sweetheart." She extended the cardboard triangle on the back of the frame and set the photograph down on the table. "Thank you. I've missed seeing it."

"I wish I could remember her."

"She's been gone a long time. You were too young to remember."

We gazed at the photo silently until she got up to put it back on the end table where it had rested for as long as I could remember. When she returned to the kitchen, she asked, "What are you doing tonight? I mean, other than vegging in the recliner with Shadow."

I let out a low groan. "Thanks for the reminder. You won't believe this, but when Rachel, Sally, and I had dinner at Doug's, the server wanted me to search for her girlfriend."

"What? Why?"

"She had a copy of that damn newspaper article about me, and she's apparently convinced I'm some kind of super sleuth. I let her talk me into doing an online search. But it's impossible. The woman she wants to find is named Smith. No recliner for me for a while. I'll spend a few minutes online, but I don't expect to find anything useful. I don't know what I'll tell her." I finished my tea.

"You'll tell her you tried. That's all you can do."

After we'd finished our meal and got the dishwasher running, Grandma Natalie went into the living room and turned the TV on to her favorite news channel. I went to the desk in my bedroom and opened my laptop. Shadow made himself at home across the keyboard, purring loudly, so I spent the next several minutes scratching behind his ears and petting his silky coat. When he'd had enough, he moved onto my bed, and I called up my email.

Much to my dismay, I already had two new messages from Mandy. Trying not to feel annoyed, I opened the first one.

"Thank u," it read. "I appreciate ur help."

"Okay," I said to Shadow, "that's nice of her." And then I opened the second one, which made me want to retract my words.

"I'm really excited ur going to find Sandy for me. I told all of my friends. We miss her tons, especially me. I showed them ur news article, and they think ur great. Thanks again."

Cursing under my breath at whoever decided dropping two letters from a four-letter word improved communication, I considered finding the reporter who'd written that misleading article and pummeling her with my fists. Then I reconsidered. I already had two homicide detectives eyeing me. I didn't need an assault and battery charge on top of it.

After ten fruitless minutes trying to use Google to identify one Sandra or Sandy Smith from the masses, I reluctantly turned to paid search sites. I picked one I could afford and could easily cancel. All to no avail. I simply didn't have enough information to go on.

Fifteen minutes later, I was done. If Mandy couldn't give me more information, I couldn't help her. I sent her a short email saying the woman's name was too common and even with more precise identifying information, I still didn't think I could help. I suggested she hire a private detective, but at the same time, I suspected she couldn't afford one. I also suspected I hadn't heard the last of Mandy and her missing girlfriend.

As tired as I was, I wasn't ready to quit for the day. I might not find Sandra Smith, but I now wondered what I could find out about Nicole Fleming. I certainly had more information about Nicky than Mandy had provided about her missing friend.

"Why didn't I do this before?"

A Google search brought up news items about her death. They were minimal and didn't include information I didn't already know. "Young woman found shot to death in a Portland alley, suspected to be drug related." That part of Portland had a long history of drug trafficking and prostitution. I didn't find any follow up, but I wasn't surprised. News organizations loved a sensational story, but they seldom provided subsequent information. Mundane reality didn't sell.

I went back to the paid search site and typed in Nicky's name, birthdate, and other information the site requested. For the first time in my life, I found my mouth agape as I viewed her place of birth, parents' names, schools she attended, places she'd lived, phone numbers, and email addresses. I already knew most of it, of course, but I was a bit surprised to find a section listing other possible relatives and associates. Big Brother, indeed. I knew a few of the names on the list, but many of them were new to me. I wondered if the list wasn't accurate, but it wasn't outside the realm of possibility she had friends and family I'd never met.

I thought about it for a moment. Maybe I could talk to them. "No and no," I said out loud. "Don't be an idiot."

I printed the information and went back to Google. I'd already seen and saved the stories about the fire at the bike shop, my father's death, and his obituary. Then I saw one I'd somehow missed about the fire investigation, where the investigators had concluded the fire was started by chemicals stored in the shed behind the bike shop, chemicals commonly used in the manufacture of methamphetamine. I knew about the source of the fire, but for the first time, I wondered how the fire investigators had identified the chemicals. Weren't they destroyed in the fire? I sent off a quick email to Sally and Rachel and went down to join Grandma Natalie in front of the TV.

Chapter Four

Two mornings later, I huffed and puffed and cursed myself for suggesting to my friends that we go for a run up the dormant volcano at Mount Tabor Park. I stopped and bent over, my hands on my knees and stars before my eyes. A few steps later, they realized they'd left me behind and circled back.

"Are you okay?" Sally put a comforting hand on my back.

I peered at her through slitted eyes. "The least you could do is pretend to be out of breath," I groused. "Saturdays shouldn't be this much work."

She laughed, a full-throated sound. At six feet and muscular, subtle she was not, but since she was a Portland firefighter and emergency medical technician, she couldn't very well be a wallflower.

"Are you kidding? Every time I get a call, I have to get into gear weighing at least fifty pounds. If we're on a fire call, I have to run with all of it on, sometimes up multiple flights of stairs. If I got out of breath easily, I'd be out of a job. This little hill is nuthin.' What happened to your bike-riding stamina?"

By then, I'd recovered enough to stand upright. "Between taking care of Grandma Natalie and working at the shop, I haven't ridden at all. And sitting on my behind at the clinic sure won't help. My bike is collecting dust in the garage."

"Joe doesn't drag you out for rides?" Rachel asked.

"He tries, but I feel bad because he's much faster than I am. He zips away and then stops and waits for me. He means well, but him waiting for me makes me feel even slower, so I don't go."

"Totally understandable. Okay, let's walk for a bit until you've at least got some color in your face."

"Maybe it's good you're an EMT," I said to Sally. "This fitness thing will be the death of me."

We walked up the steepest part of the grade and jogged to reach the top. I always loved the view from the summit of Mount Tabor Park, so we found a bench where we could admire the sight of Portland, spread out from the city's east side to the Willamette River and to downtown on the other side of the river. By the time we'd made ourselves comfortable, my pulse was out of the heart attack range, and I could breathe well enough to broach the subject with Sally that had prompted me to email her.

"You mind if I pick your firefighter brain?"

She exchanged a wary glance with Rachel. "What are you getting into now? You're not trying to find the woman you saw, are you? Nicky's twin?"

She knew me too well.

"No," I protested, but when I saw she didn't believe me, I gave up. "Okay, fine, yes. I can't do nothing, can I?" I turned on the bench to face her. "Look, the investigation into Nicky's murder is dragging on. And what if she's actually alive? I'm beyond tired of having this thing hanging over my head. She told Patrick and me there's been no new information for months. And yes"—I raised a hand to stop their objections—"I know there's a lot the detectives can't or won't tell me."

"Not even your gorgeous detective?"

I rolled my eyes. "No, not even Detective O'Brien." Maybe using her title would defuse things a bit. "And she's not mine. I wish you'd knock it off."

"Sorry, but it's too easy." Sally grinned for a moment before saying, "So?"

I resigned myself to what was sure to follow. Outrage. Demands that I "stay in my lane," whatever the hell that meant. Appeals to my safety and to how my grandmother would feel if something happened to me. Every possible objection.

"I've decided to do some investigating of my own." I waited.

"Okay. How can I help?"

"You mean, how can *we* help, don't' you?" Rachel asked.

For half a second, I wondered how I could be so wrong about their reactions. With such a poor ability to predict human behavior, I'd never make a decent detective. Good thing I had no such aspirations.

"You're not surprised? You're not going to insist I don't do it?"

"Why? It wouldn't stop you. Any progress yet?"

"Okay, remember Mandy, from Doug's?"

"You mean your new girlfriend?" Rachel's grin couldn't have gotten any wider.

"Give it a rest," I said, annoyed. "She emailed me about her missing girlfriend. Get this: she doesn't even know the woman's age or birth date. And her name is Sandra Smith."

Both of my friends rolled their eyes.

"Exactly. But I did what I told her I would do. I went online and tried some searches. I even signed up for one of those paid sites where you can find information about people."

"And?"

"Nada, zilch, zero, nothing."

"Bupkis." Rachel added to the list.

"Exactly," I said. "But then I thought, what the hell, I've already paid for it, so let's see what I can find out about Nicky."

"And?"

"Most of what I got was stuff I already knew, but there were phone numbers and addresses I'm not familiar with. And the lists of people associated with her also included names I don't recognize. I have no idea how accurate those sites are, but at least it's something."

"I'm surprised you haven't walked up to her parents' door and asked to see her." Rachel narrowed her eyes at me. "You wouldn't do that, would you?"

"Part of my brain wants me to." I told them about my semiconscious drive to the Flemings' neighborhood. "Once I realized where I was, I left, and I hope they didn't see me. Even if they did, they wouldn't recognize my new car."

"Wow, it's a good thing you don't drink and drive," Sally said. "There's no telling what you might do."

"Yeah, I was exhausted. I probably shouldn't have been driving at all. Otherwise, all I have is a couple of news articles about the fire at the shop." I turned to Sally. "Which is why I wanted to talk with you. They say the fire was started by chemicals usually used to make meth. How would they know? Wouldn't the fire have destroyed any chemicals?"

"I don't know enough about them to be able to say with any certainty. Why would Nicky have had drug-related chemicals anyway? It was like pulling teeth to get her to have a beer with us."

"I know," I said. "I can't imagine her using drugs, much less making them."

"Portland fire investigation summary reports are public," Sally said. "It wouldn't explain why Nicky would have put stuff like that in your dad's shed, but it might include an analysis or something to help us understand which chemicals they found. You can order reports from the fire department website." She thought for a moment. "It probably takes a few weeks, but I might get a full report more quickly myself. Let me see what I can do, and I'll let you know."

I wrapped her in a fierce hug.

"Thank you very much. Dinner next time is on me."

I peered out the front window again, trying my best not to disturb the curtain.

"Are they here yet?" Joe was practically dancing with excitement behind me.

I turned away from the window. "Not yet, but Liz's text said they were a few minutes away."

The last time Grandma Natalie's living room was this festive was the day she came home from the hospital. After she was moved from intensive care into a regular room, all of her friends, including many she made from the hospital staff, had showered her with gifts. The potted plants, fruit baskets, stacks of magazines and Harley catalogs, and more mylar balloons than I'd ever seen in one place took up so much room in my Subaru there was almost nowhere for my grandmother.

This time, the decorations didn't say, "Welcome Home," but instead "Happy Birthday" in bright colors. I threw in a black one from the "over the hill" collection, just for fun, but the rest were made with bright colors. Most of them sported streamers of crepe paper and ribbon.

We'd covered the kitchen counter with platters of Grandma Natalie's favorite foods and, of course, a beautifully decorated cake festooned with candles took center stage on the kitchen table. The perimeter of the table and all the chairs were filled with brightly wrapped gifts.

"Do you think she suspects anything?" Joe was trying to peek through the curtain.

Grandma Natalie was notorious for discovering what people were trying to keep secret. My band of co-conspirators and I had been as careful as we could be, never talking about a party anywhere near my grandmother, not even on the phone. In the past, I'd theorized she was psychic or able to detect radio waves or mental vibes. She could sniff out a conspiracy a mile away. It was uncanny.

"I don't think so, but the glitter you spilled on the stairs might give us away." I poked him in the ribs, as a dutiful sister should do to a wayward brother.

"It got away from me. I tried to put some on a balloon, and it stuck to everything else."

"Including your sweater." Hearing an engine, I held up a hand to quiet him and the others who waited behind me. "I think they're here."

I shooed everyone into the kitchen and turned off the lights. The only illumination in the living room was the lamp I used when I was reading alone at night. Since it was still July, the sun hadn't yet set, but Grandma Natalie wouldn't consider it unusual for me to be sitting by the lamp with a book in hand.

The front door opened, and Grandma Natalie came in, followed by Ada and Liz. The plan was for them to take my grandmother to lunch and then on some kind of excursion to keep her occupied for the afternoon. I wasn't sure what they'd decided on, but their timing was perfect.

"Hi, Annie," Grandma Natalie said. "Good book?"

From behind our mutual victim, Liz gave me a thumbs up.

I spoke the magic words. "A bit boring, actually. Maybe we could do something fun instead."

And chaos erupted. All the kitchen lights came on at once. Twenty people jumped up and yelled, "Surprise!" and "Happy Birthday!" Grandma Natalie was stunned. Joe picked her up in a bear hug, followed by Patrick, Liz, and Ada. My grandmother's other friends and acquaintances took their turns. Rachel, Sally, and Sharon, my friend from Charbonneau, joined in. The crowd pulled her into the kitchen to admire the birthday cake.

Joe said, "You might need some help blowing out all those candles."

She slapped him on the shoulder. "Not a chance, kiddo." Everyone laughed.

After a few minutes, Grandma Natalie came to me with a look of amazement on her face. "How did you do this? I had no idea."

"That right there makes it all worthwhile. You're a hard one to keep secrets from."

"It's wonderful." She held me in a tight hug and when she spoke, she sounded choked up. "I love you, Annie. Thank you for such an amazing surprise."

She went back into the kitchen and surveyed the bounty of food on the counters. Then she turned to the partiers. "Thanks to all of you for this. Knowing Annie"—she smiled at me—"you've all been working on it for quite a while. I hope you know how grateful I am, but now I also know how devious you can be. Let's eat. These two kept me busy all afternoon, and I'm starving."

Sharon and Rachel had arranged the food so the partygoers could take a plate and make their way along the counters to select what they wanted. Utensils were at the end. Liz and I moved Grandma Natalie's gifts to the living room, leaving plenty of places for people to sit and eat. I stood back to watch the homemade buffet line in action, making sure everyone had what they wanted.

"Where did you get all of this food? I know you didn't cook it, unless you've also been keeping this from me."

"Remember Freddy, the woman who owns the Charbonneau Diner?"

"Of course."

"And my friend, Mo?"

"How could I ever forget Mo after what you two went through? She's a chef at Freddy's diner now, isn't she?"

"Yep. They did all of this, including bringing it here from Charbonneau."

"Are they here?" She craned her neck, trying to see.

"No, they had to get back for the dinner rush. But the food and the beautiful cake are their gifts to you."

For the second time that evening, my grandmother was surprised. "I'll be sure to go out there and thank them."

She went to the counter and picked up a plate, taking her place in the buffet line. I was almost ready to join her when my phone vibrated in my pocket. I didn't recognize the number on the screen but answered it anyway. With the work I was doing to get the new bike shop business organized, I frequently got calls from unfamiliar numbers.

"Hi, this is Annie." I was greeted by a silence long enough for me to say, "Is someone there?" and put my finger on the "end call" button.

And then she spoke.

"Hi, Annie."

My world stopped. I was dumbstruck, unable to breathe or move.

"Annie?"

I finally took a deep breath. "Nicky?" My eyes felt as wide as dinner plates as I turned toward the people in the kitchen, but I wasn't seeing them. "Is that you?"

In a flash, Grandma Natalie appeared in front of me, looking concerned. She didn't speak, but the question was clear on her face, and I nodded. She made a beeline for Patrick and spoke to him in a low voice. His head shot around, and he gave me a piercing stare. He stage-whispered, "Nicky?" I nodded again. He grabbed his phone and went into the living room.

His urgent tone of voice carried over the conversation of the party. "Beth, Patrick Wyatt here." I returned my focus to my own caller.

"Yes, it's me. I only have a minute, but I wanted to say happy birthday to Grandma Natalie. Will you tell her for me?"

"Yes, of course I will. But Nicky, please, please talk to me. Where have you been?"

At the sound of Nicky's name, Rachel put her plate down and came over to me, her eyes wide with questions. She leaned in and I tilted the phone so she could hear the conversation. Sally also joined us.

"I'm sorry about the coffee shop. I never expected to see you there, and I freaked out."

Rachel went pale, but she put her arm around my shoulders, always the supportive friend. Sally rubbed my back in support. We followed Patrick into the living room, where it was quieter than the kitchen.

"Please talk to me. I need to understand. How could you disappear and leave me alone? Where have you been?"

"I can't explain, but I didn't have any choice. I wasn't even supposed to send you a note at all."

"Dad died in that fire. He loved you and treated you like a second daughter." I felt like sobbing, both from the shock of hearing her voice and from a sudden stab of grief for my father, for Nicky, for the losses of the last year and a half. "I've missed you terribly."

"The fire wasn't my fault, Annie." She sounded as if she might cry. "I never would have hurt Dad. Never." She paused for a moment. "Sorry. I have to go." She ended the call.

Suddenly, all strength left my body. My arms dropped to my side and my phone fell to the floor. Rachel caught me as I started to slide. Sally helped her guide me into a nearby chair. Patrick kneeled in front of me, phone still in his hand, while my friends hovered nearby, concerned.

"Are you okay?" His voice was low, but he was clearly worried. "What did she say?" He looked up at Rachel and Sally. "Was it Nicky?"

"Yes," they spoke together.

Rachel said. "I'd know her voice anywhere."

By this time, everyone was aware something had happened. Grandma Natalie quietly filled them in, and I heard low voices saying, "Nicky? Really?" and "What did she want?"

When I got enough strength back to sit up straighter, I said, "She wanted to send birthday wishes to Grandma Natalie." For some reason, it struck me as funny, and I started to laugh, sounding more shocked than amused. "How weird is that? She leaves me to twist in the wind and be investigated by the police, and what she wants is to say happy birthday."

My laughter died down as quickly as it started, and tears filled my eyes. Patrick had remained by me, so I grabbed his hand. "What did Beth say?"

He held his phone out to me. "Ask her yourself."

Hesitantly, I took his phone. "Detective?"

"Hi Annie. How sure are you it was Nicole Fleming?"

"One hundred percent. Hold on. My friends are here. I'll put you on the speaker." Patrick pushed the button after I held the phone out to him. "I'm here with my grandmother, Rachel, Sally, and a lot of other friends. It's my grandma's birthday party."

"Hi, everyone." Her voice carried nicely. "Did any of you know Nicole Fleming?"

"Rachel Simmons here, Detective. We were all good friends. We'd know her voice anywhere. It was her, no question about it."

Grandma Natalie spoke up. "I didn't hear much of the call, but I heard enough. And if Annie's reaction is any indication, it was definitely Nicky."

"Reaction?"

"She went wide-eyed and pale and started shaking. Annie's not one to take to a fainting couch, Detective."

"Yeah, I learned that some time ago. Okay, thanks, everyone. Patrick, can we talk for a moment?"

He took the phone and pushed the button to turn the speaker off. He spoke with the detective in low tones for a minute or two before ending the call.

"What did she say?"

"Not much. She wants me to get the number Nicky called from." He checked my phone. "I'll text it to her and see if there's anything she can find out from it."

"I'm impressed you were able to reach her on a Saturday evening."

"She's dedicated to her job."

I finally had enough strength to stand on my own and decided to try for humor. I waved everyone back into the kitchen. "Move along, everyone," I said in my best TV police officer voice. "Nothing to see here."

The mood in the house lightened and our friends went back to their plates. I picked up a plate and made my way down the line. With healthy servings of Freddy's excellent food—especially her famous pastrami—I found a seat between Sally and Rachel. Unfortunately while I'd always loved Freddy's cooking, I was too preoccupied by Nicky's call, and I didn't taste much. I listened to everyone's conversations while my mind tried to make sense of what had happened.

After everyone had eaten, we cleared the counters and put the leftovers away. Joe carefully carried the birthday cake into the living room and placed it on the coffee table.

"At least," Grandma Natalie said to him, "you didn't spill it like you did the glitter." So she had seen the multicolored sparkles on the carpet. Couldn't put much past my grandmother.

While Sally lit the candles, we made jokes about how we needed a firefighter at the party in case the cake got out of control. Grandma Natalie joined in, cracking wise at her own expense, but everyone went quiet when she did, indeed, blow out all sixty-six candles on the first try.

It was Sally's turn. "With lungs like yours, if this place ever catches fire, you won't need to call me." Grandma Natalie laughed heartily and hugged my friend.

Over the next forty minutes, she opened her gifts, much to the oohs and aahs of the onlookers. I enjoyed watching her bask in the spotlight, but my evening had been spoiled.

Nicky was alive.

Early the next morning, I was sitting at the kitchen table with my hands cupped around a mug of coffee long since gone cold when Grandma Natalie came in. She still wore her flannel pajamas and a flowered robe a friend had given her while she was in the hospital.

"You're up early," she said. "The sun isn't even up yet."

"I never went to bed. I mean, I got into bed, but when I couldn't sleep, I gave up trying."

She slid into the chair across from me and took the mug from my hands. "This is cold. Want fresh?"

"Yes, please." I was unable to hold back a yawn. "I made it at about one thirty. I won't vouch for it being fit for human consumption."

She went to the coffeemaker and took a whiff of the sludge I'd created. "It isn't now, and I'm pretty sure it never was." She poured it out and started a new pot. "Anyone ever say you're a hazard in the kitchen?"

"Only you," I tried to smile through my exhaustion.

Grandma Natalie came around behind me and massaged my shoulders. I leaned back against her, savoring her warmth and the solid feel of her body.

"I tried to call her back last night."

My grandmother went to the counter and put bread into the toaster. "I thought you might. Did you talk with her?"

"No. She didn't answer, and there was no way to leave a voicemail. It rang until I gave up. I tried a couple of times." I pulled my robe around me in a futile attempt to get warm. I wondered if the chill I felt was exhaustion or a comment on the course of my life. "It'll be interesting to see what Beth can find out from the number, but I'm not counting on it."

"Disposable phone?" Grandma Natalie watched a lot of police and detective shows.

"Why not?" The delectable aroma of coffee filled the room and not long after, she brought me a full mug of fresh brew. "Makes as much sense as anything else in my life these days." A plate of buttered toast and a jar of extra crunchy peanut butter joined my coffee mug. "Thank you."

"Other than getting some sleep, what are you doing today?"

"I thought I'd vacuum Joe's glitter off the stairs."

"Make him do it himself."

"He'd make it worse. But cleaning the house might help wake me up. People left dishes everywhere, though I think Shadow took his turn with the leftovers. Sugar isn't good for him, so I might have more than dishes to clean up." Grandma Natalie and I both wrinkled our noses at the thought of what my cat might produce after a night of his own partying. "And then I think I'll go to the shop. Being outside might be good for me."

"How do you feel about Nicky calling last night?"

I sat back in my chair and blew my breath out. "I can't even imagine why she called. After all this time, deserting me, letting us think she was dead, and what's on her mind is your birthday?"

"Maybe my birthday gave her an excuse to do what she wanted to do anyway, which was talk to you."

I thought for a moment. "Maybe, but it would be nice to ask her."

I spent the next hour trying to put the house back into its pre-party order. Before long, the dishwasher was full and running, with more dishes rinsed and waiting in the sink. After several minutes of diligent vacuuming, I declared Joe's glitter to be a permanent part of the carpet on the stairs. Grandma Natalie rounded up all the balloons well-wishers had brought and Shadow hadn't been able to reach and took them into her bedroom. We stood back and surveyed the results of our work and declared the job good enough.

"Why don't you go take a nap?"

I didn't have the strength to disagree. I'd barely gotten comfortable under a blanket on my bed with Shadow snuggling against me when my alarm pinged. I'd figured to sleep for about three hours, thinking I'd feel more like working at the shop after a good nap, but the alarm woke me too soon. I glared at it, trying to blame it for my inability to set a clock until I realized three hours had indeed passed.

I mumbled a tired apology to the clock and pushed the blanket back. I washed my face and went downstairs. Patrick was sitting with Grandma Natalie in the kitchen. I poured myself a mug of coffee and joined them at the table.

"You up for a road trip?" For once, he was dressed more casually than usual, jeans and a pullover instead of what I called his lawyer suit.

"It depends. Where are we going?"

"Beth wants to see us." He didn't have to tell me why.

"Shouldn't you be dressed as some kind of hotshot lawyer?" I wasn't in any mood for his shenanigans.

"It's Sunday. Even I get a day off now and then. And so does Beth, which is why she asked us to meet her somewhere other than her office. Wear clothes you don't care will get dirty."

Half an hour later, he pulled into a gravel parking lot next to a well-tended field enclosed by chain-link fencing.

"A dog park? We're meeting her at a dog park?"

"Why not? It's a nice day, and she likes to bring her dogs here."

He led me through a gate into the first enclosure, and then a second gate to a smaller area. One part of the park was for large dogs and the other was for small ones. We went into the small dog section.

"There she is." He pointed to the far corner of the park.

"Holy shit," I groused. "I really hate you more than usual right now."

He looked pleased with himself. "I can't imagine why."

Beth saw us and waved, and we walked toward her. She started in our direction, followed by two bounding fluffy balls. The dogs distracted me for a moment, but nothing would hold my attention longer than a few seconds when the woman I'd had too many dreams about came closer. She was dressed as anyone would for a visit to the dog park, but few could look that good in faded jeans and a baggy T-shirt.

Before she got much closer, I mumbled, "Asshole," to Patrick, and he chuckled.

"Hi, Annie. Hi, Patrick. Thanks for meeting me here." She bent down and took a ball from one of the dogs, and in an athletic move, threw it toward the far end of the park. Both animals ran after it, and she turned back to us. "I want to talk with you about last night, but I didn't want to go into the office today. It's too nice outside. And those two crazies needed to run off some energy."

We found a bench under a tree in one corner of the park and made ourselves comfortable. Beth's dogs returned with the ball she'd thrown, accompanied by another dog. Tired as I was, I was enjoying watching all the dogs running and playing. She threw the ball again, and they all sped after it.

"Doing this gets old after a while," she said, "but they love this place."

"What breed are they?" I didn't know much about dog breeds, but their fluffy fur and little round eyes were appealing.

"Lhasa Apsos. Their friend with the blue eyes is a miniature Australian Shepherd. He's here almost every time we are, so they play together." Her expression changed from amusement at watching the dogs play to one more suitable to our conversation. She pulled a notebook and a pen from a bag she had close by.

"I wanted to follow up on our call last night. Since you were having a party, I didn't want to get into details, so can we do it now?"

"Sure."

"You're sure it was Nicky?"

"Absolutely. Detective, we lived together for years and were planning to get married. Do you think I wouldn't recognize her voice?"

"I apologize. That came out wrong. I'm sorry." She paused and then went on. "Tell me what she said."

I related the conversation as close to verbatim as I could. "After the party was over, we talked for a few minutes about how odd it was that she called after all this time, and all she wanted was to wish Grandma Natalie a happy birthday. I tried calling her back, but she didn't answer.

To be clear, there's no way it wasn't Nicky. Grandma Natalie recognized her voice right away. You remember when I told you about my friends, Sally and Rachel?"

"Yes, I do."

"They were at the party, too, and listened in with me. Rachel told you over the phone it was Nicky, but obviously, you can talk to her and Sally yourself if you need to."

She wrote for several seconds and put the notebook away. "What I can do is try to find where the call originated. Even if the number she called from is blocked, the phone records will show which cell towers she was closest to when she called. We might be able to narrow down her location. I can't promise anything, but we'll try."

"I understand."

"But first you have something very important to do."

"Oh?"

"Look down." Both of her dogs and their friend were sitting at my feet. One of them had dropped the ball, and they all waited, almost vibrating in anticipation.

"You have to throw the ball."

Chapter Five

I arrived home after my first day behind the desk at Rachel's clinic to find a shiny, new Harley Davidson parked near the garage door. Its polished chrome reflected the sun. I wasn't surprised to see it, since Grandma Natalie's doctors had given her the all clear to resume any activities she wanted. She and Liz had haunted motorcycle dealerships almost since the day my grandmother was released from the hospital after her crash.

On the other hand, its companion puzzled me. Another motorcycle sat close by, its fenders scratched and dented. Dried mud crusted the wheels.

I contemplated the sparkling new machine with resignation. I should have known better than to think she'd wait a while before buying a new Harley.

"Grandma, what did you do?" I dropped my car keys and wallet onto the table inside the front door.

"We're in the kitchen, Annie," she called.

We. That explained the second machine in the driveway.

In the kitchen, my grandmother's guest rose from the table. At his full height, he towered over my own five foot nine. He extended an enormous hand to me.

"Hi, Annie. Nice to meet you, finally. I'm Edward Bailey, but everyone calls me Chip."

"Good to meet you." I hoped I sounded far less surprised than I was. I shook his hand, making a mental note to ask my grandmother to explain the word "finally" in his introduction. As he returned to the table, I raised an eyebrow in her direction.

No way would I let Grandma Natalie keep this story to herself. I turned to my grandmother. "I see you have a new toy." Only after I spoke did I realize it sounded as if I meant the man dwarfing our kitchen and not the sparkling Harley in the driveway.

"Toy?" Chip roared with laughter. "Hon, that ain't no toy. That there's a first-class ridin' machine. Now that Nat can ride again, we're going to have some fun."

Nat? He calls her Nat? And she lets him get away with it?

Not meeting my eyes, Grandma Natalie poured me a glass of iced tea and refilled their partially empty ones. She put out a plate of homemade cookies, peanut butter from the look of them. I took one, and while I munched on the scrumptious cookie, I sized up the man sitting across from me.

He appeared to be about the same age as my grandmother, mid-sixties. Besides standing at least eight inches taller than me, he was big, with broad shoulders. No wonder his hand had engulfed mine. The man was not a chip. He was a whole bag—a whole *display* of chips. A mane of silver-gray hair brushed his shoulders, and his beard was neatly trimmed. No wimpy goatee for him.

I turned to my grandmother and tilted my head toward the front of the house. "Is it the one you told me you picked out?"

"Isn't it beautiful? It's a Road Glide, and its name fits perfectly. I knew I'd love it, but I waited until I could take a test ride to buy it. Chip went with me, and we had a fun ride down the freeway and around town. The moment I rode it, I had to have it."

On impulse, I stood up from my chair and leaned over to give her a hug. "Promise me you'll be careful."

She patted me on the shoulder. "Always."

"You don't have to worry about Nat," Chip said. Age had apparently not affected his hearing. "She's the best rider I've ever seen. Better than me, even."

I resumed my seat at the table. "Has she told you about last spring?" Since we were "finally" meeting, I assumed she had, but I inquired anyway. "How close we came to losing her?"

"She told me, and I understand your concern. But the wreck wasn't her fault. She told me all about it, and Ada told me how she tried to avoid that truck and ended up saving both of them. You don't have anything to worry about."

Okay, so he'd been around long enough to meet at least one of my grandmother's friends. I wondered how many dinners with Liz and Ada were really dates with Chip. Nobody called my grandmother Nat, at least not more than once.

Over the next half an hour, I learned Chip was a retired truck driver. His wife of thirty years died a decade earlier, and his two grown children lived in Portland. His daughter was a nurse, and his son owned a house painting company.

"Where did you meet?"

He confirmed my suspicion when he said, "At the Harley dealership in Tigard. I've been thinking about getting another bike, and I was doing some shopping. And one day, here comes this little lady and I thought 'you're kiddin' me,' and it turned out she knows more about these machines than I do." The look in his eyes told me he was thinking, "and the rest is history."

By the time he left, having declined an invitation to stay for dinner, I'd started to understand why Grandma Natalie had invited him into our home. Almost despite myself, I'd liked him, even though it was clear they had deliberately left me in the dark.

After he'd gone, I turned to her. "You have a boyfriend?"

She blushed. "I'm sorry. I—"

"How long has this been going on?" I realized I sounded like an exasperated parent, so I tried to tone it down. "I don't mean it like that. You know I don't like surprises. And this is a biggie. He really likes you."

We went into the living room and sat at opposite ends of the sofa, turning a bit to face each other. Shadow jumped up in between us and enjoyed being the center of attention from two people rather than one. For a moment, the only sound in the house was his purring.

Grandma Natalie spoke first. "I didn't want to say anything until I knew he would be around. You know I haven't had a serious relationship since your grandfather died. It was a long time ago. And I've been fine. You and your dad were my family, and then Joe joined us. Everything was great." She amended her words after a moment. "Everything *is* great." She paused. "But your dad is gone, and Joe doesn't live with us any longer. And you'll want your own place at some point." She held up a hand as I opened my mouth to object. "Yes, you will, and you should. You should have a life with your friends and a girlfriend or even a wife. It's only right. But I need to live my own life. I wouldn't enjoy being alone in this house."

"But you have friends. And Joe and I aren't going anywhere. Sure, I'll probably get another girlfriend sometime. At least I hope so. I know Joe's been hoping to meet someone special. But we're still your family." Despite my protest, I knew she was right.

"Of course you are. Friends are great. Liz and Ada and the others are wonderful. And even a few of your friends check in with me now and then. But it's not the same." She reached over and grasped my hand. "You know it's not the same."

"Yes, I know."

"Then I met Chip, and he asked me to coffee."

We sat silently for a few moments until Shadow nudged my hand with his head. He climbed onto my lap and made himself at home, purring and kneading his paws against my leg.

"How long ago was that?"

"About a month, maybe six weeks. We've been to dinner a few times, and he gave me a couple of rides on his bike when I was in Harley withdrawal." She smiled at the memory. "He's a good man, Annie. I haven't met his children yet. I'm not even sure he's told them he's dating. You're the first to know."

The weight I'd felt in my chest when I first realized she'd kept all of this from me started to lighten.

"It's not fair, you know."

"I know. I should have—"

"No, not that. Well, yes, you should have told me. But what I meant was it's not fair that you're dating and I'm not."

"Entirely your own fault."

"He's gigantic. His name gives me the giggles. Chips are tiny, little things. He's huge. And he calls you 'Nat'."

"Yeah." She wrinkled her nose. "I've been trying to get him to stop, but so far, no luck."

My next thought made me chuckle. "Maybe," I said to her inquiring expression, "maybe he doesn't mean it as short for Natalie, but as descriptive, like a gnat." I spelled it for her. "He's big enough to make you appear even smaller than you are."

She slapped my arm but laughed along with me. "I'll ask him. Now give me a hug, and let's make dinner."

After we ate our meal and cleaned the kitchen, I went online and rechecked the website I'd found when searching for Mandy's missing friend. The fee I'd paid was good for another three weeks, so I figured I might as well get my money's worth.

I put Nicky's name in again and got the same report as before, but this time, I switched my printer on. If the Portland Police Bureau wasn't making any progress in its investigation, or at least any they'd told Patrick and me about, then I'd see what I could find for myself.

As before, I reviewed the information I already had. Where there was new information, I made notes. She'd had more addresses in Portland than I knew about, but I didn't think too much of it. New college graduates tended to move frequently. The information might not be useful, but I printed it anyway, along with a string of phone numbers and addresses. I had no way to know how accurate the information might be, but I kept all of it.

The next section consisted of possible associates and relatives. Some names were familiar to me, such as family members and mutual friends we'd had in college. My name appeared, of course, but I didn't know many of the people on the list. Maybe I could find a way to talk with them without sounding like a total lunatic.

While the printer was working, I found a section for civil judgments and any criminal background far enough down the page I hadn't seen it the first time. Curious, I scrolled down.

At first, there wasn't anything I didn't already know. She'd had a couple of speeding tickets, which didn't surprise me. She loved driving fast. I mean, who didn't?

Maybe, I mused, it's good Nicky never went for a ride with Grandma Natalie.

Then I read something that made me momentarily hold my breath. The police had arrested her three times for possession of a controlled substance. Two were for small amounts of marijuana, and they put her on probation and ordered her to pay a fine each time. The third time was for possession with intent to distribute. That charge was apparently reduced. All of the charges were before 2015, when Oregon changed its marijuana laws.

A boulder settled into the pit of my stomach. All of it had happened before we met, and she'd never told me. In all our time together, I'd never known her to use drugs. So I couldn't help but wonder how she went from minor marijuana infractions to apparently making meth in my dad's shed.

Then realization took my breath away. This new information meant she'd had connections with people who produced and sold drugs for a long time. Maybe what she'd been up to behind the bike shop was nothing new. Maybe she had more secrets than I could ever have imagined.

Maybe I didn't know her at all.

I leaned back in my chair and stared at the computer screen. The black and white letters of the words morphed into a fog before my eyes. How could I have known so little about her? We were planning to get married. I'd have pledged my life and love to her and not known any of this. What else didn't I know?

Beth must certainly have this information. Did she think I already knew?

I stood up and collected my printout. I tapped the pages into place and stapled them at the corner. The actions I took were automatic. My eyes were open, but I saw nothing. My entire focus was internal.

A split second later, I screamed in rage and threw the printout across the room. It wafted to the floor a few feet away. As I collapsed into my office chair, my bedroom door flew open. Grandma Natalie wrapped me in her arms and held me tight.

"What's wrong, Annie?" She stroked my hair. "Are you okay?"

I blinked and came back to my room. My head hurt, my chest felt tight, and my face was wet with tears.

"Annie, please, talk to me." She held me by my shoulders and looked into my eyes, worry spread across her face. "What's wrong?"

"Nicky—" Unable to speak without stuttering, I waved in the computer's direction, out of breath.

Grandma Natalie dragged me out of the chair and over to my bed. We sat on the edge, and she held me while tears ran down my face. I felt like a bereft child, and maybe at that moment, I was.

After several minutes, Grandma Natalie fetched a washcloth soaked with cold water and soothed my face with it. Nothing had ever felt so good. Once I could breathe more normally, she let me go, and I sat up straight. I took a deep breath, trying to quell my anger.

"What's this about, honey? You know you can tell me."

"You can, too, girlfriend of Chip." My attempt at humor was feeble, but I was starting to feel better.

"Touché. And?"

"Remember the woman I told you about who wants me to find her missing friend?"

"Mm hm."

"I signed up for one of those background check sites. It's not expensive, so I thought I'd check there. I mean, the woman's name is Sandra Smith, for pity's sake. I had to try something."

She waited for me to continue.

"I didn't find Sandra Smith, but I figured while I was on the website, I'd put Nicky's name in. I thought maybe I'd find something to prove she's alive, like a current address or something." Another tear ran down my face, and I wiped it away.

"Did you find it?"

"I'm not sure. But it says she has a criminal record. She was arrested for drug possession, and she was apparently a drug dealer. How could she keep that from me? She had to know those chemicals were dangerous." My anger returned. "And she put them at the shop anyway." I started crying again. "She killed Dad."

Grandma Natalie held me tight while I cried tears of grief for my beloved father and for the Nicky I'd loved but who was a stranger to me in so many ways. Sobs welled up from my chest and restricted my breathing. After what felt like a long time, I sat up, took a shaky breath, and wiped my face.

"I'm sorry if I scared you. I can never forgive her for what she did. And yes, I'm angry she lied to me." I tried a weak smile and mopped my face with the washcloth she'd brought. "I hate that I cry when I'm really mad."

She led me down to the kitchen and cut me a piece of my favorite pie, strawberry rhubarb, and poured us both mugs of steaming coffee. She sat down across from me with her own slice of pie and added sugar and cream to her cup.

"It's well-known in our family that pie can cure nearly anything." She waited until I took a bite. "Everyone has secrets."

"But—"

"Yes, I know." She headed off my protest. "This one's much bigger than most."

I took a drink of coffee. "I feel as if I never really knew her. And we talked about getting married. It's not as if she'd had a past relationship she didn't want to talk about. That's normal. This isn't. Not by a long shot." I blew out my breath. "My head is spinning."

"You should talk with Patrick about it. He can check with the detective to see if the website is accurate."

"Good point, but earlier, out of curiosity, I put in my own name, and the data it showed was right on the money. It was actually creepy, how much information they had."

"It doesn't necessarily mean Nicky's is correct. There must be other women with the same name."

I felt a spark of encouragement. "Here's hoping."

"Does it say she was arrested in Portland?"

I nodded, having taken a bite of pie.

"Here's what you're going to do. Call Patrick, tell him what you found, and ask him to confirm the information with the detective. If she's as thorough as you and Patrick have told me, then she'll know, or she'll know where to find out."

"If it turns out to be true, I wonder if Beth believes I knew what Nicky was doing." Another thought struck me. "Could it somehow make the police think I had even more of a motive to kill Nicky? That I was afraid she'd implicate me in drug dealing or something? Is that why they haven't made an arrest yet?"

She was puzzled. "How could Nicky's drug activity make you want to commit murder?"

"I don't know." I waved my hand. "I'm confused right now, so not much makes sense." I picked up my fork. "Except pie." I reached across the table and grasped her hand. "And you. Thank you for coming to my rescue tonight. I'm sorry if I scared you. I love you, Grandma. Without you, I don't know what I'd do."

⚙

Before I went to work the next morning, I sent Patrick a text. "We need to talk. I'm working at Rachel's today, so call me tonight when you have time."

The day went by more slowly than most, which I put down to leftover emotional stress from the previous evening. I simply could not focus on my work. Even Rachel noticed when she came out to the front desk to retrieve a client's record.

"Are you okay?" she asked.

"I'm fine."

"Liar. I'm concerned about you. Why don't you take the afternoon off? We can manage for a few hours. Go home and get some rest."

Grateful, I took her up on her offer. I prepared paperwork for the remaining appointments and headed out, but I didn't go home. I needed fresh air and exercise. Maybe cleaning up after the crew would help me work off some of my stress.

When I arrived, the men were hard at work, hot and sweaty in the July afternoon. With shouts of delight, they descended on the coolers I'd brought with me. Before long, they had claimed most of the drinks, and the snack bag was empty.

"You're spoiling them, Annie." Brad tried to sound stern, but he had a cold soda in his hand and two bottles of water pinned to his side by his arm prosthesis. "What brings you here so early?"

"I got the rest of the afternoon off and thought I'd get a jump-start picking up the mess." I scanned the construction site. "Your guys are great, and I love how the shop is coming along, but a tornado couldn't make this much of a mess."

"You've clearly never been in a tornado!"

"I don't mind. I enjoy being here. Joe and I are grateful for your help getting our dad's shop rebuilt. Helping out is the least I can do."

"Your dad was a great guy. We're happy to help."

"Have you had any more of your equipment go missing?"

"Yes, unfortunately. One of the guys forgot to lock up, and now we're missing another box of nails, two nail guns, and parts off our table saw. Seriously, who takes a table saw apart?" He looked disgusted and frustrated at the same time. Then he shook his head with a rueful expression. "But I can't be too mad. I put my tape measure down and forgot to pick it up."

"And someone else did?"

"Yeah. My own damn fault."

"Tell you what. I'll bug Joe again about getting a fence around the lot or some kind of barrier. It might not keep everyone out, but it's worth a try."

He chugged down the rest of his soda and got back to work. After I left Joe a voicemail about the fence, I followed Brad's example, collecting discarded pieces of plywood and other materials and sorting them into piles. As I'd hoped, the physical work was exactly what I needed. I could work without thinking about Nicky, about how angry and heartbroken I was to learn how she'd deceived me. It was much more pleasant to remember how surprised I'd been to find out my grandmother was dating. Even the new motorcycle was okay to consider.

By the time the construction crew quit for the day, the sun was almost below the horizon. I worked for another half an hour, concentrating so hard on my tasks that I jumped when I heard a voice.

"This is really coming along well."

I spun around, dropping a scrap of plywood. My heart was pounding hard, and I could scarcely breathe.

"I'm so sorry." The woman reached out a hand as if to reassure me. "I didn't mean to scare you." She was an inch or two shorter than me with dirty blonde hair caught up in a messy ponytail. I wasn't very good at estimating someone's age, but I'd have put her at about forty-five, maybe fifty. She had a friendly demeanor.

"No problem. I didn't hear you come up. Thinking too much about how messy construction can be, I guess." I retrieved the wood I'd dropped and added it to the nearby wheelbarrow. "Can I help you with something?"

"Do you work for the construction company?" She scanned the partially finished building.

"No, I'm one of the owners. The original building was damaged in a fire. It was originally a bicycle shop."

"Will it be a bike shop again?"

"Yes."

"It's the same exterior, but you're expanding it, aren't you?"

"Were you a customer?"

"No, but I used to live not far from here. I imagine the neighborhood will appreciate having it open again."

"Would you like a tour?"

When she agreed, I offered her a bottle of cold water from the cooler and took her through the new building. I enjoyed being inside, and with it now mostly enclosed, I could envision the locations of the different departments. The racks of new bikes would be the centerpiece, of course, with accessories and clothing along the walls.

"I'm putting a coffee station over there." I pointed to a corner in the back. "We'll have bike maintenance classes and maybe riding lessons for kids and adults who never learned to ride."

I showed her the rest of the shop, and she thanked me and left. After she'd gone, I got back to work until the job site was as clean as I could get it. I opened another bottle of cold water and left, taking my time to enjoy the summer sunset as well as the air conditioning in my car.

Patrick called when I was halfway home. I pushed the button on the steering wheel to answer his call.

"The last time a woman told me 'we have to talk,' I wound up single again."

I felt better enough by then to joke back with him. "Good thing you and I don't have that problem."

"So what's going on?"

While I drove, I gave him a short version of what I thought I'd discovered about Nicky's criminal past. "Can you check to see if it's accurate?"

"And why are you looking at those kinds of sites?" He sounded suspicious, which meant he knew me too well. We'd been through this when I'd decided to find out who killed my employer in Charbonneau.

"Nothing you need to worry about." I hoped I wasn't lying. "But have you ever heard whether Nicky had a record?"

"No, but why does it matter?"

"Do you think Beth would know?"

"Probably, but she hasn't mentioned it to me. And obviously not to you. I'll call her tomorrow. What are you up to? Not playing amateur detective again, I hope."

"Nope. Lesson learned." I resisted the urge to cross my fingers against the fib. "Besides, I don't have time. Between working at Rachel's clinic and keeping up with the construction guys, I'm too busy to go snooping. Plus, I'm trying to learn how to start a business. Joe keeps trying to educate me about different forms of businesses." I had to laugh. "Poor guy."

Patrick was also amused. "You've always enjoyed tormenting him."

"It's what I live for. Oh, and did you know Grandma Natalie bought a new motorcycle?"

"No, but I'm not surprised."

"Want to hear the real news?"

"I suppose." He drew the word out, sounding concerned.

"She has a boyfriend."

"She has *what?*"

For the rest of my drive home, I filled him in on the details about the shiny new Harley Davidson in the driveway and the mountain of a man in the kitchen. It was a welcome diversion from wondering how my not-dead girlfriend could carry out such a deception, letting everyone think she'd been murdered

Chapter Six

Brad had asked me to pick up another load from the building supply, which gave me another opportunity to stop at the coffee shop. I settled into a table near the window and cradled my hot latte between my hands. Never mind that it was ninety degrees outside. Hot coffee was never wrong in my book.

Nicky's picture was still on the bulletin board, with all of its pull tabs intact. I'd shown Nicky's photo to the new barista, who hadn't seen the it previously, but she didn't recognize her. I expected nothing different, but I had to try.

Not wanting to face Friday afternoon traffic, I took my time with my coffee. Brad and his crew wouldn't be at the shop by the time I got back anyway, so I could cool my heels for as long as I wanted.

I sipped my latte and tried to decide what to do next, but before I knew it, I slipped into a state where I could gaze out the window without really seeing anything. My internal monologue had taken over, whirling in circles like an out-of-control carousel.

Without warning, someone put an arm across my shoulders and held me close, as if greeting me as a good friend. Before I could turn my head, my assailant leaned in close and spoke in a low voice, close enough to feel her warm breath against my skin.

"Tell me why I shouldn't arrest your ass right here and now?"

She released me and sat down in the chair on the other side of the table. Beth O'Brien smiled at me as friends do when they meet for coffee.

I wasn't able to act nearly as cool as she did. Before I could think, I burst out, "Holy shit," and clapped a hand over my mouth. She raised one perfectly arched eyebrow.

Before my friends met her, I'd told them Beth could pass for a model on her worst day. She was always beautiful, with a heart-shaped face and chocolate brown eyes framed by perfectly wavy blonde hair. But this was too much. She wore tight jeans and a wrap-style blouse that appeared to be silk and clung to her shape as if it had been custom-made for her. The necklace she wore of blue topaz and citrine stones set in gold accented the pale lavender fabric.

"Sorry." I had no clue how to cover my embarrassment. "You startled me."

"Do you like my necklace?" She lifted it away from her skin to show it off. "It's new." When I hesitated, she said, "I'm making nice for the audience. Your little outburst has everyone looking at us, so say something."

"Entirely your fault for sneaking up on me. How did you know I was here?"

She let the pendant drop. "I didn't. I'm meeting a friend for dinner. I'm early, so I decided to stop in for an iced coffee. I didn't know you were here until I came inside." She got up, collected her cup from the barista, and retook her seat. "Why are you here?"

I told her about my errand for Brad. I did my best to look out the windows and not gawk at my companion across the table, but the deep V-shaped neckline of her blouse didn't make it easy. I also tried not to think about who she might be having dinner with. To my eyes, she was dressed for a date, not a casual meal with a friend. It was Friday, after all.

"Annie," she finally said in a skeptical voice. "What the hell are you thinking? What's really going on?"

I was fairly sure she didn't really want to learn what I had on my mind right then, but I was also confident about what she did want to know. She gazed at me until my inner resolve crumbled.

"I can't help it. She was here, and I keep hoping she'll come back. When I'm in the neighborhood, I come in and show them this." I handed her the photo of Nicky. "They put it up for me." I gestured toward the flyer on the bulletin board.

She drank some coffee, narrowing her eyes at me over the rim of her cup.

"You have to stop this nonsense. If you're right"—she held up a hand when I started to speak—"if you're right and she sees you, what do you think will happen?"

"I don't know. We'd talk, and maybe I'd find out what was going on with her."

"No. What would most likely happen is she'd disappear. She'd see you from outside or across the room and turn right around and be gone. And then we'd never know what happened, and the case would never be closed."

"But she called me. Doesn't it mean she wants to talk?"

"Did she answer when you called her back?"

"No, as you know perfectly well." I was trying to avoid sounding defensive—and failing. "What am I supposed to do? She's alive, she called me, and what? I should shrug my shoulders and say 'oh well' and get on with my life?"

"Of course not. You're supposed to do what you've already done. You've told Ted and me about it, and now you let us do our jobs. We're the experienced ones here who can be objective and follow the evidence. It's completely understandable you want to find her, but I'm asking you to stop."

I felt foolish. "You're right, of course. You'd think after my last escapade, I'd have learned I have no business acting like some kind of half-assed detective. I'm sorry. I didn't think of it that way." The episode I mentioned was my misguided attempt to discover who had killed the doctor I cleaned house for in Charbonneau.

She smiled reassuringly. "I know you're smart enough and motivated enough to do this kind of work if you wanted to. You just lack training and experience and," she paused long enough to tilt one extended hand from side to side, "and maybe the tiniest bit of common sense."

Embarrassed, I said, "Thank you, sort of." And then I remembered. "Oh, have you talked with Patrick today?"

"No, but I took most of the day off. Why?"

I suddenly wished I hadn't spoken. Here she'd busted me for being in amateur sleuth mode, and now I had to admit she was right. Me and my big mouth. "Okay, here it is. After I got home from Charbonneau, a local reporter wrote a news story about me, and it refuses to die. Since then, two or three people have asked me to find someone for them. Once I explained the actual situation, they dropped it." I shook my head, frustrated at the thought. "It happened again about ten days ago. A server at a sushi restaurant I like asked me to find her missing girlfriend."

"What did you say?"

"The same as the others. I told her the newspaper story was bogus, but she insisted. She refused to take no for an answer, so to make her leave me alone about it, I agreed to do an online search, but I made it clear to her I wasn't promising results."

Beth shook her head slightly. "Annie, really."

"I know. I'm an idiot. So I signed up for one of those websites where you can get information about people." Beth started to speak, but I held my hand up to stop her. "I didn't find anything about the missing girlfriend."

"Okay. And you're telling me this why exactly?"

"Since I paid for the website, I put Nicky's name in."

She waited.

"Did you know she has a criminal record? The site showed three arrests for drug possession and intent to distribute. The dates were from before we met, and I knew nothing about it." I paused long enough to take a sip of my now lukewarm coffee. "I don't know how accurate those sites are, so I asked Patrick to call you to see what you knew about any record she had. I thought it might be important because of the chemicals that burned down my dad's bike shop." I didn't add *and killed my beloved father*.

"I haven't talked with him, but I don't usually answer my work cell if I'm off the clock." She paused, clearly considering what to say. "Okay. To answer your question, when your case was first assigned to me, I read her file."

"From when she was murdered?" I put air quotes around the last word.

"Yes. And to be honest, it's been long enough I don't remember a lot of the details. I'll go through it again when I'm back in the office, but on two conditions. First, if someone asks you to find a person for them, refer them to the police bureau."

"Done. My sleuthing days are over."

"All current evidence to the contrary."

I conceded the point. "What's the second condition?"

"Tell me the name of your sushi restaurant."

I complied with her second request and mentally crossed my fingers for the first one. She got up to leave when I remembered something else.

"Wait, what did you say about arresting me?"

"I had to get your attention somehow."

"A simple hello tends to work."

"What I mean," she said with exaggerated patience, "is if Nicky does come in here and she sees you and takes off, I could charge you with interfering with an official investigation." She waved it away. "At the very least, you might risk our witness taking flight. I need you to stop what you're doing."

"So you believe me?"

"I promised I'd take your story at face value and do what I can to either prove or disprove it." She put a hand on the back of my chair and, leaning over slightly, looked directly into my eyes. She said, "I keep my promises," and then she left.

The next week flew by in a blur. Between working long days at Rachel's clinic and picking up after the construction crew in the evenings, I barely had time to breathe. Most days, I didn't see my grandmother. She was either out with Liz or her new boyfriend by the time I dragged myself home, and I was usually sound asleep when her nights ended. When I took the job at the clinic, I'd told Grandma Natalie it would be beneficial for me to be busy, but I wondered if it was possible to have too much of a good thing.

Shortly before seven Friday evening, I slid into our usual booth at Doug's Café and grabbed a menu. The familiar seat comforted my weary back, and I relaxed while deciding what to order. As usual, dozens of tiny illustrations of delectable sushi mesmerized me until Rachel arrived.

"Did you forget?" She narrowed her eyes at me.

"Oh, no." I clapped my hand over my mouth and quickly scanned the restaurant. "Crap. You're right. I did. I must be operating on autopilot."

After I'd locked the door to the clinic, she and I decided to risk eating at our favorite restaurant but agreed to find a table as far from our usual spot as possible. I'd completely blown it.

"Maybe we'll get lucky, and she won't see us. Or maybe she has the day off."

We picked up the tall, laminated menus, hoping to use them as camouflage, but to no avail.

"Hello, ladies." Mandy's voice was unmistakable. "What can I get you to drink?"

I lowered my menu to the table, as did Rachel. We ordered our drinks, and Mandy bustled away with her usual efficiency.

"Damnation. Bet you dinner she asks me about her friend when she comes back to take the rest of our order."

"I'm not dumb enough to take you up on that one. Do you want to go somewhere else?"

"No, let's stay." I lowered my voice. "I'm not letting one little nutjob ruin my favorite celebration food."

"Is she still pestering you?"

"It's so frustrating. I get an email from her about every other day. I've told her time and again I won't be able to find her friend. I don't know if she's ignoring what I'm saying or truly doesn't hear me, but I'm beyond tired of it."

Before I could say more, Mandy returned with our drinks, and we gave her our list of sushi selections.

"Anything else?" She waited expectantly.

"No, I think we're good."

She thanked us and headed for the kitchen.

"Guess you should've taken the bet after all."

"It's still early," Rachel said. "Give her time." She took a sip of her iced tea. "Is this a celebration?"

"Yes. I survived two weeks of you as my boss." I grinned at her over the top of my glass of tea. "Definitely celebration worthy."

"Yeah, well, about that." Rachel drank more tea, clearly trying to avoid my gaze.

"Don't give me your innocent routine. What's up?"

She put her glass down, bit her lip for a moment, and finally met my eyes. "You're not a quitter, are you?"

"No. Don't say it." The relief I'd felt at finishing my stint as a veterinary hospital receptionist vanished in an instant.

"Becky isn't coming back."

"What? Why not?"

"While she was on vacation, she found out she's pregnant for the fourth time, and she decided to quit. I guess I get it. Childcare is expensive, and at some point, it costs more than she can make working for me."

"Four kids. Yikes."

Rachel was amused. "Yeah, better her than me." She grew serious again. "What do you say? Will you stay?"

Our sushi arrived before I could answer. I held my breath for a moment, waiting for Mandy to ask about her friend, but she surprised me and left without mentioning it. Rachel and I made our selections from the bounty on the table.

While we ate, I considered my friend's entreaty. The two weeks I'd worked at her clinic were a whirlwind. The work was exhausting, but never boring.

When I said, "Okay, I'll stay on," Rachel let out a gusty breath, as if she'd inhaled and not let it out.

"Don't throw a party just yet. I'll fill in, but you need to find someone to hire right away."

"Okay, not a problem."

"And whether you've hired someone or not, I'll have to quit when we open the shop. It has to be my top priority."

"Totally understand. Any idea when that will be?"

"Not really." I grabbed my phone to check the calendar. "Okay, it's almost August. If I had to guess, and I do, I'd say end of August, maybe early September." I put the phone down and picked up my chopsticks. "I'll have to see what Joe thinks."

"Sounds good. I'll get an ad out right away. And I'll call some of my colleagues to see if they can recommend someone."

I was suddenly struck by something I hadn't realized. It must have shown on my face because Rachel asked, "What?" through a bite of spicy tuna roll.

"Something occurs to me. I've been so busy during the day and evenings I've hardly thought about Nicky since the other day when I saw Beth at the coffee shop."

"Maybe that's good. Beth said she'd look into what you told her, didn't she? Why not let her do it? She's the professional, after all."

I didn't have a response for Rachel, so we finished our meal and asked Mandy for boxes to take the leftovers home. Far be it from me to leave perfectly good sushi behind. She returned with two boxes and our bill. Rachel took the bill to calculate who owed what for the night's repast, while Mandy packed up our remaining food.

"Annie?"

I cringed inside at the tentative sound of Mandy's voice. Trying not to sigh, I looked into her eyes. Frustration bubbled barely below the surface, and I hoped it didn't show.

"Have you made any progress finding Sandy?"

Rachel stopped doing her calculations but didn't speak.

I paused, mostly to remind myself not to cause a scene, and then I spoke deliberately. "Mandy, I've told you at least half a dozen times I can't find her. The very first thing I told you was I'm not a detective."

"But you promised you'd find her."

"I absolutely did not. In fact, I told you clearly that all I could do was search online with the information you gave me. Nothing else."

"I was here, too, Mandy, "Rachel said. "She only promised to look, not succeed."

"And as I've told you," I said, "the information you gave me is completely inadequate. She has a common name. You don't even know her birthdate with any certainty or much about her family. I'm sorry, but I can't help you." She grew teary-eyed. "I'm sorry. I really am, but please stop asking me about it. If you haven't done it already, you need to make a missing person report with the police."

Mandy pulled a tissue from her pocket and dabbed at her eyes. "Thank you for trying," she whispered.

Rachel handed her the bill and a credit card. After Mandy left, I asked, "What do I owe for dinner?"

"My treat since I derailed your celebration." She glanced in the direction Mandy had taken. "That girl does not have all of her wheels on the ground." She looked back at me. "You haven't heard the last from her."

The next morning, I awoke to find my room bright with sunlight. When I read the time on my bedside clock, I leaped out of bed, startling Shadow.

"Jeez, I knew I was tired, but eleven?"

I put on a bathrobe and went downstairs to the kitchen. The second surprise of my Saturday was finding it unoccupied. No Grandma Natalie. Not even any cold coffee. The kitchen was unchanged from the way we'd left it after dinner the night before.

Almost. Next to the coffeemaker, I found a slip of paper with my grandmother's writing on it.

Chip and I are spending the weekend at the beach. See you Monday.

A bit nonplussed, I made coffee and toast and opened a can of Shadow's favorite food.

"It's you and me, bud," I told him. "Eat up."

I was following my own advice when I heard the front door open and close. Joe came into the kitchen, dressed as usual in his cycling gear.

"You been out for a ride?"

He raised an eyebrow at me as he took a bottle of water from the fridge and pointed the bottle at the logo on his chest. "What was your first clue, Sherlock?" He sat at the table and filched my last piece of toast. "What are you up to today? Want to go for a ride? I promise not to leave you behind. Brad and I drove out to Hillsboro this morning and rode up to Vernonia and back, almost sixty-five miles, so I'm kinda tired." He tried and failed to look weak.

"You don't fool me. You never get tired. I think you have more replacement parts than your leg. You're the bionic cyclist." He grinned at me, and I relented. "Maybe a short ride later if it's not too hot out. I need to see what I need to do at the shop first since I haven't been there for a couple of days."

He got up to put more bread in the toaster. "Don't bother. Brad got a contract for a new project that'll pay him buckets of money, so he has to slow-roll the shop for a while."

"Oh." I tried not to be disappointed. Brad was doing us a huge favor by building our new shop for very little money. We'd agreed he'd work on it when he wasn't busy elsewhere, but I was still hoping for steady progress. "I'm glad for him."

Joe dropped into a chair. "It's actually good timing. They got the building enclosed, so it won't hurt to wait. And now with a fence up, it should be secure enough. In the meantime, I'll get your bike cleaned up and ready to go. Where's Grandma Natalie?"

"Having a dirty weekend, it seems." I had to chuckle at his puzzled expression. "She went out to the beach with Chip. Coming home Monday."

He threw his head back and let out a roar of laughter. "Good for her. It's about damn time she let loose."

We finished our breakfast and Joe promised to return with his car to collect my bike, long since collecting dust in the garage. "If we're going to own a bike shop, you have to ride. It's the law."

After he left, I washed the few dishes we'd used and went upstairs to my computer. While I waited for it to wake up, I had time to think.

My stint as Rachel's receptionist was continuing, but I had the next two days off. Work at the shop was pretty much on hold for the time being, so I had no crew to clean up after or supplies to pick up. I'd already set up accounts with the suppliers Dad had used for the shop, so they were ready, as were the business bank accounts. Grandma Natalie was off with her boyfriend. Rachel and Sally had plans for the weekend, as did Joe and Patrick. Even my friends in Charbonneau were busy.

Just like that, my life went from sixty to zero. "Maybe I need to get a new hobby. Or friends who are as boring as I am."

Great. I'm alone for fifteen minutes, and I'm already talking to myself.

Mentally crossing my fingers, I checked my email, swearing when Mandy's name popped up in the "from" column. Her note read, "Any progress?"

I swore again when I saw she'd sent it a mere three hours after Rachel and I saw her the evening before. "Rachel's right. She really is nuts." Shadow seemed to agree with me, but he didn't offer any solutions. Frustrated, I closed her email. "Deal with it later," I muttered to myself.

I went through the rest of the emails, deleting ads for insurance and roof repairs. I also received a few emails related to the shop, which I scanned. Those could wait.

Then I saw the email confirmation of my subscription to the site I'd signed up for when I was looking for Mandy's friend.

I read it, my mind suddenly whirling. I grabbed my phone and texted Patrick. "I forgot to tell you I saw Beth and asked her if she knew about Nicky's record. She said she'll review the file again." I threw the phone onto my bed and turned back to the computer. I'd previously printed all the information the search site had about Nicky, so I retrieved those papers as well.

I leafed through the printout again. There must be something I could use, some action I could take. I unearthed a tablet of paper and a pen to make notes. After a time, I realized my desk was insufficient, so I collected my laptop and all the papers, and took the whole works downstairs.

Suitably fortified with a tall glass of iced tea, I opened my laptop on the kitchen table, flanked by the computer printout and the tablet I'd been writing on.

Picking up my pen, I divided my sheet of paper into sections. Phone numbers, addresses, name of friends and acquaintances, all associated with Nicky, according to the website I was using. Other than the few details I recognized, I didn't know how accurate any of the information was. Of the dozen phone numbers on the printout, I recognized Nicky's parents' number and my own. The rest were new to me.

Only one way to find out.

I grabbed my phone and tried the first number on my list. When it rang, I realized I didn't know what I was going to say.

"Hello?" The voice on the line sounded as if it belonged to a child.

I went for it. "Is Nicky there?"

The child said, "No," and then yelled, "Mom!" at a deafening volume. After some rustling sounds, a woman's voice asked, "Who's this?"

"I'm trying to find my friend, Nicky. Is this her number?"

"Sorry, no. I don't know anyone by that name."

"Thanks anyway. Sorry to bother you."

The next number I called was answered with "Jorgensen Upholstery. How can I help you?" The third belonged to a pizza restaurant, which sounded busy. I apologized to both of them for calling a wrong number, but I made a note of the pizza place. Far be it from me to pass up the possibility of good pizza.

The next two numbers resulted in one abrupt hang up and one exasperated, "Damn it, I told you to leave me alone. My number is on the Do Not Call list. Do I have to report you?"

This wasn't going well.

I took a break to make myself a sandwich and refill my glass. While I ate, I wondered if I was wasting my time. My phone rang. *Patrick.*

Before I could utter a greeting, he said, "You saw Beth? Without me? Where?"

"I was at that coffee shop across town yesterday, and she stopped in on her way to meet a friend. Pure coincidence. While we were talking, I asked her if she knew whether Nicky had a criminal record. She said it had been long enough since she read the file she didn't remember many details, but she'd check it."

"Did she tell you to quit stalking the coffee shop?"

"Oh, so you did talk with her."

"No, but I know she wants you to stop behaving like a half-assed Miss Marple."

"Not one of you has any confidence in my abilities."

"The last time I checked, your abilities got you tied to a cot in an old barn, eating cold soup out of a can and peeing in a bucket. Maybe it's time you took up a different hobby."

"Okay, fine," I said, grumpy. "When I find Nicky, you'll eat those words."

He started to speak, but I ended the call. Still out of sorts, I watched a cat video on YouTube while I ate my sandwich. Once both were finished, I changed my clothes, grabbed my keys, and headed for the door.

Once in the car, I realized I had no more idea of where to go than I did how to approach the information on the printout. Regardless, I started the engine and backed out of the driveway. My car was apparently in charge, because it took me to my favorite drive-through for a cold drink and a large order of fries. I wasn't hungry, but nothing got between me and hot, salty fries without taking a bruise or two. I munched on fries while my car took control again.

Fifteen minutes later, my car parked us next to the bike shop. I licked the last of the French fry salt and grease from my fingers and, with cold drink in hand, got out to survey the construction site. True to his word, Joe had gotten a six-foot-tall chain-link fence put up around the entire lot. "No Trespassing" signs were wired to the fence every ten feet. A brass padlock nearly the size of my hand secured the single gate, but since he'd previously texted me the code number to open it, I was inside in no time.

The site was eerily quiet. Even weekend traffic on the busy streets bordering our property seemed more subdued than usual. I'd spent a lot of time there in the evenings after the construction crew had packed up for the day, but quiet in the afternoons was new. I walked around the building and then inside. Since Brad and his men had enclosed the exterior with plywood, it was much easier to see how the completed building would appear. The interior walls were still studs, but I could visualize the layout of the total floorplan. Bikes there, accessories here, clothing and shoes along the wall. Coffee bar in the corner. For half a moment, I felt a pang of grief for my father, but knowing he'd have loved the new shop helped to soothe my hurt.

Back outside, I saw Joe was right. Inside and out, the place was pretty clean, but I still took a few minutes to pick up stray nails and scraps of plywood.

I was pulling my work gloves off when two people came through the open gate, the woman pushing a stroller. I remembered them from a previous visit, when I'd dubbed them the N Plus One family.

"Hello," the man called out. "How are you today?"

I met them halfway and shook their hands. "It's nice to see you again. Something I can help you with?"

"We were walking by and we're wondering if you've picked an opening day yet."

"My brother, always the optimist, is hoping for late August, but I think September is probably more realistic."

The woman said, "We'll be here for your grand opening."

"Thanks!"

After they made their way down the street, I surveyed the lot for any debris I might have missed. Satisfied, I locked the gate and headed home, this time making sure I was driving the car and not the other way around.

A persistent rattling noise woke me. Bleary-eyed, I peered toward the sound, which I foggily realized was my phone set on vibrate mode. I picked it up, pulled the blankets back over my head, and pressed the screen somewhere in the vicinity of the call button.

"Hello?"

"Don't tell me you're still sleeping." Joe sounded annoyed.

"Why are you calling me at zero dark thirty?"

"It's almost ten."

"Morning is in the eye of the beholder. It's not morning until I've had my coffee, especially on the weekend."

"Have you been to the shop in the past couple of days?"

"Yeah, I was there last night for a while." I pulled the blanket down and sat up against the headboard. "Why?"

"Did you lock the gate?"

"Of course. Why are you interrogating me?"

"Get your lazy ass out of bed, grab some coffee, and get down here. You're not going to believe this."

I pushed the blankets back and sat on the side of the bed. "Okay, all right. Give me half an hour. What's going on?"

"Get a move on." He ended the call.

I peered at my phone for a moment, wondering at his uncharacteristic brusqueness. "Come on, Shadow. We're under orders."

When I arrived at the bike shop, I left my car on the street near the open gate and walked onto the property. Joe was standing in the middle of the eight-slot parking lot, fists on his hips, staring at the building.

"Look." His voice was harsh, and he waved his hand toward the shop.

I turned in the direction he pointed, and "Holy shit" popped out of my mouth unbidden.

Multicolored spray paint covered the entire building. Red, black, yellow, green, even some gold-colored paint. Whoever had done this had worked hard at it. Almost no bare wood showed through the graffiti.

"How?" I was nearly speechless. "I swear I locked the gate when I left."

"I know. It was locked when I got here. Whoever did it must have climbed over the fence."

"And spent three hours painting. There's no way this was done quickly, unless it was a group of people. Do vandals run in packs?"

I turned in a circle where I stood, surveying the corner lot. Our lot was flanked by businesses on two sides, a gas station on one and an auto body repair shop on the other, both separated from our property by privacy fences. The third and fourth sides of the lot faced the streets, but there were trees along the sidewalks, outside the chain-link security fence we'd had installed.

"You'd think someone would have seen them. If nothing else, the streetlights should have given them away."

Joe made the same survey I did. "I wonder if the trees on the corner block the light. I've never thought about it before."

We turned back to the damaged building.

"Now what?"

Joe took his phone from his pocket. "I'm going to take pictures and call Brad. I hope the wood doesn't have to be replaced."

When he left to walk around the structure, I went inside.

"Joe, did you see in here?" The new windows hadn't been installed yet, enabling him to lean in through the lower openings. Our visitor hadn't spared the interior of our new shop.

Joe swore eloquently as he took pictures. While he was documenting the damage, I went outside the fence and walked along it to see if I could figure out where someone could have easily climbed over it without attracting attention. Near the end of the fence closest to the neighboring gas station and behind two of the more mature trees, I found what I sought. I called my brother over.

"Mystery partially solved," I said as he joined me.

The vandal had cut a section of the fence away, making a flap large enough for a person to crawl through. A casual observer wouldn't have noticed it.

We went back inside the fence and sat in the shade on the tailgate of Joe's truck.

"Did you call Brad?"

"Yeah. He'll come over tomorrow and check it out. I sent him some pictures. I think he's more pissed off than we are since it's his work being damaged." He gazed at the defaced building. "And we have more stuff to do."

"Starting with a call to the police, right?"

"Yes. There probably isn't much they can do, but we should get a report filed anyway." He blew out a breath with disgust. "But more important for the moment is getting security cameras and lights now. They're already on our list of stuff to buy, but I thought we could wait until we were closer to having a finished building. I'm very clearly wrong."

"You don't think this is a one-off? Kids with time on their hands and money to spend on paint?"

"Who knows? At this point, it shouldn't be too expensive to fix, but once we have windows in or siding on, it's a whole different ball game."

"We also need to get the fence repaired."

Chapter Seven

"This is no way to start a Monday." Brad was as frustrated as I was, perhaps more, since it was his work being damaged. "It's two steps forward and one step back here."

"Feels like it, doesn't it?" I'd taken an hour away from Rachel's clinic to meet him at the shop. Fortunately, she was understanding about my commitment to it.

"I want to check inside. Did you say Joe's coming?"

I glanced at my watch. "He should be here any time. He had one meeting this morning, and then he's taking the rest of the day off."

Brad disappeared into the building as Joe pulled up. He emerged from his truck still wearing the button-down shirt and khakis he'd worn to the office.

"Brad inside?" he called.

"Yes. We got here a few minutes ago, so he is just seeing it now."

Joe started to follow his friend, but he turned back for a moment.

"Is Grandma Natalie back from her weekend? Did she have a good time?"

"She got back late last night. She stammered a bit when I asked if she had fun, so I'm thinking she had a very good time. If you know what I mean."

Joe laughed. "Good for her." He ambled into the shop.

After a few minutes, both men joined me in the middle of the parking lot.

"Have you made those calls yet?" Joe asked. When Brad raised an inquiring eyebrow, Joe said, "We're filing a police report and getting the security equipment installed. Between the thefts and now this"—he made a sweeping motion toward the paint-stained building—"I don't think we should wait."

"Yes, all done. The woman who took my call at the nonemergency number for the Portland Police Bureau told me unless we had video or witnesses, there wasn't much they could do, but she said an officer will contact us in the next day or two to take the information for a report. If nothing else, we'll have a record of it. Then I called about the security lights and cameras and requested them to expedite delivery and installation. They might be able to get to it by tomorrow, but we'll have to pay extra."

"Fine by me," Joe said.

"They asked whether we had power run to where we want the equipment installed, but I told them the cameras we ordered have battery backup."

"Good thinking." Joe rubbed his hand over his face. "What about the fence company?"

"As you might expect, they were none too pleased when I told them about the cut section, but the man I spoke with promised to send someone out right away to repair it. We might have to pay extra for it, since the rental agreement doesn't cover vandalism."

While we talked, the rest of Brad's crew arrived.

"Well, shit," one of them said. The other men uttered an even more impressive array of expletives when they saw the carnage that had been loosed on the unprotected plywood. I agreed with every syllable.

"What will it take to fix it?" Joe asked.

"We'll paint over it. Annie, do you have time to visit the building supply?"

"Sure. Let me know when. I'm working for a short time at a friend's veterinary clinic, but I'll figure it out. I think the building supply is open until nine."

"I already have an order in to them, so I'll call them and add primer, and we can get this cleaned up."

"Hey, boss?"

Brad turned to the man who wanted his attention. "Yeah?"

"The load of vapor wrap and the windows are supposed to be here tomorrow or Wednesday, and the siding by Friday. What do you want to do?"

"Let's get to work on this for now, Ryan. Do we have room at HQ to store everything?"

"We can make room." Ryan pulled his phone from his pocket. "I'll divert the deliveries."

"Thanks. Between the thefts and now this, it's clear we have a serial vandal on our hands. Ryan, schedule a quick meeting with the guys for later today so they know what's going on." Brad turned to Joe and me. "I think we need to speed up the work here. I'll see about moving up the electrical and plumbing work, now that the building is almost fully enclosed. It's likely to cost extra."

"Not a problem," Joe said, "but what about the other job you took on?"

"Let me worry about that. I can chew gum and walk at the same time."

"Sounds good to me," Joe said. "I have a ton of vacation time saved up, and the boss has been on my case to use it. I'll take as much as he'll approve so I can help out here."

Brad clapped him on the shoulder. "Thanks. If you're okay with it, I'll hire a few more guys I know who do good work, which will cost you more in labor costs, but barring any more surprises, we'll get this baby finished."

"Good. Do it." Joe turned back to the eyesore that was our new bike shop. "You've already saved us a small fortune. Getting the shop open as soon as possible is the best thing we can do."

Brad was true to his word. By the time I visited the site on my lunch break the next day, his crew had painted over the offending graffiti and had put up more than half of the vapor wrap. After work that day, I headed to the building supply for Brad's order.

Although I'd promised myself I wouldn't stop at the coffee shop where I'd seen Nicky, I decided a visit was harmless. After all, I deserved some of their excellent coffee.

As I walked toward the counter, I saw the photograph I'd tacked to their bulletin board. Soy latte in hand, I gazed at the picture for a moment. One of the pull tabs on the bottom was gone. I took the photo down from the board and went back to the counter.

"You didn't happen to see who pulled this tab, did you?" I knew I was asking for the impossible, and I wasn't wrong.

"No, sorry." The barista wrinkled her nose. "We're way too busy to notice if anyone pays any attention to the board."

"I can see why." I lifted my cup into view. "This is the best coffee I've ever had, so it makes sense you'd have a lot of people through here."

She thanked me. "Yeah, some days I think a flash mob Mariachi band could start playing in here and we wouldn't notice."

I liked the mental image. "I'd love to know the secrets of your coffee. My brother and I are opening a bike shop across town, including an espresso bar. I am almost clueless about making coffee except for our drip pot at home."

She glanced around furtively for a moment and grabbed a pad of paper.

"First," she said, almost whispering, "get the best beans." She jotted a name on the paper. "Do you have a supplier?"

"Yes," and I told her the name.

She nodded approvingly. "Good." She wrote a few more lines and slid the paper across to me. "Those are the machines we use here, and my cell number. When you're ready, call me. I'll come to your place and show you my secrets."

I tucked the paper into my pocket. "Do you like to ride bicycles?"

She seemed surprised for a moment. "Yes, but I haven't ridden in forever. I miss it sometimes."

"Maybe we can exchange favors."

"It's a deal." Then a bell chimed, and she dashed to the drive-through window.

When I arrived back at the construction site with Brad's supplies that evening, the vapor wrap was nearly complete. Joe had also arrived and was up a ladder and hard at work. When he saw me, he climbed down and met me in the parking lot. I told him about my information coup at the coffee shop, and he laughed aloud as he hugged me.

"Good job, Annie. I always knew you were hiding an entrepreneur inside you somewhere."

"What's going on here?"

"We'll finish the wrap today. The fence guy was here and replaced the damaged panel, but honestly, there's nothing to keep someone from cutting another hole."

"What about the security cameras?"

"I called them to see how our request to expedite installation was going. They told me the cameras came in, and as you reminded me, they'll work on the battery backup until we can get power run out to them. They might be able to install them in the next few days. Did you ever hear from the police department?"

"No, not yet," I said. "It might be a day or two."

"I don't imagine graffiti is real high on their priority list."

"Hey, Annie!" Brad waited near my car, so I pressed the button on my key fob to open the rear gate of my Outback. He and two other guys got busy unloading the boxes of nails and whatever else he'd ordered. They also unloaded my cooler filled with cold drinks and two canvas totes loaded with snacks. When they were done, Brad joined Joe and me, water bottle in hand.

"What's next?"

Brad drank half his water in one swallow and wiped his face with his sleeve. "After we finish the wrap, then the windows and siding will go up."

"It already looks much better with the spray paint covered."

We chatted for a few more minutes about the progress and then went back to work. With construction in high gear, I had more to do than usual, picking up after the crew. By the time they were gone for the day and I'd finished picking up everything I could, I was worn out. I stretched my back and headed for my car. Time to call it a day. Grandma Natalie had mentioned possibly grilling burgers outside tonight, which sounded great to me.

I locked the gate and stood for a moment, gazing at the bike shop building. I was grateful to see how much progress Brad, his crew, and my brother had made.

"Dad would have loved it," I said aloud.

On my way home, I thought more about him, how he'd built the original shop from an old former fruit stand and turned it into a vibrant business popular with the local neighborhood. After a few years, he had repeat customers from all over Portland, and once he'd had a website made, he received inquiries from farther afield.

As I drove, the photo of Nicky I'd retrieved from the coffee shop caught my eye, and I impulsively changed my plans. I wasn't going right home.

I made a quick detour through a convenient drive-through. Armed with fries and an icy cold Diet Coke, I headed across town.

In short order, I was parked on the street across from Nicky's parents' home. The Fleming family had always welcomed me with open arms. I'd been to their home more times than I could count. They had even invited me to one of their family reunions. Grandma Natalie had always done everything she could for me as grandmother, mother, and friend, and I loved her fiercely, but after her, Nicky's mother was the closest I'd had to an actual mom. What was the phrase—the one about Family of Choice?"

But now I was an outsider. I could no longer walk up to the door and ring the bell. Once I came in contact with Nicky, I realized I'd somehow been deceived into believing Nicky was dead, though I couldn't imagine why. And I still had no idea whether Nicky's family knew she was alive. I couldn't very well ask them. What if they were unaware of her being alive? What would I say? Oh, by the way, the child you've mourned for the last year and a half has scammed us all. Surprise! She's still alive after all.

I sat in the car while the sun went down, and finished my cold fries while I gazed at the house. My heart ached for the familial closeness I'd once felt for the people inside the tidy home. I missed them.

"What the hell am I doing here?" Suddenly angry with myself, I straightened up in my seat and was reaching for the button to start the engine when my phone rang. I didn't recognize the number, but with so many bike shop suppliers calling me, I was getting used to receiving calls from unknown numbers.

"Annie," an all too familiar voice said, "go home."

"Nicky?"

"You shouldn't be here. Go home." Her tone was serious, almost cold.

That answered one question. Her family knew. Had they always known? Had they lied to the police when they identified the dead woman found with Nicky's belongings? Was I the only one left in the dark?

"Nicky, why won't you talk to me? What's going on? Where have you been?"

She took a deep breath and blew it out in what sounded like frustration. "I can't tell you." Her tone softened. "But please, you need to leave."

"Why? What's the big secret? Did you know the Portland police think you're dead? They found some woman's body downtown with your bag and the sweater I gave you. Your parents identified her as you. Did you know that?" She was silent, which felt like an admission to me. "Did you know her? How did she get your stuff?"

"Someone stole my car about a week after the fire, and my bag was inside." She was quiet again. "Maybe it's good the police think I'm dead." She sounded as if she were talking to herself.

I felt my anger growing. "For you, maybe. Not so much for me."

"What? Why?"

"The fire inspectors said your meth stuff in the shed caused the fire."

"What? No, that's not possible."

"Oh, it gets even better." I was past trying to be reasonable. Eighteen months of grief and anger took over. "The cops think I killed you as revenge for Dad's death. I've had homicide detectives up my ass for a year and a half because of you."

"Annie, no." She sounded near tears.

"Oh yes, it's been a real joy ride, let me tell you. And when I saw you at the coffee shop, I told everyone, and now Grandma Natalie and Joe and all of them are worried about me, wondering if I hallucinated seeing you. And those damn detectives either think I'm off my rocker or I'm lying to get them to lay off."

"I'll take care of it, Annie. I'll do whatever I can."

"Except be honest with me, apparently." I started my car and put it in gear. My anger dissipated and morphed into sadness. "You know, I've realized I never really knew you at all. I knew nothing about your involvement with drugs, making meth, dealing, whatever it was you were doing." I let the car roll slowly. "I can't imagine what else I don't know. But even with that, I don't understand how you could disappear with no explanation. You told me you loved me, we talked about getting married, and that's how you treated me? And on top of it all, you bailed right after Dad died." She started to speak, but I cut her off, my anger returning. "I don't want to hear it. I obviously can't believe anything you say, so I'm done. Have a good life."

I ended the call. As I drove away, the form of a slender woman running out into the street was reflected in my rearview mirror. I kept driving.

My trip home was a blur, not least because of the tears streaming from my eyes. I grabbed a paper napkin off the seat next to me and wiped my face, only to discover it smelled like French fries. I was amused for a moment, realizing I'd smeared grease and salt on my skin, but my lighter mood disappeared, and the tears resumed.

About the time I reached home, I'd finally stopped crying. I wiped the last of the tears from my face and turned into the driveway, relieved to be home.

That feeling lasted about four seconds. Smack in the middle of the driveway, blocking my path, was Chip's dirt-encrusted motorcycle. I stopped and glared at it, my previous anger back full force.

"Damn it all to hell. Just what I need." Fuming, I backed out and parked on the street.

I slammed the car door hard enough to make the whole vehicle rock. Halfway up the driveway, I stopped long enough to glare at the offending Harley, seriously considering how satisfying it would be to knock the damn thing over. Common sense prevailed, so I left it where it was and went into the house, slamming the door and throwing my keys onto the nearby table. They clattered to the floor, and I left them there.

Grandma Natalie met me a few feet inside the door with an alarmed expression on her face.

"Annie, are you okay?"

"Do I seem okay to you?" Even in my anger, I knew I was being unfair to her. "Sorry, Grandma." I moderated my tone. "It's been one of those days."

She reached out toward me, but I avoided her hand. "Have you been crying?" Her expression changed from alarm to concern. "Do you want to talk about it?"

Chip rounded the corner from the kitchen. "Is everything okay?"

I pulled my grandmother in for a hug. "I'm going to bed. We can talk tomorrow." I released her and ignored Chip, instead heading up the stairs.

When I was halfway up to my room, I heard Chip say, "Is there anything I can do?"

At that moment, my anger flared. I knew it was irrational, but the accumulation of the day's insults overrode any common sense I had remaining. I turned around and went back down the stairs.

"Yes, there is." I glared into his startled eyes. "You can have some simple consideration for the people who live here. There are two of us, in case you forgot. We have a huge driveway with enough room for four cars, and yet you parked that monstrosity of a machine right in the middle. Not close enough to the house to let me pull in behind it and park without blocking the sidewalk. Not far enough to one side so I can get around it. No, right in the most inconvenient place possible. My car is on the street again, thank you very fucking much. How about you learn you're not the center of the damn universe and think of others for a change? I have had it up to here"—I held my hand at arm's length above my head—"with people who have no consideration for how their actions affect other people."

Throughout my tirade, Grandma Natalie tried to placate me or at least slow me down, but I ignored her. After I finally ran out of steam, I turned and went upstairs. Before I slammed my bedroom door behind me, I heard my grandmother say, "Maybe you should go." A few moments later, I heard the welcome sound of a motorcycle fading away.

By the time I emerged from a long, hot shower, I was feeling on more of an even keel. I put my favorite pajamas on and fired up my computer. When I opened my email, I almost lost it again. Goddamn Mandy was inquiring about her friend for what felt like the billionth time.

I hit reply and typed, "I'VE TOLD YOU SEVERAL TIMES I CAN'T HELP YOU," but then I thought better of it and deleted the words. I'd deal with her when I was in a better frame of mind. Shadow jumped onto my desk and started purring. I stroked his soft fur and felt the day's frustrations begin to melt away.

"Did you know cats have medicinal qualities?" He purred as if such a thing were universally understood.

Though not sure if I should, I ventured downstairs, where Grandma Natalie was sitting at the kitchen table with a cup of coffee.

"Are you waiting for me?" I poured myself a cup and joined her.

"I figured you'd come down once you were over your tantrum. You're too old to be having your first teenage screaming fit, but I figured it was for a good reason. And I bet it's not entirely because of Chip."

"I'm sorry I yelled at you," I stirred my coffee for no reason. "And I'm sorry I yelled at him, but his parking is almost mathematical. He couldn't pick a more inconsiderate place to park if he'd measured it out ahead of time. I'll apologize the next time I see him."

"Thank you, dear. I appreciate it. Now, what was that all about? I mean, other than Chip's parking."

I told her about my visit to Nicky's parents' home.

"So her parents do know she's alive." Grandma Natalie appeared confused and sad all at once.

"What I don't know is whether they knew all along and lied to the police or if she let them think she was dead for some time, like she had the rest of us. I mean, they had a full-on funeral for her. If they knew she was alive, they're excellent actors."

We sat quietly for a few moments while I contemplated what I'd learned. I finally said, "I don't know what to do with this information."

"Call Patrick. He'll know what to do."

"He usually does. But first, I want to bring my car in off the street." I wasn't quite ready to admit I'd been back to the Flemings' home.

She held my phone out to me. "I put it in the driveway while you were upstairs."

With my delay tactic defeated, I took the phone.

Thirty seconds after he answered his phone, Patrick said, "Wait a sec," and put me on hold. The next thing I knew, I was explaining myself yet again to Beth O'Brien. She wasn't amused.

"Let me make sure I understand. You went to the Flemings' home and sat outside like some kind of stalker?"

"No, of course not." I started to babble. "Well, yes, sort of, but not really."

"Oh, yeah, that's clear." Her tone was wry. I decided it was better than angry. "And what exactly did you think you'd accomplish? Did you think she'd rush into your arms and confess everything?"

"Look, I've told you repeatedly she's alive, and now I've seen her at her parents' home."

"You saw her? Patrick told me she called you and told you to leave."

"She did, but when I was leaving, I saw her run out into the street."

"And you didn't stop."

"No. She wouldn't tell me anything about where she'd been or why. No details at all. I was angry so I left."

"How can you be sure it was her?" Patrick asked.

"Who the hell else would it be?"

"How about a neighbor who was concerned about the strange woman sitting in her car staring at the houses?"

I was silent for a moment. "The important thing here is she's in town at her parents' home. Doesn't it matter that I've proved her mom and dad know she's alive? Don't you want to know if they've known all along?"

Beth and Patrick were quiet for longer than I'd have liked, until Beth sighed audibly. "Do I have to put you in protective custody?"

Alarmed, I blurted out, "Protective what?"

"Yeah, I clearly need to protect you from yourself."

For a few seconds, I heard the muffled sound of Patrick laughing.

"Very funny," I said. "I hope that was some kind of sick joke."

"It won't be if you don't cool your fucking jets and let me do my goddamn job."

Her choice of words and harsh tone took me aback. I couldn't recall ever hearing Beth use any kind of strong language. I must have gotten under her skin pretty seriously this time.

"I'm sorry." I meant every syllable. "I'm sure you understand how important this is to me. I didn't kill Nicky. I've been saying it for a year and a half, and now there's proof. She is alive and in her parents' home. It doesn't make sense otherwise that she'd call and tell me to leave, would it? And I do believe I saw her in the street." I paused to take a calming breath. "I'm sorry for going over there, I am, but I can't apologize for feeling the need to do something. Being me hasn't been a lot of fun since my dad died."

"I understand, Annie. I'm asking you to remember you're a civilian. I'm the cop here, you know?" She paused. "Annie, I'll follow up on what you've told me. I've met with her parents multiple times. They used to call me about once a week or so about Nicky's case, but over time, they've called less frequently. It's been a month or so since I heard from them, so I'll get in touch with them. If she's there or they know where she is, I'll find out."

I slumped back in my chair in relief. "Thank you."

"But make no mistake. If you interfere again, I might have to take action. You're only hurting yourself with what you're doing." When she spoke again, her voice was lowered, as if she didn't want to be overheard. "I shouldn't say this, but since I met you, I've come to believe you didn't kill Nicky or the woman in the alleyway. I can't say it officially because I still have to follow the evidence, but the more I've gotten to know you, the more the suspicion on you doesn't feel right to me. And I'm a big believer in listening to my gut." Then she resumed a more normal tone. "But I will do what I need to do to keep you out of the investigation. Are we clear?"

"Very." I felt chastised but also relieved. "I promise to keep my nose clean and the rest of me out of your way."

She actually laughed. "Good. That's what I needed to hear. I do appreciate you giving me this information. You can be a real pain in my ass, but perhaps you got the information I need to close this whole thing out. But only if"—she said with added emphasis—"you stay out of the way. Deal?"

"Deal."

For all the relief I felt after talking with Beth and Patrick, I couldn't help thinking about Nicky. My emotions were constantly in flux. One moment, I was angry she'd let me believe she was dead, and the next moment, I was relieved not only for her but for myself. Then I'd remember the woman whose body was found downtown, someone who was probably missed—a daughter, a mother, a sister—but without some way to identify her, the police were unable to notify her family. Knowing as I did the devastating impact of such a loss, the unknown woman reminded me yet again of my dad, and grief left me breathless. Under it all was disillusionment. Nicky had an entire past I knew nothing about, and she was still withholding information.

I had to find a way to avoid spiraling into an obsession about her. Fortunately, my job at Rachel's clinic kept my mind occupied over the following days. Work at the bike shop continued, which also kept me busy. Brad brought in electricians, plumbers, and other trades to make the building functional. I spent some time trying to pick paint colors for the interior and exterior of the shop, but in the end, Joe and I found some photos of the original bike shop and decided to emulate the colors Dad used.

At breakfast with Grandma Natalie and Joe, I checked the list Joe and I had created to track what remained to be done. We still needed display shelving and racks, an inventory system, and ways to take payment. I made them my next priority.

Joe and I also discussed whether we'd need to hire anyone to work in the shop and decided to wait and see how busy we were.

"Don't want to be too confident," Joe said. "We might need to open slowly, only a few days a week or shorter hours. For now, the two of us can do the work and see how it goes." He eagerly anticipated quitting his accounting job and working full time at the bike shop.

"If we open slowly, do you think your boss would let you work part-time? I'd hate to see you give up your job if we're not making any money."

Grandma Natalie weighed in, offering to lend him money for rent and other expenses during the transition time. "Or you could move in with us."

He scooped her off her feet in a whirling hug, and she laughed with delight. He put her down and gave her a noisy kiss on the cheek. "Thank you, Grandma. But you better be careful what you ask for."

The harder days were those when I wasn't working at Rachel's clinic or trying to keep up with the mess the construction workers made. Brad's requests for me to pick up materials from the building supply had all but stopped since the building was nearly finished. On those days, I was often at loose ends with too much time to think.

And to get into trouble.

Despite my promise to the detective, I was still tempted to drive by the Flemings' home on the off chance I'd see Nicky. Fortunately, I remembered the words "protective custody" and behaved myself. It wasn't easy

.

Chapter Eight

A week later, Rachel and I parted ways after we closed her clinic, glad to have finished another week. She had plans for the night, so I headed to the bike shop. The final stages of construction were moving along more quickly than before. The original dumpster had been replaced with a smaller one, which made sense since most of the debris I picked up comprised discarded strands of electrical wire and bits of white pipe. A sizable stack of unused plywood and a couple of boxes of roof shingles were ready for Brad to collect. He'd told me he'd be able to reuse the materials I'd piled up for him, which would save him money while keeping them out of the landfill.

On this Friday, there wasn't much work for me to do, so within an hour, I was dusting off my hands and closing the dumpster lid. On slower days, I liked to take a cold drink and find a place to sit where I could contemplate the front of the new building and visualize the end result. I particularly liked the bricks on either side of the door. They were one of the few parts of the original bike shop that survived the fire. I remembered how proud my dad had been putting them in place himself.

I'd settled myself in a shady place at the edge of the parking lot when Joe rode up on his bike. He dismounted and propped his bike carefully against a nearby tree before joining me. I got a bottle of water out of the cooler I'd left nearby and handed it to him.

"Gotta love the August heat, right Annie?" He opened the bottle and took a long drink.

"Nope. Not me. Anything over eighty degrees should be a violation of Oregon law." I nudged him with my shoulder.

We'd always disagreed about hot weather and probably always would. We also enjoyed bantering about it, much to the amusement of those around us. It worked for us.

"It's getting there." He pointed his water bottle at the shop.

"I know. For the first few weeks, any progress seemed to take forever, but now I think it'll be finished in no time."

"Brad has lined up the painting contractor, so as soon as the utilities are in, they'll get to work. The suppliers have our first shipments ready to go. I've been thinking about getting a storage locker delivered here to hold the initial shipments, but I don't want to do it too soon."

"You don't think it might be broken into?" I'd previously expressed concern about the security of the inventory, even when it was in the shop. "Brad told me he's had nothing else go missing, but his guys have been extra careful about not leaving their tools lying around."

"That's partly why I'm waiting. If we pull the trigger too soon, we'd also have inventory on the books and no way to sell it. Judging the timing isn't easy."

"I'm glad we'll have a security system. Dad never thought it was necessary." I didn't want to say it aloud, but I'd often wondered what we might have learned if Dad had fitted the original shop with security cameras. "Do you think we should put up signs? You know, a grand reopening or a barbecue to let everyone know. Since we're on this corner with lots of car traffic, we could put one on each side. What do you think?"

"Good idea. Let's check into it. We already have the attention of the neighborhood."

"I know. Pretty much every day I'm here, someone stops by to say they're glad we're coming back or to ask when we're opening. I'm even seeing the same people coming through multiple times. They all say how much they anticipate us opening."

"I've seen a lot of people, too, including someone who actually drove up to the gate and parked, as if waiting for someone to open it for her."

"How odd. Isn't it obvious we're still building?"

"Especially since we were actually working. It made no sense, but there she was, sitting in her minivan with the engine idling. When I went to tell her she couldn't be in a construction area, she took off." He shrugged as if to say, "Go figure."

His mention of the woman in the minivan got my heart beating until I reminded myself how common minivans were. "A plague upon the land" was a phrase Rachel liked to use.

But I couldn't dispel the sense of dread I felt at his words. What if the woman I'd seen at the coffee shop was also the woman Joe saw? What if the mystery driver was Nicky?

"Joe, any idea when the cameras will be installed?"

He turned to me, eyebrows raised. "Why do you ask?"

"When I saw Nicky, she was driving a silver minivan. Was the one you saw here silver?"

"Annie, those things are a dime a dozen."

"Was it?"

"Yeah," he drew the word out, "it was. You don't think she'd come back here, do you?"

"Hell, I don't know what to think. Maybe seeing me made her think of the shop, and she came back to check it out. You knew Nicky. Did the woman in the van look like her?"

He shook his head. "I didn't see her well enough to know." He took my hand in both of his and held it tight. "I'll call Brad, and we'll get some security put in right away. Better safe than sorry, right?"

Early the next morning, I was awakened by the sound of voices downstairs. I pried one eye open and peered at my alarm clock. Seven. Who has company at seven in the morning, especially on a Saturday?

I closed my eyes and pulled my pillow over my head, but the damage was done. My innate curiosity would always get the better of me. I flung the pillow aside, narrowly missing Shadow, who jumped off the bed in protest.

"Welcome to the club, buddy." I brushed my teeth and hair and got dressed. Someone would pay big time for waking me up.

As I went down the stairs, I realized I was hearing Joe and Grandma Natalie making breakfast. I had to admit there were worse ways to start the day because Joe made the best waffles ever.

"You two are making enough racket to wake the—"

Joe gave me a smooch on the cheek and handed me a mug of steaming coffee, already dosed with sugar and my favorite almond creamer. He stood there appearing satisfied with himself.

"Okay. You're forgiven. And I hope you're making waffles."

My wish came true when Joe delivered a plate of hot, crisp waffles to me with his usual flourish. "Your morning repast, madam." He bowed and I laughed at his truly terrible attempt at an English accent. "May your humble servant add your favorite accouterments for you?" With a dish towel draped over his forearm, he indicated the butter dish, maple syrup bottle, and a jar of raspberry jam.

I tried to act the part of a snooty, upper-crust lady, but it was too much. I laughed out loud and waved him away. "I think I can manage, you goofball. Go away."

He and my grandmother joined me at the table while I poured syrup on my waffles. Not much—but enough for a taste of good quality maple syrup. They brought some crisp bacon with them, and I added a few slices to my plate, making sure to get some syrup on them. I took a bite of waffle. "You're hired. You can make waffles for me any time you like."

"You realize you say the same thing every time, don't you?" He tried but failed to look modest.

"Yes, because it's true."

The three of us chatted about our plans for the day while we ate. When we'd finished, we remained at the table, coffee mugs in hand, taking our time.

Joe sat back in his chair and squinted his eyes at me.

"What?" He never did that unless he was up to something.

"It occurred to me," he said after a moment, "you're a bike shop owner."

"Not exactly a news flash." Now I was definitely suspicious.

"Soon to be talking with customers. About bicycles."

"We won't be selling hot water heaters or cucumbers. What are you getting at?"

"And you'll be taking their money, and hoping they become regular customers, buy more stuff, sign up for rides, and such."

"Are you getting to the point any time this decade? I have today and tomorrow off from Rachel's place, but I have to be at work Monday morning."

"So you should be a good example of a bicycle shop owner."

"And?" I was getting an inkling of where he was heading.

"A good bicycle shop owner should know everything about bikes and the gear that goes with them."

"Okay."

"A good bike shop owner should also set an example as a professional in the bicycle industry."

"I'm aging beyond my years here."

The shoe finally dropped.

"A really good bicycle shop owner should," he leaned forward, put his elbows on the table, and stared me right in the eyes, "ride."

I couldn't think of a witty retort quickly enough, so he asked, "When was the last time you rode your bike? I saw it when I came in this morning. It's totally covered in dust and one tire is flat. That's no way to treat a good bike."

"You know I've been really busy. Between working at the clinic and at the shop, I haven't had time."

"Bullshit." He looked determined. "You've had plenty of time. I've asked you a hundred times to ride with me, and you never do. What gives?"

I didn't want to tell him why I refused to ride with him, but I saw I wouldn't escape unscathed. I took a deep breath and blew it out.

"Okay, fine. You're eighty times faster than I am. I can't keep up with you, but I also don't like it when you stop and wait for me."

"Eighty times?" He raised an eyebrow with amusement.

"Measured by NASA." I tried to sound defiant, but he laughed.

"Why didn't you say something before?"

"I don't know. I guess I should have. But why do you want to ride with me when I'm so slow?"

"You're my sister, you dingbat. I enjoy spending time with you. But I am sorry for leaving you behind. I get used to going as fast as I can, especially when Team Three and a Half is training."

"I do miss riding." I rode my bike far more consistently when I lived in Charbonneau. When I first moved back to Portland, caring for my grandmother had consumed all of my time. As her injuries healed, I found my days taken up elsewhere, mostly the bike shop and working at Rachel's clinic.

"Tell you what," he said, "let's get your bike tuned up and go for a ride a couple times a week. He held up two fingers like the Boy Scout he never was. "I promise I won't leave you behind." The twinkle in his eyes put me on guard. "At least that's my promise if you'll promise me something in return."

I was wary. "What?"

"You'll work on riding faster."

Skeptical, I reached across the table with my right hand to shake his. "You have a deal, on one condition."

"Which is?"

I held up my empty plate. "Make me one more waffle." While I waited for my waffle, I peered at my phone, reading the list of emails that came in overnight.

"Oh no. Not again."

"What is it?" Grandma Natalie asked, concerned.

"Remember the server at the sushi place who wanted me to find her girlfriend?"

"Yeah."

"She's back. I've told her at least three times, by email and in person, I can't help her." I met my grandmother's eyes. "Even a professional detective would have trouble tracking her down." I pushed the phone away in frustration. "And here she is, asking again if I've made any progress. I swear, I'm hunting down the reporter who wrote that damn article and—"

A deep voice interrupted me with "and what?"

I almost jumped out of my chair. In mid-rant, I hadn't heard Patrick come into the house.

"I'm going to take your key away if you come sneaking in here again," I said, annoyed.

"Waffle?" Joe tried to intervene.

"No, thanks, I already had breakfast." He paused. "I called Beth about the van at the bike shop and—"

"And I told him I needed to talk with you about it." Beth O'Brien stepped into the kitchen from behind Patrick.

"So here we are." He tried appearing chagrined, as if it would buy him absolution for bringing an unannounced guest to the house so early in the day. Especially *this* guest.

"Nice try," I said, and he gave up.

At Grandma Natalie's prompting, they made themselves comfortable at the table. She poured coffee for them and refilled my cup as well, before joining us.

After everyone was settled, Beth asked, "What were you saying about an article?"

"You know, the newspaper article I told you about before." I tried to wave it away. "Remember I told you I'd agreed to search for someone for the server at Doug's Café?"

"Did you have any luck?"

"No, none at all. The paid search site was useless. I told her I couldn't help, and now it seems I have a cyber stalker. I guess I'll have to wait her out. Eventually, she'll have to give up. I even stopped eating at my favorite sushi place to avoid her."

"Which of the paid sites did you use?"

I named it, and she said, "As far as I know, that one is usually fairly accurate."

"I put my own name in, and it was right on." I thought for a moment, and said, trying to be casual, "As I had the site paid for, I put Nicky's name in, too, thinking I might find a current address or something."

"Did you?"

"No, but as I told you at the coffee shop, I was surprised to find she apparently has a history of drug-related arrests. Have you had a chance to review her file?"

"After we talked, I did check her file, and now I have a bit of a mystery on my hands. The information you found appears to be correct, from what I can see, but there's nothing in the case file about it. And I didn't find any other records of her being arrested. Unless the online source is wrong, I don't know what it means. I have a friend in the Drugs and Vice Division, so I'll see if she can help me sort it out, because this makes no sense to me."

"If it's true Nicky has that kind of record, I guess I didn't know her as well as I thought I did."

"Do we ever?"

Her diversion into what felt like a personal observation made me uncomfortable, so I changed the subject. "Patrick told you about our mystery guest at the bike shop. I wasn't sure we should bother you with it. I told him homicide detectives wouldn't care about trespassing."

"I agree with you it might be nothing more than a coincidence, but you should always err on the side of telling me more rather than less. Let me decide if it's relevant. I'm glad you're getting security cameras."

"Also here at the house," Patrick said.

"Good. I know it's an expense, but you're doing the right thing. I still need proof Nicole Fleming is alive, but maybe cameras could help us find out."

She and Patrick got up, and I walked them to the door. As they stepped out onto the porch, Beth turned back to me with a trace of a grin on her face.

"And Annie? Whatever you were going to do to that reporter? Just don't. I really would hate to have to arrest you."

"She likes you."

"Oh please." I turned to Grandma Natalie. "Why does everyone I know have more interest in my love life than I do?"

She gave me her "I'll never tell" smile and went back to the kitchen.

I followed her to the table. "I know what it is. All of you have a secret society dedicated to pawning me off on some unsuspecting woman.

What do you do? Have meetings at an undisclosed location to plot against me?"

"Not at all," she said, settling into her chair. "We use Zoom."

"Not funny." I poured each of us fresh coffee. "And no, she doesn't like me. Not that way anyway."

"You like her, don't you? That way?" She made air quotes around her last words.

"No. I'm only trying to keep her on my side."

"You keep saying it and someday you might even believe it. But I see how you look at her, and so does Patrick. She's far too observant not to have noticed. You're the one in denial here."

"Grandma, she's a cop. She could lock me up for murder. You don't see a problem here, some kind of conflict of interest, some issue with her job? Seriously?"

"She told you herself she thinks you're innocent." She waved my objection away. "And if you're right and Nicky is alive, then what's the problem?"

I glared at her for a moment, wishing I had an answer.

"What are you up to today?"

"I'm going to the shop. Joe told me the painters finished the exterior yesterday, and I want to see it. Some of the fixtures were also delivered. Maybe I can put shelves up. Joe's meeting me there in a while. Want to come along?"

"Absolutely. It'll be fun to see how it's coming along."

An hour later, I parked my car on the street near the shop and got out to unlock the gate. The parking lot was empty, except for the dumpster, but the ground was littered with debris left behind by the latest tradespeople who worked there.

"I have some work to do here, Grandma. I hope you don't mind hanging out for a while."

"Not at all. I'll give you a hand."

As we got out of the car, a bicycle whizzed by. Its rider turned expertly toward the open gate and stopped with a short skid of the tires in front of us. Titanium leg prosthesis gleaming in the sunshine, Joe stepped off his bike and waved at us.

Seeing my brother always lifted my spirits. "Hey there, speedy," I called to him. "You ever scare anyone off the road with that metal contraption you call a leg?"

His booming belly laugh filled the air. "No, but I do amaze them with my blazing speed and superb bike-handling skills."

"And you wonder why I don't ride with you."

"Come on." He put his arm around Grandma Natalie's shoulders. "The painters finished the outside, and I'm anxious to see it. Let's go check out our shiny new bicycle store."

We walked through the lot toward the newly painted building, but we stopped in our tracks after a few steps.

"What the—" Joe's jaw dropped for a moment at the sight before us.

We'd had the new building painted the same colors as my dad had painted the original, creamy white with the other colors of the Mexican flag, red and green, accenting the windows and doors. I'd long anticipated seeing it.

But what I saw now was heartbreaking and enraging at the same time. Someone had desecrated our beautiful new building with streaks and blobs of yellow and black spray paint. Even the windows were painted over.

Joe ran around the building. When he came back, he was boiling angry. "They ruined all of it. All of it." He let loose with a string of invective mirroring my own rising rage. "I wish we'd had those security cameras up by now." He paced back and forth, waving his arms and swearing.

I could only stand still in shock, with tears streaming down my face. I wiped them away with the back of my hand, but my efforts were useless since more followed. Grandma Natalie tried to comfort both of us, but it was several minutes before any of us could speak.

Joe had his phone in his hand. "I'm calling the police." He walked to the far end of the parking lot. When he returned, he said, "They're sending someone to take a report. I called Brad, and he's on his way. I'll take pictures while we're waiting. Unbelievable." He walked toward the building, his phone held up before his face.

"Why would someone do this?" I knew my question was rhetorical, but I couldn't help it. "We're so close to opening." I had another thought and called to my brother, "Do we have insurance for this?"

"Good question. I'll have to check. All this and we're not even open yet." He blew out of a gust of air and went back to taking pictures.

Through my angry tears, I looked at the damage until I couldn't stand it any longer and turned away. "We'll have to wait a while for the police to get here. I might as well clean up. Better than standing around."

"Maybe you should photograph it first," Grandma Natalie said. "In case there's any kind of evidence. Paint cans maybe."

"Good idea. Maybe you should be a detective." I looked at the trash scattered on the ground. "Worst case, I'll have pictures of old coffee cups on my phone. If you want, you can wait in the car, Grandma. It'd be more comfortable than standing out here. Too bad we don't have a bench or something to sit on. Maybe I should keep folding chairs in the car."

"I'm fine, Annie. I'll help you clean up. We'll both probably feel better getting some work done."

Of course she was right. We spent the next forty-five minutes cleaning up the bike shop lot. The heavy construction was done, so what we found was mostly used paint stirring sticks, strips of blue painter's tape, a few discarded paint brushes with the red and green colors of the shop trim, and a lot of empty coffee cups and water bottles. I'd hoped the vandals had discarded spray paint cans when they were finished, but we didn't find any.

We'd finished when a Portland Police Bureau car pulled up. The officer introduced himself as Carlos Martinez. We gave him our names and shook hands all around.

"Are you the property owner?"

"Yes, with my brother, Joe."

Joe went into the shop and returned with a drawing of the planned paint job. He handed the paper to the officer. "The painting was finished yesterday. We didn't even have time to photograph it."

"The Mexican flag?" Martinez asked.

"Dad was an immigrant and very proud of his origins. The bike shop was originally his, and we wanted to honor his memory with these colors."

He gave me a kind smile. "I understand. My parents came from Mexico, too, before I was born. If I showed them this picture, they'd be repainting their house in no time." He handed the drawing back to Joe. He shook his head with a sad expression on his face. "I've only been a police officer for a few years, and I will never understand why people put so much effort into being destructive. I hope this wasn't a response to the colors you chose." He left us to walk around the structure. When he returned, he said, "I'll take some pictures and file a report. I probably don't have to tell you it's unlikely we'll ever know who the perpetrator was." He scanned the property, focusing on the eaves of the shop and nearby utility poles. "No security cameras?"

"Not yet," Joe said. "We've had a couple of minor incidents here, a few thefts and some trespassing, so we've already decided to put them up. They've been delivered, but we're having some trouble getting the installers scheduled. They're all booked up."

"If I were you and this was my property, I'd be calling every day until they got someone out to do the installation," Martinez said. He looked through the windows into the building. "They didn't go inside?"

"No, they didn't. I checked it out when I went in for the drawing. All of the damage is on the exterior."

"Yeah, that's bad enough." The officer left us to take his photos and when he was finished, he shook our hands again and, wishing us good luck with the bike shop, he left us with a wave and an "*adios.*"

As the police cruiser disappeared around the corner, a truck with a familiar logo on the side pulled up. When Brad saw the damaged building, he stopped and stared.

"What the everlasting hell?"

"That's kind of what I said, though Joe was more eloquent."

"I bet he was."

"Do you blame me?" Joe joined us after going back inside to put the painting scheme away.

"The painters will be as pissed as we are," Brad said. "They worked hard on it." He ran his hand through his hair, leaving it standing on end. "We can fix it, but the painters are all booked up for a couple of weeks. I'll see if I can get them here before then, but I can't promise anything."

"Thanks, man," Joe said. "In the meantime, since the interior wasn't damaged, we can start putting up shelves and whatnot."

"And I'll see if I can clean the paint off the windows," I said. "Less for the painters to do."

Brad said, "Good idea. And maybe it'll help to have people here."

We talked for another few minutes before Brad left, promising to get painters back as quickly as he could. We watched him drive away, and Grandma Natalie grabbed my arm.

"I haven't seen the inside. Give me a tour, and then let's go shopping and try to shake this off."

Chapter Nine

The next morning, I wheeled my bike out of the garage and into the Sunday sunshine. True to his word, Joe had given it a thorough tune up and cleaning, and its dark blue paint gleamed in the sun. I'd ridden it a time or two around the neighborhood to get used to being on the bike again after a few months, but today's ride was different. This time, Joe, Sally, and Rachel were joining me.

They were due to meet me at eight, but I was ready to go fifteen minutes early. Instead of standing around waiting, I mounted up and rode around the block a couple of times. Our neighborhood streets were quiet and fairly flat, good for warming up. I'd been looking forward to riding with my friends and my brother, but truth to tell, my favorite rides were the solo efforts. What I missed most about living in Charbonneau was easy access to country roads with little traffic. Riding outside the town was enjoyable, except for the occasional macho idiot who felt it was necessary to blow diesel exhaust, called "rolling coal," my way. Fortunately, it had happened only a couple of times, and I wrote it off to testosterone poisoning.

I'd wheeled back up to the house when Rachel's car followed me into the driveway. As she got out of her car and joined me, Sally arrived, parking on the street next to our driveway. She called hello to us when she got out of her car and started untying the straps holding her bike to the roof of her car.

"Joe's not here yet?" Rachel asked.

"No, but he told me your bike is ready to go." I gave her a once over. "New riding shorts?"

"And a helmet and gloves. It's been long enough since I rode I figured new stuff was in order. Your bike is beautiful."

"Joe does good work."

As I spoke, he drove up and parked behind Rachel's car. He jumped out and waved before he went to the back of his SUV, where he unloaded two bikes. His own was the color of burnished gold, a custom paint job he'd commissioned after winning a hundred-mile bike race, called a century. Rachel's bike, a red beauty shining in the sunlight, followed his bike. She met him at the car and wheeled her bike up to where I stood. By then, Sally was also ready to go.

Joe joined us. "It's about time we did this, sis."

"Remember, you promised not to fly away and leave us in your dust."

He rode down the driveway and back before we could follow him. "And you promised to train yourself to ride faster." He sped away before I could respond.

Sally, Rachel, and I rode onto the street in the direction Joe had taken. The morning was perfect for a ride. Sunshine and cool breezes. The August heat would come later, long after we'd finished.

"Where'd he go?" Rachel strained to see Joe in the distance.

"Never mind him," I said. "He'll come back and find us."

We rode in silence for a couple of miles, enjoying being in each other's company. It wasn't the same as riding in the country, but since it was an early Sunday morning, traffic was light.

"I keep forgetting to ask you," I said after a while. "How's your search for a receptionist going?"

"Pretty good," Rachel said. "I have three interviews lined up next week, and one of them seems especially promising. Are you looking forward to being a free woman again?"

"It's been fun, mostly, but yes, I'll be happy to hand the reins to someone else. Your timing is good. Work at the bike shop is picking up. I need to spend more time there from here on out." I told my friends about the vandalism and the mystery van in the parking lot. "Joe ordered security cameras, but getting them installed is taking forever. In the meantime, our shelves and bike racks are being delivered, so we can get them assembled. We also have some stuff from the original building we're going to use."

"It's terrible about the paint," Sally said. "I really don't understand people sometimes, you know?"

"Me, neither. The painting contractor is scheduled to come back in the next few days, but I'm wondering if we should wait until the security cameras are in place. It won't do us much good to paint if the vandal ruins it again." I glanced around as best I could without losing my balance. "Where's Joe? I need to talk with him about this."

"Sounds like a good idea to me." We pedaled on for another few minutes before Sally asked, "Any more news about the van?"

"I'm seeing silver minivans everywhere I go," I said with disgust. "It's really hopeless."

"Who's hopeless?"

I almost fell trying to see behind me. Joe had joined us at some point, and none of us had heard him.

"Apparently you are," I said. "You promised to stay with us."

"I didn't say for how long," he said cheekily.

The four of us rode together for another five miles, circling back through the city streets to where we'd started. With the day warming and traffic picking up, we agreed it was a good time to end our ride.

We turned our bikes into the driveway and pedaled up to the house. We'd dismounted and pulled our helmets and gloves off when Rachel directed my attention toward the street. "Is that who I think it is?"

After a moment, I saw her—a young woman standing behind the rhododendron occupying a corner near the end of the driveway. She was peering at us through the leaves, but when we saw her, she stepped back, seeming to seek more cover.

"What's she doing here?"

Mandy had gone from cyber stalking to the real thing.

"Mandy, what are you doing here?"

When she heard my voice, she bolted down the street. Joe mounted his bike and chased her down, and after a few minutes, hauled her back to the house by her wrist. She pulled and twisted, trying to get away, but to no avail. I met them halfway down the driveway, with Rachel and Sally not far behind.

"What the hell are you doing here?" I tried not to sound as angry as I felt. "Have you been following me?"

Again, she tried to pull away from Joe's grip, but she gave up when Sally stepped up and grasped her other arm. She glared at me defiantly. "You told me you'd find Sandy for me, and you haven't. You promised."

"I did nothing of the sort. I only promised to search online, which I've done. I also told you I couldn't promise to succeed."

"That's right," Rachel said. "All of us were there and heard her, and you said you understood."

"And then you gave me almost no solid information to go on. I've told you many times since then that without better information, it's hopeless. And here's another thing." I was gaining momentum. "You don't even know your own girlfriend's birthdate or her age. Did you make it all up?"

I hadn't realized until the words left my lips that I'd subconsciously wondered whether she'd deliberately sent me on a wild goose chase.

She stuck her chin out. "I did not." She sounded like a stubborn child.

"Let's get a few things straight." I tried to calm myself. "For the last time, I am not a detective." I emphasized each word. "I agreed to try to help you and I did what I could, but I'm done." I stepped forward, causing her to back up, at least as far as she could with Joe's grip on one of her arms and Sally's on the other. "Leave and do not come back here. I don't like being followed, and I don't like people spying on me, not anywhere, but especially not my home. And here's something else for you to keep in mind." I stepped forward again, now less than a foot from her face. "Trespassing and stalking are crimes in Oregon. If I see you here again, I'll file a complaint with the police, and I'll talk to your boss at the restaurant. Got it?"

Wild-eyed, she looked at Joe, Rachel, and Sally, as if in supplication, and then at me. When she didn't speak, I repeated in measured words, "Do you understand?"

She refused to meet my eyes, but she finally mumbled, "Yes." She tried in vain to wrench her arms free until I said, "Let her go."

She ran down the driveway and out of sight.

Joe said, "The sooner we get those security cameras up, the better I'll feel."

I seconded his sentiment and turned to Rachel. "Remember when you said something wasn't quite right with her?"

"Sure."

"Bingo."

Rachel loaded her bike into her car. "See you tomorrow," she called as she backed out of the driveway. Joe helped Sally tie her bike down, and she departed as well.

Joe and I went into the house where Grandma Natalie had already laid out sandwich fixings for us. The enticing aroma of homemade bean soup met us at the door, and my mouth was watering even before I saw the bounty she'd prepared.

"Who was that young woman?" she asked. "Not your friends," she clarified. "The one you were putting the fear of Odin into."

I shook my head, too frustrated to comment on her reference to her favorite Norse god. "Mandy. Remember I told you about the server from the sushi place who asked me to search for her girlfriend?"

"Yes. That was her? What was she doing here?"

"She apparently followed me home at some point. If you ever wanted proof I shouldn't ever try to be a detective, there you have it. I never noticed I was being followed."

"I don't like it one bit," she said.

"I don't, either, which is why I hope I scared her enough to keep her away."

I busied myself setting the table while Joe changed out of his cycling jersey. When he appeared in jeans and a T-shirt, he took over my kitchen duties while I changed my own clothes. By the time I was back downstairs, enough time had passed that my ire at Mandy's unwelcome visit had begun to fade.

"You have a good ride?"

"Speedy here," I punched Joe playfully on the shoulder, "took off and left us, as usual, but otherwise, we had fun. I'm glad I invited Sally and Rachel. At least I had someone to ride with." I gave Joe a mock glare.

"They're excellent riders." He opened the fridge and returned with a pitcher of iced tea. "I had fun fixing up Rachel's bike."

"You're a born bike shop owner," I said.

"Don't I know it." He poured tea for all of us and claimed a seat at the table as Grandma Natalie served bowls of soup all around. "I can't wait until we can open."

I piled sliced turkey and vegetables on my sandwich until Grandma Natalie gave me side eye accompanied by a raised brow.

"Never you mind." I gave her the eye right back. "I'm a growing girl."

"Yeah, sideways."

Joe laughed out loud, rocking back in his chair.

"Neither of you are very funny." I tried to look stern.

"I think we're hilarious."

"Like an ingrown toenail."

"Children." Grandma Natalie occasionally spoke to us as if we weren't adults approaching thirty. Exchanging amused glances, Joe and I settled down and tucked into our food, proving yet again that her admonitions still worked.

"So," I said after a few minutes, "what's left to do?"

Joe took a small spiral notebook from his pocket and leafed through it. "The construction is done except for the last inspection."

"And painting." I took a bite of my sandwich. "Well, repainting."

"Yeah." He was sad for a moment and then brightened again. "I have a thought about that." With my mouth full of sandwich, all I could do was raise an inquiring eyebrow. "We have the interior painters scheduled to come in a couple of weeks, but maybe we should let the exterior wait for the time being."

"You won't believe it, but Rachel and I talked about exactly the same thing while we were riding. Why tempt the vandal if we don't have to? If we leave it the way it is, maybe they'll think it's not worth messing with again."

"One can hope." He consulted his notebook again. "The parking lot is in reasonably good condition, but I'd like to get it striped." He met my eyes. "At some point, we'll need to have it resurfaced, but it's fine for now." Back to his notes. "Storage shelves for the back, racks for the front, places for customers to sit and try on shoes and whatnot."

"And have coffee."

"Yes, coffee bar. Do we have a source for coffee and snacks?"

"All done." I'd arranged for a local coffee roaster to deliver to us, and I knew where to buy good cookies and muffins. "I can get us stuff like energy bars and fruit from the store. That should work while we see how popular they are."

He made a note.

"We have the payment system ready to install." His phone dinged, and he looked down to check it. "Good news. The security system will be delivered tomorrow. Finally. I'll get the installer scheduled right away." He looked back and forth between Grandma Natalie and me. "Which should we do first, the shop or here?"

Grandma Natalie spoke up for the first time. "Do I get a vote?"

"Of course."

"Please have the first ones installed here. For as long as I've lived here, I've always felt safe, but I'm not at all happy about that woman showing up here uninvited. From what I could see, she didn't appear to be very stable."

"You got it," Joe said. "If we're lucky, maybe we can get both locations installed the same day. And I agree with you. Our little Annie has a stalker."

"Oh, now I'm little. Earlier, you were on my case about my sandwich. What was that you said? I'm growing sideways?"

Grandma Natalie got up from her chair to hug me. "Just more of you to love." She laughed aloud before returning to her seat.

"Fine. Have your fun." I turned to Joe. "Want to ride again tomorrow?"

Wednesday evening, Grandma Natalie met me at the door when I got home after work. "Did you see them?" She seemed pleased.

"Them who?"

"Not who, what. Joe put a rush on the security camera installation here at the house and it's done. Let me show you."

We went back outside and stood in the driveway. Try as I might, I couldn't spot anything new about the house until she showed me where the cameras were. "They're so small. The ones at Doc Wentworth's house were much larger and clearly visible."

Doctor Carlton Wentworth had been my main housekeeping client when I lived in Charbonneau. His foresight to install security cameras outside his home had led to the identity of his murderer. I felt a momentary pang of loss thinking about him. He'd always been kind to me and everyone around him, including his shrew of a trophy wife. I still occasionally missed his sense of humor.

I looked again at the tiny cameras peering at us from the house. "If someone doesn't know they're there, they'll never see them."

"I know. It's perfect. Sensors on the doors and windows will trigger the alarm if they're opened without the security code. They linked all of it to a security company who monitors it round the clock."

"Security code?"

"Let me show you."

We went back inside, where she showed me a small panel inside the door. I hadn't noticed it when I came in.

"Once we set this, an alarm will go off if someone opens a door or window, and the security company will call. All we have to do is remember to set it when we go out or at night."

"Amazing, but I wish it wasn't necessary."

Grandma Natalie hugged me. "Me, too, but I already feel better. From what you've told me, the young woman who was here isn't the type to take no for an answer. Maybe she's harmless, but better safe than sorry."

Unfortunately, I had to agree. "I wonder how many times I'll set this thing off before I get used to it."

"Not more than once, I bet. The installer demoed it for me, and it sounds like an air raid siren."

"Shadow will lose his mind. He hides when he hears a doorbell on TV."

We went into the kitchen, and I got a cold drink from the fridge. I sat at the table and called Joe.

"Hey, the cameras here are great. I like how small they are. I wouldn't have seen them if Grandma Natalie hadn't pointed them out. Do you know when the cameras at the shop will be installed?"

"Tomorrow," he said. "We'll start with the ones covering the outside of the building and the parking lot, and they'll put in the rest after the painting is done."

When we ended our call, I wrapped my arms around my grandmother. "Here's the important question. What's for dinner?"

She spoke in a tentative voice. "Well, about that."

"Oh?" I held her at arm's length for a moment. "What's up?" We sat at the table.

"We're having company for dinner."

"Okay."

"It's Chip. He wants to talk with you."

I sat back in my chair. "Why?" My voice was plaintive.

"He wants to apologize. He seems sincere, but you can decide for yourself."

"Trust me, I will." I took a deep breath before continuing. "He seems to make you happy."

"He does."

"I promise to be polite, but I won't lie, there's something about him I find off-putting." She started to speak, but I extended a hand to forestall her. "I don't know what it is, a gut feeling. And I'm surprised he hasn't asked me why I'm not married with kids by now."

Her gaze slid away from mine.

"No. He didn't."

"Yeah, he did. He asked me."

"Coward. What did you tell him?"

She met my eyes again with a wicked grin. "I told him he'd have to ask you himself. Maybe tonight he will." She got up and went to the fridge. "How does lasagna sound?"

"Like you're baiting me with my favorite dinner, that's how."

Our meal with Chip started amicably enough. When he arrived, he seemed somewhat quieter than usual, and after I brought him a cold drink, he asked to talk with me. We went into the living room, where I sat in my grandmother's recliner, and he took a spot on the couch.

"What do you want to talk about?" I had a pretty good idea, but I figured I'd leave it open-ended for him.

He stuttered for a moment and then said, "I want to apologize for being inconsiderate and blocking the driveway. I have no excuse. I honestly didn't think about it. You were right to call me on it."

"Thank you. I accept your apology. And I owe you one as well. I shouldn't have yelled at you the way I did. I'd had a bad day, and I took it out on you when I shouldn't have. I'm sorry."

We stood and shook hands, and when I turned toward the kitchen, Grandma Natalie was standing in the doorway with a satisfied expression on her face.

"Who's hungry?"

Chip helped me set the table while Grandma Natalie got the hot food out of the oven. I put the salad bowl out with two different dressings alongside it. We made our beverage selections—iced tea all around—and sat down to eat.

At first, the only words spoken were "please pass the vinaigrette" and "I'd like another piece of bread, please." At least three times, Chip exclaimed my grandmother made the best lasagna he'd ever eaten. As I ate, any tension remaining after my talk with Chip receded somewhat, and I resolved to try to be more welcoming of my grandmother's boyfriend.

They told me about their latest ride, this time to Astoria. I enjoyed how they each filled in details of the ride, the weather, how light the traffic was on the usually busy highway, and what good burgers they'd had at a local restaurant.

"How was your day?" Chip asked after they'd finished their tale. "I hear you're building a bicycle shop with your brother, but Natalie here"—I noticed he no longer called her 'Nat'—"says your bikes don't have engines. What's up with that?"

I laughed. "Our bikes are people-powered."

"Slow and poky," he said.

"Quiet and peaceful. No fumes."

"Grunting up the hills. Sweating."

"Good exercise, plus you can actually hear birds singing and enjoy nature."

"All right, you two." Grandma Natalie interrupted what was turning into a competition. "No fighting or no pie."

I gave her a grin. "You wait. I'll convert you yet."

She snorted. "As if." She sounded just like a teenager.

We got up to clear away our dishes. She brought out a perfectly baked pie, and I was delighted to find it was my favorite strawberry rhubarb. A scoop of vanilla ice cream alongside each slice resulted in perfection.

Which lasted until Chip spoke again.

"So why aren't you married?"

Even with Grandma Natalie's warning, I almost choked on my pie. When I'd taken a drink of tea and cleared my windpipe, I met his eyes. "What?"

"I know, I know." He waved a meaty hand. "None of my business. Natalie told me you've never been married. You're a pretty girl with your blue eyes and dark hair, and I can't help but wonder why some young man hasn't put a ring on your finger. Don't you want kids? A family?"

So much for our new détente.

"First, I'm twenty-eight years old, which makes me a woman, not a girl."

He was taken aback, his eyes going back and forth between my grandmother and me, a deer in the headlights.

"Annie, please."

"Second," I continued as if my grandmother hadn't spoken. "There's not a man anywhere, young, old, or in between, who could convince me to marry him, because my relationships, when I have them, are with women." I paused and took a breath, reminding myself he was our guest, and finding I didn't care. "And third, you're right about one thing. None of it is any of your business."

If I'd been any younger, especially still in my teenage years, I'd have stormed out of the room in a dramatic exit, but I didn't. I gave him my best "don't fuck with me" glare and took another bite of pie.

He sat stock-still and slowly put his fork down, indecisive.

"Chip," my grandmother said, "it's okay. I could have told you the other day, but it's not my information to share. That's why I wanted you to talk with Annie yourself."

She reached out to him, but he brushed her hand away and rose from his chair.

"It's okay?" he asked. "Exactly what is okay? That I ask an innocent question and then I'm being lectured? Sure, she's right, it's none of my business. But she dates women? How is that okay?"

"How is it not?" I couldn't restrain myself any longer. I stood up and faced him, feet planted, fists on my hips. "Who are you to judge me?"

"I'm not judging anyone," he said. "It's not natural. You should marry a man and have children, raise a family. That's how the world works."

"Does it now? Maybe that's how your world works, but here's a news flash: there's not only one way to be in the world. There's no such thing as one kind of family. Grandma Natalie, my adopted brother, and I are a family. We were a family when my dad was alive, and we have been since he died. And nobody, not you, not anyone else, can tell us otherwise. Yes, I'm a lesbian. Always have been. Always will be. It's what's natural for me. It's not up for debate."

He stood there gaping at me, clearly unable to respond. Grandma Natalie came between us and made soothing sounds, all in vain. After a minute, I stepped back and took a deep breath, blowing it out forcefully. My heart rate was decreasing and the red haze that had come over my eyes was receding.

"I'm sorry, but I have to apologize to both of you. Grandma Natalie, I'm sorry for ruining dinner." I turned to Chip. "And I apologize to you for how I reacted, but I will never apologize for who I am."

Grandma Natalie put her hand on my arm. "It's okay, Annie."

I gave her a hug. "No worries. I don't expect you to introduce yourself and then say, 'My granddaughter is a lesbian.'"

"Maybe you should." Chip finally spoke. His eyes were hard and angry.

My grandmother stood straight, shoulders back, chin up. "Chip, it's time for you to go."

He headed out the front door without another word, closing it harder than was necessary. A few seconds later, we heard the roar of his motorcycle engine and listened as it faded into the distance.

Grandma Natalie and I stood there for another few moments, neither of us quite sure what to do, until she said, "I'm so sorry, Annie. I had no idea he'd react so badly."

I couldn't help but chuckle. "Maybe it's a good thing Joe didn't invite himself to dinner. I don't know what Chip would think of a

Scandinavian grandmother, a half-Mexican lesbian granddaughter, and a Black grandson with a metal leg. His head would have imploded."

She laughed with me for a moment. "Probably so." She sighed. "Oh well. It was fun while it lasted."

As August wore on, the days became noticeably shorter than earlier in the summer. The weather was still too hot for my liking. Rachel hired a regular receptionist, so in another week, I would be a free agent again. As much as I enjoyed talking with Rachel's clients and spending time with their pets, I happily anticipated having more free time.

Her timing couldn't have been better. The painters had completed their work inside the shop, and the walls and trim gleamed. We'd carried the exterior color theme inside but in a more understated way. The walls were white to show off the bicycles and related accessories and clothing. Three courses of green and red horizontal pinstripes encircled the public area, one near the ceiling, one near the floor, and the third midway between. It was perfect.

I arrived on a sunny Saturday morning to clean up after the painters and to start assembling shelves. After collecting the discarded paper and painter's tape that lay on the floor and the ground outside the door, I went into the back of the building where we'd set aside space for storage. Joe and I had agreed three sets of floor-to-ceiling shelves would be sufficient, at least at first.

I set to work laying out the pieces of shelving. The aluminum uprights were unwieldy, but once I got the first shelf bolted into place, the rest went together easily enough. After another hour, I had the first unit assembled, but still lying on its side on the floor. At six feet tall and ten feet long, it was too heavy for me to lift on my own. Time to enlist my brother.

After I called Joe for help with the shelves, I got a bottle of water from the cooler I'd brought and stepped outside. I tried not to look at the ruined colors on the outside of our new shop. I retrieved an empty five-gallon paint bucket from the pile I'd made of the painters' detritus and, turning it on its top, made myself a place to sit near the front door.

Leaning back against the bricks we'd salvaged and had installed at the front of the shop, I surveyed the property as we'd see it from inside. We were fortunate enough to have a corner location with two entries into the small parking lot. Established trees flanked the driveways on two sides. The third side of the lot was fenced, creating a demarcation between our shop and the gas station next door. The shop itself formed the fourth side of our property, also fenced.

While I sipped my cold water and waited for Joe, I imagined how it would appear when it was finished. The concrete parking lot needed to be re-striped, but we'd have at least a dozen parking spaces. Joe hoped to have enough room for kids to try out their bikes without having to go out onto the street, and it appeared as if he might be right. I got up to examine the windows, still marred by spray paint. I scraped at one of the lines of paint with my fingernail and some of it came off. Maybe I could clean the windows with a razor blade scraper and some elbow grease.

I turned to scan the trees and nearby utility poles, wondering where the security cameras would go, when Joe arrived.

"Wow, you do know how to drive," I said, as he emerged from his car. "I almost don't recognize you without Team Three and a Half written across your chest." He was dressed for working at the shop, wearing a raggedy pullover and jeans that had seen better days. The shining metal of his titanium prosthesis showed through a tear in his jeans.

"Smart ass." He hugged me briefly. "Got another one of those?" He pointed to the water bottle in my hand.

"Inside."

He stood back and, much as I'd done, surveyed the place. "Paint job sucks."

"We should fire the designer."

"Agreed." He started toward the door. "What's happening in here that means I'm indispensable?"

I showed him the assembled rack of shelves lying on the storage room floor.

"It's too heavy for me to stand up."

"Annie, Annie, Annie." He shook his head with a sad expression on his face. "Never decide to become an engineer."

"I won't, but why not? It's put together and ready to put in place, isn't it? I know I assembled it correctly, so what's the big deal?"

"Think about it for a moment. If we tilt it up, the top edge will hit the ceiling. There's not enough clearance. Why didn't you put it together standing up?"

Embarrassed at my mistake, I said, "I was standing up."

He had the good grace to laugh.

"Well, hell. I suppose this means we have to take it apart."

He put his arm around my shoulders. "What would you do without me?"

"Probably have much better self-esteem."

We got to work and had the top part of my newly assembled shelf unit in pieces in short order. We stood it up, put the top shelf back on, and slid it into place. Over the next ninety minutes, we unpacked and assembled the other two units.

Joe declared it to be break time, so we went outside for some fresh air. He found another paint bucket to use as a chair, and we settled down, enjoying the late afternoon sun. I brought the cooler outside, and we each opened a can of soda and bags of tortilla chips.

"The perfect snack," Joe said with satisfaction.

"Totally agree." Surveying the property, I asked, "Where do you think the cameras will go?"

He scanned the trees and utility poles. "I have no idea, which is why we hired someone to do it. Hey, I almost forgot." He turned his improvised chair to face me. "How'd it go with Chip?"

"Oh, Grandma Natalie filled you in? Well, first he apologized for blocking the driveway with his motorcycle."

"Yeah, I heard you tore him a new one about it."

"What can I say? I had a bad day. He sounded sincere enough, so I accepted his apology, but then he wanted to know why I wasn't married and popping out kids."

"Seriously?"

"Yeah. What can I tell you? He's a troglodyte."

"Did you set him straight?" He laughed. "So to speak?"

I flashed him a quick smile. "I did, and he didn't seem to take it well. When I gave him a dose of lesbian reality, he tried telling me I'm unnatural."

"I bet you took it well."

"I'm tired of people who refuse to join the century. The man's in his sixties. There's no excuse for willful ignorance. Anyway, I tried to be patient—"

"Not your strong suit," Joe said with a grin.

"You know me too well. We'd had a good enough time before then. He likes Grandma Natalie, and I can tell she likes him, but she made him leave. If he's ballsy enough to come back, I'll be polite, but I reserve the right to tear his kneecaps off if he ever says anything else stupid to me."

"Or if he hurts Grandma Natalie."

"That's a death sentence offense." But Joe and I both laughed. Since neither of us believed in the death penalty, we couldn't keep straight faces. Even though we laughed at our joke, we knew we'd move heaven and earth to protect our grandmother, and we knew she'd do the same for us.

We'd returned to our snacks when a familiar form approached.

"Someone really didn't appreciate your new paint job," she said. It was the blonde woman I'd spoken with before. "It was beautiful when it was finished."

Joe and I stood to greet her. "You must live close by, I remember you from before. I'm Annie and this is my brother, Joe."

She smiled uncertainly and shook Joe's hand when he held it out to her.

"Annie here keeps trying to tell me I'm adopted," Joe said, "but I don't believe her. The family resemblance is too strong. What do you think?"

The blonde woman blushed, obviously caught off guard.

In many ways, Joe enjoyed disturbing the preconceived notions of people he met. I was used to his jokes about being a Black man in a white and Hispanic family, but most people seemed too self-conscious to comment. The only part he left out of his usual comedy routine was showing her his prosthetic leg.

Joe's easy manner seemed to give the woman a moment to regain her equilibrium. "What happened here?" She pointed to the building.

"Jackson Pollock wannabe." Joe was on a roll. "But," he said more seriously, "someone with money to spend on paint and too much time on their hands would be my guess. We're going to wait until we're closer to opening to get it corrected."

"When will that be?"

"Soon, we hope," I said. "We're down to the last details here, and we're getting anxious to get started."

"I'd imagine so," she said. "With fall coming, you'd probably like to be ready for holiday shopping."

"That's the plan."

Chapter Ten

Glaring with disgust at the sight before me, I turned and stomped back into the house, almost slamming the door behind me. Grandma Natalie rushed in from the kitchen.

"What's wrong? Are you okay? I thought you were on your way to work."

"I would be, if I didn't have two flat tires."

"What? Two? How is that even possible?"

"Damned if I know." I dropped onto a chair at the kitchen table. "I can change one, but who has two spares?" After taking my phone out of my pocket, I went to my list of contacts. "I have to get Triple A out here, and I need to call Rachel. I'm supposed to open the clinic this morning. Her Monday schedule is always jam-packed."

A few minutes later, I'd made both calls, and my grandmother tried to calm me with a mug of fresh hot coffee and toast with peanut butter on it. She always knew what to do, so I was in a much better mood when she joined me at the table.

"Do you need a ride to work?" She had a mischievous glint in her eye.

"Have you been tested for Alzheimer's lately?" I knew where this was going.

"What? Of course not. Why?"

"Because you've obviously forgotten who you're talking to."

She laughed. She knew very well there wasn't enough money on the planet to get me onto the back of her Harley. I knew better than most what a skilled rider she was, but I was never comfortable on a motorcycle. Just me being me.

"I had to try."

"Why don't you buy a car?" We'd had this conversation several times over the years, but since I'd definitely inherited my stubbornness from her, I couldn't resist trying again.

"Too many wheels. How are you getting to work?"

"Rachel will pick me up on her way to the clinic. I'd ride my bike, but it's been a while since I've ridden that far."

"And you'd be a bit aromatic when you arrived. The clients might not be too pleased."

"Oh, I don't know. Dogs and cats like stinky stuff." I finished my toast and refilled both our coffee cups. "If Rachel gets here before the tow truck, will you talk with the driver? If they'll take my car to the tire place,

I'll make arrangements to have them fixed." I put my car key on the table.

"I can't figure out how you could get two flats."

"Unless I drove over some leftover nails at the shop or something, neither can I." A horn beeped outside. "Rachel's here." I stood up and gave my grandmother a kiss on the cheek. "You behave yourself today, hear me?"

Outside, Rachel was standing next to my disabled car, surveying the damage. She had her fists on her hips, shaking her head in disbelief.

"I'll give you this much," she said. "When you set out to do something, you tend to overachieve."

"I know. It's weird, right? Two flat tires at the same time."

"And on the same side."

We got into her car and headed to the clinic. Since Rachel's appointment calendar was full, the morning flew by. Not long after lunch, I answered the phone, expecting to hear another client needing an appointment or a medication refill. What I heard instead was, "Is this Annie?"

"Yes. What can I do for you?"

"This is Ryan at Leo's Tires. We have your Subaru here."

"What did I do, run over a couple of nails?"

"Not even close. Someone cut your tires right through the sidewalls. There were no nails."

"Cut? What do you mean cut?" I couldn't quite wrap my head around his words.

"Plain and simple, someone slashed your tires. Unfortunately, we can't fix them, so you need to buy new tires."

I pushed my chair away from the desk and ran my free hand through my hair. "Well, hell and damnation."

"Yeah, your grandmother thought you'd say something like that. She asked me to tell you what we found. She said you shouldn't worry. She gave us a credit card number, so we're replacing your tires."

"Oh, that's my grandmother for you. She's incorrigible." So I hadn't run over nails at the shop. Someone had vandalized my tires. I hoped the security cameras had recorded the miscreant in action.

"Your car will be ready by four, and we're open until seven. And let your grandmother know if she ever wants to adopt, we're available. She seems like an amazing lady."

I laughed out loud. "I'll be sure to tell her. And thanks for taking care of my car. I'll come by after work to get it."

I hung up the phone and found Rachel looking at me with a puzzled expression. "What was so funny?"

I told her what the tire shop had found and about Grandma Natalie's largesse.

"I'll pay her back, of course, but this is typical of her. She bought the car for me, you know."

My next thought must have shown on my face, because Rachel said, "What?"

"I'm wondering whether my favorite little stalker slashed my tires."

Her eyes widened. "Do you think she's capable of it?"

"She definitely lives in her own universe, so who knows what she might do?" I grabbed my phone. When my grandmother answered my call, I thanked her for the tires, and then asked, "Will you check with the security company? I'd like to know if the cameras recorded whoever did this." After we ended our call, I said to Rachel, "I wanted to go to the shop tonight. Damn, it's always something."

"I have an idea. When we're done here, let's go get your car, and you can show me your fancy new bike shop. I haven't seen it yet. And then we can treat ourselves to dinner. What do you think?"

"I think that's the best plan I've heard all day. Where do you want to eat?"

We both paused and at the same moment said, "Not sushi," and laughed.

After we closed the clinic and collected my car, we caravanned to the shop, with me leading the way and Rachel behind. My new tires looked great, but I promised myself to tease Grandma Natalie mercilessly about making the decision for me. Of course I was grateful, but I'd string her along for a few minutes before letting her know I'd repay her.

We got out of our cars, and I unlocked the gate. With a grand gesture, I swept my arm in an arc. "Behold, Velasquez Cycles. Paint by unknown local artist."

Rachel turned toward the multicolored building. I expected her to comment about the pain, but she looked shocked.

"Uh, Annie, the paint is not the only problem."

Only then did I look at the building myself.

"No." I ran toward it, saying, "No, no," repeatedly. I whirled around to meet Rachel's eyes. "No, this can't be happening." Tears ran down my face as I stood with my friend and stared at my still unfinished bicycle shop.

The plate glass windows we'd installed on either side of the door were shattered. Some of the glass had fallen away, leaving large openings, but any remaining glass was marred with long cracks and smaller holes. A hundred square feet of glass in each window, destroyed.

I broke from my trance and ran around the building. All of the windows were damaged, though the worst of it was in the front. Even the glass in the front door was broken out.

I ran back to my car and grabbed my phone. "Joe, I'm at the shop. Get your ass down here. Now." I ended the call.

Stepping carefully around the glass littering the ground, I peered through the shattered windows.

"Any damage inside?"

"No, not that I can see from here. The glass door is broken, too, but I want to wait for Joe."

While we waited for my brother, I paced back and forth in the parking lot, stopping only briefly to survey the damage in disbelief. Rachel tried to placate me, but I wasn't having it. After several minutes, I stopped moving and met my friend in front of the broken door.

"I'm glad we didn't eat first. My stomach is in knots. First the tires and now this."

"Annie?" Rachel's voice was tentative. "Does Mandy know where the shop is?"

I stared at her. "I don't know. She followed me home, so I suppose it's possible." I spoke slowly, thinking it through. "We had thefts here, and now vandalism three different times. Maybe she's more off her rocker than we've been giving her credit for."

After a short while, Joe drove into the lot and emerged from his car. He was still dressed in the business casual he wore to his accounting job. When he saw the recent damage, he let loose a string of epithets that would have made George Carlin proud, ending with "Annie, what the everlasting fuck?"

"I know." I raised my arms and let them drop in a gesture of helplessness. "Is this how it's going to be here? Dad never had this problem." Tears flowed down my face again, and I wiped them away with the back of my hand. "Can we even open? Has all of our hard work been for nothing?"

He stared at the damaged windows, much the same as Rachel and I had. Then he walked all the way around the building, swearing with each new discovery. When he rejoined us, he was still angry but calmer than before. "We obviously need to file another police report. I'll take some pictures." He took his phone from his suit coat pocket and poked a few buttons. His first call was to the police, and then he made a second call.

"Brad, we've had more vandalism at the shop." A pause. "No, not paint. Windows. All of the windows are damaged. Looks like they'll all need to be replaced." Another pause. "Come and see for yourself. We'll wait. I'll call the security company to see if the cameras caught anything. Damn it, I'm sick of this shit."

He ended the call and turned to Rachel and me. "Have you gone inside?"

"We looked through the windows, but I didn't want to go inside until you got here."

He pulled a small ring of keys from his pocket. "Let's check it out." His voice sounded resigned, as if he expected more bad news.

Inside, we found glass on the floor in the main public space, which I expected from the damage to the front windows. Broken glass was scattered in other areas as well, but not as much. Not all of the windows had been broken completely, though those without missing glass were cracked.

"Someone worked very hard at this," I muttered.

Joe emerged from the back room. "I don't see any other damage. If they used a gun, it must not have been a very powerful one. I don't know enough about guns to know what kind of damage they'd do to plate glass. Maybe rocks?"

"I don't see any on the floor," Rachel said. "But wouldn't someone need a pretty strong arm to break those windows with rocks? Good quality plate glass is thick."

"Damned if I know." He locked eyes with me. "We're not even open, and the insurance company will jack our rates through the roof."

By the time we emerged from the building, Brad had arrived. His reaction mirrored ours. He took the same walk around the building we had. "This is so wrong. You guys decided to rebuild, which was a great decision and a wonderful way to honor your dad, and now this. I don't understand it." He turned back to us. "To hell with it. We'll fix all of it, and you'll have the best damn bike shop in the city. Whoever's doing this will not win."

After Brad left, we made ourselves comfortable in my car to wait for the police.

"Maybe an officer will get here faster if there's a chance a gun was involved," Joe said. "Shooting a gun within the city limits is illegal."

"I'm wondering if it was Mandy." I told him about my slashed tires. "We know she followed me home. She could have also followed me here."

"This is some pretty determined vandalism for a twenty-something food server."

"I know, but she's been very insistent about me finding her friend, even after I've told her many times I can't. Logic and reasoning aren't her strong suit."

"Let's talk with the police about her when they get here. If she's stalking you, which she certainly is, maybe a restraining order would help. Here's hoping the video from the security company shows who did this."

"And who cut my tires."

A Portland Police Bureau car rolled into the lot, and two officers emerged. The driver was Officer Carlos Martinez, who had responded to our first instance of vandalism. The second officer was unfamiliar to us. He was tall and slender with red hair and a baby face. He introduced himself as Cameron Stewart.

Martinez said, "You guys are too popular with all the wrong people."

"It's a ploy to get you back here so you'll buy a bike from us," Joe said. They shook hands, and Martinez slapped Joe on the back as he would a friend. "We don't know what they used to do this damage, but there are some small holes. Could gunshots have done this?"

The officers inspected all of the broken windows, and Joe took them inside as well, where Officer Stewart took pictures.

"We'll write up a report," Stewart said. "That way, you'll have an ongoing record with the bureau."

Martinez said, "Yes, we're happy to help, but same as before, it's unlikely we'll ever know who the vandals are. I'll send these pictures to the experts for their opinion on whether a firearm was used." He looked at the building, his expression a mixture of sadness and consternation. "How much longer until you open? You definitely need more activity around here, or this might not stop. An unoccupied building is an easy target, even with the fence and cameras."

"We've been planning to open soon, but stuff like this keeps happening," I said. "Here's hoping the cameras caught something useful."

"I agree," Martinez said.

"Besides," Stewart said with a genial smile, "I need a new bike."

We promised we'd find one for him when the shop opened, after which we all shook hands and with an "*adios*" from Martinez, the officers drove away.

Joe locked the shop door and, realizing the absurdity of what he'd done, laughed without a trace of humor. "Seems useless, doesn't it, to lock the door when all someone would need to do is crawl through a window? I am glad we don't have any bikes or anything portable in there."

As we walked to our cars, I had a thought. "Hey Joe, Rachel and I are going to find the cheesiest pizza we can. Want to join us?"

Twenty minutes later, we were shown to a table in a small restaurant that was new to Rachel and me, but Joe claimed they made the best pizza he'd ever had. The enticing aroma of pizza sauce and fresh crust made my mouth water. We ordered our pie and drinks and settled in to wait.

I said, "I didn't realize how hungry I was until we came in here."

"Me too," Rachel said. "What are you doing?"

My brother had stuffed about a dozen paper napkins into his collar, unfolding them so they hung down his chest. He looked up, surprised. "What?"

"You're ridiculous," I said.

"Off my case." He tried to appear offended. "This is a new shirt. The pizza here is fifty percent sauce. You'll see."

Our server refilled our water glasses and, spying my brother's antics, shook her head with amusement and brought him a stack of napkins. "You've eaten here before."

Once he'd finished embellishing his chest with a tree's worth of paper, he looked back and forth between Rachel and me. "I've been thinking a bit since the police left. They're right. We need more activity around the shop. Most of the work is done, but it's still vacant, which makes it an easy target." He paused and a smile grew across his face. "But I have the perfect solution. Two, in fact."

"Oh, do tell." He was entirely too pleased with himself, which usually meant the evil schemer side of his brain was fully engaged.

"First plan, we could hire security to supplement the cameras. If we have someone on the premises when Brad's crew or we aren't there, maybe the vandals will leave us alone. If not, we'll have witnesses who can help us figure out who's doing this."

"It'll be terribly expensive."

"Hence, my second plan. I'll give my notice at work tomorrow. I've wanted to do it ever since we decided to rebuild. We'll pay for security for two weeks, and then I'll move into the shop."

"Let me make sure I understand. Your plan is to hire security people and then pay for it by quitting your job." I squinted at him. "Do I have that right?"

He was almost bouncing in his seat. "No more stuffy bosses. No more endless meetings. I can get inventory delivered and put in place, and keep the lights on, car in the lot, and whatnot. Make the place look busy."

"And be really stinky." I was unable to resist pointing out another potential flaw in his plan. "There's no shower in the shop. Or laundry."

"Isn't that what Grandma Natalie's house is for?"

When I arrived home after dinner, Grandma Natalie was standing in the middle of the driveway, right where I'd normally park. I rolled the window down to ask what she was doing when she pointed toward the garage door.

"Park in there," she called.

I was confused. The last time I'd been in the garage, it was jam packed with boxes of my dad's documents from the shop, unused motorcycle gear, and three or four bicycles. There'd never been room for a car.

I pulled up to the garage door. She walked alongside my car and opened the door.

"Wow." I was amazed. "You've been working hard."

"From now on, you park inside."

"You'll get no argument from me." I did as she told me and eased my car into the garage. I collected my doggie bag from the front seat, and we went into the kitchen, where I put my pizza leftovers into the fridge.

"How did you get all of this done so fast?"

"I called in a few favors. Turns out we had a lot of junk taking up space for no good reason. They hauled it away, which I should have had done long ago. I put your dad's stuff in the spare room in case you still need it. And they put up bike racks, so now all the bicycles have their own places. It's amazing how much space we freed up once we organized it."

I gave her a tight hug. "You always surprise me, and I love you for it. But what prompted you to do this?"

"The guy at the tire store told me what happened. I checked with the security company, and the camera recorded someone cutting your tires."

"Could you tell who it was?"

"No, but it looked like a woman. Made me wonder if it's the same one who was here before, but I couldn't tell. I decided it's best if your car is safe and sound in the garage."

I hugged her again and followed it with a resounding smooch on her cheek.

"Thank you for paying for my new tires." I abandoned my earlier plan to tease her about it. "I'll pay you back."

"No need. Merry Christmas."

"In August?"

"Now I don't have to shop for you."

"Cheater."

"Whatever works. Dinner will be ready in about half an hour. Let's go relax in the other room."

We made ourselves comfortable in the living room, Grandma Natalie in her recliner and me on the couch. I'd barely sat down when Shadow jumped into my lap and started purring.

"Joe told me about the windows," she said. "He called me when he was on his way to the pizza place."

"Did he tell you what he decided to do?"

"Yes. He's wanted to quit his job for a long time, and I'm happy for him. He asked me to research storage places for his furniture, but he can store smaller stuff here until he gets another apartment. I hope this stops the vandalism, but I mostly hope he'll be safe there."

"The cameras are in place, and the rest of the security system will be up and running pretty soon, so he'll be okay. What I don't understand is why we're having so much trouble. Dad never had stuff like this happen, did he?"

"Not that I knew of. But he never had a crazy stalker like you do." She gave me a playful wink. "Hey, on another topic, have you heard anything from the police about Nicky?"

"No. It's all surreal, isn't it? If she hadn't called, I'd think I imagined all of it, but I know I didn't. How do you find someone who truly does not want to be found?"

"I hope you know you owe me big." Brad, Joe, and I watched as the glass company workers finished replacing the vandalized bike shop windows. "I think I've called in every favor I had to get this done. Only a week to get these huge windows is nothing short of a miracle." Brad gave us his version of a stink eye. "You guys are a shit ton of work." And then he laughed.

"Don't you even worry about it," Joe said. "Free bikes and all the gear for life."

"And," I said, "free espresso or whatever you want from the snack bar."

Brad nodded with satisfaction. "In that case, it's worth it."

He was mostly joking, but we were serious. He'd done miraculous work for us for very little in return. The window replacement was almost finished. With the electrical system completed, the security company had tied the cameras to their power source and had also installed motion-activated exterior lighting. All of it was linked to a local security company, as was the security system at Grandma Natalie's house.

"A mouse won't be able to walk through the parking lot without us knowing about it," the lead security technician had boasted. While I couldn't take his comment literally, I certainly appreciated the sentiment behind it.

After the work was done, Joe started moving a few of his possessions into the bike shop. He'd sublet his apartment to a friend and rented a storage unit for most of his furniture.

"I don't need much here," he said, as we brought boxes in from our cars. "My bikes, of course. A place to sleep, some music, maybe my TV. You know, the essentials."

We made him a makeshift bedroom in the storage area and used a shelf for his clothes. The main area of the shop held his bicycles and an impressive array of related gear, such as his helmet and cycling shoes. He also had a toolbox filled to the brim with the instruments of his trade:

spanners, Allen wrenches, and a host of mysterious objects I couldn't identify.

"You need to learn to use those tools, Annie. I want to have bike maintenance classes here, so you need to know this stuff."

"Yeah, right. We'll see about that." He knew very well I was the least mechanically inclined person he'd ever met. Still, he kept trying.

By the time we were finished, he'd hung his flat-screen television on the wall facing the front door. He'd also hooked up an old boombox he found somewhere. We added four small tables and three lamps I bought for a song at a local secondhand store. I laid down an old area rug Grandma Natalie had stored in the garage, and Joe added two folding yard chairs. If it hadn't been for the bike racks and shelving, the place could have passed for a sparsely furnished home with extra-large windows.

"All you need now is that ugly recliner you love entirely too much. Why didn't you bring it?"

"I won't be here very long. Between the light from the TV and the music, it should be obvious someone is here. And I'll park my car out front. Move it around now and then. The only reason I need it is to get food and to visit Grandma Natalie."

"To get your laundry done, you mean?" I had to tease him, even while recognizing he was sacrificing his own comfort for all of us.

He surveyed his temporary home with satisfaction. "Let's hope this works."

Chapter Eleven

That evening, Grandma Natalie, Joe, and I had finished a late dinner and were sitting at the kitchen table, trying to find the energy to clean up the kitchen. So far, no luck.

"How was your first night at the shop?"

"I bet he didn't get any sleep at all, Grandma," I said. "All alone in the spooky shop."

"You're hilarious," Joe said. "It was amazingly quiet, especially compared to my apartment. That place must have the world's thinnest walls. You'd be amazed at the stuff I've heard."

As we gave in to the inevitability of hauling our overfed selves out of our chairs to load the dishwasher, Joe's phone rang. A few seconds later, mine did as well. Joe went into the living room to answer his call, and I stayed in the kitchen. I didn't recognize the number.

"Hello?"

"Is this Annie Velasquez?"

"Yes. Who's this?"

"Tyler, from Stumptown Security. There's been some kind of disturbance at your commercial property. The cameras showed someone there, but in the dark, we couldn't see any details. Would you like us to call the Portland police?"

I turned around and found Joe looking at me with a concerned expression. I stage-whispered "security company" and he pointed to his phone.

I went back to my call. "Yes, please. We'll go down there right now. Thanks for letting us know."

We arrived before the police did, so we unlocked the gate and drove into the lot. I backed into a spot where we could see the shop from the safety of my car.

"I don't see anything. Do you?"

"No, but the lights aren't working."

"Maybe the motion-activated ones will come on if we get closer." I opened the car door and stepped out, and Joe did the same on his side.

I walked cautiously toward the shop door, trying to remember where the parking blocks were. Late August overcast made the evening darker than I expected. I stopped about six feet from the door, wondering why the floodlights weren't shining. I stepped forward another foot or two, getting my door key ready, when I tripped.

My knees hit first, landing on something solid, yet yielding.

My outstretched hands followed, ending up on the walkway near the door. When I pushed myself up, I realized my hands were damp and sticky.

"What the hell—" Without thinking, I wiped them on my pant legs.

Joe joined me a moment later. "Are you okay?"

"Yes, but there's something here. I can't tell what it is. I can't imagine Brad's guys would have left anything outside the door like this."

Joe took his phone out and switched on the flashlight function. When he turned the beam on the ground in front of my feet, the world swam around me. Joe grabbed my arm as I staggered.

The body of a young woman lay face down on the walkway, one arm outstretched and the other beneath her. The sticky dampness I'd felt was her blood, which had pooled around her head.

I turned to Joe, wide-eyed, and held up my blood-covered hands for him to see.

He quickly called 911 to report what we'd found and request police assistance, and then he made a second call.

"Patrick? Annie and I are at the shop. You need to get down here now."

I heard Patrick's voice. "Why?"

"You won't believe this, but Annie just tripped over a dead body."

In what felt like an eternity, but was probably less than ten minutes, a Portland police car and an ambulance with lights flashing pulled into the parking lot, followed by an unmarked car. Beth O'Brien drove the unmarked car with Ted Winston in the passenger's seat.

I stood where I was while Joe went out to meet them.

"I hope you have flashlights," he called out. "The power is out."

One of the uniformed officers said, "On it," and opened the trunk of his cruiser. Within minutes, the officers and detectives stood around the body I'd found, shining powerful flashlights. They also activated the spotlights on their cars. More headlights announced Patrick's arrival.

The ambulance crew immediately went to work. I walked away a short distance, refusing to look at the body any longer. The paramedics quickly confirmed what seemed obvious. She was dead.

"Has anyone touched her?" The paramedic scanned our faces.

I held up my hands. "I tripped over her in the dark. Otherwise, we haven't touched her or anything around her."

He came over to me. "Are you hurt?"

"I might have scraped my hands when I fell, but otherwise, I'm fine." In the glare of the flashlights, I finally looked down at myself. My hands and forearms had blood on them. My clothes were also stained, apparently at least partly from when I fell, but also when I'd reflexively wiped my hands on my pant legs.

"Annie, are you okay?" Beth had joined us while I spoke with the paramedic. Patrick must have called her.

"No, I'm not okay." I started to shake, and my voice quavered. "I might never be okay again." I looked up at her. "Why do people keep dying here?" I sensed I was being irrational, but there I was, standing in the dark, covered with someone's blood, surrounded by police officers, and somehow all I could think about was the last person who died here shouldn't have died at all, and now someone else was dead. Tears slipped down my face.

"Here," the paramedic said. "Come and sit down." He led me to the ambulance and made me a place to rest. When he saw me shaking harder, he wrapped me in a blanket and handed me a small packet of tissues. "I'm Adam. Yell if you need anything, okay?" I nodded weakly, and he went back to work.

Joe came to check on me. My normally unflappable brother, who had been through combat and lost a leg in an explosion, seemed almost as shaken as I was.

"They'll take pictures of everything and then take her away. Apparently, there are people who clean up crime scenes, so after they're done here, they'll call someone to take care of it for us." He paused for a moment. "Well, shit."

"What?" I was alarmed by what appeared to be an unpleasant realization.

"This is a crime scene. The whole place will be off limits until the police investigation is done."

The words had no sooner left his mouth when I saw the uniformed officers roping off the front of the shop with yellow plastic tape. I'd watched enough police shows to know it meant we couldn't do any work there until the police decided they'd done all they needed to do for the investigation.

"We're never going to open." As I'd always done, I defaulted to the worst-case scenario.

Joe put his arm across my shoulders and hugged me. "Sure, we will. Don't know when or how, but we will."

"Or not." I let out a deep sigh.

"Or not."

We watched while the police officers photographed the body and surrounding area. When they were satisfied, the paramedics rolled the body over and officers took photos of her face up. The paramedics zipped her into a body bag and lifted her onto a gurney, which they wheeled in our direction. They paused near us.

"Are you willing to see if you know her?" Adam looked at me with a doubtful expression.

I took a step away from the gurney. "I'm willing to help, but can I see photos instead?" I'd seen two too many dead people in my life, and now here was a third.

"Totally understandable." He pushed the gurney into the ambulance and closed the doors behind it.

The ambulance left, followed by the marked police cruiser. Beth and Patrick joined Joe and me in the parking lot.

"What now?" I asked.

"They'll take her to the medical examiner for an autopsy," Beth said. "They'll assign the case to a detective, but probably not me. I'm sure whoever it is will want you to go to the precinct to make a statement, probably within a day or two. Maybe even tomorrow."

"Why not you? We already know each other."

"That's why. They'll want someone who can be completely objective."

"You can do it."

"You know it and I know it, but it's best to avoid any appearance of a conflict of interest. If it turns out somehow your case and this one are related, then it would be different." She touched my arm briefly. "Don't worry. I'll keep an eye on it as much as I can. You'll be okay."

One of the officers who had taken photos of the body approached us. "Are you willing to look at a couple of pictures for us?"

"Yes."

I tried to steel myself for what I might see, but when he turned the camera screen toward me, the world swayed. I gasped, "Mandy," and everything went black.

My next memory, though not a clear one, was of Joe carrying me to Patrick's car.

"Put her in the back."

Joe laid me down on the seat, and when I struggled to sit up, he pushed me down. "Just lie here."

"I'm fine. Let me up."

I tried to get up again, but he got into the back with me and propped my head and shoulders up on his lap.

"Drive."

As Patrick got the car moving, I shook my head to clear the fuzziness. "Where are we going?"

"Emergency room," Patrick said. "You need to get checked out."

Yet again, I tried to sit up, but I was struck by a wave of dizziness, so I lay back on Joe's lap. "I'm fine. Take me home. It's freezing in here." I pulled the blanket the paramedic gave me more closely around me.

"No, you're not fine," Joe said. "I'm no expert, but I think you're in shock."

He had his arm across my upper chest keeping me from moving, but by then I realized I shouldn't try to sit up. During the short drive, the cloudiness in my brain began to fade.

"Oh my god. Mandy." Tears ran down my face again. "Who would do such a horrible thing to her?"

"The cops are already working on it," Patrick said. "When we get you settled, I'll call Beth and see if she has any new information."

I closed my eyes and wiped my tears with the blanket.

The next I knew, my brother lifted me into a wheelchair. The bright lights of the emergency department made me squint.

Within moments, I was wheeled into an alcove, and what felt like a legion of nurses descended on me. They checked my pulse and listened to my heart. They checked my pupils with more blindingly bright lights. They asked me who I was and did I know who the president was.

I tried telling the nurse who questioned me I wasn't injured, but she said, "We're required to make sure." I knew I was outnumbered when the nurses started cutting my clothes away despite my protests. Within minutes, they dressed me in a hospital gown—if dressed was even the right word—and covered me in layers of blissfully warm blankets.

Unfortunately, I wasn't allowed to rest. A young man in a white lab coat pulled my arm out from under my blanket cocoon and drew some blood. He left as silently as he'd arrived, but a friendly woman took his place and told me it was picture time.

"Wait, what do you mean? I'm not hurt."

"Honey, the doc wants x-rays, and he's the boss."

A ride through the hallways later, she positioned me expertly under the machine and went to work. Fifteen minutes later, I was back in the emergency department. I thought I'd have a few minutes of quiet, but a nurse came in pushing a pole with a bag of clear liquid hanging from it.

"I don't need an IV."

"Doctor's orders." Within half a minute, she'd inserted the IV catheter, which I barely felt, and got the fluid running.

Mercifully, I was finally alone and able to relax. Or at least I tried to relax. Images of Mandy's pale face framed by blood would not leave me. Maybe they never would. I lay in the bed, trying to see through the spaces between the curtains for some kind of distraction.

Suddenly, the curtain was swept aside, and a tall man in a white coat and a stethoscope in his pocket strode to my bedside. He held a clipboard in one hand.

"Annie Velasquez?" He checked the name band on my wrist. "I'm Doctor Higgins, one of the docs here in the emergency room. How are you doing?"

"Please tell me your first name is Henry," I said.

"Sorry, no. My mother loved plays and old movies, but even she wouldn't take it that far. She settled for Harold, which I suppose is close enough," he replied with a smile. "Are you feeling any better?"

"Yes, much. Though I don't know what all the fuss was about. I tried to tell everyone I'm not injured, but they didn't seem to believe me."

"You did come in covered in blood, my dear."

"But it wasn't mine."

"We still had to check. And regardless, you were definitely in shock, so it's good you came in. Care to tell me what happened?"

No point in trying to sugarcoat it. "I tripped over a dead woman's body in the dark. The blood was hers. And she turned out to be someone I know…I mean, knew. When I realized who she was, I guess I passed out."

"I'm an emergency room doctor, and I'm not sure I'd have reacted any differently than you did in those circumstances."

"You'd think I'd be more used to it by now. She's not the first dead person I've found." When he raised an inquiring eyebrow, I continued. "She's the third. The first was my father, and the second was my employer."

He took my hand in between both of his and gazed at me closely. "No wonder you had such a strong reaction. If you haven't already, you might want to consider counseling. You could very well have PTSD or something like it. Few people could have those experiences without some kind of aftereffect."

"Thanks, doc." I knew he was right. "When can I go home?"

"I want to monitor you for a while. In the meantime, there's an entire entourage of people waiting to see you. I'll send them in if they promise to let you rest."

A few moments after he left, Joe and Patrick came to my little alcove, followed by Grandma Natalie, Rachel, and Sally. They gathered around my bed, and they all started talking at once.

"Are you okay?"

"Why do you have an IV?"

"When can you go home?"

I tried to shush them without effect, but after only thirty seconds of them piling one question after another, Doctor Higgins flung the curtain aside and glared at them. He seemed taller than when he'd visited with me and was definitely more fierce.

"Didn't I tell you to let her rest?" He fixed each transgressor with a stern stare, and each of them had the good grace to look abashed. Then he saw Grandma Natalie. "Wait, I recognize you. Have we met?"

"I don't think so," she said. "I was a patient here several months ago, but you don't look familiar."

"That's it! Motorcycle Grandma. Am I right?"

"Yes, but how could you remember me?"

He peered at her more closely. "You look great. I was working when they brought you in. You were unconscious, but I remember thinking you must be an amazing woman to ride such a powerful machine." He reached his hand out, and she shook it. "I'm glad you're doing well." He scanned the group again. "Now keep it down." He smiled broadly at my grandmother and left.

"Hey, guys," I said, "I'm doing fine. I was apparently in shock, but I'm okay now. Any news about the shop?"

"No," Patrick said, "but I wouldn't expect any. It's only been a couple of hours."

"I asked them to close and lock the gate before they left. I think they were happy to have the fence there," Joe said. "Still no idea why none of the lights were working, but we'll figure it out. What matters now is you're okay. When they release you, we'll take you home."

"What about my car?"

"Patrick and I will go back tonight and get it. The police tape is only at the front of the shop, so it's not blocked in."

Grandma Natalie had pulled up a chair next to my bed and was holding my hand. "Are you really okay?"

Pensively, I waited, not sure how to word what I wanted to say. "Mandy wasn't my favorite person. In fact, I'd started to wonder about her mental health, what with the way she was following me and not hearing me when I told her I couldn't find her friend. But she didn't deserve to die."

My grandmother squeezed my hand. "Of course she didn't. I hope the police can figure out who did this."

I was feeling tired again. "Will one of you see if you can find a nurse or the doctor? I'd really like to go home."

Two o'clock Wednesday afternoon found Patrick and me once again waiting in familiar surroundings: the Portland Police Bureau Homicide Division. Two nights previously, before I'd been whisked away to the hospital, one of the police officers had told me I'd be expected to give a statement about finding Mandy's body. Patrick had scheduled the time for us to take care of it. He'd also mentioned that Beth wanted to talk with us about something else, so my interest was piqued. Did I dare hope it was good news for a change?

"This is surreal," I whispered to Patrick. "They might as well put our names on these chairs."

"Hush," he said quietly and took my hand. Suddenly concerned, he ran his fingers over the back of my hand. "Why is your skin so rough?"

I hesitated, but I also knew he wouldn't let it go.

"I've washed my hands a few times, that's all." What I didn't say was I'd spent hours in the bathroom scrubbing my hands with hot water and soap. Grandma Natalie threatened to put gloves on me and lock me out of the bathroom if I didn't stop. I was starting to understand Lady MacBeth. I was guilty of nothing, but I kept seeing and feeling Mandy's blood on my hands and clothes.

After a few minutes, Beth emerged from the depths of the department. Unlike our previous visits, we didn't go to her office. This time, we followed her into a nearby conference room. She waved us to one side of the long table, and we sat side by side.

She put a stack of folders and a couple of pens on the table across from us and settled into the leather chair.

"The main reason for this meeting," she said, "is for you to meet the detective who's been assigned to the new case. Before he joins us, I want to give you an update."

"Is this about Nicky?" Patrick asked.

"Yes, but the mystery deepens."

"Oh?"

She picked up her pen and tapped it on the tablet, thinking for a moment. "As I mentioned to you at your home, Annie, I found the same information online you did about Nicky's arrests. But I didn't find anything in the files about them."

"How can that be?" Patrick asked.

"An excellent question. I searched for separate files, wondering if the information had been archived apart from the murder case." She flashed me a smile. "Alleged murder case. Anyway, I got nowhere with it. So I called my friend in Drugs and Vice, and she went through their files and also came up empty."

"So the online record is wrong?" I asked. "She doesn't have an arrest record?"

"I guess it's possible, but I don't think so. The information I have access to is more detailed than what you saw on the commercial site, such as case numbers and the like that wouldn't exist without there being an actual case. Something isn't quite right here, and I don't know what it is. Anyway," she dropped her pen and sat back in her chair. "I wanted to let you know I am looking into it. I really don't like loose ends, and this is fraying everywhere."

"I appreciate the update. Not much has made sense to me since the day I saw Nicky, so I appreciate your help."

"Okay, let's get on with the program." She picked up her phone and pressed a few buttons. After a few seconds, the text chime rang, and she checked her phone. "They'll be here in a minute."

Something in her voice made me nervous. Maybe I was about to be arrested after all.

After about three minutes that felt like thirty, Beth's partner, Ted Winston, entered the room, along with another man I didn't recognize. He appeared to be in his forties. His impassive expression and buzzcut hair told me he was also a detective, probably one who had seen it all and had little patience for any of it. My nervousness ratcheted up to fifteen on a scale of ten. The detectives took chairs at the table opposite us and produced notepads and pens. The new man also had a laptop computer and a manila folder holding a sheaf of papers.

"Patrick, Annie," Beth said, "you know my partner, Ted Winston. This is Detective Charles Grant. He's been with the Portland bureau for many years, longer than I have." She turned her attention to Detective Grant. "Chuck, I've known Annie Velasquez for almost a year now. In the interest of full disclosure, she has been a person of interest in a murder related to an arson fire at that same location about a year and a half ago. Patrick Wyatt is her attorney."

We extended our greetings. Patrick stood long enough to pass a business card to the new detective and shake his hand.

She turned back to us. "Detective Grant is the lead on this new case. I'm here as a courtesy only, so unless he finds some link between our cases, I won't be involved."

"Detective Grant," Patrick said, "I assume we're here so Miss Velasquez can tell you what she knows about what happened at her property Monday night. What would you like to know?"

Grant tapped his pen on his notepad for a few seconds before opening the folder he'd brought with him. Without acknowledging Patrick's question, he focused on me.

"How well did you know Brittany Tucker?"

Surprised, I looked at Patrick first and then at Beth. I turned back to Grant. "I don't know anyone by that name."

"No?"

"No."

He consulted the papers from the folder. "Her cell phone and email records show she contacted you several times over the past few weeks."

"There's some kind of mistake. I haven't gotten any messages from anyone with that name. I can show you my phone, if you'd like." I held it up briefly, despite Patrick shaking his head slightly, as if trying to stop me.

Detective Grant frowned. "It's right here." He tapped the papers with his pen. "Brittany Amanda Tucker called or texted this number"—he recited my cell phone number—"multiple times, sometimes more than once a day. That's your number, isn't it?"

"Yes." I drew the word out as realization dawned. Amanda. "You're talking about the woman who was killed at the bike shop, right?"

"Yes." His voice carried a heavy undertone of, "of course, you idiot, who else?"

"I only knew her as Mandy. I never heard her full name."

"And how did you know her?"

"She was a server at a restaurant my friends and I went to."

Grant consulted his notes. "Doug's Café?"

"Yes."

"And you got to be friends?"

"No, not at all. In fact, she'd been stalking me recently, including at my home."

"Why would she do that?"

I tried not to show my frustration. Would it never end? I looked at Patrick and he gave me a curt nod. Beth opened a file folder and extracted a slip of newsprint.

"She wanted me to find a friend of hers who had been missing for some time. I told her multiple times I'm not a detective, but I agreed to search online to see if I could find any information. I also told her at the same time I made no promises about what I might find, but she kept pressing me to try, so I agreed. When I couldn't find out anything about her friend, she refused to believe me."

"And why would she ask you to find her friend? Have you had training in locating missing people? Or job experience?" He was becoming sarcastic.

"Chuck," Beth said quietly. "Take a look at this."

She handed the newspaper article to the detective. Fortunately, it was as short as it was misleading.

"You're kidding me, right?" He raised an eyebrow in my direction.

"Most of that article is exaggerated and simply wrong. Yes, I got carried away with myself and decided to find out who killed the doctor in Charbonneau. I was ultimately successful, but only because of sheer dumb luck. I suspected the wrong person, for one thing. And for another, the actual killer drugged me and tied me up in an old barn. I still don't know why he didn't kill me. After all, he'd killed his own father for money, and I was just the nosy housekeeper." I pointed to the article.

"That makes me sound like some kind of sleuth, but what I am is lucky to be alive."

Grant leaned back in his chair and stared at me. "And a server in a restaurant came to you because of this?" He lifted the article and then let it drop, dismissively. "You expect me to believe you?"

"I know it's weird, but it is what happened. It wasn't the first time someone approached me after reading that article. I can't tell you how I wish people would forget about it." I exchanged a glance with Patrick. "Look, two of my friends were there when Mandy asked for my help. They'll confirm what I told you."

"Sally and Rachel, right?" Beth asked.

"Yes."

She turned to Grant. "I have their contact information. I'll forward it to you when we're finished here."

Without acknowledging Beth's offer, Grant changed the subject. "You own the bike shop where the body was found?"

The body. No name. No humanity.

"Yes. I own it with my brother."

"Your brother?"

"Yes," Patrick said. "Joseph Velasquez. You should have his contact information already. He was at the scene as well."

"Why isn't he here?" He glowered at all of us in turn.

"I think he's scheduled for later today," Beth said. "After he gets off work."

"Okay." Grant turned back to me. "When was the last time you saw her, uh, Mandy?"

I thought for a moment. "About two weeks ago. She showed up at my home and wanted to know if I'd found anything about her missing friend. I'll be honest. I was angry at being followed, so I told her in no uncertain terms if she kept stalking me, I'd call the police and talk to her boss at the café. I hadn't seen her since then."

"Have you been to the restaurant recently?"

"No. She was so persistent about me finding her missing friend I decided not to go back. I probably told her half a dozen times I couldn't help her, but she didn't listen."

Detective Grant put his pen down. He glanced at the papers in front of him and at Beth and her partner before turning to Patrick and me.

"Then this is all good for you, right?"

I was floored. "What?"

Patrick leaped to his feet. "What are you saying?"

"Down, cowboy," Grant said with a lopsided grin. He was apparently happy to have gotten a reaction from Patrick. "I'm talking to your girl here."

I glared at him without speaking, but Beth intervened.

"Chuck, what are you doing?"

"I'm trying to solve a case, Beth. This little girl knows more than she's letting on, that's all."

I started to stand, but Patrick put a hand on my shoulder.

"Do you have any evidence to back up this ridiculous accusation?" Patrick had resumed his seat.

"No, not yet." He leaned back in his chair and put his knee against the edge of the table. "But I'm right, aren't I? You don't have to worry about her stalking you anymore. It's a win-win for you."

His callousness was appalling. Even Beth was surprised at his words. He wasn't finished.

"Why were you at the bike shop Monday night?"

I took a deep, calming breath before answering. "We got calls from the security company monitoring our cameras about seeing someone at the shop. We've had several instances of vandalism, so we put up a fence with signs and got cameras and floodlights to try to stop it. So far, it hasn't worked."

"When the security company called, you and your brother went down there?"

"Yes." I didn't say "of course," but I wanted to.

Grant opened another file and took out a sheaf of photographs. "These don't show any floodlights."

"I know. They weren't working."

"Why is that?"

Patrick spoke up. "We don't know, and we won't be able to find out until your investigation is done and we can have access to the site."

Grant put the photos down in a tidy stack. "What did you do when you arrived?"

"Joe and I decided to go into the shop to see if we could figure out why the security company called us. I was a couple of steps ahead of him, and in the dark, I didn't see Mandy lying on the walkway. I tripped over her body and fell."

"And then?"

"First, Joe helped me up. He turned on the flashlight function of his cell phone, and that's when we saw her. She was face down on the ground, surrounded by blood."

"And that's how you got her blood all over your hands, arms, and clothes."

"Yes." I tried not to remember the sight of Mandy's body or how her blood felt on my skin, but when Patrick reached over and touched my forearm, I realized I was rubbing my hands together.

"And then you called 911."

"Yes, Joe did."

"And then?"

"Uniformed officers and paramedics arrived within a few minutes. Patrick joined us shortly afterward." I glanced up at him. "At that point, I didn't know whose body I'd found, but one of the officers showed me a photograph, and I knew it was Mandy."

"And then?"

"And then I passed out, and my brother and Patrick took me to the hospital. I was there overnight, being treated for shock."

"I don't suppose it's easy to fake that," he muttered.

"Why don't you quit dancing around it, detective?" Patrick stood and leaned on the table with his hands spread. "Are you saying you think my client killed that young woman?"

Detective Grant leaned back in his chair and crossed his arms.

"Down, counselor," he said again, still sarcastic. "But let's face it. The alleged stalker is dead and from what you've told me, she could have been the vandal. Two for the price of one."

Patrick stood up straight and collected his briefcase from the table. "This meeting is over. If you want to talk with my client again, call me first. You have my card."

He took my arm, and we left the room.

Outside the conference room, I started to speak. "Patrick—" but he cut me off.

"Not here."

He led me through the building and outside.

"But—" I tried again.

"Wait until we're in the car." His voice was tense, as I knew it would be only if he was trying to tamp down rage.

Only then did the enormity of what had just happened explode in my mind. I started to cry, and my knees felt wobbly. "Not again. I can't do this. Patrick, please, I have to sit down."

"In the car." He helped me cross the parking lot to his car. He climbed into the driver's seat, started the car, and drove us out of the parking lot toward home. "Okay, now."

"Holy fucking shit." I was almost shouting, and tears ran down my face. "He thinks I killed her. That bastard as much as accused me of murder."

"Yeah, he did." He seemed to have calmed down somewhat, and I tried to follow his lead. I took a deep breath and let it out slowly.

"Does he think I'm some kind of criminal mastermind? That I'd kill a woman, and then pretend to trip over her. And for what? To cover up why I had her blood on me?"

"Honestly, I don't know what he's thinking, but if he contacts you, don't talk to him. Tell him to call me. The last thing we need to do is give him ideas."

"No worries there. He has plenty of his own."

At home, we went into the kitchen where Grandma Natalie and Joe were squabbling over which of them had hoarded more jigsaw puzzle pieces. She took one look at my face and Patrick's, and asked, "What happened?"

I sat at the table with a glass of iced tea while Patrick explained. By the time he finished, my grandmother and brother were as outraged as I'd been.

"I'm sorry she's dead," Grandma Natalie said, "but how could anyone think Annie had anything to do with it?"

"I know it's hard, but try to consider it objectively for a moment," Patrick said. "First, she's been a person of interest in another case for over a year and a half. Second"—he held up a hand to forestall her objection—"second, she knew the victim and didn't have a good relationship with her."

"Relationship?" I couldn't keep the sarcasm out of my voice. "Is that what stalking is? A relationship? I'm sure millions of women would disagree."

"I understand, Annie. I don't agree with it. All I'm trying to do here is explain what I believe he's thinking. I wish you'd had cameras installed when she turned up here."

"So do I."

When Patrick stepped into the living room to make a call, I sat at the table with Joe and my grandmother, my mind whirling in confusion. I sipped my tea and pushed puzzle pieces around aimlessly.

"A penny," Grandma Natalie said.

"I was wondering how many times I can be accused of murder before one sticks."

"Not funny," Joe said.

"No shit." I handed him a puzzle piece, grateful for the distraction.

Patrick joined us at the table. "I called Beth to see what she thought of our meeting. She has to tread lightly, but I thought it wouldn't hurt to ask."

"What did she say?"

"Not much. She's being careful not to step on her colleague's toes. She did say he made it clear I'm not his favorite person. Like I care."

"Any idea how long the shop will be off limits?"

"She said it could be a few days, but she'd check with Detective Grant about it. You should take time to rest anyway after what you've been through. Grant won't be easy to work with, so I'm glad she was there. She'll try to reason with him."

"Good luck," I said, disgusted. When he objected, I waved him off. "Sorry, I didn't mean it that way. I'm exhausted. The past year and a half has worn me down, Patrick. I try to be optimistic that everything will work out and I'll finally be clear of all of it, and then this happens. A person can only take so much."

Joe put his arm around my shoulders. "You know what would help you work off some angst?"

I raised an eyebrow at him, suspecting I knew the answer. "Okay, I'll bite."

"A nice long bike ride."

"What a surprise."

"And I know just the route. It has hills you will hate, so you can yell out all the anger and frustration you like on the way up, and then have fun descending the other side, where you will laugh and love going fast. There's no better medicine."

"And we haven't left yet?"

Chapter Twelve

Beth O'Brien was right. The investigators estimated they'd need about a week to wrap up their work, less if the experts they needed were available. Even though we'd been told to stay away, I couldn't resist driving by. The day after our meeting with Detective Grant, I parked on the street and watched them work.

One man took photos of the ground where Mandy's body had lain and also of the front of the shop. I wondered what he thought of the paint covering the exterior of the building since it still looked as if it was painted by forty coked up kindergarteners. Another man and a woman examined the walkway and the adjacent ground. They scraped at different spots and put the results into test tubes and other small containers, presumably for testing.

I wondered if they also tested any of the nearby surfaces for fingerprints. I'd have been interested to know if whoever spray painted the shop had touched any of the windows or siding. I made a mental note to ask Patrick.

I called Rachel at her clinic. "Do you need me to work? I can come in, you know."

"No, you stay home and rest. I bribed Becky to come back for a few days, and the new receptionist starts next week. You're a free woman."

"That's the problem. You know how I like to keep busy. I can't do any work at the shop. Joe's off on one of his epic rides with Team Three and a Half, and Patrick is at work. Grandma Natalie is out with Liz somewhere. I don't need to rest. I need something to do." I didn't say I wanted something—anything—to take my mind off the image of Mandy's body surrounded by blood.

"Okay, tell you what. It's almost lunchtime. Come pick me up, and let's go eat. Harvey is always ready for a visit to the dog park, if you want to take her. Maybe walking around with her will do you some good, though she will expect you to throw her tennis ball about a zillion times."

"See you in a few."

Lunch with my friend and a couple of hours with her energetic female pit bull, improbably named Harvey, turned out to be exactly what I needed. When I got home, Grandma Natalie was still out, so I went for a ride. I wheeled my bike out of the garage and, after checking my tire pressure and putting my helmet on, I rode down the driveway to the street. The day was lovely, sunny but not too hot, and I spent a pleasant six miles exploring nearby neighborhoods. It was a welcome distraction.

I had removed my helmet and was putting my bike up on its rack in the garage when my phone rang.

"Hey, Patrick. What's up?"

"Can you meet me at Beth's office in half an hour?"

"I suppose so, but why? We were there only yesterday." I dropped my riding gloves onto the seat of my bike and went into the house.

"She didn't give me any details, but there's someone she wants us to meet."

I hesitated, remembering the last person she introduced us to. "Okay. It might be closer to forty-five minutes. I just got back from a bike ride, so I need a quick shower."

"I'll let her know," and he ended the call.

I dashed into the house and set a new land speed record for making myself somewhat presentable, all the while wondering what could have changed in twenty-four hours. I pulled into the parking lot across the street from the police bureau building in forty minutes.

Patrick greeted me with "How many speed limits did you break?"

"All of them. I sure hope this isn't another session with Detective Grant."

"I don't think it is, or she would have told me."

We went inside and within a few minutes, we were seated in the same conference room as the day before. The receptionist brought us bottles of cold water, which I particularly appreciated after my ride.

Five minutes later, Beth came into the room accompanied by a woman I didn't recognize. She was perhaps forty years old, with short brown hair and a friendly face. She and Beth took chairs across the table from us.

"Annie, Patrick, let me introduce Detective Barbara Raymond. She's a senior investigator in our Drug and Vice Division. Barb, this is Annie Velasquez, and her attorney, Patrick Wyatt."

After a round of "good to meet you" greetings, Beth turned to us. "After our meeting yesterday, I called Detective Raymond and explained your situation. I also asked her to help me figure out why I can find no drug-related records for Nicole Fleming, despite the information we both found online. Barb?"

The new detective exuded an air of calm confidence, which I hoped meant she had good news for me.

"You gave us a bit of a mystery to solve," she said. "I reviewed the information Beth gave me about Nicole's record, but I also found nothing in our division files. I'm sorry to have to tell you I wasn't surprised, and here's why.

"We've had a higher than normal personnel turnover in the past year. Getting everyone accustomed to our policies and procedures hasn't been a smooth transition. To add to the fun"—she gave me a rueful smile—"one of the detectives who left had been with the Drugs and Vice Division for decades, probably before it was put in place in its current form. Detective Nelson was an excellent investigator, but he had one eccentricity that caused all of us a lot of grief." She paused to take a sip from her water bottle. "He liked to squirrel files away, and we never knew where for sure. I never knew how he got away with it, but the head honchos refused to do anything about it, so we all had to manage as best we could.

"After he retired, he moved to Florida or Arizona or somewhere, and left his daughter to clean out his house before it was sold. She found boxes of files in the house and called my boss. We took a department SUV over there to bring them into the department.

"This happened two weeks ago, and nobody has had time to go through them. So when Beth called me and I didn't find anything in the usual files, I started digging through those boxes." She exchanged glances with Beth.

Patrick, never the most patient person in the best of times, started to fidget. "You must have found files about Nicole Fleming, or we wouldn't be here. Am I right?"

"Yes, you are."

At her words, I let out a breath I hadn't realized I was holding. She was quite a storyteller.

"And?" I couldn't keep myself from prompting her.

"The information you found is accurate. She had—or has, if what you've told Beth proves to be true—quite a history of drug-related arrests. Almost all of them were misdemeanor possession charges, but she also had at least one for possession with intent to distribute."

"Was she ever prosecuted?" Patrick asked.

"She pled guilty and got probation is most of them, and the others were dropped." Detective Raymond turned to me. "Beth told me some of your situation, especially what you're saying was incorrect identification of a woman whose body was found a few weeks after the fire at your dad's bike shop. Correct?"

"Yes. I've been hoping Nicky's arrest records would have her fingerprints in the files so we can finally clear up that the dead woman wasn't Nicky."

"But her parents identified her."

"I know. I guess they could have been mistaken, what with the injuries the woman had and the emotions associated with the death of a daughter, but since I saw Nicky, I'm questioning everything."

Detective Raymond appeared pensive. "Unfortunately, there are no fingerprint cards in the files. Her cases are old enough to predate electronic fingerprints, so we would have needed the cards."

"Is it normal for them not to be in the files?" Patrick asked.

"No, and that's also a mystery. I tried contacting Detective Nelson, but he hasn't responded. I called his daughter and, of course, she doesn't have any information. She was as surprised as we were at how many files he'd stashed in his house, and relieved when we took them from her."

"Is there anything in the files about the detective's conclusions about Nicky?"

"Not much, counselor. He noted Nicole Fleming's death, and closed the file."

Another dead end.

Detective Raymond collected her belongings and stood, and we followed suit. We shook hands again and she said, "I'm sorry I couldn't have been more helpful. Feel free to contact me if you have any more questions."

The next three days passed slowly, made even more glacial by my persistent insomnia. Learning more about Nicky's past was unsettling, but I was also frustrated by the absence of the fingerprint cards from the files. Patrick tried to be encouraging, pointing out the new information we'd gained, but in the end, nothing about my situation had changed.

Daily bike rides, including one in the rain and another with Joe, didn't help. I cleaned the house and cooked dinner over Grandma Natalie's objections. I read. I made bread from scratch, which even my picky grandmother gave a thumbs up. I watched far too much TV. I even filled a bucket with soapy water and washed my car. Joe tried to show me how to tune up my bike, but my sleep-deprived brain couldn't grasp the details.

At breakfast on the fourth day, Grandma Natalie looked at me with concern. "Are you awake? You've almost gone face-first into your plate a few times."

I sat back in my chair and blinked hard, wiping my eyes. "I'm sorry. I haven't been able to sleep much. Every time I do, I dream about dead faces and hands covered in blood. And then I lie awake thinking about fingerprints." I shivered.

She got up and refilled my coffee mug. "Maybe this will help."

The hot liquid was restorative to a point, and the pancakes and eggs on my plate also helped.

"The doctor in the emergency room thought I might have PTSD."

"I'd be surprised if you didn't. You're usually not one to let things get to you, so for you to go into shock must have been frightening."

"And it's far from over. The detective assigned to Mandy's murder is definitely the bulldog sort, gets an idea and won't let it go. He might as well have come right out and accused me of killing Mandy. Patrick backed him down, but I can't imagine it'll last."

"What about Beth?"

"They didn't assign her to the case, so we have to deal with Detective Hardass."

"What's your plan?"

"Mostly hoping Patrick will get me out of the detective's crosshairs. Otherwise, I'm hoping the police will release the shop back to us soon and we can get to work. We're very close to opening."

"Are you sure you want to go back so soon?" She hadn't lost her concerned expression.

"No, but what choice do I have? We have to get the place stocked and ready to open. Hell, Grandma, I went back after Dad died."

"Not right away."

"No, but I did it. I'll be okay." I stirred the remnants of my egg yolk around with my fork and looked into her blue eyes. "The doctor suggested I might want to find a therapist. I think it's a good idea, don't you?"

Before she could answer, my phone rang. Joe.

"Hey, guess what?"

"Let me see," I said, playing along. "You won the lottery. No, wait. You found a camel on the street, and you named him Alice, and you're bringing him home."

"You have it all wrong. His name is Florence." No matter what, my brother always made me laugh when I needed it most. "No, goofball. I went by the shop after we got back from our ride and talked with one of the investigators for a minute. It's not official yet, but they think they'll wrap up today. He told me they've already scheduled a company that cleans crime scenes to come in either late today or early tomorrow, and after they're done, they'll release the shop back to us. We could be back at work in a couple of days." I was quiet until he asked, "Are you still there?"

"I'm here. How clean do you think it'll be?" I didn't want to see any residue on the walkway. Nightmares of bloody hands and dead eyes were more than enough.

"I've heard those crime scene cleaners are amazing at what they do, but I'll see what I can find out."

We'd no sooner ended our call than Patrick arrived at the house with much the same news, but he also had something else he wanted to tell me.

"We got the autopsy report." He took a seat at the table with us. "Do you want to know what it says?"

I took a deep breath and let it out slowly. "I suppose."

He tapped his fingernail on a file folder he'd laid on the table. "Someone shot her." He spoke slowly, watching for my reaction.

"Go on."

"She had two gunshot wounds, one to the chest and one to the neck. That one went through one of the carotid arteries."

"Which accounts for the blood," I said. "Someone could have shot her from the street, right? But then why cut off the lights?"

"I've wondered about it as well. It doesn't make sense, unless the person was actually inside the fence. Maybe he's not a good shot?"

"Or she?"

"Sure, but women rarely use guns to commit murder. I mean, yes, it happens, but it's not as common as men shooting someone."

"I don't even want to know why you'd know that."

"I didn't. Beth told me." He grinned sheepishly for a moment.

"What's next? I'm surprised Detective Hardass hasn't kicked in the door to arrest me."

He was puzzled for a moment until comprehension dawned. "Really?"

"It fits, doesn't it?"

"Don't even joke about it. Beth told me on the down low he's laser-focused on you, as if we couldn't tell when he met him." When I protested, he waved me down. "I know, I know. But what he believes doesn't matter if he doesn't have the evidence."

"And besides," Grandma Natalie said, "you were here with Joe and me all evening until the security company called."

Patrick reached over and grasped my grandmother's hand. "He will want to interview both you and Joe about it. If he hasn't called you yet, he will. I've also put in a request for the video from the cameras here, to show you didn't go out."

Grandma Natalie grabbed her phone off the nearby counter. "I turned this off last night when the battery was almost dead, and I forgot to turn it back on." She pressed the buttons and when the phone lit up, she sighed unhappily. "Yeah, he left me a voicemail."

"Maybe I watch too much TV," I said, "but if they thought I shot her, wouldn't they test my hands and clothes for residue?"

"They may have wanted to, but your hands and arms were pretty bloody—"

"Don't remind me."

"Sorry. Unless they tested your clothes. Do you know what they did with them?"

"No. I don't think they even mentioned them since the nurses in the emergency room cut them off me when I got to the hospital. I hadn't thought about it, but wouldn't they have given them to the police? It's not as if I'd want them back."

Patrick stood and gathered his files. "I'll see what I can find out. If Detective Grant calls you, tell him to call me. Don't talk to him or any other cop without me present."

"Yes, boss," I said, trying to lighten the mood. "I'm far too familiar with how it all works." I got up and gave him a hug. "Thank you for looking out for me."

He hugged me back and took his leave.

Patrick called a short while later to tell me we'd have access to the bike shop by the next morning. The police had finished their work.

"They got a top-notch crime scene cleaning company to start today. In fact, they're probably already working on it."

"How long do you think they'll be there?"

"It's a relatively small area, so I don't know, a few hours at most? But it's good they're on it so quickly."

"I'll call Joe, unless you already did. What's next for the police investigation? They'll have to wait for the evidence to be examined, right?"

"Yes, and I don't know how long it will take. Depends on how backed up the lab is."

"Do you know if they checked for fingerprints?"

"I can ask. Why?"

"I've been wondering if our junior Jackson Pollock would have left any prints behind, maybe on the windows or even in the paint."

"Interesting idea. Let me see what I can find out."

I called Joe with the news, and we decided to head over to the shop first thing in the morning to start organizing the inventory we'd received.

"Maybe we can get the place opened in a few days," he said.

"What about the exterior paint?"

"I'll call Brad. He might be able to work some more magic with the painters."

The next morning, after a quick breakfast, I drove to the shop to meet Joe. I was anxious to get some work done so we could finally open, but I was also dreading seeing the place where Mandy's body had lain. I called Joe while I drove.

"Are you there yet?"

"Yes. Are you coming?"

"I'm about halfway there. How does it look?" I didn't have to explain why I was asking.

"They did an amazing job, Annie. It's so clean nobody would ever be able to tell what happened here."

Relief flooded my body. "Thanks. See you in a few."

By the time I arrived, I'd done what I could to prepare myself to walk where we found Mandy's body. With no other way to enter the shop, I tried not to look at the ground as I passed. All I could do was steel myself and try not to think about it. It wasn't easy.

When I got inside, I breathed more freely. Joe and Brad were opening shipping cartons and emptying their contents onto two nearby tables. Sally was there, too, taking what the men had piled up and filling shelves. They greeted my entry loudly.

"About time you got here!"

"Get to work, lazy butt."

That last one was from Joe, but he looked regretful when I showed him the cooler I was carrying.

"If you don't want cold drinks, more for the rest of us," I said, trying to shake off the remnants of how I'd felt outside. I scanned the chaos, especially the pile of empty shipping boxes. "Where do you want me?"

Joe pointed to the tables. "What doesn't fit out here goes into the stockroom. I labeled the shelves. If you're not sure what something is, give me a holler."

"Oh, because the words on the box are in Swahili?" I held up a box plainly marked to contain bike tubes.

"Smart ass." He went back to work.

After about two hours, we took a break and surveyed our handiwork. We'd emptied all the shipping cartons and shelved most of their contents. The rest were piled on the tables or stashed in the stockroom. Brad and I grabbed box cutters and started breaking the empty shipping cartons down, stacking the flattened boxes near the front door.

"We need a dumpster for recycling," I said.

"Should be delivered tomorrow." Joe was always on top of things. "We're also getting more deliveries this week, which I think will be the last for a while. Almost all of this will go into the stockroom."

We raided the cooler I'd left on the checkout desk and opened well-deserved cold drinks. Even with all the doors open and a couple of fans blowing a breeze through the place, we'd kicked up a lot of dust cutting boxes. Cold water had never tasted so good.

"It's looking very much like a bike shop in here." For a moment, I thought about my dad's shop and how I'd always felt at home there.

Joe seemed to read my mind, because he put an arm around my shoulders.

"He'd have loved it, Annie," he whispered, and I got tears in my eyes. He let me go. "Know what's next?" We all looked at him inquiringly. "We build bikes."

Joe and Brad made a beeline for the bike boxes he'd stashed in the stockroom, and Sally and I went outside for some fresh air.

"I don't know a thing about assembling a bicycle," she said.

"Neither do I, but I'll bet Joe will show us how. Otherwise, we'll be relegated to watching."

"Fine by me. I'm a born supervisor."

We basked in the midday sun, sitting on folding chairs Joe had brought to the shop when he moved in. I set them up in a corner of the parking lot, away from the walkway. It would be a while before I was at ease there.

"Joe told me what happened," Sally said. "Are you okay?"

"No, not really, but I will be. Mandy wasn't my favorite person. In fact, she was stalking me, and I wondered if she was the one who slashed my tires. Even if she did, she didn't deserve to die."

"And you don't deserve to be suspected." Sally's loyalty made my throat tighten.

"Thanks. From your lips to the detective's ears."

We rested for another few minutes, but as I was thinking we should get back to work, Rachel drove up.

"You have good timing," I said. "We finished everything except bike assembly."

"Okay, then. My plan worked." She pulled up a chair next to me and took my hand. "You okay?" She looked skeptical when I nodded, but apparently decided not to push it. "There's still stuff to do, though, right?"

"Plenty. We probably need to check the shelves to make sure it all looks good. The coffee bar needs to be organized and supplies loaded into the checkout area. Joe found a cool old bike he wants to mount on a wall somewhere. Maybe we can do it. And I think he's inside right now, ready to give us a university course in bike assembly."

"Then we should go in and get started."

As I'd predicted, Joe showed all of us how to assemble a new bicycle, and before long, we had nearly a dozen shining two-wheelers in the display racks. The sun was setting, so we called it a day.

"Not yet." Joe pulled the bike I'd admired most down from the rack and put my hand on the bars. "Try it. You've almost been drooling on it for the last hour. I think you'll love it."

The bicycle was beautiful. The frame was polished aluminum, and the saddle and handlebar tape were black. It called my name.

He adjusted the seat and handlebars to fit me well enough for a test ride, and I took it outside. He was right. Riding it felt like flying. I circled the parking lot a few times to get used to the feel of it. After a few minutes, Rachel came out with a red one she'd been eyeing. A couple more circles and then we headed down the street.

After a few blocks, we circled back to the shop. Joe was standing out front, feet apart, arms crossed, with a knowing expression on his face. "What did I tell you?"

"You're absolutely right. As much as I like my old bike, this is like riding magic. I'm not sure I'll be willing to sell it."

He threw his head back and laughed, a deep belly laugh that lifted my spirits. "Then don't. Take it home. It's yours."

"But I have a bike already."

"N Plus One, remember? Consider it a perk of being an owner of a bike shop."

I stood over the beautiful silver bike and tried to think of a good reason not to do what he suggested. I failed, and he laughed again when he saw it on my face.

"Tell you what. Leave it here for now. I think you'll need a different saddle for longer rides, and we should talk about pedals. But it's yours. We have another one like it in the storage room."

I stepped off the bike, and he took it and the one Rachel rode into the shop. Brad had also taken a ride on one of the new bikes, and he took his indoors as well.

Back inside, I went to work putting the flattened boxes outside. I started stacking them outside the door, thinking it would be easy to put them into the recycling dumpster the next day, but before long, the more boisterous in our number made a game of trying to see who could throw a box the farthest, frisbee style. I did my best to ignore their silliness but, of course, I joined in. I'd set no records in Olympic box-flying, that was certain.

About the time we ran out of boxes, a Portland police cruiser pulled up. He started to drive into the lot but gave up and parked on the street.

"Hey, guys, we have company," Brad said. "Can we be charged with littering for filling up your parking lot with cardboard?"

Joe looked outside and called out, "Hey, Carlos! Coming to join in the fun?"

The officer and his partner waded through the corrugated debris as best they could.

"What's all this about?" he asked, surveying the mess.

"It's all Annie's fault," Joe said with a straight face. "She told us to put the empties outside."

"Yeah, put, not throw." I rolled my eyes at my goofy brother. "All I wanted was to clear some working space in here. It was your idea to turn it into a competition."

"You're only grouchy about it because you lost."

I had to laugh. "Okay, fine, you're right." To Carlos, I said, "And what brings you here? Did the neighbors complain?"

"As it happens, yes. Well, maybe complain is too strong a word. One of the tenants in the apartments across the street was worried another vandal might have gotten inside and was ransacking the place." He scanned the room. "She might have been right."

Joe laughed and clapped him on the shoulder. "Ask her to come over when we're open, and we'll make her a latte. I like neighbors who look out for us."

After he gave Carlos and his partner a quick tour of the shop, Joe and I went outside with them.

Carlos scanned the parking lot and adjacent streets. He looked back at the bike shop building. "I see you haven't repainted yet. I hear the graffiti look is on trend." He smiled at his own joke.

"Hopefully, fresh paint tomorrow," Joe said. "And then we open, probably within a day or two. You should come by."

Joe went back inside to check with Brad about the painting schedule.

Carlos peered at me closely. "How are you doing?"

"About like you'd expect. Even being here"—I indicated the now-clean walkway—"isn't easy."

"I wouldn't think it would be. I'm a patrol officer, so I don't have a lot of visibility into homicide investigations, but I'll see if I can keep an eye on it. After all, I was here, so they might want to talk with me once they read my report." He put a comforting hand on my shoulder. "You take care of yourself, okay?"

After the officers left, I went back inside. Joe was hanging a vintage bicycle on the wall above the merchandise racks. I poked him in the side.

"Carlos, is it? Not Officer Martinez?" I arched an eyebrow at him. "Something here we should know about?"

"He likes to race bikes."

"But he seems to have all of his body parts," I said. "Doesn't that disqualify him from Team Three and a Half?"

"We don't discriminate against the able-bodied."

"You're such a humanitarian." I went outside with my friends to collect the results of our box-throwing contest.

Chapter Thirteen

I was yawning by the time I pulled into the driveway. The stress of the past few days caught up with me, and by Wednesday evening, all I wanted was dinner and snuggling with my cat in my warm bed. The universe had other plans.

When I turned into the driveway, there it was, parked right in front of the door to my garage, the garage Grandma Natalie had cleared for me to protect my car from being vandalized again. Unfortunately, it could still be blocked from its safe haven. By a dirty Harley Davidson. Chip's motorcycle. I parked and turned the engine off, glaring at the offending machine.

"What the hell is he doing here?" I muttered. If I hadn't been about to fall asleep, I'd have backed out of the driveway and hit the nearest fast food place for some fries. Swearing under my breath, I locked the car and went inside.

Grandma Natalie met me at the door, looking uncharacteristically tentative.

In a low voice, I asked, "What's he doing here?"

She glanced over her shoulder as if to ensure Chip wasn't listening. "He wants to talk with you, so I invited him to dinner."

I whispered, "I'm too tired for any of his crap tonight. I wish you'd warned me."

"But you'd have stayed away, wouldn't you?"

"In a heartbeat." I wanted to run, but let out a sigh. "All right. Let's get it over with."

We went around the corner into the kitchen, where Chip was setting the table. He extended a hand for me to shake, and after a momentary hesitation, I complied.

"Good to see you, Annie. Did Natalie tell you why I'm here?"

"Only that you want to talk."

"Can we go into the living room?"

I glanced at my grandmother, who tried to look encouraging, and led the way. I sat at the far end of the sofa, and Chip took Grandma Natalie's recliner. She stood in the kitchen doorway where I could see her but he couldn't.

"What do you want to talk about?"

"I owe you an apology for what I said the last time I saw you. I have no right to judge you for who you are. No excuses, but it's how I was raised. I'm afraid I've had blinders on for a long time. I apologize, and I hope you can forgive me."

All I saw on his face was sincerity.

Glancing at my grandmother, I saw her with tears in her eyes and a tiny smile.

"What's changed? In my experience, people don't go from judgmental to accepting so quickly. I accept your apology, but I'm trying to understand such a sudden change of heart."

He looked down at his hands for a few seconds. "I won't lie. I was angry about what you said, and at Natalie for throwing me out. When I got home, I was still mad. My son was there, and he asked what the problem was. I probably ranted at him for ten solid minutes before he shut me up. And then, well, he told me he's gay." He looked into my eyes. "I had no idea. He told me he knew I'd disapprove and throw him out if I knew, so he kept it to himself all these years. He was too afraid to tell me, and he's almost thirty. Damn near broke my heart." He rubbed his eyes with the back of his hand. "We talked for a long time. Then I thought about you and what I'd said to you, and I knew I had to try to make it right. Well, first I had to persuade Natalie to talk to me." He looked over his shoulder at my grandmother. "She's a tough nut to crack." He turned back to me. "That's it. That's my story. I am truly sorry."

Shadow jumped into my lap, giving me a distraction. I stroked his silky coat for a few seconds. "Thank you. I'm sure it wasn't easy for you, and I appreciate it."

We both stood, and for a split second, I thought he might try to hug me, but I stepped around him and into the kitchen.

"What's for dinner? It smells scrumptious."

Grandma Natalie ran down the menu. "It'll be done in about fifteen minutes, so let's set the table. The salad is ready and in the fridge."

During the meal, Chip and Grandma Natalie told me about the ride they'd taken up the Columbia Gorge and through Oregon wine country. As tired as I was, I was happy to let them carry the conversation.

After Chip left, we cleaned up the kitchen, started the dishwasher, and went into the living room to watch television. Shadow climbed up into my lap, which was the last thing I remembered until Grandma Natalie shook me awake.

"Go to bed."

"Good idea," I mumbled. Carrying Shadow, I kissed my grandmother good night and made my way upstairs to my room. Five minutes later, I was under the covers with my cat nestled against me.

An insistent buzzing sound interrupted my slumbers, but it took several moments before I understood the source of the annoying noise. I opened one eye halfway. The only source of light in the dark room was the faint numbers on my clock. Three in the morning.

The buzz repeated itself. Swearing under my breath, I reached over and picked my phone up. I peered at the screen with one partially open eye and saw an unfamiliar number. Ordinarily, I'd have rejected the call, but I was annoyed enough to tell whoever was calling to go to hell.

"Who is this? Do you have any idea what time it is?"

"Hi Annie. Sorry it's so late."

"Nicky?" Her voice jolted me awake. I sat up and, piling a couple of pillows behind me, leaned against the headboard of my bed. My pulse was going a hundred miles an hour.

"I want to talk to you for a minute."

"I'm happy to hear from you, but it's three in the morning."

"I need you to understand something. I know you have no reason to believe me, but it's important."

"What is it?" Shadow snuggled closer to me. His purr was calming.

"I didn't start the fire. I don't know who did. I never would have done anything to hurt Dad. I loved him as if he were my own father."

"But you were making meth in the shed. How does that not hurt him? Or me and Grandma Natalie?"

"I wasn't making anything in the shed. I was only using it for storage, which I know doesn't help." She paused, and I heard her take a deep breath and blow it out. "I never wanted you to know, but I've had problems with drugs off and on for a long time."

"Nicky, I loved you. We were going to get married." A tear ran down my cheek. "How could you keep something so important from me? Didn't you trust me?"

"I'm a coward, Annie. I couldn't risk your rejection." She paused. "In retrospect, I know it sounds stupid, but it's how I felt at the time."

"The report says spilled or leaked chemicals used in making methamphetamine started the fire. Are you saying you didn't put that stuff in the shed? Dad wanted you to clean it up, but it seems you got rid of his things and put yours in. Am I right?"

She paused for long enough for me to wonder if she'd ended the call, but when I checked the screen, the timer still ticked.

"Yes. You're right. That's what I did. But I only stored those chemicals in the shed. I didn't use any of it there." Another pause. "The meth was made somewhere else."

"Oh, well, that changes everything." My tone was sarcastic. When she didn't speak, I went on. "You kept dangerous chemicals in an old shed attached to my dad's bike shop. How is the fire not your fault?"

"All of those chemicals were tightly sealed in containers made specifically for them. There's no way I spilled any and I never would have deliberately poured any of it out. Annie, you have to understand. I've been dealing with those chemicals for almost ten years. I know exactly how to keep them safe." I started to speak, but she cut me off. "You're absolutely right. I deceived you and Dad, and I put dangerous chemicals in the shed. But they were as safe as they could be. Someone had to have tampered with them and started the fire. You know how easy it was to get into the shed. A second grader with a safety pin could pick that old lock."

She sounded so certain I almost started to believe her. She'd lied to me and kept information from me, to be sure, but I'd also lived with her for several years. We'd been inseparable. Despite the lies, some part of me wanted to believe her.

"I was horrified when I heard about Dad." She started crying. "But it wasn't me, Annie. I promise."

I tried to be objective, but it wasn't easy. We were talking about my beloved father, after all. "And then you disappeared."

"I can't explain why, but I had no choice. Did you get my note?"

"Yes. And then they found a dead woman downtown, dressed in your shirt and with your bag and driver's license. Your own family identified her as you. So imagine my surprise when I go to a coffee shop and there you are, alive and well. Who was she?"

"I don't know. I told you before. My car was stolen, along with everything I owned." She was crying again.

"What are you going to do now?"

She sniffled as her tears stopped. "I don't know. There isn't any way for me to prove I didn't start the fire. I didn't kill that woman, which I also can't prove. It's impossible."

"Will you do me one favor?" I didn't think she'd agree, but I figured it couldn't hurt to ask.

"Depends." She sounded wary. "I'm not going to the police, if that's what you're thinking."

"I wish you would. The detective working on the case seems to believe me when I tell her you're not dead, but she needs proof. If you won't talk with her, then help me prove you're alive. Get a newspaper or something with today's date and take a photo or make a video and send it to me. Something I can give her. I've been under this cloud for a year and a half, and it's fucking up my entire life. You can make it stop immediately. You owe me that much consideration, if nothing else."

She was silent for several seconds. "I'll see. I can't make any promises."

When she ended the call, I felt a flash of anger and came within a split second of throwing my phone against the wall. Shadow pressed his head against my hand, which brought me to my senses. Stroking his fur and listening to his deep purr, I lay back down and pulled my blankets over me. Before I got too comfortable, I retrieved my phone and sent Patrick a text.

Nicky just called. Call me tomorrow.

I shut my phone off and settled under the blankets. Shadow resumed his usual position alongside me, and I lay there, staring at nothing until the morning brought dim light into my room. Only then did I sleep.

"Out of bed, sleepyhead."

I pulled the blankets over my face and mumbled, "Go away."

"It's almost eleven, Annie. Are you sick?"

I surrendered to the force of nature known as Natalie Lindberg and let her pull the covers out of my grasp. She put her hand on my forehead, as she'd done a thousand times before, and declared I was fine. Her actions comforted me, as they always had.

"Okay, I'm up." I tried to sound gruff. "Why can't a girl sleep in now and then?"

"Except you almost never do. What's going on?"

Only then did I remember. I grabbed my phone to see if Patrick had tried to call. He'd texted me that he'd call after he finished work.

I rubbed my eyes to clear the bleariness away. "You won't believe it, but Nicky called last night. I mean this morning. Three o'clock." I stood up and stretched, and my grandmother stood by my bedroom door. "Let me wake up a bit."

Fifteen minutes later, I was seated at the kitchen table, coffee mug in hand and a sandwich on the plate before me. A hot shower had done wonders to revive me, and my grandmother's excellent coffee was finishing the job.

"Nothing from Patrick yet?"

I checked my phone to be sure. "Not yet, but he's at work. He's probably up to his ears in law books and whatnot."

"What did Nicky want?"

"To talk, apparently. She insists the fire wasn't her fault. Get this, her reason is she has too much experience with chemicals for making meth for it to be true. That's about two steps from 'I didn't rob that bank because I was robbing another bank at the time.' I don't know what to think about any of it right now. I mean, how could we have been together for so long and I never knew this about her."

"I wonder why she's calling after all this time."

"I've been wondering the same thing. Maybe she's tired of hiding? Or homesick? I don't know." I refilled my coffee mug. "I'm meeting Joe and Sally at the shop in a bit. We've recruited a few people to help us get everything set up so we can open. Brad was hoping to get the painters there today."

We chatted while we ate our lunch. I started to help her clean up afterward, but she shooed me away.

"Go get the shop finished."

As I walked toward the door, my phone rang. It was Patrick.

"Nicky called, did she? What did she want?"

I gave him a rundown of the call. "I don't know what to think about what she said, but I imagine Beth will want to know." I gave him the number she called from, which differed from before.

"I wonder why she's calling you now." He paused for a few seconds. "I'm not sure which is worse, Nicky letting her family believe she was dead or if they've been covering for her and lying to the police."

Having grieved the loss of my father and feeling as though I always would, I knew which one I thought was worse, but I kept it to myself.

"Well, they know now for sure. I told Beth about it when she was on my case about going over there. I asked Nicky to provide some kind of proof, like a photo with a current paper or something. I don't know if she'll do it, but I had to ask."

"Sounds like a good idea to me. I'm glad you thought of it."

"Well, I am my own detective."

"Or you watch too much TV," he said with a laugh. "I'll let you know what Beth says when I hear from her.

"Be careful. It's hot." The barista placed a paper cup with a cardboard collar on the counter. She put a small plate holding a poppy seed muffin alongside it.

"Just the way I like it," I said.

I'd long since promised myself—and Beth—not to haunt the coffee shop where I'd run into Nicky, but there I was. Brad sent me to pick up a few small items from the building supply company, which gave me an excuse to stop in for some well-deserved caffeine. Let Joe and the rest of my friends work on organizing the shop. I had no interest in braving Friday afternoon traffic, and I needed a break.

While I ate my muffin and savored my latte, I watched the cars and trucks pass by. I'd long since given up looking for silver minivans. I tried playing sudoku on my phone, but found it difficult to concentrate while watching the world pass by outside.

Of course there was no sign of Nicky.

I was almost ready to give up and go home when my phone vibrated on the tabletop. The display showed the caller to be Beth O'Brien, which piqued my interest, because she seldom called me directly.

After I greeted her, I asked, "Have you talked with Patrick today?"

"Yes, he called me earlier about your late-night phone call. We're working on it. That's not why I'm calling." Her next words caught me off guard. "Why are you at the coffee shop again? Didn't we talk about this?"

"Yes, we did, but since Nicky called—" I stopped. "Wait one damn second. How do you know where I am?" I stood and scanned the parking lot and nearby sidewalks. "Are you here?"

"No, I'm at my desk."

"You have got to be fucking kidding me." Seeing other customers looking my way, I lowered my voice and turned away from their prying eyes. "You put a tracker on my car? Or are you tracking my phone?"

"Does it matter?"

"Hell yes, it matters. I thought I could trust you." My anger was starting to override any common sense I might have exercised. "Even more, I thought you trusted me. Shows you what I know, doesn't it?"

"Annie—"

"In case you hadn't noticed, this is a free country, and I'll go wherever the hell I want to. If you're not going to arrest me, then get off my ass. Nicky is alive and damn it, I'm going to find her. If it means I sit in a coffee shop half the afternoon, then that's what it means."

"Annie—"

"What?" I ran out of steam.

"You're right when you say your car has been tracked. It's one of those magnetic GPS gadgets. I didn't put it there, but I know who did."

"Oh, let me guess. Macho and Mini-Macho."

"Is that what you call them?" She sounded amused.

"If the size fifteen shoe fits. They did it, didn't they?"

"Yeah." She drew the word out, as if reluctant to implicate them. "Winston and Grant can be overzealous sometimes. I made Winston show me the website."

In the background of Beth's phone, I heard Winston's voice. "I'm sorry, Annie."

"Not good enough. Not nearly good enough."

"I do trust you, Annie," Beth said. "I can't say this officially, but you know I don't think you killed Nicky."

"Good thing, since she's not dead." I knew I was digging my heels in, but I didn't care.

"Don't get me wrong, I did believe she was dead, and I still need proof otherwise. For her to surface like this, if indeed she has, changes everything."

"Not everything. There's still the question of whose body was found wearing Nicky's shirt and carrying her bag. What's to keep you or the macho twins, or anyone else in the department, from thinking I killed her?"

"It's an open question, no doubt about it. But other than Nicky's belongings, no one has found evidence of any connection to you at all."

"I still need to know what happened. Nicky insists she didn't start the fire. If that's true, who did? Or was it an accident? The fire investigation report said it wasn't clear whether the fire was arson or accidental. And why would she disappear? There's still too much we don't know."

"I agree, absolutely, but I still think you're wasting your time at the coffee shop."

"It's mine to waste." My anger was giving way to stubbornness.

"True enough." She paused for a moment. "Call me when you get back over to this side of town, and Winston and I will meet you. He'll take the tracker off your car. He and Grant owe you an apology, and I'll make sure you get it face to face."

I'd calmed down by then, but I had one more thing to say.

"Fine, but I won't call you."

"No? Why not?"

Before I pushed the button to end the call, I said, "I don't need to. Ask your buddies, Macho and Mini-Macho, to tell you where I am."

By the time I got home, my anger had morphed into a general, all-purpose bad mood. When I marched through the front door, Grandma Natalie took one look at me and said, "What happened? Are you okay?"

I threw my phone down on the sofa and plopped down next to it. "Remember I told you Beth has a new partner, some guy from another police force? And the detective who accused me of killing Mandy?"

"Yes."

"Those two geniuses got their pointy heads together and put a GPS tracker on my car. I went back to the coffee shop where I saw Nicky, and Beth called me and wanted to know why I was there. I'm afraid I told her off. Might not have been my smartest move, but damn, it felt good."

"After the last year and a half, I bet it did."

I stood and paced the length of the room. Then I stopped and faced her. "You know, ever since Dad died, I've been a saint. I've cooperated with everyone. I've told the police everything I know, and not once, but several times. I haven't made waves or demanded anything. I'm nicer than Doris Day and Debbie Reynolds and what's-her-name, the TV housewife who vacuums in heels and pearls. And what has it gotten me? Nothing. Not a damn thing." I sat down again. "Just more questions and more suspicion and more of my life in suspended animation, because I could be arrested at any moment. And not for one murder, but also for the dead woman who had Nicky's stuff and now Mandy. Remember all the times when I was in school we talked about visiting London?"

She nodded.

"How could we do that? Would the police think I was running away from prosecution? Would it look suspicious if we got on a plane and left? Hell, for all I know, they have me on a no-fly list. I've been as careful as I know how. But today, finding out there's a GPS tracker on my car was the last damn straw." I sat back down on the couch. "She wanted me to call her when I got home and she'd meet me to have the damn thing taken off. I told her I didn't have to call since they knew where I was, and I hung up on her. She might arrest me out of sheer exasperation."

By now, Grandma Natalie was trying hard not to laugh, but she had tears in her eyes from the effort. She reached over and gave me a bear hug. "I know it's not funny, but it's either laugh or cry. I will say, it's good to see you stand up for yourself. No wonder Chip's half afraid of you."

"Yeah, well, he deserves it."

"What does Patrick think about this?"

I picked my phone up off the couch and checked it. "I don't know yet. Before I headed home, I left a message for him. My guess is he'll be pissed. I'm pretty sure the cops need a warrant to put a tracker on someone's car, and if he ever got one, he didn't tell me about it." My phone rang. "Speak of the devil's attorney," I said, when I saw Patrick's name on the display. I gave him a rundown of my conversation with Beth, and as predicted, he was angrier than I'd ever heard him be.

Even from halfway across the room, Grandma Natalie heard him swearing. "Sit tight. I'll call you right back."

Ten minutes later, he let me know we had a meeting with all three detectives first thing Monday morning.

In between phone calls, I'd had an idea that improved my mood considerably. I put my phone in my pocket and picked up my car keys.

"Where are you going?"

"Back to the shop. I'm pretty sure Joe is still there, and I have an idea."

Chapter Fourteen

This time, we knew the way to the conference room. Beth greeted us by the door, her tone more subdued than usual, and she ushered us into the room without further conversation. Patrick and I had talked beforehand about how to proceed.

When we took our seats, Patrick whispered to me, "What's with the bag? I thought you hated carrying a purse."

"I do, but I need one today. You'll see."

He gave me a suspicious look, but any further comment he wanted to make was interrupted when Beth spoke from where she stood at the other end of the long table.

"Patrick, Annie, you already know my partner, Ted Winston, and also Detective Grant."

We greeted them as professionals, but they avoided eye contact.

"And this," she said, indicating the dark-haired woman seated next to Winston, "is Alicia McKenna. She's an attorney for the police union."

The attorney appeared to be in her mid-forties and had an air of confidence and experience with a serious but not forbidding expression. She had a slim file folder on the table before her, a pad of paper, and two pens.

"Alicia, this is Annie Velasquez, of course, and her attorney, Patrick Wyatt."

"Nice to meet you," she said.

Beth took her seat. "Patrick, we all know why we're here, but I think it might be helpful to lay out the overall situation. Ms. McKenna is new here and while I've given her a brief rundown of events, it might be good for her to hear it from you."

Patrick rolled his chair forward a few inches and rested his elbow on the table.

"Ms. McKenna, my client has been a person of interest in a homicide investigation for a year and a half, and I have represented her the entire time. For most of that time, we've worked with Detective O'Brien, as I'm sure she told you. Recently, Detective Winston became her partner, and we've worked together in good faith to resolve the case." Patrick paused and looked down at me for a moment before continuing. "My client has reason to believe the woman who was allegedly murdered, Nicole Fleming, is alive, and as any reasonable person would do, she has set about trying to find Miss Fleming and put the matter to rest. Part of her activity has included going back to the coffee shop where she first saw her." He paused again. "Several days ago, a young woman was found murdered on a property owned by Annie and her brother. In fact, Annie found the body. The woman's name was Brittany Tucker. She and Annie had a somewhat troubled relationship, which I suspect you've already heard about."

The lawyer nodded. "Detective Grant was assigned to work on that case."

"Yes. Yesterday, Annie went back to the coffee shop, still hoping to see Miss Fleming. While she was there, she got a phone call from Detective O'Brien, during which Annie learned a GPS tracker had been placed on her car. During the call, she heard Detective Winston apologize, clearly establishing his involvement in putting the tracker on the car.

"Ms. McKenna, you know as well as I do that in order for the police to put such a device on a person's car, a judge must issue a valid warrant based on probable cause. I know of no such warrant being issued. Do you?" He sat back in his chair.

Alicia McKenna took her time to respond, clearly thinking through Patrick's words. "Mr. Wyatt, you are correct. A warrant is required, but there's an exception for exigent circumstances. Detective Grant, as part of his duties, felt it wise to monitor Ms. Velasquez's whereabouts, and Detective Winston agreed. Unfortunately, they did not consult with Detective O'Brien, which they should have. Regardless, surely you can see it's somewhat extraordinary for one woman to be at the center of two apparently unrelated homicide investigations."

"It is, but I don't see any exigence here. Annie has been the focus of the first investigation for many months, and she's shown no inclination to flee. She's been cooperative throughout."

"She did move out of town last year."

"Yes, to Charbonneau, which, as you may know, is less than forty miles from here. And she kept in touch with the Portland Police Bureau, her friends and family, and me the entire time. Even the Charbonneau Police Department knew where she was."

"Yes, they did." She opened the file folder. "Detective Dean Jarrett of the Charbonneau Police Department learned of Annie's residence when she inserted herself into the investigation of the homicide of her employer. She has quite a penchant for—what should I call it?— involving herself where she doesn't belong?"

"You're right. She did try to find her employer's killer and got herself into some trouble doing it, but the only relevance of those events to today's discussion is that yet another law enforcement agency was aware of her whereabouts. The person she's trying to find now is someone she had a long personal relationship with and who may have been connected with a fire leading to Annie's father's death. There's a significant difference between playing amateur sleuth, which I will agree is not wise for her to have done, and trying to find an old friend and clear her name.

"And again," he said, "Annie never gave any of the investigators or her family members reason to believe she even considered taking flight. As Detective O'Brien can confirm, Annie has been a model of cooperation throughout the investigation. In the days since Brittany Tucker's murder, she has also cooperated fully with Detective Grant. Even if the detective thought she might flee, he had plenty of time to get a warrant for the tracking device, and he didn't do it. I don't know why. Maybe he thought he didn't have sufficient probable cause? I can only speculate. He had no justification for putting an illegal tracking device on my client's car. So my question now is, what are the next steps?"

McKenna closed the file folder and put her pen on top of it. "What I need to do is confer with these detectives, as well as with their superior officers, and then decide what's appropriate."

"I trust you will keep me informed?"

"Of course." She turned to Grant and said, "Detective."

Grant cleared his throat. "Miss Velasquez, Mr. Wyatt, please accept our sincere apologies. Detective Winston and I acted inappropriately. We have no excuses for our violation of your trust."

"And the law," Patrick said.

"Yes, sir," Grant said, clearly chastened. He shifted his focus to me. "If you'll bring your car to the precinct, I will personally remove the tracking device."

My moment had arrived. "No need, Detective." I stood and put my purse on the table. Patrick gave me a worried glance, but I did my best to keep a straight face. "It's okay," I said quietly, but knowing me as well as he did, he still looked concerned. I opened the purse and removed a clear plastic bag that held multiple pieces of plastic and metal. "I brought the device with me."

Grant jumped up from his chair. "You destroyed police property."

"Not at all." I did my best to appear completely unperturbed by his outburst. "I merely disassembled it." I walked the length of the table and put the bag in front of him. "It's complete, including the inventory tag declaring it to be the property of the Portland Police Bureau." I gave him a small one-shoulder shrug. "It'll work fine once you put it back together, if you do it right. Think of it as a three-dimensional jigsaw puzzle." I made as if to walk back to my chair, but stopped and turned back. "By the way, those screws are really tiny. You might need a magnifying glass."

I went back to my seat while Grant blustered impotently. Patrick whispered, "Wow." Winston looked as if someone had coldcocked him. The police attorney tried to maintain her professional demeanor, but there was amusement in her eyes.

Beth's reaction was by far the best. She'd swiveled her chair away from her colleagues and her shoulders shook. After half a minute, she turned back and reached for a tissue to blot tears from her reddened face. She stifled the laughter threatening to overtake her, but only barely. She met my eyes and shook her head, as if to say, "I don't believe you did that."

Patrick and I stood to take our leave, but I wasn't finished.

"I have one more thing to say. You can believe what you want about me. You can think I'm guilty as hell. And you know what, I'm fine with it, because I know after all is said and done, you're required to follow the evidence. And please do, because if you do it without bias or preconceived notions, you'll find I haven't harmed anyone.

"But understand one thing. I might look like a young woman who will roll over and not protest when you violate my rights, but perhaps this little demonstration"—I pointed to the bag of parts—"will help you rethink that notion. I've been through hell and back in the past couple of years, and through it all, I've learned not to take shit from anyone. You do not scare me. If you want to destroy your own careers by pulling stunts like this, feel free.

"Keep this in mind. Treat me fairly and with respect, and I'll give you the same in return. I don't think it's too much to ask."

With that, Patrick and I left.

"What are you doing today?" I held my coffee mug between my hands and inhaled the delectable aroma.

"On this beautiful early September day," Grandma Natalie said, "Chip and I are thinking of riding south to visit a few wineries and see the fall colors."

"How is Chip these days? Still trying to join the century?" I wasn't sure I could trust his newfound enlightenment. Maybe learning he had a gay son would bring him around, but I had my doubts.

"Be nice. He's trying."

"I know, and I hope he's sincere. I still have to tweak you about it now and then for fun. I can see you enjoy his company, and he seems to treat you well."

"Sure, once I pounded it into his head not to call me 'Nat.'" She grinned. "And what's on your agenda today? Working at the clinic?"

"No, I'm all done there. Rachel hired a new receptionist, so as of today, I'm a free woman." I put my coffee down. "I'm meeting Joe at the shop, and we're spending the day getting more stuff sorted out. We're almost ready to open."

"No more vandalism?"

"No, thank goodness." I finished my coffee and stood. "It must have been Mandy the entire time." I felt somber for a moment, thinking of how violently her life had ended. She'd been difficult to deal with, but she didn't deserve to die. "Joe still wants to stay there until we open. He seems to prefer the company of bicycles to humans. Brad scheduled the painters to come back today. It's time to ditch the Jackson Pollock look."

"And then you can open?"

"Finally. Do you believe it?"

"Your dad would have been so proud of you and Joe. I know I am." She rose from her chair and hugged me, while I tried to stop the tears that formed in my eyes at her mention of my father. Sometimes I wondered if I would ever hear his name or think about him without tears.

A few minutes later, accompanied by my cat, I settled in front of my computer with a refilled coffee mug in hand to check my email. I'd tried calling Nicky on the numbers she'd used when she called me, but she never answered. Acting on a whim, I emailed her at the last address I had for her. I nursed a faint hope Nicky would email me back. I didn't know if the address I had was still valid, but my note wasn't bounced back, which I interpreted in my favor. She hadn't responded to my past emails, but I still checked every day, just in case.

An hour later, I parked my Subaru at the far end of the bike shop parking lot in a space I liked because it was shaded. Since Joe was living at the shop, he was already hard at work. Music was blasting from the open doors, and boxes were strewn everywhere, some spilling out into the parking lot. He had his back to the door and was singing along to whatever that cacophony was he called music while he slit the packing tape on another carton.

I walked up behind him and tapped him on the shoulder. He whirled around and lost his balance. I caught his hand before he toppled over and pulled him upright, but not before I started laughing. I found the source of the raucous noise and shut it off.

"Not funny, Annie."

"Oh, I disagree. I think you're hilarious. I heard whatever that is"—I pointed at his old boom box—"halfway down the street. You wouldn't have known it if I set off a bomb in here. How do you even have any hearing left?"

"Clean living and a pure heart."

We both laughed.

"New delivery? What's the plan?" I surveyed the chaos. "You don't appear to have a plan."

"*Au contraire.*" He tried and failed to sound lofty. "My plan is to open all the boxes, and see what's in them, and then put stuff away. Most of this will go into the stockroom anyway."

"How can you do that when there's not even a path to walk?"

He looked around, appearing to see the mess for the first time. "You might be right. But," he pointed at me, "I put all the bikes in the back, so the rest should be shoes, clothes, and bike parts. It's sort of a plan, isn't it?"

"Yeah, you're Mister Organization here. Let's see what you have already. Do you have another box cutter?"

We spent the next few hours trying to sort the new inventory by category, which required a lot of lifting and pushing boxes around. After a time, we had some semblance of organization. By midafternoon, our pace had slowed considerably. Where we'd started out by opening a box and saying, "Helmets go over there," before putting it with the other ones, we were now taking them out of their boxes to admire.

"We're never going to finish at this rate. And I'm starving."

I hadn't realized it until he mentioned it, but I was also hungry.

"I have an idea." Joe took his phone from his pocket. "Double duty call." He pressed a button and waited. "Hey, Brad, Annie and I are at the shop. What are you doing?" A pause. "What are the chances you could give us a hand unpacking stuff? Yeah? Great. And if a couple of burgers and fries should happen to accompany you, we'd be forever grateful. We've been here all day, and neither of us was smart enough to bring anything to eat." He laughed and ended the call. "Help is on the way."

Half an hour later, we were happily eating the food Brad brought and trying to show him our system—or what would pass for a system if we ever actually had one.

"If you made a mess like this at my place, I'd fire your butts immediately," Brad said. "How do you expect to run a business when you can't even organize a few boxes?"

Before long, we were back to work, and even Joe had to admit Brad had a point. Within a couple of hours, we were filling shelves with shiny new helmets and pedals and row after row of bicycle tools. The stockroom was filling up as well.

We stood back and admired our handiwork.

"Wow. We're really doing this."

Joe put his arm around my shoulders. "Yep. No turning back now. One more thing, Brad."

"Exterior paint?" Brad checked his watch. "They should be here within the hour. When's the grand opening?"

"As soon as the paint dries," Joe said. "We have the rest of what's here to unpack and put away, but this should be the last for a while. There are more bikes in the back room to assemble." He grabbed me by the shoulders and turned me around. "And what, missy, have you done about the coffee bar?"

I pulled myself from his grasp. "The espresso machine is in Grandma Natalie's garage, along with a supply of syrups and other nonperishables. I have an order in with a local supplier for coffee, and muffins, and fruit, and the like. All I have to do is schedule a time to pick it up." I scanned the walls. "We need artwork. Do you have any race posters?"

"In fact, I do. They're packed away safely in Grandma Natalie's garage. I'll get them tomorrow. And before you ask, the payment system is here and needs to be installed. I'm glad Dad's checkout stand survived the fire. You were smart to save it."

Brad checked his watch. "Time for me to go, but listen, if you want more help here, call me. And Joe, I can help assemble bikes, so let me know. Only next time, you buy dinner."

"Deal," Joe said. "But you're not fooling me. You want to see the new bikes first and test ride some of them."

"*Moi?*" Brad tried to look innocent but failed. "You're right, but it's a small price to pay for free labor." He slapped Joe on the shoulder, gave me a quick hug, and left.

"It's beautiful."

Three days later, Joe, Grandma Natalie, and I stood together in the parking lot of the newly christened Velasquez Cycles. The exterior paint was finished, the colors of the Mexican flag gleaming in the September sun. The new windows sparkled. Even the yellow stripes in the parking lot, their edges wavering a bit from my status as an amateur painter, glowed. The new sign over the door had been installed, only this time the small print in the lower corner read "A. and J., Proprietors." Otherwise, the sign was identical to Dad's original. Seeing it made me nostalgic.

"We're ready."

"One more day to recheck everything," Joe said.

"You've rechecked all of it half to death." I poked him in the ribs with my elbow. "It's perfect now. Enjoy it while you can, because once it's open, it'll be messy."

"Fine by me because that'll mean we have customers."

"You will," Grandma Natalie said. "From what you've told me, you've had a steady flow of visitors this whole time. They'll be back. Your dad would have been so proud of you both."

We were silent for a time, each of us thinking of the man who had built the original shop from the ground up. A tear ran down my face. Joe also had tears in his eyes.

"I can't imagine what my life might have been like without him, Annie." His voice was thick with emotion. "This is for him."

We admired our shiny new building for another few minutes and then went inside. We had stocked the shop to the rafters. The stockroom was jammed full, leaving no room for Joe's cot. He moved it to the front of the shop near the windows.

"You should move in with us tonight, Joey," Grandma Natalie said. "There haven't been any more problems here. Most of your stuff is at the house anyway."

"I will, Grandma, but I want to stay until we're open."

"Yeah," I said, knowing I was in for it. "He's nesting with the bikes. Mama Joe and his babies."

He spun around to grab me, and I shrieked, but he was faster than I was. The next thing I knew, he'd wrapped his arms around my waist and was whirling around fast enough to make my feet fly out from under me. When he finally put me down, I was laughing so hard I couldn't breathe.

"Is someone here?" Grandma Natalie went to the window and peered out. "Looks like we have company."

I got to the door as Brad and his entire crew emerged from their trucks. They hadn't made it far when three more cars pulled in. Rachel and Sally got out of one, and Sharon out of another, along with her husband and two children. Another car joined the fray, one I didn't recognize. Its driver was Carlos Martinez, dressed this time in civilian clothes. Cameron Stewart accompanied him, also in jeans.

"What's going on here?"

Grandma Natalie was smiling. "You didn't plan a grand opening party, so I did."

A van drove into the lot and parked near the door. I definitely recognized this one.

"Freddy! Mo!" The owner of the Charbonneau Diner and my friend who was her chef had arrived, along with two of Freddy's employees, who went right to work unloading the amazing bounty hidden in the back of the van.

Joe and I tried to make room for everyone. He set up a couple of folding tables to hold the food that came through the door in waves. One of Freddy's employees set up a barbecue grill in one corner of the rapidly filling parking lot, and before long, the aroma of burning charcoal and wood filled the air.

"Did you know about this?" I asked Joe.

"No. Seems like our grandmother knows how to keep a secret or two."

Grandma Natalie wasn't the only one who had kept mum. More familiar faces followed Freddy and her crew. Chip rode in on his Harley with Natalie's friend, Liz, riding behind him. A few minutes later, Hal and Ada Brownlee from Charbonneau arrived. At some point in the chaos, Patrick appeared, as did Beth O'Brien. Neither Winston nor Grant appeared, which suited me fine.

I stood outside greeting everyone, and Joe set up his old boom box outside. Music blared into the neighborhood. After a short while, employees from the gas station next door and the auto body shop behind us joined the crowd.

I found Freddy supervising the food. I hugged her and told her how good it was to see her. "I hope you brought tons. We seem to have attracted the entire population of this part of town."

"The more, the merrier," she said. "Natalie hoped this would happen. You know I know how to feed a crowd."

I went back outside and found Patrick talking with Beth. "This is amazing, Annie. You really had no idea?"

"Not a single one." I scanned the crowd and the nearby streets. People driving by slowed down, craning their necks to see what the excitement was about. Pedestrians were also drawn to the noise and enticing aromas of the barbecue. The N Plus One family joined us.

Patrick called me over and directed my attention to the front of the shop. Joe and Chip were standing on ladders, putting up a large red and white banner emblazoned with the words, "GRAND OPENING" and the following day's date.

"There are two more, for the fences. If they don't get some attention, nothing will," Patrick said.

Joe joined us in time to hear his comment. "I wanted fireworks, but they're illegal this time of year."

I was glad but kept my opinion to myself, considering the history of fire at the shop.

Half a dozen people in the apartment building across the street had come out onto their balconies to see what the noise was about. Joe went out to the street and with his booming voice, invited them to the party.

"If they want to complain about the noise, too bad," Beth said. "There are already three police officers here. What are they going to do? Call more? They should grab a plate and have fun. I know that's what I'm doing."

Half an hour later, the noise had died down somewhat as the partygoers filled their plates and settled down to eat. Someone had set up folding chairs and a few tables, so everyone had a place. Joe had turned the music down a bit so people could converse without having to raise their voices. I marveled that so many people who didn't know each other and from different walks of life had come together for a common purpose, and all got along fine. I didn't see anyone who seemed left out.

I took my plate, which I'd happily filled with Freddy's famous pastrami as well as an assortment of salads and vegetables, to a chair designated for me near the door to the shop. Joe and I, as owners of the new shop, had reserved seats near one another. I was sure Grandma Natalie had arranged it, along with everything else.

After a time, everyone seemed to quiet down a bit, perhaps from having eaten their fill in good company. I picked up my glass of iced tea and a spoon and, standing near the door, tapped the glass to get everyone's attention.

"I can't thank you all enough for being here and being so supportive. First, thank you to Grandma Natalie for being sneaky." That earned me a smattering of laughter and my grandmother some applause. "This hasn't been an easy journey for us. My dad's spirit will always be here"— I choked up for a moment—"but I think he'd be proud." I raised my glass, as did everyone else. "To my Dad. This is for you."

The others echoed my words, and glasses and bottles clinked together. I wiped my tears away. This happy moment only existed because of tragedy. While nothing would ever erase my memories of the terrible events that had occurred here, I could only hope happiness could, over time, mitigate some of the pain from the past.

Chapter Fifteen

After the party wound down, Joe and I spent an hour fine-tuning the merchandise layout, making sure everything looked as good as it could. Many of the partygoers had meandered through, admiring the shop layout and talking about the bikes. I hoped they would return after we opened. Joe hung my silver bicycle in one of the front windows.

"It's ready for you, Annie. It's a beautiful bike, and maybe it'll entice people to come in." For fun, he'd made an old-fashioned "sold" tag out of a manila folder and some string and hung it on the handlebar. I couldn't help myself: I took a photograph.

That evening, Grandma Natalie and I had an early dinner. Joe joined us for a while, but he left to sleep at the shop "just one more night."

When I went to bed, I propped myself up on a couple of extra pillows to read. Shadow assumed his usual position at my side, creating an extra warm spot. I stroked his fur and listened to his rumbling purr while I turned the pages on a recent novel I'd picked up.

I was awakened by my phone ringing. I had fallen asleep with the book open under my hand. The bedside lamp was still on. My phone was next to my alarm clock, and when I reached for the phone, I saw it was about two in the morning. Was Nicky calling again?

When I answered the phone, an unfamiliar voice said, "May I speak with Annie Velasquez?"

"This is she. Who's this?"

He introduced himself as Tyler, from the company monitoring our security system. "An alarm went off at your second location, your bike store."

I sat straight up. "What happened?"

"It appears there's been an accident. We've called the police, but you should go down right away."

I got dressed as fast as I could and bolted down the stairs. Grandma Natalie was in the kitchen, dressed in jeans and a pullover.

"They called me too. Let's go."

At that time of night, traffic was almost nonexistent, and we arrived at the bike shop in record time. Flashing lights were everywhere, blue and red. At least three Portland Police Bureau cruisers were parked at angles in the street, blocking our access. I had to park half a block away.

"Go check on Joe." Grandma Natalie gave me a gentle push. "I'll catch up."

I ran down the street toward the parking lot. Two more cruisers occupied it. A uniformed police officer stopped me at the entrance to the lot.

"This is a crime scene, ma'am."

"I'm the property owner." I tried to push my way past him, but he held onto my arm with an iron grip.

"Please, you need to stay out of the way." His tone was kinder but firm. "Let them do their work."

I pulled against his grasp. "My brother—"

"The EMTs took the man who was inside to the hospital. The ambulance left a few minutes ago."

By then, Grandma Natalie had joined us. I wrapped my arms around her and held her tight. "They took Joe to the hospital."

When I released her, she asked, "How bad is he?"

The officer said, "I don't know, but the EMTs didn't waste any time getting him out of here. I hope he's okay."

The scene before us was like something out of a movie. Police cruisers in the parking lot had their spotlights trained on the front of the shop. The swirling red and blue made the area look surreal. At first, my brain couldn't comprehend what I was seeing.

"Is that a truck?"

The back end of an enormous black pickup truck protruded from the front of the shop where the front door should have been. The windows flanking the door were shattered. The brick we'd so carefully saved from the original shop and reused was broken and scattered. The truck sat at an awkward angle, front end higher than the rear.

"Where's the driver?" I asked, worried that more than one person had been injured.

"As far as we can tell, the driver is gone. When we got here, a man was inside the shop. For a second, we thought he was the driver, but he was lying on the floor in his pajamas, obviously injured. It's clear someone else drove the truck into the building and took off. What we don't understand is why he was in there at all."

"The man who was in the shop is my brother. We own the place together."

"Why was he here in the middle of the night?"

"We've had trouble with vandalism, so he moved into the shop temporarily to try to discourage further damage. Do you know which hospital the ambulance went to?"

"The closest is Portland General, but I'm not sure where they'd have taken him."

"Give me your keys, Annie." Grandma Natalie held her hand out. "I'll find him." I passed my keys to her. "I'll call you as soon as I know anything."

After she left, I stood with the officer and watched the police work around the shop. After a few minutes, an officer approached us. As he came closer, I recognized him.

"Officer Martinez," I was relieved to see a familiar face. "Do you ever get time off?"

"Call me Carlos, please. When I heard the call, I had to come down here." He looked back at the building. "This wasn't an accident. Someone would have had to make a ninety-degree turn into the front of the building. It's hard to envision an accident happening that way."

"Someone did this deliberately? Why?"

"Good question." He turned to me, a serious expression on his face. "Joe was apparently sleeping right inside the front window. The left truck tire rolled right over his cot and smashed it flat. I don't know how he survived."

"Any idea what his injuries might be?"

"The paramedics thought he had a broken leg. Otherwise, I don't know. He's lucky to be alive."

"My grandmother's on her way to the hospital." I held my phone in my hand in anticipation of her call.

He led me to the building where I could see the damage for myself. The truck had rammed through the front wall of the shop. It sat at an angle through the door and partly through one of the adjacent windows. Most of the front wall was damaged, and the central part was demolished. The front eave was resting on the truck's roof.

Carlos stepped through the open windowpane and held out a hand so I could follow him inside. The remnants of Joe's cot lay flattened beneath the truck's front wheel. A crumpled blanket and a pillow lay nearby, covered with glass. The other tire rested on an overturned bike rack, having settled into a space previously occupied by the new bicycles, which lay crushed underneath. My beautiful silver bike, bent and broken, lay across the hood of the truck.

Most of the rest of the space was untouched, though the impact had moved several of the shelf units out of place. One had toppled over. The rest of the shop appeared intact. Joe's phone lay atop the checkout stand, and I pocketed it.

"Can you tell if anything was stolen? Except for the obvious damage, it looks the same to me from when we were here for the party, but you'd know better than I would."

I scanned the room. "No, but it's such a mess, it's hard to be sure."

"You saw the crash reconstruction guys working in here?"

"Yeah, I did. I'll bet it's interesting work."

"If they decide this was intentional, why would someone want to do it? You've had several incidents of vandalism and now this."

"But we haven't had any problems since Brittany Tucker died. We'd pretty much concluded she was our vandal. I guess we were wrong, unless this is a one-off, entirely unrelated? Maybe a drunk driver?"

"No way to know. I hope your cameras show something useful."

We went back outside, where one of the other officers approached us.

"Do you recognize the truck?" he asked me.

"No."

"We checked the plates. The owner reported it stolen yesterday. When we're done here, we'll have it towed. You have security cameras out here, but nothing will keep people from taking what they want once we're gone." He rejoined the rest of the officers still taking photos and measurements.

I grabbed my phone. "Patrick—"

"It's three in the morning, Annie." He sounded groggy.

"Yes, I know, it's the middle of the night. I'm at the shop. Someone drove a massive truck right into the building—"

"What?" Now he was awake. "Was Joe there?"

"Yes, he's been taken to the hospital. Grandma Natalie is checking on him now. But—"

"I'm on my way."

We didn't have to wait long before he rushed into the parking lot. He hugged me while he got his first look at the damage.

"Holy shit." He released me to survey the mess.

"Pretty much sums it up."

"Any word about Joe?"

"Not yet. Grandma Natalie said she'd call when she knew something." I grabbed his arm to get him to focus. "They'll tow the truck out of here pretty soon. Check out the roof."

"To say nothing of the gaping hole in the wall. I hope it fell on the driver." He took his phone from his pocket. "Do you know Brad's number?"

"No, but I found Joe's phone. I hope it's not password protected." I tried the screen and was relieved when it lit up.

I pressed the speed dial number. "Brad, it's Annie. Yes, I know what time it is. This is an emergency. Some idiot drove a truck into the front of the shop, took out most of the front wall. Once the—"

"Twenty minutes," he shouted.

"Brad?" When he didn't respond, I held Joe's phone away from my face and looked at it for a moment. "I guess he's on his way."

"He's quick on the uptake," Patrick said.

"He's had a lot of practice putting this place back together."

"Too much."

One by one, the police officers finished their work and left until only two police cars remained. One belonged to the officer assigned to stay and wait for the tow truck. The other car belonged to Carlos, who said, "I'll hang here until you hear from your grandmother."

The coolness of the September night made us decide to wait inside the shop. We found chairs and sat facing the intruding vehicle.

"Doesn't add to the ambiance at all." I tried to make a joke, but the late night and the aftereffects of the shock were catching up with me. I checked my phone. "Come on, Grandma. Call me." I got my wish ten minutes later.

"How is he?" I didn't even say hello.

"His leg has at least two fractures and he's in surgery," she said. "He has a couple of broken ribs and maybe a concussion. They did a CT of his head before they took him to surgery, and they didn't see any bleeding in his brain or skull fractures." She took a deep breath, which seemed to help calm her. "He was a bit out of it on pain meds when I saw him, but he asked me to make sure we find his prosthesis. Did you see it anywhere?"

"No, but there's so much damage I'm not surprised. I'll check again after the truck is gone. We're waiting for them to tow it." I took a deep breath. It felt like the first one I'd had in hours.

"They told me to go home. It'll likely be the afternoon before we can visit him. Do you want me to pick you up?"

"No, go on home and try to get some sleep. Patrick is here, and he can give me a ride."

We ended our call, and I gave my companions the news. While we were talking, a tow truck pulled into the lot, amber lights flashing. We went outside to meet the driver.

"The roof has collapsed a bit." He pointed to where it rested on the top of the truck. "I hope it doesn't fall in when I pull this out from under it."

"We have a construction crew on the way," Patrick said. "If you can wait, I think they might shore it up."

The tow truck driver backed his truck close to the black pickup. He was hooking onto the intruder when Brad and his crew showed up in their work vans. Brad emerged from the first one and joined us.

"First things first. How Joe?" I filled him in, and he continued. "That's a relief. Please keep me posted." He turned back to the building and ran his hand through his hair. "Isn't this a first-class pain in the ass. What's it been since we finished? Twelve hours, maybe? Who'd you piss off anyway? Somebody sure hates this place."

He went to where his crew had gathered. They started unloading sheets of plywood and boxes of tools. Two of the men came back to the front of the shop with lengths of lumber and, propping up the roof, nailed them into place.

When they were done, the tow truck driver pulled the black pickup out of the shop. He started slowly, checking over his shoulder to make sure the roof stayed up. The black truck protested its way out of the shop with metallic screeches and wood creaking, but it was fully outside the building within a few quick minutes. We were happy to see the roof bracing had held. We cleared debris off the truck, including splintered wood, a lot of glass, and my damaged silver bike. The front of the pickup was caved in with its fenders pushed against the tires, which refused to roll. Its windshield was cracked, and the hood was warped from the impact. The tow truck driver released his chains from the pickup and moved the tow truck to the front of the pickup for towing. He extended the wheel lift, added safety chains, and the next thing I knew, the front of the black pickup was off the ground. He accepted our thanks and after wishing us well, he left.

Carlos and the other officer stayed long enough to watch Brad's crew at work on the temporary repairs.

"If we learn anything about the truck or its driver, we'll call you," Carlos said. "Are your security cameras monitored?"

"Yes, they are."

"Good. I'll see about getting the video from them. I hope it'll help. Too often, those pictures aren't too useful."

"Joe made sure to buy top quality. Maybe we'll get lucky."

"We can hope."

After he'd gone, Patrick and I did our best to stay out of the way of Brad's crew. They had the front of the building enclosed faster than I'd have thought possible. Even so, the sky was beginning to lighten by the time they finished.

"It'll do for now," Brad said. "We'll come back tomorrow—I mean later today—and assess the damage. We can fix it, Annie, but there's no way you can open when you'd planned."

"It's okay, Brad. We'll manage." I turned to the men who had done the work. "Thanks, guys. I really appreciate you coming out here in the middle of the night."

They all spoke up to say they were happy to help and wished Joe a speedy recovery. We shook hands all around, with a couple of the men giving me bear hugs. Brad waited with us until his crew left, promising to return after they'd gotten some sleep.

"One more thing left to do," I said to Patrick. "Let's go take those banners down."

After lunch, Grandma Natalie and I went to visit Joe. He was propped up in bed, his leg encased in a cast from hip to toe. The cast was attached to a contraption that elevated the leg and also appeared to apply traction. He had bandages on both arms, and another one over his left eyebrow.

I was most concerned about his demeanor. His normally unflappable personality was nowhere in evidence, replaced by melancholy, downcast eyes, and an initial refusal to talk. I gave him an awkward hug and held his hand. Grandma Natalie and I settled into chairs next to his bed.

"Are you in any pain?" Grandma Natalie asked.

After a long pause, he said, "It's not too bad. I have a headache from the concussion, but the worst is the ribs. I've never had broken ribs before. I can't recommend it." He shifted against his pillows and grimaced. "What's the latest from ground zero?"

"We haven't been back yet today," I said. "Last night, well, early this morning, Brad and his crew closed up the hole where the front wall used to be. They braced the roof to keep it from caving in. Which reminds me." I took his phone from my pocket and gave it to him. "Thank you for not password protecting your phone."

"No idea if my leg was damaged?"

"Not yet. I didn't see it when the truck was towed away last night, but it was too dark to see much. When we're done here, I'll go check on the damage and see what we can salvage. I'll look for it then. Brad's going back today, too, to get an idea of what needs to be fixed." I felt sadness flood through me. "So much for our grand opening."

"Oh, we have a grand opening," Joe said. "It's the entire front of the building, thanks to one asshole truck driver." He hadn't sounded that bitter when he lost his leg to an IED.

"What do you remember?"

"Exactly what I'd like to know." Carlos Martinez joined us, accompanied by his partner, Cameron Stewart. He gave Joe's cast a playful thump. "I'm glad you're okay."

Thanks, bud." Joe considered the question for a moment. "I was asleep when a really loud engine woke me up." He shook his head and squinted his eyes in pain. "It was as if someone was accelerating hard, and then I had bright lights in my eyes. Some kind of instinct kicked in, and I dove away from the window."

"The truck landed on your cot," I said. "Smashed it flat. Thank you for having instincts."

He laughed humorlessly. "Yeah, but my stupid instincts forgot to remind me I only have one leg, and I crashed hard on the floor. Face first. Not my most graceful moment. And I must have blacked out because the next thing I remember is being put into the ambulance."

"You know, falling might have saved you," Carlos said. "The truck was one of those macho pickups that's three feet off the ground with a solid flat front grill. If you'd stayed upright, you'd be in worse shape than you are now. If you even survived."

That sobered us up for a few moments.

"Still," I said, "I'd have paid good money to see you fall down." My sisterly teasing made Joe smile.

"You might get to," Joe said, "if the cameras were working."

"You know what else? That bastard ruined my pretty bike you hung in the window. Bent it all up and broke part of the frame."

Joe patted me gently on my shoulder. "We can replace the bike. I'm sorry about it, but I'm more concerned about my prosthesis. The last time I had to get a new one, it cost almost fifty grand. The custom work it needs so I can ride really adds to the cost. This one isn't very old, so I hope it isn't damaged."

"So do I."

I dropped Grandma Natalie at home and went to the shop. Brad was there with two of his men. They'd removed part of the supports they'd installed the night before, exposing splintered wood and shattered window frames. They were inspecting the opening, and Brad was making notes on a clipboard.

"What's the verdict?"

He made another note before answering me. "It could have been worse. I guess the good news is the truck was tall enough to support the roof, or it would have caved in."

"And the bad news?"

"It'll take at least a couple of weeks to get it all fixed. We can close it up enough to temporarily protect what's inside, but full repairs will take longer, especially for those damn windows. You should take the inventory out and store it somewhere else. Maybe get two or three of those portable storage pods, like you had before. I can round up a few guys to help you move everything. Once I have a better idea how long the repairs will take, I can get the painters and the other trades scheduled."

He looked so dejected that I reached out and patted his shoulder.

"I can't tell you how grateful we are you're helping us, especially on a Sunday. I'm glad you're Joe's friend—and mine." I scanned the wreck of my bike shop and spotted something else that made me want to cry.

The bricks my dad had mortared on either side of the door to his shop, the ones we had preserved, were scattered across the property. Many of them were broken, some ground under the wheels of the truck.

I took a deep breath in an attempt to hold back my tears. Brad put his arm around my shoulders.

"We'll get through this, Annie. It'll be okay."

"I know, but look." I held back a sob. "They were Dad's."

"Do you want us to see how many we can save?"

"I'll work on it. You have a lot to do already. But as much as I love using part of Dad's shop here, what's more important is Joe is alive and he'll be okay."

"Speaking of Joe, I have something for you." He went to his truck and returned carrying Joe's titanium prosthesis, his cycling shoe still in place. "Joe might like to have this."

I wrapped my arms around it, as if I were hugging my brother. Any bit of good news was welcome. "Is it damaged?"

"Doesn't look like it. I found it between a couple of bike racks. It apparently got knocked away by the impact."

I put the prosthesis into my car and texted Joe. "Found your leg. No damage I can see. Looks like you'll be putting your race competitors to shame again." I got a smiley face emoji in return.

Brad went back to work, and I retrieved a couple of empty paint buckets and started to sort through the damaged bricks. The work was therapeutic. My initial sadness disappeared, replaced by resolve, fueled by anger. Someone was intent on destroying what we were trying to build. I couldn't imagine who it could be or why our bike shop was the focus of so much animosity. Brick by brick, I became more determined to defeat the person who had vandalized the building and almost killed my brother. That person could not and would not prevail, not if I had anything to say about it.

True to his word, Brad made sure the shop was closed up as securely as it could be. While his crew worked on the front wall of the shop, he and I sat down together inside and made a list of needed repairs and estimates about when they might be completed.

"The good news is your electrical system is working, but I'd still like to get the electrician to check it out to make sure it's safe. Same for the plumbing. Some of the air conditioning ducts were damaged. I'll get repairs scheduled."

"Will windows and paint take the longest?"

"I've ordered the windows." He let out a short laugh. "When I called the glass company, the sales guy said, 'Let me guess. You want the usual?'"

I managed to smile. "I hope he appreciates the business, but I also hope this is the last time. We've probably already spent our first year's profits on glass."

"He's a good guy, really. I told him the situation, and he said he might come by and check it out after you're open. You've given him a lot of business. Maybe he'll return the favor."

"And painters?"

"Yeah, they're the long pole in the tent, as usual, but they need to be last anyway. I got us on the calendar, but it'll be at least two weeks. I asked them to call me if they have any time before then, but I wouldn't count on it."

We worked on the plan for another few minutes and called it good.

"Have you been to see Joe?"

Brad opened a bottle of cold water and took a long drink. "I saw him this morning. Looks like he'll be released in the next day or two. He was worried about having to be in a wheelchair until his leg is healed. He said your house has lots of stairs, and he sure can't stay there. I told him he can stay at my house. It's all one level, and he'll have his own bedroom and bathroom."

Without thinking, I reached over and clasped his hand. "Thank you, Brad. You're a good friend. Grandma Natalie will be relieved. She and I spent some time trying to figure out how to manage. We thought he could sleep in the living room well enough, but there's no bathroom on that floor."

"Hey, he's my buddy. He and I became brothers in Iraq, and again in rehab, and now with the cycling team. Of course I'll make sure he's taken care of. He'd do the same for me. Have you heard anything from the police?"

"No, not yet. The truck was reported stolen. I don't know if they found fingerprints or anything that would let them figure out who drove it. They're getting the recordings from the security cameras. I don't know how long it'll take."

"I hope it helps."

"Me, too, but you've seen those videos. The pictures are always bad. It's a wonder anyone is ever identified from them."

"Joe told me he got the best you could afford. He knows his stuff, all those electronics. Fingers crossed we'll get lucky."

"Fingers crossed," I said. "So you want Joe in your house, do you?"

He tipped his chair back on two legs and laughed. "At least until he's feeling better and turns back into a major pain in the ass, at which point he's all yours."

"You wouldn't have a knitting needle handy, would you? A yardstick? A stiletto?"

"What are you talking about?" I was sitting in a chair near Joe's bed in the hospital. His broken leg had been set and encased in a cast. The traction device was gone, so he could shift position and be somewhat more comfortable.

"I have an itch right below my knee. I need something to poke under this infernal cast and scratch it." He squirmed, frustrated. "The damn nurses won't give me anything to scratch it with."

"Yeah, and probably for good reason."

"A lot of good you are." He sounded grumpy, but the humor in his eyes gave it all away. "Tomorrow, I get to blow this pop stand. They want me to stay one more day to make sure the concussion is better." He tapped his forehead with one finger. "Important stuff in there, you know."

"Wait a sec. Do that again."

With a look of suspicion on his face, he tapped his forehead again.

"That's what I thought. Hollow. They should discharge you immediately."

"You're not very funny," he said, trying to appear hurt.

"I'm delightful, and you know it."

We both laughed, always amused by our own antics.

"How's the shop?"

I showed him a few pictures I'd taken with my phone. "Brad and his crew are hard at work. If the painters don't refuse to work with us again, we might get the place up and running in two or three weeks. Sooner, if we get lucky, but what are the odds?"

Joe's good humor disappeared when he saw the photos. "What a mess." He had a pained expression. "Who is doing this to us? And why? You know," he grasped my hand, "at first, I thought it was the stalker, Mandy. She was obsessed with you finding her friend or maybe with you, so I thought it was probably her."

"I did, too, but we were either wrong about her or we have more than one problem. Or this is some drunk driver and not at all related to the other vandalism."

"Yeah. I'd sure like to know who has it in for us this bad. I mean, what was to keep the driver of the truck from being hurt? There's something seriously wrong with a person who would take such a risk out of—what?—hate? Anger? Batshit craziness?"

"The police are checking with the security company to see if our cameras show who the driver was. Maybe we'll get lucky."

"There's a first time for everything."

Startled, I whirled around to find Carlos and his partner standing in the doorway. Their police uniforms were uncharacteristically dusty and wrinkled, but both of them were grinning ear to ear. Carlos held a ribbon attached to a colorful mylar balloon with "Get Your Lazy Ass Out of Bed" across it in bright colors.

"Think the nurses will let this stay?" He tied the ribbon to the railing on Joe's bed.

"I think it's better to ask for forgiveness than permission," Joe said. "Your sergeant shouldn't see how you two look. Have you been spelunking?"

Both officers made futile efforts to dust themselves off.

"We went by your bike shop. Brad showed us the extent of the damage and how much they've repaired so far. It's coming along pretty well, faster than I'd have thought. I swear, construction dirt is worse than cat hair. I have two cats, so I know what I'm talking about."

"I'm out of here tomorrow, and I'll be able to help."

I gave Joe an incredulous look. "From a wheelchair?"

He stuck his chin out, stubborn. "You found my leg, didn't you? I'll be fine."

"You think you're going to get around a construction site on a prosthesis and a cast?"

Before he could answer another voice spoke up.

"He will not."

A stern-looking man in a white coat stood at the door to Joe's room. His name tag read V. Patel, M.D. "Joe, we talked about this. You have to use a wheelchair until your fractures heal." He spoke in that weary, patient tone people use when they're tired of repeating themselves. "I don't care how good your balance is, you can't support your entire weight on a prosthesis, especially not on uneven ground."

"But—" Joe started to protest.

"If I hear you're trying to do it, I'll slap your ass into a rehab facility. Is that what you want?"

I couldn't get Joe to behave, but now I had hope.

"You can't do that, doc. I'm a patient, not a prisoner."

Doctor Patel stood at the foot of Joe's bed. "Okay, you're right. I can't. But I worked for hours in surgery to fix the only human leg you have. You had two severe fractures, and I'm not entirely sure there isn't nerve damage. If you fuck around"—he seemed amused at our reaction to his choice of words—"you could make it worse. You don't want to risk another amputation, do you?"

For a moment, Joe looked like the stubborn child he used to be, but then he relented.

"Fine, doc. I hear you. I promise to be good."

The surgeon was skeptical. "The rest of you are my eyes and ears, okay? If he misbehaves, duct tape him to his wheelchair and call me."

I got up from my chair. "I have to go. Grandma Natalie will come by later to see you. I'm going to the shop to see if I can help." I leaned over and gave him a hug and a noisy smooch on his cheek. "Be good and don't torment the nurses any more than you have to." I turned to Carlos. "Please don't give him anything pointy. He wants to scratch under the cast."

When I left the room and passed the nurses' station, the nurse who was taking care of Joe asked, "Is he always this persistent?"

"You have no idea."

I worked the rest of Sunday at the bike shop. Brad's crew had built a temporary replacement for the damaged wall, though without window openings. They'd installed a plywood door, enclosing the building and protecting the merchandise inside while we waited for the storage units to be delivered. I'd salvaged as many of dad's bricks as I could, but the pile was small.

"I have a present for you." Brad emerged from the improvised door with a grin on his face.

"A present? What is it?"

He led me to a tarp-covered pile I hadn't noticed. With a "ta da!" flourish, he flung the tarp aside. What he revealed took my breath away.

"Where did you find them?"

Before me were the prettiest blond bricks I'd ever seen, apart from the ones my dad had installed on either side of his bike shop door. I looked at Brad, eyes wide, and then back at the bricks.

"They're exactly like Dad's. I didn't think anyone made them anymore."

"They don't," he said. "I know someone who salvages old buildings. He keeps the good stuff to be reused rather than taking them to a landfill. I took one of the originals to him, and he had these. There are enough to replace the broken ones, and maybe a few spares."

Without thinking, I threw my arms around Brad in a bear hug. Laughing, he hugged me back. "I thought you it might make you happy."

Tears welling in my eyes, I picked up one brick in each hand. "You're a miracle worker." After I'd finished admiring his find, he replaced the tarp.

"I hear Joe is out of the hospital tomorrow."

"Thanks again for letting him stay with you. He's under orders to stay in his wheelchair, but I half expect you'll find him up a ladder on his cast and prosthetic leg."

We shook our heads at my brother's foibles and went back to work. I found some comfort in the familiar routine of cleaning up after the construction crew. The physical labor helped me take my mind off my worries. Now that I knew Joe would be okay, I wondered yet again who would want to destroy our little store.

"What's so damn offensive about a bike shop?" I was talking to myself again. "I don't get it."

Brad's crew left at about six, and I picked up what little they'd dropped before going home myself. After dinner, I crawled into bed with a book and my cat. It felt good to relax after the past few days, though my mind refused to stop obsessing about who our nemesis might be.

The phone ringing startled me awake. For the first few seconds, I was disoriented until I realized I'd fallen asleep with the light on and my book on my chest. Half asleep, I grabbed the phone and answered it without checking the screen.

"Hello?"

"Hi, Annie."

"Nicky?" I peered at the clock and decided on feeble humor. "At least it's not three a.m."

"No, it's one thirty. Did I wake you?"

"I fell asleep reading. How are you doing? Are you okay?"

"Yeah, I'm fine. I just wanted to talk. I miss you."

I sat up and propped my pillows behind me, buying myself a moment to think, surprised at the anger I felt. When I spoke, I tried to keep it from my voice. "It's been a year and a half, Nicky. You let me think you were dead for a year and a half, and now you want me to believe you miss me?"

"I know." Her voice sounded restricted, as if she were trying not to cry. "I'm sorry. How can I make it up to you?"

"If you want to even begin to make amends, do what I asked you to do the last time. Take a photo or make a video with something showing the current date, so I can prove to the cops you're alive. Why won't you do it?"

"It isn't that I don't want to. I can't."

"Why not? It would be simple."

"I can't explain."

"Can't or won't?" When she didn't answer, I said, "Then find another way."

"How?"

"I don't know. There has to be a way to do it. Without it, I might never get out from under their suspicion. I guess I don't need to tell you what it's like to have your every move examined by police detectives. And for what? For something I didn't do? Would never do? That never happened?"

She was quiet for what felt like an hour but was probably less than twenty seconds.

"I'll think about it."

"No, not nearly good enough." I took a deep breath to calm my anger. "I'll let it go for now. But promise me one thing."

"What?" I didn't blame her for sounding wary.

"Keep in touch. Answer the phone when I call. Don't disappear again."

"What about the police?"

"Look, I already told them you contacted me, including that you called when I was at your mom and dad's house. So they're aware your parents know you're alive. If the detectives haven't contacted them yet, they will. But the real bottom line is I want these cops out of my life, and proving you're alive is the best way to do it. I don't understand why you won't help me. I hope someday you'll trust me enough to tell me."

I felt the last of my anger dissipate. "I can't keep living the way I have since the fire and since Dad died. Only you can change it. Please find a way. It's all I'm asking for."

Chapter Sixteen

Over the following week, Brad and his men made near miraculous progress on restoring the bicycle shop building. The framing was finished, and the new front door was installed. On Monday, by some miracle only a week after the truck crash, our third round of windows arrived. I watched the men from the glass company expertly wrangle the massive sheets of plate glass into place. Their exertions told me just how heavy those windows were, and I was impressed with their work.

Once the windows were installed, the construction crew finished the trim and got the building ready for painting.

"Again," Brad said.

"It's a good thing those guys like us."

"So does the paint supplier. When the lead painter picked up the paint, the store manager rolled his eyes and hoped the third time was the charm."

"So do I."

Brad took pictures every day to show to Joe. For all of his bluster about getting back to work, Joe quickly realized he needed to rest and heal. In a rare display of common sense, he hadn't tried to visit the shop. Brad tried to keep him mollified with photos.

As repairs progressed, I had another idea, and I called Joe.

"Hey, sis, what's up?"

"Did Brad show you the latest pictures?"

"He did. It's looking good. I tried to get him to set up a live feed so I could watch the work being done, but he didn't do it."

"You would think of something like that, wouldn't you? How's our budget?"

"You know what a basement is, right?"

"Um, of course I do. How many pain pills have you taken today?"

"Our budget is at least four levels below the basement. Why?"

"We need to hire security for the shop. You can't live here now, and we can't afford any more problems. The cameras are great, and I'm glad we have them, but they didn't stop someone from driving a truck into the building."

"True. One more incident and we're out of business for good." I could almost hear him thinking. "Tell you what. I'm bored witless doing nothing, so let me research security companies. It'll give me something useful to do between naps."

"A nap sounds wonderful."

"Yeah, say that with thirty pounds of plaster on your leg. Brad hid everything I could use to scratch under the damn cast, and it's driving me batty."

"Short drive." I couldn't help myself.

"You're not funny." Despite himself, he laughed. "Okay, I'll get on this security thing and let you know what I find out. But I want to see the shop."

"Tell you what. After your doctor's appointment, I'll drive you by here. Okay?"

"You're a peach, sis." He made noises that sounded less like a brotherly smooch and more like a newly unplugged drain.

"Now you're being disgusting," I said, though I was laughing. "Get to work."

🚲

Two days later, Patrick and I waited in the reception area of the Portland Police Bureau Homicide Division. I'd been here often enough I was getting used to it, but this time, I was feeling unsettled, though I couldn't articulate why. Always supportive, Rachel had agreed to accompany me, but since it was her first time, she was more nervous than I was.

"Any idea what this is about?"

"None," Patrick said. "All I know is she asked all of us to meet her here. She wouldn't do it without good reason."

"Yeah, that's what worries me."

We settled into the chairs and waited for the rest of our companions. Grandma Natalie had offered to bring Joe, and before long, they arrived. Between her pushing the wheelchair and him trying ineffectively to turn the wheels, they made quite a show getting off the elevator.

Beth led us to the conference room. Detective Winston was seated at the long table, as was Detective Grant. Officer Martinez and his partner were also in attendance. Before I took my seat, I spoke with Beth to explain Rachel's presence. The window blinds at the far end of the room had been partially closed. A viewing screen on the opposite wall was drawn down from the ceiling.

Introductions were made all around, mostly for the benefit of Grandma Natalie and Rachel. Someone had placed bottles of cold water on the table, and I was glad to have one. Nervousness had dried my mouth to where I wondered if I could speak. The bottle also gave me something to do with my hands. Grandma Natalie sat next to me and kept her hand on the small of my back, which was comforting.

Everyone settled into their chairs and waited. Beth sat at the head of the table, clearly leading the meeting. She had a closed laptop and a manila folder before her on the table, alongside a couple of pens and a clean notepad. After we were all settled, she stood.

"We're here to talk about the latest episode of vandalism at the Velasquez bike shop. You're probably wondering why we have three homicide detectives involved in an episode of vandalism, and I'll explain it shortly. As you can see, we also requested Officers Martinez and Stewart to join us since they were on scene that night.

"As you know, we asked for copies of security recordings from the company you hired for the shop and for your home. We included the dates your tires were slashed, Annie, when Brittany Tucker's body was found on your bike shop property, and when the truck was driven into the building. We hoped to find a common thread that might help us solve Ms. Tucker's murder." She paced slowly back and forth as she spoke.

"First, the tires. The camera at your home showed only a dark figure by the car. The person appears to be a woman, but that's about all we can tell. The outside lights you had installed are good ones, as are the cameras, but the angle put that side of the car into shadow. So we don't have anything there, except a general description of a woman of average height and build. Not very helpful, unfortunately.

"Next, Brittany Tucker. Whoever shot her was either very lucky or knew where the cameras were. The shots came from the sidewalk, outside the fence. One camera shows some of the street, but not enough to be helpful."

She picked up a water bottle and took a sip before asking, "Any questions?"

"Yes," Patrick spoke up. "Was there any evidence with the body? Fibers or fingerprints?"

"No, unfortunately, though some of the evidence is still being examined. The forensics team cleaned up all the debris in the area, which was mostly leaves and some bits of stuff from the construction. They even took the top layer of soil to examine under a microscope. So far, their work has revealed nothing helpful, but again, they're not finished. That said, even though the cameras captured the moment she was shot, this isn't the proper venue for showing that video."

I breathed a sigh of relief.

Beth opened a manila folder that lay before her on the table and removed a sheaf of papers.

"Our luck changed when we saw the recordings of the truck crashing into the building. Joe, when you bought good quality gear, you did a superb job. I'm going to show you two security recordings, one from outside and one from the inside."

Joe held up his hand. "Wait, does this mean everyone gets to see me fall on my face?"

Beth smiled. "Indeed, it does." Then she became more serious. "And it's a damn good thing you did. You'll see what I mean." She held up the papers in her hand. "We actually got a good look at the driver, which you will see in the video, but I also printed a screen shot of her. It's good enough to use for facial recognition. First, I'll play the recordings, and then if you want a copy of the photo, you can have one."

After she dimmed the lights in the room, she sat in front of the opened laptop and pressed a few buttons. "This is from outside."

The picture on the screen showed an empty parking lot and the front of the shop in the dark of the night. A small blue light shone through one of the front windows.

"My phone on the counter," Joe said quietly.

A few seconds later, chaos erupted as the truck sped into the parking lot. It scarcely slowed when it burst through the gate, made an abrupt left turn, and slammed into the front of the shop. Debris flew in all directions and the wheels spun ineffectively. Several seconds later, the wheels stopped, the exhaust dissipated, and the driver's side door opened.

A woman slid out of the driver's seat, supporting herself with the open door. She glanced at the damage she'd caused and walked away. She brushed her hair away from her face as she neared the camera, and then she was gone.

Joe and I locked eyes. Was that who I thought it was?

"Annie? Joe?" Beth focused on us. "You seem surprised. Do you recognize her?"

"I think so," I said. "Can we see it again?"

"Of course. But take one of these." She handed the sheaf of photos to Joe, who sat nearest her. He took one and passed the rest down, and they made their way around the table. She replayed the video.

"Before we talk about it, let's see the inside view first."

My mind was racing, and I felt short of breath, dimly aware Grandma Natalie's hand was no longer on my back. I steadied myself with a sip of cold water.

The second video was no less dramatic. For the first several seconds, it showed the dark interior of the shop. Joe's still form lay on the cot near the front window. The rest of the picture showed the bike racks we'd positioned so customers would see them first when they entered the shop.

Then bright lights lit up the parking lot and when the truck turned abruptly, the interior of the shop itself blazed with light. Joe leaped up and made an obviously desperate attempt to escape the incoming threat. As the truck smashed through the window and wall, he fell to the floor. The vehicle came to rest on a toppled bike rack, only inches from my brother's prone body. He tried to scramble away but could only propel himself a short distance with his arms, and then he was still.

Through the remains of the window, I saw the woman emerge from the damaged truck. She surveyed the carnage for a few seconds with a disinterested expression and turned to walk away, almost strolling.

Only then did I pick up the photograph. Joe and I stared at each other again in disbelief.

"Joe? Annie?" Beth's voice was sharp. "Do you know her?"

I finally turned to her, trying to comprehend what I'd just seen.

"I don't know her name, but during construction, she visited at least two or three times." I turned to Joe. "You saw her, too, didn't you?"

"Yes, but she never told me her name."

"Wait, I need to understand this," Beth said. "She visited with you?"

My incredulity was giving way to anger. "Yeah, she did. I think I told you I did some cleanup work for the construction crew. And Joe did some of the actual construction. Lots of people came by to talk. Some of them remembered the old shop and told us they were happy to see us rebuilding. Some of them remembered Dad." I got a momentary pang at the memory. "Most of them wanted to know when we were planning to open. She was one of those, even though she told me she'd never been a customer." I wrinkled my brow, trying to remember. "I think she said she lived in the neighborhood and how nice it was to have the shop back. Something like that."

"Joe?"

"Same here, except I only spoke with her once. I wasn't there much in the evenings like Annie was."

Beth was silent, as were the other two detectives.

"It doesn't make any sense," I said. "Why would she come by and visit and then do this? She seemed friendly enough. I don't understand it at all."

"Here's what I think we need to do next." Beth spoke deliberately, as if thinking it through. "The video and the photograph I made from it are good, better than most security recordings. Since you two have met her, would you give a detailed description to us?"

"Of course."

"And maybe she has a record. If you wouldn't mind looking at some photos, I'd appreciate it. Even if she'd introduced herself to you, she might not have used her real name, so we'll have to use other ways to identify her. I'll try facial recognition software."

"You don't need to do that." Grandma Natalie spoke for the first time, getting everyone's attention. Her voice was tremulous.

"No?" Beth was intrigued. "You know who she is?"

Before she spoke again, Grandma Natalie turned to me. She took my hand in both of hers and held it tight. "I'm so sorry" she whispered. "I hope you can forgive me." She released my hand and turned her chair to face the detectives.

I said, "What do you mean?"

She ignored me, keeping her focus firmly on Beth O'Brien.

"Her name is Laura Natalie Lindberg Velasquez. She has a criminal record going back more than thirty years and probably as many aliases. She's my daughter, my only child."

The room was silent. The rest of its occupants disappeared from my vision as I stared at my grandmother, eyes wide. She didn't return my gaze. She kept her eyes on Beth, with her back turned partly toward me.

I felt an arm around my shoulders. Rachel had come around the table and sat next to me. She looked almost as shocked as I felt.

She took both of my hands in hers. "Breathe."

I inhaled deeply, only then realizing I'd been holding my breath since my grandmother spoke. "My mother. My *mother?*" Tears ran down my face.

Rachel pulled me close and wrapped her arms around me. "It's okay, Annie." She held me, as if trying to comfort an upset toddler, rubbing my back and murmuring, "You're okay."

I let her hold me until reality crashed in. I pulled away from her and stood, my chair banging into the wall, and faced my grandmother. "My mother?" I was almost shouting. "My fucking mother?" When she looked down at her hands, I yelled, "Don't you dare look away from me." She finally met my eyes. Tears wet her face. "You've been lying to me my whole life. You told me she was dead, and now I learn not only is she alive, but she's been coming to the shop and talking to me."

"Annie—" She reached for my hand, but I pulled away.

"Don't touch me." I took a step back.

Joe wheeled his chair next to me and wrapped an arm around my waist. I put my arm around his shoulders. "Did you know?"

"Of course not. I'm as surprised as you are."

I turned to Patrick. "You?"

"Not a clue."

Their faces told me everything I needed to know. "I believe you." To Beth I said, "I can't be here. I have to go." I turned to Rachel. "Will you come with me?"

"Of course. Whatever you need." She gave me a handful of tissues, and I wiped away the tears coursing down my face as I tried desperately not to break down sobbing. I squeezed Joe's hand and released it, and spoke to Patrick. "Talk later?"

Rachel and I went to the conference room door and pushed it open.

Beth met me at the door and laid a gentle hand on my forearm. "Annie, please stay."

I pulled away from her and stepped through the doorway, and she followed me. When the door closed, the floodgates burst. Sobs wracked my body. She stood with me, holding my hands.

Rachel hugged me tight, steadying me. "It's okay, Annie. You're going to be all right."

After a couple of minutes, my tears abated for a moment, and she let me go.

"How?" I was asking myself as much as her.

"It's okay if you want to go," Beth said, "but there's a lot here I need to understand. Will you come back inside for a few minutes and talk with me?" Concern shone in her eyes.

"I can't talk to her. Not right now."

"You don't have to talk to anyone else, but I'd appreciate it if you would talk to me. Sit next to me, and let me ask you a couple of questions. I promise, you don't have to talk with anyone else."

"Why can't we do it in your office some other time?"

"We can, but why not take two minutes and get it over with now?"

I paused and then relented. "Okay. Two minutes, but if anyone but you or Patrick or Joe or Rachel says anything to me, I'm leaving."

She opened the door for me, and I went back into the conference room. I scanned the faces of the occupants long enough to locate Patrick and Joe. They looked worried. I did not meet my grandmother's eyes.

Beth pulled a chair up for me next to hers. "Focus on me. Ignore everyone else."

"Okay."

Patrick had come around the table to stand behind me. Rachel and Joe were nearby.

Beth turned to the rest of the room's occupants. "Annie and I are going to talk. Please have some respect and don't interfere." Her tone made it clear she would tolerate nothing less. She turned her chair toward me and took my hands in her own.

"Annie, how do you know the woman in the video?" Her voice was soft, kind.

"She came to the bike shop two or three times, asking about the construction. I didn't think anything of it, because lots of people did the same thing."

"But why didn't you know who she is?"

I wiped away fresh tears. "I've never known her. My earliest memory of her was asking my dad and grandmother where my mom was when I was maybe four years old." I clamped down hard on the anger that arose suddenly. When it receded enough to let me breathe, I said, "They told me she was gone. I remember wondering when she'd be back, but as I got older, I realized people used that word as a euphemism, rather than saying someone had died. They let me think she was dead."

"So you've only now learned she's alive? Nobody's ever told you otherwise?"

I looked down at my hands. "That's right."

Beth sat up straighter in her chair and in my peripheral vision, I saw her give my grandmother a frown that conveyed deep disbelief. She turned back to me.

"Annie, I am so sorry. I would never have done this had I known."

I gave her a teary smile, feeling calmed by her presence. "Thank you." She released my hands, and I stood. "I have to go now. Call me if you need anything else."

As I left the room, followed by Rachel, I heard my grandmother say, "Annie, please." Her voice was tremulous. I did not look back as the conference room door closed behind me.

Only when Rachel and I got to her car did the emotions I'd barely controlled erupt again. I burst out crying in the police department parking lot, almost wailing, sobbing like a heartbroken child, which perhaps I was. Rachel held me and let me cry. I was dimly aware when a concerned officer approached us, but she waved him away. "It's okay. I'm taking care of her."

She gently persuaded me to get into the car and handed me a box of tissues. It must have been a fresh box, because by the time I reached the hiccup stage, the passenger's side of her car looked as if a blizzard had blown through.

"I made a mess of your car." My voice was weak.

"As if it matters."

I picked ineffectively at the pile of sodden tissues. "I think I might be dehydrated after all this."

"Want me to take you to the clinic and give you fluids under your skin, like we do with cats?" She gave me an evil grin.

"Yeah, I don't think so. How about we get some cold drinks? Maybe a snack?" I'd always been an emotional eater, but today wasn't the day for personal improvement.

She started the car and took us to Burgerville, our favorite local fast-food joint. Once she'd collected our orders, she parked under a tree and rolled the windows down. The breeze felt wonderful on my skin. My cold drink felt even better in my achy throat.

We unwrapped our burgers and ate. I knew she was waiting for me to speak first, but I didn't know what to say. Turned out I didn't have to.

"Well, that was a kick in the head," she said, pointing at me with a French fry.

"No shit." I stared off into space, momentarily taken back to the moment my life changed. A weight had settled onto my shoulders, and I had the beginnings of a headache. My thoughts were whirling.

"What do you want to do?"

"No idea. Should I try to meet her? I mean, as who we really are, no subterfuge? Should I ask Beth to see any criminal records she finds? Do I even want to know her? And why would Grandma Natalie lie to me for such a long time? My dad, too, come to think of it. What is so bad that they would keep me in the dark? I'm an adult. I can handle tough conversations. There must have been a million times they could have told me the truth." I looked into her eyes. "I hate surprises, and this is a whopper."

"All good questions, but what I meant was, what do you want to do right now? You're my dearest friend and I love you, but you can't live in my car while you solve your existential crisis."

Her description made me smile, and her logic brought me back to the practicality of here and now.

"Sorry about that." I touched the end of a crispy French fry to my forehead. "Too much going on in here."

Always the practical one, Rachel got right to the point. "You have a decision to make. You can go home and face your grandmother and get it all out, or if it's too much, too soon, you can come and stay with me while you decide what you want to do. You're welcome to use my guest room for as long as you want."

"What about Shadow?"

"Bring him with you. You already know how sweet Harvey is. She loves cats. Maybe they can play together."

I paused, thinking. "I don't think I can try to talk with Grandma Natalie about this right away. As angry as I am with her, I don't want to say anything I'll regret." I looked up at her. "I will talk with her, I promise. I need time. Will you take me back to my car and then come home with me so I can pack a few things? I don't want to be in the house alone if she's there."

Twenty minutes later, I pulled into my usual spot in the driveway, and Rachel parked behind me. I was relieved to see Grandma Natalie wasn't home yet. I opened the garage door, and we went inside. The time we had taken to eat and drive home had let me form a rudimentary plan.

I pointed to Shadow's carrier. "Grab that."

Rachel obliged and followed me into the house and up to my room. I flung my closet door open and grabbed my suitcase. I unzipped it and started throwing clothes into it.

"It's not too late to stay and hear her out. She must have a good reason for keeping the truth from you."

I added underwear into the suitcase and reached for my favorite pajamas. Rachel's words made me slow for a moment, and I sat on the bed. "I'm twenty-eight years old, Rachel. In all that time, she couldn't find a way to tell me my mother was alive? Would it really have been so difficult?"

I got up and put more clothes into the case. I put my laptop on the bed, along with two pairs of shoes. I got a tote bag out of the closet. I'd need it to carry Shadow's litter box and dishes.

"Any chance the new receptionist won't work out?"

Rachel looked puzzled. "What? Why?"

"If we can't get the shop open, I'll need a job."

She waved my feeble attempts at humor away. "You'll get the shop open, but if worse comes to worse, I'll put you to work cleaning kennels. Holidays are coming up in a couple of months. Lots of dogs boarding. Get it?"

"A perfect description of my life as late, piles of crap." Even I had to smile at that one. "There's cat food and litter in the garage, and then I'll go find Shadow."

"He's right here." My grandmother stood in the bedroom door, holding my cat.

Rachel took him from her and put him into his carrier.

"What are you doing?"

Without looking at her, I said, "Isn't it obvious? I'm packing. Shadow and I are going to stay somewhere else." She didn't need to know where.

"Please don't." She sounded as if she might cry.

I'd finally had enough. I spun around so we were face to face. "I'm leaving. You have lied to me for my entire life. And then I find the woman I've been talking with is my mother, and of course she knows who I am, but she wasn't honest with me either. You're both liars." I went back to my suitcase.

"Please stay."

"I can't. I need time to think about all of this, what it means. Dad lied to me, too, didn't he?"

She didn't reply, which was an answer in itself. She reached out to touch me, but I avoided her hand.

"Please stay. I'll tell you everything. You can ask me whatever you want. But please don't leave."

"You can tell me over the phone." I picked up my bags and, with Rachel following with Shadow, I left the only home I'd ever known.

Chapter Seventeen

Two hours later, I'd settled into Rachel's deep leather recliner with the footrest up. I had a warm blanket across my lap and a tall glass of ice water on the table next to the chair. She brought me two aspirin, and I washed them down.

"How are you feeling?"

"At the moment, I'm convinced ice water is the drink of the gods," I said, knowing I was sidestepping her question. When she didn't speak or look away, I gave up. "Honestly, I don't know how to feel. I'm so angry with her I'm afraid of it, if you know what I mean. It's like a coiled snake in my chest, wanting to strike out, but it wouldn't do anyone any good."

"Keeping it bottled up won't do you any good."

"I know. Yes, I'm mad, I'm livid, but I'm also heartbroken. She lied to me my whole life. Who does that?"

"The good news is you can stay here as long as you want. Take time to work through it. You'll have to talk with her at some point, but there's no rush."

"But what if all I can do is scream and yell and say terrible things? This calm exterior"—I waved my hand around my face—"is a façade. I'm angry inside, and heartbroken."

"Then you should scream and yell, if it's what you need to do. You have every right to be angry and to feel betrayed." She picked her coffee mug up and held it between her hands. "But think about it logically for a moment. Ask yourself a couple of questions."

"Such as?"

"Do you think your grandmother would ever intentionally hurt you? Have you ever known her to do anything without a good reason?"

I opened my mouth to answer, but she cut me off. "Motorcycles don't count. But she even does that for a reason, because she loves them. And she loves you. Didn't she kick her boyfriend out of the house for you?"

"You know I hate you when you make sense."

"No, you don't. You love me, and you know I'm right." She stood and took her coffee cup to the kitchen. "Think about it. You don't have to run into her arms and proclaim all is forgiven, but I do think you should talk with her. Call her. Give her a chance to explain. You're not a vindictive person, Annie, and you're not normally one to wallow in self-pity. Hear her out, and if you don't like what she has to say, then so be it. But give her a chance."

"Okay, I'll think about it. You might be right." I felt the need to change the subject. "Does it look to you like our furry kids will be okay?"

While I was unpacking my clothes in Rachel's spare bedroom, she had put Shadow's carrier in the middle of the living room floor. She knew Harvey would inspect the newcomer, and we both thought it was safer for them to be introduced with a barrier in between. At the moment, Harvey was lying on her side on the floor with her nose pressed against the door of Shadow's carrier. Her tail waved slowly, making quiet thumps on the hardwood floor. Shadow eyed the dog warily.

"Shadow stopped growling," Rachel said, letting me get away with the distraction. "That's progress."

"I need to trim his claws. I don't want him to hurt Harvey, and those little daggers can be lethal."

While we watched our pets get acquainted, I couldn't help but think about the events of the past few months. Grandma Natalie's motorcycle crash, Nicky showing up out of the blue not dead after all, Mandy's obsession with her missing friend and then turning up dead, and wave after wave of vandalism at home and at the shop.

But it wasn't all bad. My grandmother was well and had a boyfriend, even if he had troglodyte tendencies. The shop was lovely, or it would be once it was finally open for business. Joe was mending well. Patrick was doing just fine. I had the best friends a woman could have, and my cat was happy and healthy.

Well, I amended, Shadow would be happier if that dog would remove her nose from his carrier door.

But this latest firebomb to strike my life was foremost on my mind.

Rachel, ever the perceptive one, said, "Give it time. You're one of the most resilient people I've ever known. You'll be okay."

"You know, I always thought she and I would live together for the rest of our lives, or at least the rest of hers. When she met Chip, I thought maybe I was wrong. But it was all right. That's how life is. Things change."

"What if you met someone?"

I waved a dismissive hand. "I suppose it could happen, but the way my luck has run, I never gave it much thought." When she started to speak, I cut her off. "Don't even mention the detective." I tried giving her a stern look, but she laughed.

"She likes you, Annie, and I think you like her." I started to deny it, but she went on. "I've known you a long time. Maybe you can fool some people with that 'butter won't melt' attitude, but not me. Don't even try."

I gave up. "Okay, all right, fine, I like her. If you tell anyone what I said, I'll deny it. But it doesn't change the fact that she could arrest me for murder and who knows what else. She seems to believe Nicky is alive, but what about the woman who was identified as Nicky? Who killed her? And what about Mandy? That little nutball was stalking me, including at my home—well, former home—and I've told everyone, including Beth, how angry I was with her. And now she's dead, too, and I have a new detective to deal with. I seem to collect homicide detectives. I'm a murder magnet. I should have a T-shirt made."

Rachel tried not to laugh, but she failed. "Murder magnet? What the hell's that?"

I couldn't help it. I started laughing, too, and before long, both of us had tears running down our faces. Maybe it was the stress of the day, but "murder magnet" put an end, even if only a temporary one, to my somber mood.

"Annie, look."

I wiped my eyes and followed Rachel's gaze. Shadow had curled up against the carrier door. He put a paw out through the bars and rested it on Harvey's nose. When the tip of Harvey's tongue snaked out slowly and touched the cat's paw, Shadow started purring.

Maybe the day wasn't a total loss after all.

I spent the next day doing very little. Rachel left for her clinic before eight, anticipating a full schedule. She took her dog with her, enabling Shadow to explore the house without Harvey following his every move. He'd spent the night locked in the bedroom with me, tunneled under the blankets and curled up next to my leg. The change in accommodations made him nervous, so I was glad to see him exploring, checking each room in succession.

Before she left, Rachel admonished me to take it easy for a few days. I had every intention of complying, as I had no energy to do anything, including driving to the bike shop to check on the repairs. I spent most of the day in the recliner. If I wasn't zoning out on mindless television, I was sleeping, except when my phone rang. Every two hours, I'd hear the chirping bird ringtone I'd assigned to Grandma Natalie. I couldn't bring myself to answer her calls.

About midafternoon, a different ringtone woke me from a nap.

"Hello, Detective," I said, trying to sound alert.

"I'm sorry. Did I wake you? I wanted to see how you're doing."

"I'm okay." She had to know I lied. "Thanks for asking."

"Your grandmother is worried about you," Beth said. "She says you're not answering your phone. She told me you moved out, and she doesn't know where you are."

"I'm sorry she's bothering you. This situation is her own doing. I couldn't stay there."

"I understand, but you'll have to face her sometime."

"I know. Just not now." I paused, wondering if I should ask. "Is it true? That Laura—my mother—has a criminal record?"

"Yes, unfortunately, but our most recent record of her is almost twenty years old. She must have left town. Your grandmother doesn't know where she might have lived, so unless Laura tells us herself, we might not get the full picture."

"Or maybe she didn't commit any other crimes?"

"Maybe." She sounded doubtful. "I could be wrong, but to my eyes, she has all the appearances of a habitual criminal. Thefts, burglary, at least one armed robbery of a convenience store, possession of a controlled substance with intent to distribute, and some other stuff."

"I won't ask what other stuff, at least not today. I'm still trying to wrap my head around it all."

"Understandable." She paused. "Where are you staying? I thought I might find you at the bike shop, but the men working there said they hadn't seen you."

"I don't mean this the way it sounds, but these days, I'm not sure who I can trust. If I tell you where I am, you won't tell my grandmother?"

"Promise. Totally under detective-person of interest confidentiality."

I laughed out loud, a belly laugh that felt amazingly good.

"I'll hold you to your promise. Don't make me sic my lawyer on you. I'm staying with my friend, Rachel." I gave her the address.

"It's good of her to help you out."

"She's the best. I'm glad you were okay with her being at the meeting. I'm not sure what I would have done without her."

"You also had Patrick and Joe with you. After you left, they let your grandmother know in no uncertain terms what they thought of her deception. For what it's worth, I thinks she's truly remorseful."

"Thank you for telling me, but I'm not feeling particularly charitable toward her right now. All I can think of is an old line about being sorry for what someone did or sorry for getting caught."

"That'll wear off in due time."

"I hope so."

Beth was quiet for a moment. "Confidentially, I was surprised at the identity of the vandal. Nicole Fleming appearing out of nowhere after a year and a half seems to have coincided with the incidents of vandalism at your home and at the shop. I thought it was possible she was behind it. Then I thought it was Brittany Tucker, after you told me she was stalking you. To find it was someone else entirely was unexpected."

"I know what you mean. Before, I'd have sworn Nicky wouldn't waste time with any kind of vandalism, that it's not who she is, but now I've learned things about her I never knew, so I could have been wrong. And my friends and I did think Mandy, I mean Brittany could have done it. We even talked about it after she died, that the vandalism would stop, but we couldn't have been more wrong. Jeez, my life has a theme, and it's not one I like very much."

"I've noticed."

"I guess we all have secrets. Some are more earth-shattering than others."

"What's yours?" Her voice had taken on a playful tone.

"You're the detective," I said, appreciating the lighter mood. "You figure it out."

🚲

"You look better this morning." Rachel settled into a nearby chair, her hands wrapped around her steaming mug of coffee.

"I feel better. I'm still unhappy about what happened. I don't know what I'll do about it, but lying around feeling sorry for myself doesn't accomplish much." I didn't tell her my mood improved after my bit of banter with a certain detective.

"Are you going to talk with your grandmother?"

"No, not yet. I do want to get out of the house, though. A change of scenery and some fresh air will do me good. I'll check on Joe to make sure he's not misbehaving and swing by the shop to see how the repairs are coming along."

"Sushi dinner says Joe will try to talk you into calling her."

"I'm not taking that bet. He tried last night. Why don't you leave Harvey with me? She and Shadow are getting along okay, and when I go out, I'll take her with me."

"She likes you. She's shy with most people, but not you."

We didn't need a detective to figure it out. As Rachel and I were talking, her dog had laid her head in my lap and looked up at me with supplication. Those puppy eyes were irresistible.

"She wants my bacon."

"She absolutely does, but she also wants you to pay attention to her." Rachel laughed. "If you're not careful, she'll wind up in your lap. Sure, I'll leave her with you today. She loves car rides and if you really want some exercise, take her to the dog park over on Moody. She'll run off a lot of energy chasing balls and playing with the other dogs. There's a supply of poop bags in the cupboard. Oh, and you'll need some paper towels."

After Rachel left for the day without explaining her last comment, I called my brother. "What are you doing today?"

"Oh, not much. Skydiving. Free-climbing El Capitan. Training for the Tour de France. The usual boring stuff. You?"

"I thought I'd take Rachel's dog to the park and then go to the shop. Want to come along?"

"You're a wild woman. Of course I want to go."

Half an hour later, we did a Keystone Kops routine getting him into my car. Maneuvering him with a hip to ankle cast wasn't ever easy, and Harvey insisted on helping. By the time he was seated in the car, we were both soaked with sweat and laughing.

"Next time, you're riding in the wayback. It's too damn much work getting you in the seat."

"I'm not cargo." He tried an expression of wounded dignity.

"Thirty pounds of plaster qualifies."

After another comedy scene getting Joe out of my car, we spent the next hour at the dog park, throwing soggy tennis balls and well-chewed toys for Harvey. After I picked up yet another slimy ball to throw, Rachel's advice made sense. I was glad to have paper towels handy. The dog was fun to watch, though I saw more than one other dog owner look at her with concern. The reputation pit bulls had acquired was sad. I'd never known a more lovable dog than Harvey.

Joe had sent her running after another tennis ball when my phone vibrated in my pocket. The number display was unfamiliar, but I answered it anyway, thinking the caller might have bike shop business to discuss.

"Hi, Annie."

"Nicky." I locked eyes with Joe, who mouthed "speaker." I pressed the button so he could listen. "How are you doing?"

"I'm okay. Where are you? Am I hearing barking?"

"Yeah, I'm at the dog park with Rachel's dog and Joe."

"Hey, Nicky," he said.

"Hi, Joe," she replied. "How is Rachel these days?"

"Busy with her clinic," I said.

"How's Sally?"

"Oh, you know Sally. Kicking butt and saving lives."

I exchanged a puzzled look with Joe. Were we having a casual chat, as if nothing had ever gone wrong?

"That's good." Nicky paused for a moment. "Can I see you sometime? I mean"—she spoke faster, as if hoping to head off any objection I might have—"only if you want to."

"Um, sure. Do you still like sushi? We could have dinner at Doug's, if you like."

"Yes, let's do that. I'll call you, and we can pick a day." She ended the call without warning.

"Okay, that was weird."

"Maybe she thinks the two of you will pick up where you left off?" Joe sounded as confused as I felt.

"Yeah, not gonna happen. But what the hell? It's only dinner, right?"

"It's done. Our lovely, little bike shop is finally finished. Again." I looked across the breakfast table at Rachel. "Do you believe it?" Ever the mooch, Harvey nudged my arm. "No, you can't have my bacon." I tousled her ears and her tail thumped against the table leg.

"I think you've stolen my dog." She drank some of her coffee. "I'm happy for you and Joe. If getting the shop built and ready to open hasn't been a labor of love, I don't know what is."

"Maybe we should have another party to celebrate." I slipped Harvey half a slice of bacon, which Rachel pretended not to notice. "We picked an opening date, and Joe ordered new grand opening banners." I tried not to think about the events that stopped our last attempt to open the shop. "I almost don't believe we're ready to open." Despite my best efforts, I yawned.

"Still not sleeping well?"

"You know, the days are okay because I've been busy. Between organizing the shop again and making sure Joe doesn't hurt himself, I haven't had time to think. But at night…" I shook my head slowly. "My mind refuses to shut up. Over and over, I think of what Grandma Natalie said at the police station, and I get angry again, and sad. So no, I don't sleep much."

"And you won't until you talk with her." Rachel took her dishes to the sink and turned to lean against the cabinet. "Call her. It's been three days already. Give her a chance to explain. If it goes well, then fine, but if not, I meant what I said. You can stay here as long as you like." She nodded in Harvey's direction. "You might as well since my dog has adopted you."

After she left for work, I washed the breakfast dishes and fed the animals. I put a load of laundry in and vacuumed the house. The mundane work gave me time to consider Rachel's words.

"Okay, fine." Before I could talk myself out of it, I grabbed my phone.

Grandma Natalie answered immediately. "Annie, thank goodness. I'm glad you called. Joe told me you're okay, but—"

"Please stop talking." When she was silent, I continued. "You have to understand something. I need time to think this through. What you said about Laura—"

"Your mother."

"Laura," I repeated with emphasis. "What you said turned my life upside down. Can you even begin to understand that? Do you have any idea how it feels to have everything I've believed my entire life turn out to be a lie?"

She didn't speak.

"And not just one lie. Years and *years* of lies, of letting me believe something that wasn't true. And it seems as if you and Dad were in it together." I was getting upset, so I took a deep breath. Harvey sat down next to me. She leaned against my leg and put her head in my lap. Stroking her silky ears helped to calm me. "Rachel said you wouldn't have deceived me without a good reason. I'm only calling now to see if she's right. I truly believe you wouldn't deliberately hurt me, but hurt is all I feel right now."

"We were only trying to protect you." Her voice was weak and sounded as if she might be crying. A rustling over the phone sounded like a tissue.

"We?"

"Your dad and me. We sent her away and refused to let her see you." She sighed deeply. "It's been my greatest heartbreak that my only daughter—my only child—is not a good person. Your grandfather and I could never understand where we went wrong. She started stealing when she was in elementary school, and she only got worse as she got older. She stole, she hurt people, and she didn't seem to care. I always thought she had some kind of mental illness. We took her to doctors and therapists many times, but we never got an answer that made sense. I always expected someone to tell us she's a sociopath or a narcissist, but they never did. From what little I know, it seemed to fit, but I could never get the doctors to listen." She took a deep breath, sounding shaky. "And then for a while, she was fine. She met your dad, and they got married. A couple of years later, you were born. We thought she'd had a long bad phase and she'd finally gotten her life on track." Another silence. "And then she started again. Drugs, thefts, men, worse."

"And you made her leave? That's how you treat your own daughter? To banish her from her family?"

"We didn't know what else to do. We put up with her destructive behavior, bailed her out of jail more times than maybe we should have. But when she put you in danger, your dad called the police. She was arrested, but they usually let her go without bail. It was the last straw. You weren't safe with her."

"How was I not safe?"

"She would take you with her when she met men she slept with or when she bought drugs. A couple of times, she left you in the car by yourself. One time was on a hot day, and paramedics were called. Another time, she left you alone in a car overnight when she'd bought drugs and passed out in the dealer's bed. The police arrested her both times. That's why your grandfather and I took you in. Your dad tried to make their marriage work, but she'd made her choices. He moved in with us. Finally, the court took away her parental rights, and we refused to let her see you. You were too young to understand what was going on, so we told you she was gone."

"And I thought you meant she was dead." My anger rose. "You let your lie rest on semantics, on the assumption made by a child that 'gone' was a nice way of saying 'dead.'"

"Yes. I'm not proud of it, but it was easier that way. If you'd known she was alive and living somewhere else, you wouldn't have let it go. It was still hard. You were upset and sad for a long time, and it broke our hearts, even though we did it to protect you. Your dad and I wanted you to have a good life, a normal life, and we didn't think you would if you spent your time looking for your mother. We only did it because we loved you and wanted you to be happy and safe."

I was silent for a moment. "I have to go."

"Please come home." Her tone was pleading. "Please."

"I can't. Not for a while. I need time to work through this. And to be honest, I don't feel I can trust you right now."

"I understand." She was almost sobbing. "I'm so sorry."

"And please don't call me. I need more time. I'll be in touch."

I ended the call.

Chapter Eighteen

That evening, I sat in my usual booth at Doug's Café, waiting for my dinner companion to arrive. The server brought menus, but I was too distracted to pick one up. Between flashbacks about Mandy and nervousness at seeing Nicky again, I'd drunk half of my ice water by the time Nicky came through the door.

Seeing her from across the busy restaurant was jolting. For the past year and a half, I thought she was dead. The few seconds of our encounter at the coffee shop had been a shock and made me question my sanity. Of course, her phone calls had settled that question.

Then there was her appearance. If I hadn't known she was meeting me for dinner, I wouldn't have recognized her at first. She was rail thin with an unhealthy pallor to her skin. She'd always been slender, but now she appeared almost anorexic. Her hair, which had always been lovely, was lank and dull. Only her smile was unchanged. The split second look I'd gotten at the coffee shop hadn't revealed any of this. While I waited for her to join me, I also reminded myself she'd been wearing a hoodie, a garment that could conceal a lot of details about a person.

I got up to meet her, and we hugged awkwardly for a few seconds. I resumed my seat, and she slid into the booth opposite me. We waited while the server brought Nicky a glass of ice water and topped mine off.

"It's a bit surreal, seeing you after all this time." I wasn't sure I could conceal my concern about her appearance.

"I know what you mean."

An uncomfortable silence descended, so we picked up our menus. Choosing our meal gave us something to talk about for a few minutes, dispelling much of my discomfort by the time we gave our order to the young woman who waited on us. Nicky seemed to relax as well.

"Do you mind if I ask a few questions?"

"I'll tell you whatever you want to know, if I can." She started to reach across the table to take my hand in a familiar gesture, but then thought better of it. "Sorry. Old habits."

"It's okay," I said, but I still put my hands in my lap. I thought for a few moments, deciding where to start. "Why did you run away? After the fire, I mean. Where did you go?"

She bit her lip before answering. "I was afraid. I'd stashed those chemicals in the shed, and when I saw the news report about the fire, I knew the police would be after me. I couldn't risk being arrested."

"Again." I said it before I could edit myself.

"Yes," she conceded. "Again. I'm sorry you had to find out about that the way you did."

"I wouldn't have if you'd trusted me enough to tell me about it." I took another long drink of water. At this rate, I'd need to find the ladies' room soon. "In all the years we were together and with all the plans we made, you'd completely hidden an important part of your life from me. When I found out, I was upset and angry. I questioned whether I'd really known you at all. Can you understand that?"

"Yes, and I'm sorry. I was afraid to tell you. You were amazing to me, and I loved you so much. I thought you'd leave me if you knew." She met my gaze. "I should have trusted you, and I apologize. It's entirely my fault."

"Did you leave town after the fire?"

"Yes, I stayed for a few days, and then I had to go. I'd been back here less than a week when I saw you at the coffee shop."

"Did you know about the woman who was found with your bag?"

"Only later. From what I was told, by the time she was found, I was nowhere near here."

"Your parents identified her as you. Did you know that?"

"They told me after I came back."

"So you let them think you were dead?"

"It was easier for everyone."

"For you, you mean." I started to feel angry. "Not for me. Not for your family." I made myself calm down. "They had a nice funeral for you."

"Mom told me about it." She wiped a tear away. "I'll never be able to make it up to them. Or you."

"Why come back now?"

"Mom is sick. She's had two major surgeries and has been in and out of the hospital. Her prognosis isn't very good, so I had to see her, in case it was the last time." She looked down at her hands. "I can't explain why, but I still shouldn't be here. It's not safe for them or anyone around me."

"Why?" Nicky had never been one for hyperbole, so her words definitely piqued my interest.

She shook her head. "I can't say. You have no reason to trust me, but I'm asking you to anyway. I'm sorry."

I decided to let it slide, at least for the time being. "How is your mom doing?"

She brightened. "Much better. Seems like she'll be okay, though she has a long recovery ahead."

Our conversation was interrupted by the arrival of our food. The server put two serving platters of assorted sushi rolls and sashimi before us and left. We didn't talk much while we ate, and by the time our meal was over, I'd lost almost all the desire I'd felt to grill her for information.

Nicky also seemed more relaxed, as well.

There was one more thing I wanted to know. "Are you using?"

She was surprised. "What?"

"Your product. Are you using it?"

She gazed across the restaurant for a moment before meeting my eyes. "Not anymore. Before I came back to Portland, I had a job cleaning offices at night and flipping burgers during the day. I'm clean."

I tried to choose my words carefully. "I don't mean this the way it sounds, but you don't look too good."

"I know. Working on it." She paused, thinking. "I need to tell you something."

"Okay." I waited, wondering what was next.

She appeared to debate with herself for another few seconds. "I wasn't sure I should come here tonight."

"Why?"

"You mentioned trust? Why I didn't tell you about my police record?"

"Yes, and other stuff."

"And you told me before about the police investigating you, thinking I was dead? And you've asked me to provide proof I'm alive? I didn't have any way to know if you'd have the police here waiting for me." She blew out a breath. "I guess I had to trust you after all." She tried a faint smile.

"I wouldn't do that." I decided not to mention I'd considered it. "After I saw you at the coffee shop, I told the detectives I'd seen you. They were skeptical. But then you called during Grandma Natalie's party"—I shoved the thought of my grandmother out of my mind—"and Rachel and Sally heard your voice, and confirmed it for them. They know you're alive, but they still need proof before they'll close the case and let me off the hook."

"But do you believe I didn't start the fire?" She had more tears in her eyes. "I loved your dad, and I loved the bike shop. What I did was wrong, putting that stuff in the shed, but I would never have hurt him."

On impulse, I reached across the table and took her hand. "I believe you." For a split second, I wondered if I should, but perhaps it was a subject for another time.

Our conversation ebbed and flowed while we ate, and our initial awkwardness faded. She asked about Sally and Rachel, so I filled her in on their lives. When she wanted to know how Grandma Natalie was doing, I hesitated. I saw no need to tell her about the most recent events, discovering how I'd been blindsided by the news that my mother was alive, but I told her about the motorcycle crash and my grandmother's boyfriend. Through all of it, she seemed relaxed and happy to have news of old friends.

For myself, I noticed she was far less forthcoming about where she'd been. I was sure there was a story there, but I'd apparently have to be patient to learn it.

We debated ordering dessert and decided against it.

"How about showing me the shop?" She smiled, looking more like the Nicky I remembered and had loved. The memory made my heart ache. "I drove by a couple days ago. It looks good."

"Sure, let's go. I'll tell you the long story about what it's taken to get it this far. It's a tale of trial and tribulation, and of woe." I tried to sound melodramatic, which made her laugh. It was good to hear, but even her laugh was sad.

We paid our bill and went to our cars. I smiled to myself when I saw hers. Damn silver minivan. I made a mental note to tell Rachel.

Twenty minutes later, we parked side by side in the bike shop lot. When we got out of our cars, the security guard approached us, flashlight in hand.

"Can I help you ladies? This is private property."

"Hi, Dave," I said. "It's just me. I'm showing my friend the shop, and then we'll get out of your hair. I didn't mean to worry you."

"Oh, sorry, Annie. I didn't recognize you at first. Sometimes those motion-activated lights still don't work right."

I scanned the lot, noticing for the first time it wasn't as well-lit as usual. "Interesting. I thought the electricians fixed it. Thanks for letting me know." I took my phone from my pocket and texted Joe about the lights. He responded with a thumbs-up emoji.

Dave aimed his flashlight at the front of the shop. Without the floodlights on, it was difficult to see the colors we'd painted.

"It looks like the original," Nicky said. "It's perfect."

"It's even prettier in the daylight. We wanted to recreate what Dad built, but we expanded it. I had to have the original colors."

"My dad would have liked it too," Dave said. "He brought us here from Mexico City when I was a baby." He handed me a flashlight. "You can give it back to me when you leave." Moments later, I heard his car door close.

"He stays here all night, mostly sitting in his car." I told Nicky about our vandalism problem. "Even though we have a first-rate security system, I'm glad he's here."

My phone rang before we went inside, where I switched on the lights. "Go ahead and look around. I'll be there in a moment." As she moved away, I answered the call.

"How's it going?" Rachel's curiosity had gotten the better of her.

"You couldn't wait for me to get home?"

"Yes, but I didn't want to. Details. Now."

I gave her a quick synopsis, including my surprise at Nicky's appearance. "She said she's not using, but I don't know. Anyway, I'm giving her a quick tour of the shop, and then we're done. I should be home in an hour or so. Oh, and get this. She drives a silver minivan."

"Damn rolling boxes." Minivans were Rachel's favorite *bête noire*. "Hurry up. Harvey's taken to standing by the door waiting for you. Even Shadow biting her tail won't make her move."

We ended our call, and I joined Nicky. She was standing in the middle of the main room, turning in a slow circle and taking it all in. We still needed to put a couple of the bike racks back up, but the rest of the shop looked good.

"It's beautiful. Your dad would have loved it."

I had to agree. "Joe wants to have bike maintenance classes here. Dad always wanted to, but the space was too small. That's partly why we enlarged the building." I led her toward the back of the main room. "Here's the checkout stand, of course."

"Isn't this the counter your dad built?"

"Yes, it is. I don't know how it survived the fire, but it did. We also saved a few other things." I thought about where this project had started. "We tried to salvage part of the original building, but in the end, it made more sense to tear it down and start fresh. There was too much water and smoke damage, and the new building let us expand."

I point to another corner. "Coffee and snack bar, complete with a fancy espresso machine. It's all set and ready to go. When we open, I'll stock it with fruit, and muffins, and whatnot."

"You dad would have liked this."

"He always wanted his shop to be a place where bike riders could socialize, hang out with their friends, maybe meet before going on a ride. And he got some of it, but the snack bar will help to promote it even more, I think. We'll have coffee and cold drinks, and a place for riders to refill their frame bottles."

"Will you have bottles with the shop name?"

Every knowledgeable cyclist took at least one bottle of water on each ride, safely tucked away in a holder attached to the bike frame. It was common practice for shops to sell bottles with their name on them. They were an excellent marketing tool.

"Good idea. I'm surprised Joe never suggested it." I took my phone from my pocket and texted my brother. *We need Velasquez Cycles frame bottles.*

Within seconds, he texted back. *Great idea. Look at you thinking like a bike shop owner!* I sent him an emoji with its tongue sticking out and pocketed my phone.

I was showing Nicky the stockroom, now almost overrun with the new bikes Joe had assembled, when I heard a sharp noise from outside. It sounded almost as if someone had dropped a book on a hard surface. I stopped talking for a moment, but I didn't hear anything else. Situated as we were in a mixed residential and light industrial neighborhood, unusual noises were—oddly enough—not unusual.

But I still waited to make sure the noise wouldn't repeat. Even with Dave in the parking lot and security cameras everywhere, I was wary. The shop had a long history of violence, starting with the fire that destroyed the original building and took my father from me up through my own mother driving a stolen truck through the front of the building and almost killing Joe, to say nothing of repeated thefts and vandalism, culminating in the death of a young woman at the front door. There was too much history in the place for me to be completely at ease there.

I waited another several seconds and even though I didn't hear anything else unusual, my nerves were tingling and the hair on the back of my neck and arms was raised. I shook it off and tried not to think "what now?" and continued talking with Nicky.

"This room is for merchandise we don't have room for out front. There's a restroom in the far corner near the back door." I turned back to her to say, "And that's the whole thing."

Or that's what I would have said.

Instead, I found myself looking into Nicky's terrified eyes, the words stuck in my throat. Someone behind her had put an arm over her shoulder and a gloved hand over her mouth. The other hand pointed a gun at me.

"Sit down." The gun waved toward a nearby folding chair. "Now."

Unable to take my eyes off the gun, I did as I was told.

The intruder shoved Nicky toward a second chair. "Sit. Don't move."

Only then did I tear my eyes away from the gun and focus on the person's face.

Laura Natalie Lindberg Velasquez.

My mother.

"Aren't you going to say hello to your long-lost mommy?"

I didn't speak, but looked into her eyes as long as I could without wavering. What I saw was worlds away from the pleasant blonde woman I'd met outside. Where before she'd worn her hair up in a style reminiscent of 1960s Doris Day movies, now she had it pulled back in a severe bun at the nape. Anger, if not hostility, replaced her previously friendly expression. And the coldness in her eyes was, in a word, frightening.

"I asked you a question. Answer when your mother speaks to you."

I decided cooperation might be in my best interests. "Hello, mother. It's been a long time."

She appeared slightly mollified. "Not long at all, Annie." She waved her gun toward the front of the shop. "Out there, while you were working."

"True, but I didn't know it, did I?"

Laura shifted her attention to Nicky. "And who are you?"

"I'm Nicky, Annie's friend."

"You used to be pretty, didn't you? Now you look like shit. What happened to you?" Nicky didn't speak until Laura barked, "I asked you a question."

"Um, poor choices, I guess."

"I should say so. At least one of those choices has to do with methamphetamine. Am I right?"

Nicky nodded.

"Speak up, young lady. Use your words when an adult asks you a question." Laura's voice was loud and sharp.

"Yes, ma'am." Nicky sounded as if she might cry. "You're right about the meth. But I'm clean now."

"I'm clean now." Laura mocked her with a high tone. "Yeah, right." She leaned forward until her face was mere inches from Nicky's. "And a little streetwalking here and there? Am I right?"

Nicky's eyes met mine briefly.

Laura grabbed Nicky's shoulder and shook her. "Don't look at her. Look at me. Answer my question."

"Yes, ma'am."

"Yes, ma'am, what?"

"Yes, ma'am, I worked the streets when I had to."

"Pimp?"

"I'm sorry?"

"Did you have a pimp?"

"No, ma'am."

Laura stood up straight and backed away a few steps. "Good. At least you could keep your own money. You earned it, right?"

"Yes, ma'am."

"Damn straight." She laughed humorlessly. "Straight. Did you hear that? I made a joke." She looked back and forth between Nicky and me. "Yeah, I know what you are, you two. Cute little girlfriends, making like an actual couple." Animosity shone in her eyes. "Well, you know what? Who gives a fuck? Life shit on you anyway, didn't it? That's how it always is. There ain't no Hallmark moments in the real world."

She put her gun down on a nearby shelf and slid a worn backpack off her shoulders. Opening the bag, she took out a pack of cigarettes and a disposable lighter. She offered the pack to us, and when we declined, she shook one loose and lit it. The sharp smell of the smoke made me sneeze.

She pocketed the gun and stood with her back to us in the doorway leading to the main room of the shop. To the left of where I sat, I could see out the nearest window toward the front. Where was Dave? I remembered the sharp sound I'd heard, and dread pervaded my body. Laura had a gun and seemed willing to use it. Had she shot him? I hoped he was alive, but I started to lose hope that he could help us. We might be on our own here.

To my right stood the back door, a tempting sight. I exchanged glances with Nicky and tilted my head toward the door.

"Don't even think about it." Laura was more observant than I realized. She finished her cigarette and threw the butt on the floor, never taking her eyes off us. "Move from those chairs and I'll shoot you. Don't think for a moment I won't. You can ask your friend outside."

My worst fears confirmed, I believed her, and if Nicky's terrified eyes were any indication, she did as well.

Laura went into the main room. She apparently stepped outside briefly, because I heard traffic noises for a few seconds. Before we could move, she came back in, and I heard the front door lock mechanism turn. She returned to the stockroom, lit another cigarette, took the gun from her pocket, and put it back on the shelf.

"So you're a part owner now?"

"Yes."

She pulled up another folding chair and sat directly in front of me, close enough that the stench of burning tobacco made me want to back away.

"What's wrong with you?" Her hostile tone was back.

"The cigarette—" I tried not to sneeze but couldn't stop it.

She slapped me hard across the face, rocking my head back far enough to strike the metal back of the chair. I shook my head to clear it.

"How many owners are there now?"

"Two." I tried breathing shallowly. If I sneezed again, she might very well knock me to the floor.

"Where's the other one?" She turned to Nicky. "You?"

Nicky shook her head before remembering to speak. "No, I'm visiting from out of town."

"Then get the other owner down here. Where's your phone? I know you have one."

"It's in my pocket." I carefully reached in and extracted it.

She grabbed it from me and activated the screen. "Who's Rachel? Another one of your dyke friends? Who else do you have on here? Natalie, of course. My own dear mother. She couldn't get rid of me fast enough. Old bitch should have died long ago." She scrolled some more. "Joe, Brad. Oh, here we go. Dad." She thrust the phone into my hand. "Call him. Tell him to get his ass down here."

I took the phone, not sure what to do. Unable to help myself, I glanced at Nicky.

"What? It's a damn phone call. So call already."

"Um, I—I can't call him."

"Why the hell not?" She stood up abruptly, knocking her chair over. "I want him here, and I want him here now." She started pacing back and forth, toward the gun and away from it again.

I gave Nicky a warning shake of the head when I saw her looking at it.

"I burned that bastard out of this place once before, and I'll do it again." Laura was ranting, almost as if she'd forgotten we were there. "Him and his precious bike shop. Center of the fucking universe." She wheeled and got back in my face. "Except for you. You were the only thing more important to him than this place." She waved an arm to indicate the shop. "Bikes and sweet little Annie. Did he know you played for the pervert team?" She didn't wait for an answer. "Of course not. Nice Catholic boy would have been disgusted with you."

I couldn't keep quiet. "He knew I'm a lesbian. He and Nicky were good friends, and he also liked my other friends."

She slapped me again. "Don't lie to me."

"I'm not lying." I tasted blood at the corner of my mouth. "He was good to us."

"He was good to his own dick, you mean. Couldn't keep his pants on to save his life." She righted her chair and sat down. "And you know what? I was so stupid I still loved him, no matter what, even when he took up with that Black bitch down the street." She seemed introspective for a moment, the woman I'd met outside surfacing briefly. But then she was gone, and the angry woman who held us captive was back.

"Then they made me leave. Had me arrested on some kind of fantasy charge. They actually called me an unfit mother. Can you believe it?"

"I've never heard—" I started to say, but she slapped me again, harder this time, hard enough to cause stars to appear in my vision. I blinked tears away.

"Lies and more lies. The more you talk, the more you sound like your grandmother. Now shut the fuck up and call. Get that philandering bastard down here."

"I'm telling you, I can't do it."

She got right in my face, her nicotine breath making me wince. "Why the fuck not?"

I was afraid she might knock me out if she hit me again, so I rushed to say, "He's dead."

She sat back and squinted at me, as if trying to decide if I was telling the truth. "You're lying to me. You still have him in your phone."

"I'm not lying. He died in the fire here about a year and a half ago." My throat tightened at the memory, but I refused to let it show.

"Are you lying to me?" She leaned in, staring into my eyes with a malevolence I'd never thought possible.

"Call Natalie. She'll tell you I'm not lying."

She leaped to her feet, laughing and sounding delighted. "My plan worked. I got rid of the shop and Manny, and totally got away with it." She danced around the room, hollering with glee, apparently unconcerned she'd confessed to murder and arson.

Nicky and I exchanged glances of disbelief. She might have hated my father enough to want him dead, but this much glee was frightening. She danced through the shop, while Nicky and I sat frozen in place.

"She's nuts," Nicky whispered. "Or high."

"Or both."

"The gun?"

In celebrating my dad's death, Laura had neglected to take her gun off the shelf. "No, don't . . ." but Nicky was already moving.

Keeping an eye on the door, Nicky crouched down and crabwalked rapidly toward the shelf. She reached over its edge and almost had the gun in her hand when Laura returned.

"Get away from there," she bellowed, and kicked Nicky in the chest. When Nicky toppled backward, Laura grabbed the gun. In one smooth move, she shot her.

The sound of the shot was so loud, I hardly heard when Nicky screamed and fell to the floor. I sat frozen in the chair, scarcely able to breathe. Blood spread across Nicky's chest. After a few moments, her arms collapsed at her sides. She went still.

I leaped up. "No!"

Nicky lay on her back, motionless and bleeding.

Laura grabbed me by the shoulder and shoved me back into my chair, gun pointed inches from my face. She was screaming, but I couldn't make out her words. I dared not move, afraid I might suffer Nicky's fate. Tears poured from my eyes.

Laura went back to the front of the shop and peered out the front windows, muttering "I hope nobody heard that." All I could do was sob.

After a few seconds, Nicky's fingers twitched, and she inhaled sharply, gasping. She was alive. She opened her eyes and started to speak, but I could see Laura coming back to the stockroom.

"Play dead," I whispered, hoping Nicky could hear me. "Don't move."

Laura came into the room and nudged Nicky with the toe of her shoe. "Bet you didn't think your mom could do that, did you?"

My hearing had returned enough to let me hear her, but I didn't answer. My head was pounding. A trickle of blood ran down my neck from where the back of my head had impacted the chair when she hit me.

She shrugged dismissively. "Not like she's the first one. And not even the first one here, since I took care of that little girl who was following you everywhere. I couldn't let her hurt you, now could I?" She barked out another humorless laugh. "But getting Manny off the planet is the real prize." She pocketed her gun. As she left the stockroom, she said, "Don't even think about moving."

My mind was whirling. *She killed Mandy? Out of some misguided impulse to protect me?* The irony was mind-boggling.

She went out the front door of the shop again. I started to hope she wasn't coming back when the door opened and she returned, carrying two red cannisters. She disappeared from view toward the back of the shop. After a minute, maybe less, the distinctive odor of gasoline filled my nose, and tendrils of smoke wafted near the ceiling of the main room.

I bolted from my chair and knelt beside Nicky. I had to get her outside. The back door was only a few feet away. As I pulled her toward me, hoping I could lift her, the front door shattered. What appeared to be a dozen police officers burst into the shop. I leaped to my feet and yelled for help. All but one of the officers rushed past the storeroom door toward the back of the shop.

The last one ran to me, and I almost fell into his arms from relief.

"Come with me!" Carlos shouted over the noise of the confrontation outside the storeroom. "We have to get you out of here."

"No, help Nicky." I pointed to where she lay. "She's been shot."

He grabbed his radio, and within seconds, paramedics surrounded Nicky. Carlos tried to pull me from the room, but I refused to go.

"Is she alive? Please tell me." I was pleading, tears streaming down my face again.

"Yes, but she's weak," one of the medics said. "We have to get her to a hospital now."

The paramedics put her on a stretcher and took her out the front door. Carlos and I followed. I watched as Nicky's ambulance left with lights flashing and sirens wailing.

Carlos led me away from the shop and behind one of the cruisers. He stayed with me, standing guard, his eyes riveted on the door of the shop and his hand hovering near his holstered gun. When I stepped away from him, he grabbed my arm.

"Stay here." His tone of voice was commanding.

Chaos reigned inside the shop. Officers shouted "gun!" Through one of the windows, I saw an officer with his weapon in his hand. I suspected he wasn't the only one. They repeatedly commanded Laura to drop her gun, apparently in vain. She kept screaming her defiance.

Smoke began to stream out the door, but the firefighters held their position, hose at the ready.

Two gunshots rang out, and an officer fell to the floor. One of his colleagues knelt next to him. Multiple shots followed, and then none.

"Drop your gun!"

"Get on your knees!"

Through the window, I saw the officers rush toward the back of the store, where the checkout stand was. After another minute, two police officers led Laura from the burning shop with her handcuffed hands behind her back.

As soon as Laura was outside the building, the paramedics rushed in. I was relieved to see the fallen officer standing by the door. He was alive.

Blood ran down Laura's arm, but she still struggled against the restraints and screamed she'd done nothing wrong.

The officers held her against the cruiser and called to the remaining paramedics. One of the EMTs ran over to examine her bloody arm and wrapped a bandage around it. From where I stood, I heard them say she had a minor bullet wound and would need treatment. The officers shoved her into the back seat of their cruiser and closed the door.

Carlos said, "And that, ladies and gents, is why we wear vests."

The sight of the wounded officer up on his feet and Carlos's slight attempt at humor helped me breathe easier.

After the last of the police officers left the building, the firefighters rushed in with their hoses gushing water and put out the flames. They reported only minor damage from the fire, limited to the area around the snack bar, but I knew there had to be water everywhere. I was happy to see that Sally was one of the first responders.

"Damn, Annie. What do we have to do to keep this place in one piece?" She enveloped me in a hug, not easy with her firefighter gear on. "Who was that woman?"

"My mother." At her shocked expression, I nodded. "It's a long story. I only found out myself four days ago."

"I'm going to want to hear about it." She held me at arm's length by my shoulders. "Your face looks like someone's used it for boxing practice. She do that to you?" When I nodded, she said, "Wow," and pushed me toward the second ambulance. "Go get checked out." When I protested, she insisted. "Go or I'll carry you. And don't think I won't."

While the paramedic was tending to me, Patrick arrived with Joe and Rachel. I filled them in about what had happened. Even though I'd lived through it, the story sounded unreal to me.

"Young lady." The paramedic interrupted my tale. "You have to go to the hospital."

"What? Why?"

"I'm pretty sure you have a concussion, and you need stitches on the back of your head. You might also have some facial fractures. Did someone bounce your head off a concrete floor or something?"

"Yeah, something like that."

He pointed to the ambulance. "Hop in."

"I don't need an ambulance," I protested. "I'm not that badly injured."

The paramedic turned to my brother and friends. "Will you make sure she gets to the emergency room?" To me, he said, "A concussion is nothing to fool around with. And while I think you have some fractures, I can't tell how bad they are. You need x-rays."

"Okay, fine, I'll go."

"And," Patrick said, "we'll make sure she gets there immediately."

They did.

Chapter Nineteen

The first thing I saw the next morning was a phlebotomist jabbing a needle into my arm.

"Did you want to be a vampire when you were a kid?"

He put a bandage over the puncture mark. "I'll never tell," he said archly as he took his kit and left my room.

I rubbed my eyes, trying to get them to focus. My head ached, and my face felt three times its normal size. I found a plastic cup of water on the bedside table and tried to drink, but half of it dribbled down my face. Fortunately, the nurse arrived in time to rescue me from a near drowning.

"You need a straw." The nurse put one into the cup, and I tried again with better results. "You'll probably have to use one for a while."

She took my temperature and blood pressure, chatting amiably. "You're doing okay. Better than I would have thought for someone who looks as if she went twelve rounds with Mohammad Ali." She gave me a reassuring smile.

"Not Ali. My mother."

Her smile disappeared. "Yeah, I heard. I'm sorry you had to go through that." She put her stethoscope into her pocket and turned to leave.

"What about my friend, Nicky? She was shot. Do you know how she is?"

She paused before speaking. "Depending on how bad her wound was, she's probably in the ICU. I'll check for you." She paused at the door. "Your friends were here earlier, but it was before visiting hours, so they're coming back this afternoon. The doctor will be in to see you in a while, but the police detectives are already here. You okay to talk with them?"

I nodded and tried to drink more water. Straws were definitely the way to go.

"Hi Annie." Beth O'Brien and Ted Winston stood beside my bed. In a few moments, Detective Grant, who took up a position at the foot of the bed, joined them. If my head hadn't felt like an entire drum corps was practicing inside, I'd have rolled my eyes. Macho and Mini-Macho were not who I wanted to see first thing in the morning.

Or any other time, for that matter.

"How are you feeling?"

"The nurse told me I look like a punching bag. What do you think? Do you know how Nicky is doing? Did she make it?"

"Yes, she is alive." Beth smiled. "Funny how often we say that about her."

"She's a survivor. What did the doctors say?"

"She was in surgery for several hours last night. The bullet missed the most important stuff, like her aorta, but it did puncture a lung. She had some internal bleeding, but she's expected to make a full recovery."

"Is she awake? Have you talked with her?"

Beth paused before speaking. "To say we're not her favorite people is an understatement. She insisted all she'd talk about is what happened last night, about your mother—"

"Laura," I said, knowing I sounded harsh. "She doesn't deserve to be called my mother."

"Nicky told us what Laura did, even though she's none too happy about the officer we posted outside her room. I think she only talked to us for you. Despite everything, she cares for you." She glanced at her partner, who held a notepad and pen. "Even though Nicky told us her version of what happened, we need to hear it from you. Are you up for it?"

I sat up in my bed, propped up with pillows. "Sure, as long as you'll get me some more ice water." Beth dispatched Macho and Mini-Macho to find some ice water for me, much to their displeasure. I didn't care. They owed me big time. Then I laid it all out, from Laura's appearance in the shop with a gun in her hand, what she'd said, how she struck me repeatedly, when she shot Nicky, and her attempt to burn the shop. When I told her she'd admitted to killing Mandy and setting the fire that killed my dad, the detectives exchanged significant looks.

"Would you testify to that?"

"Of course, but isn't a lot of this stuff hearsay?" Maybe I watched too many police shows. Where was Alan Shore when you needed him?

"It's up to the prosecutor. The good news is your security cameras probably caught all of it, including audio, so I don't think it's much of a problem. Anything else?"

I was suddenly sleepy, but then I remembered. "Wait, what about Dave? She didn't kill Dave, did she?"

"Who's Dave?" Detective Grant spoke for the first time.

"The security guard we hired. He was outside when Nicky and I went into the shop. He's a good guy. Please tell me she didn't kill him."

"No, he's fine, or he will be," Beth said. "He told us he got out of his car to ask why she was on the property, and she shot him before she went inside. He called for help before he passed out. The paramedics found him on the ground near his car. By the time you were outside, he was already in the emergency room and heading into surgery."

"I heard the shot, but I didn't realize what it was until she showed up inside the shop with her gun. I'm glad he'll be okay. Where's Laura? I know she was arrested. I hope she's still in jail."

"She is currently sitting in a holding cell downtown. The district attorney is waiting for us to finalize our investigation, and then he'll work up appropriate charges. We'll need to talk with you in more detail when you're feeling better. Since we got great video and audio, it shouldn't take long to move the case along. I think it's safe to say she won't be on the streets for years to come, if ever." She turned to the detectives who had accompanied her, but who'd had the good grace to stay quiet. "Let's go, guys. Let Annie rest." She took my hand in hers. "We'll talk more when you're feeling better." She squeezed my fingers briefly and left the room, trailed by the other two detectives.

They'd been gone only long enough for me to promise myself never to wash my hand again and start to doze off when the doctor came in.

"Well, young lady, you had quite a night." He was the cheerful, friendly type, and I liked him immediately. "How often do you get into fistfights?"

"Never, including this time, which I suspect you know." I would have given him my best squinty-eyed expression, but the swelling in my face prevented it. "What's the verdict?"

"You'll live." He tried to look somber but couldn't pull it off. "I mean, it's true, but it isn't what you want to know. You have a severe concussion, and four hairline fractures in the bones of your face. That woman knows how to throw a punch." He tried for humor again. "What did you do to make her so mad?"

"I was born." When he looked concerned, I waved it away. "That's my working theory at the moment. It's either that or she's nuttier than a fruitcake."

"I imagine you have a whopper of a headache."

"Yes." My voice was raspy. "It even hurts to talk."

"I've prescribed some pain medications and something to take the swelling down." He touched my face carefully. "I want you to stay another night and if you're feeling better tomorrow, you can go home. Deal?"

I gave him a thumbs up and fell asleep before he made it out the door.

True to their word, my brother and friends returned to visit. By the time they arrived, I'd had some sleep and was feeling better. The doctor's pain pills had banished most of my headache, and I could almost drink water without drooling on myself.

Patrick arrived first, pushing Joe in the wheelchair. Rachel and Sally weren't far behind. Sally carried the biggest fruit basket I'd ever seen.

"There's enough stuff in here to supply a small country with fruit," she said, putting the basket on a side table.

"I know what's better than fruit." A new voice came from near the door. I didn't see anyone there, but an arm extended into the opening, holding a plate of one of my favorite foods.

"Freddy? Mo?"

They stepped into the doorway. "Of course. Who else would bring you the world's best pastrami?"

My mouth watered, despite the doctor's orders to eat only soft foods until my face healed. "You're torturing me, but I love both of you anyway. Come on in. Everyone remembers everyone, right? I don't think I'm up to introductions right now."

Freddy sat the plate of pastrami near the fruit basket, close enough I could smell it but far enough out of reach to keep me from trying to eat some.

The nurse came into the room. "You know you're restricted to two visitors at a time, right?"

My latest dose of pain medication was taking hold, so I said, "There's only two." She raised a skeptical eyebrow, which I ignored. "There's those two," pointing at Patrick and Joe, "and those two," pointing to Sally and Rachel, "and those two," pointing to Freddy and Mo. I looked at the nurse in triumph bolstered by pain pills. "See, two."

The nurse shook her head. "You know, I remember you from when your grandmother was a patient here. I'll give up now and save myself a lot of stress."

"Joe, where's Grandma Natalie? Isn't she going to come visit me?" I'd asked her to give me space, but didn't circumstances call for a détente, even if only briefly?

"I called her and got her voicemail. I told her what happened, a short version anyway. She hasn't called me back. I've tried her again a few times, but no luck."

I let his words sink in for a moment. "It would have to be hard for her, wouldn't it? To know her own daughter did this? Maybe she doesn't want to face me." Despite the depth of my feelings of betrayal at my grandmother's deception, I could still have some empathy for her. "Maybe she needs space as much as I do."

They all stayed to visit for well over an hour, ignoring the disapproving glares of the hospital staff. I reminded them several times to keep the noise down, but my efforts were largely in vain.

After a while, the nurse returned. "You really have to leave now. Visiting hours are almost over."

"Will you let them do me one favor before they go?" She raised an inquiring eyebrow, which I took for assent. "Will you let them take me to see my friend who's here? Her name is Nicole Fleming. She had surgery last night. I don't know her room number."

The nurse stepped out of the room to get the information and returned with a wheelchair and a slip of paper with a number written on it.

"Ten minutes. And not all of you. Two, tops, and a real two this time. Then you're back in bed." She wasn't much older than I was, but her tone still said "young lady" at the end of her sentence.

After some minor squabbling about who would have the honor of pushing me around the hospital, Rachel and Sally prevailed. Patrick and Joe left, followed by Freddy and Mo. Before they left, the two women made me promise to visit them in Charbonneau as soon as I was well enough.

Encumbered by the IV line and the pole holding the bag of fluid, I managed to get into the wheelchair without too much of my backside showing.

"Good thing I can go home tomorrow. No more drafty gowns for me."

"Plus, Harvey is downright despondent," Rachel said. "She sits by the front door and refuses to move until I make her." At Sally's questioning look, Rachel explained. "Annie stole my dog."

"I can't help it if she loves me," I said. "How's Shadow doing?"

"He tries to act sad, but then he pesters Harvey to play with him, which ruins the effect for both of them."

"Shadow's always been a drama queen. Okay, let's go."

They wheeled me into a nearby elevator and up to the floor where Nicky was being treated. Her room was easy to spot since it was the only one with a police officer outside the door.

We approached the room, and the officer stood in front of the door, stopping us from going in. I explained that Nicky was a friend, and she and I had been injured in the same incident. "I need a few minutes to check on her." When he hesitated, I said, "Please call Detective Beth O'Brien. She'll tell you it's okay for me to visit. Two minutes. Promise."

He relented and let us inside, but I heard him talking on his phone.

Rachel leaned down and whispered, "Name dropper."

"Whatever works."

Nicky lay still under the blanket, which was to be expected since she'd had surgery only the night before. Her face was even more pale than before, accentuating the dark circles around her eyes. She had multiple IV lines running into her arms. Wires snaked out from under her blanket and up to a machine with a multicolored screen. It beeped quietly.

All of it was too familiar from the time Grandma Natalie was injured in the motorcycle crash. Seeing it made me miss my grandmother.

Rachel pushed my wheelchair close to the side of the bed. I gently took Nicky's hand in my own, being careful of the IV lines.

She stirred and opened her eyes a slit. She managed a small smile when she saw me.

"How are you feeling?" I was almost afraid to ask.

"Like someone shot me." Her voice was hoarse. She cleared her throat and asked for some ice chips. I gave her a few and moistened her lips with a small sponge that lay on her bedside table. "Thank you."

"The docs say you'll be okay."

Nicky clutched my hand. "Hard to believe someone that terrible is your mother."

"I'm still trying to figure it out myself."

"What does Grandma Natalie say?"

"Not much, since I haven't spoken with her yet."

Nicky let go of my hand and relaxed into her pillow. "One thing's for sure. Your mother's apple tree was definitely at the top of a cliff."

"What?" I glanced at Rachel and Sally. Maybe Nicky's pain medications were addling her mind. "What do you mean?"

"When you fell off, you fell a long way away from her." She closed her eyes, but kept talking. "Down the cliff, into a creek, over a waterfall, into a river…" Her voiced faded away, but she roused herself long enough to say, "I'm glad you did."

"I couldn't agree more," I said, but she was asleep.

We sat with Nicky for a few more minutes until the police officer encouraged us to leave.

"I'm glad you're okay," he said. "Detective O'Brien told me what happened. If you want to come back tomorrow for another visit, I'll be here."

We thanked him, and Rachel pushed my wheelchair back to my room.

The next afternoon, I was living in luxury at Rachel's house. The doctor had come by my hospital room in the morning to let me know he was discharging me, but only if I agreed to take things easy. My headaches had reduced to a dull roar, easily treated with Advil, and a lot of the swelling in my face had abated. I was so happy to be released from the hospital I'd have agreed to almost anything. I was on the phone with Rachel before he left my room.

At Rachel's home, my biggest concern, apart from the multicolored bruises covering most of my face and the stitches on the back of my head, was Harvey, who insisted on sleeping on my lap. Shadow also joined us. Between the two of them, no way was I getting out of the recliner without help, much less overexerting myself.

"Why did you ever teach this big hunk she's a lapdog?" I peered at my friend over the dog's head.

"Teach? You think it was my idea? She figured it out for herself when she was a puppy. The only problem is when she was young, she was eight pounds and now she's more like eighty."

"Trust me, I'm fully aware." I stroked the dog's silky coat.

"What are you doing today? I mean, other than spending the day covered in animals."

"I'll probably fall asleep right here. These two are warm, and I'm still pretty tired. The doctor ordered me to rest, so I will. Will you take me to see Nicky after lunch?"

"Sure. Nicky's one lucky girl. A gunshot like that should have killed her immediately."

"The paramedics told me if they'd gotten to the shop two minutes later, she'd have died. She lost a lot of blood. What's amazing is the bullet missed the most important blood vessels and her heart."

I shifted my position, or at least I tried to. Harvey lifted her head and gave me a disapproving frown.

"Looks like you're eating lunch in the recliner," Rachel said.

"Which means I won't get any lunch." I tried moving again. "Help me up, and let's get something to eat."

Getting Harvey off my lap turned out to be no more difficult than offering her a treat. Shadow followed with his usual fear of missing out. Once we'd bribed the animals, Rachel heated some soup, and I put sandwich makings out.

"Have you heard from Grandma Natalie?" Rachel blew on her soup to cool it.

I shook my head. "No, and I'm starting to worry. Joe and Patrick both tried calling her, but she didn't answer, so they left voicemails. Even with everything that's happened, I can't imagine she'd stay away. I think they were going by the house to make sure she's okay, but I haven't heard if they did yet."

"Yeah, that doesn't sound like her at all."

After lunch, we arrived at the hospital and took the elevator up to Nicky's floor. When we rounded the corner, I instantly noticed the nearly empty hallway. The police officer wasn't there. The chair he'd used was gone, and in its place stood a housekeeper's cart filled with clean linens. At one end hung a bin lined with a plastic bag. Rumpled sheets spilled over the top.

I approached the door and peered inside.

A uniformed woman with dark hair was smoothing the bed, having apparently remade it. She looked up expectantly when I entered the room. "Can I help you?"

"Where is the patient who was here before?" I asked. "Nicky Fleming?"

"I don't know. She must have been discharged, or they wouldn't have told me to clean the room."

"Discharged?" Rachel and I looked at each other in disbelief. "She just had surgery. Why would she be discharged?"

"I don't know." She pointed down the hall. "Check at the nurse's station. They should be able to help you."

We went to the desk where a clerk and two nurses were conferring.

"Excuse me," I said. "We're here to visit Nicole Fleming, but she's not in her room. Do you know where she is?"

The nurse tapped on a nearby keyboard and consulted the results on the monitor. "She was discharged this morning."

"But she had surgery for a gunshot wound." I was incredulous. "How could she be discharged so soon?"

"You saw her yesterday, didn't you?" I nodded. "So you saw the police officer." She checked the paper again. "According to this, she was discharged to the care of law enforcement. Maybe they took her to another hospital? I'm sorry I can't be more helpful. We don't always have all the information."

We thanked her and turned away from the desk. I was totally flummoxed.

"Law enforcement?"

"You told me she has a police record," Rachel said. "Sounds as if there's something here we don't know about."

Given what I'd learned about Nicky since our first encounter at the coffee shop, I had to agree with Rachel. Since there was so much I hadn't known, it was entirely possible I still didn't have the full picture. Maybe I never would.

Chapter Twenty

This time, when Patrick and I pushed through the doors at the homicide division, I was greeted by name. In a matter of seconds, my mind flashed over the events that had led to the receptionist recognizing me on sight.

"Hi, Annie. You're looking much better."

"You saw the pictures?"

"I hope you don't mind. It's part of my job sometimes to file stuff, and sometimes I'm curious," she said with a smile. "I'll let her know you're here."

We'd scarcely settled into our chairs when Beth came to collect us. We followed her to the conference room. Detectives Winston and Grant were there, along with Detective Barbara Raymond from the Drugs and Vice Division, but I was surprised to see three unfamiliar faces. Two of them, a woman and a man sitting side by side, were serious in dark suits. The third was a pale woman in a light blue plaid shirtwaist dress and low heels, nervously clutching her purse in her lap. I could empathize.

"Annie, Patrick, good to see you. Annie, I see you're mending well." When we'd taken our seats, she continued. "You remember Detective Raymond."

"Yes," I said. "Good to see you."

"And you know Detectives Winston and Grant." They nodded their greetings, but didn't speak, which was fine with me. Beth extended her hand toward the woman and man, who gazed at me impassively. "Let me introduce you to Jennifer Barker and Christopher Jones. They are with the US Marshals Service."

I glanced at Patrick, trying not to show the alarm I felt. He shook his head slightly.

"And this," Beth held out her hand toward the last new person in the room, "is Amanda Tucker, Brittany's mother. She asked to speak with you, Annie." She turned toward the older woman. "Mrs. Tucker, why don't you go first?"

The pale woman stood and approached me, perching on the edge of the chair nearest me. She put her purse on the floor and took my hand in both of hers and gave me a faint smile.

"They told me you knew my daughter. That you tried to help her find her missing friend."

"Yes."

"They also told me you found her body."

"Yes, I did. I'm so sorry for your loss. She seemed like a nice person."

Mandy's mother relaxed slightly. "She was, but she was also troubled. That's why I wanted to talk with you, to help you understand her better. When she was on her medications, she was fine. She was happy and outgoing. But she didn't like taking them, so sometimes she'd stop without talking to her doctor or her therapist." She looked down for a moment. "Or telling me. I didn't know at first, but I guess she was off them again." She held my hand tightly and leaned forward, her nervousness replaced by a sense of urgency. "I wanted to make sure you know you did nothing wrong. She asked you to find Sandy Smith, didn't she?"

"Yes, how did you know?"

"She always did that when her meds wore off."

"But I couldn't find her."

"Because Sandy Smith never existed. She was Mandy's invisible friend when she was three or four years old, but when she was older and started having mental health problems, she became obsessed with finding her long-lost friend." She released my hand and patted me on the arm. "You were searching for a figment of my daughter's imagination, a ghost, if you will. The police told me she was stalking you and may have slashed your tires." She reached into her purse and took an envelope out. She offered it to me. "This is for the tires."

"What? No, you don't have to do that." Tears stung my eyes.

"Please, it's the least I can do."

She still held the envelope toward me, but I gently pushed it away. "Mrs. Tucker, you're so kind, but this isn't necessary. The fact is we don't know for sure if she cut my tires. We were having problems with someone else vandalizing our properties, so it may not have been Mandy at all. Please, you're very sweet and you obviously mean well, but I can't take your money."

She dropped the envelope back into her purse and smiled wanly. "I'm sorry for what she put you through." She pushed her chair back, collected her purse, and stood. "Thank you for trying to help her and for talking with me. You deserved to know the truth."

I rose to stand before her. "Again, I'm sorry for your loss. My dad died a year and a half ago, so I can empathize with you. I'm sure you'll always miss her."

Mandy's mother hugged me tight and whispered, "She's at peace now." She released me and turned to Beth. "Thank you." She left the room, leaving behind only the faintest whiff of perfume and a measure of peace of mind for me.

I settled back into my chair and met Patrick's eyes for a moment.

"She's a brave woman," he said.

Beth waited for a moment before speaking. "I'm glad you got to meet her."

"Thank you for arranging this. Whatever she may have done, Mandy—Brittany—didn't deserve to die. I hope her mother will be okay."

"I think she will. It can't have been easy having a child with mental illness."

I paused and took a deep breath. "And now I'd really like to know why there are marshals here."

"First, Detective Raymond has an update for you and Patrick."

Barbara Raymond sat up taller in her chair and tidied the two manila folders she had on the table before her.

"After our meeting, I tried several times to get in touch with Detective Nelson, who had worked on Nicole Fleming's case. He finally responded." She grinned. "I can be persistent, so I think I wore him down. Anyway, he remembered the case pretty well. He'd met Nicole several times and even arrested her once himself. He said he was saddened by her death, even went to her funeral. He thought she was fundamentally a good person who had made some poor choices."

"What was her involvement with drugs?" Patrick asked. "When she's spoken with Annie, she's claimed not to have been making meth, but otherwise, she hasn't been forthcoming. Was she using?"

"Originally, yes," Detective Raymond said. "She was taken in by her dealer, a man associated with a local gang, and she started making deliveries for them in exchange for a steady supply. That's how we became aware of her. Patrol officers stopped her for speeding several times. Had she stayed within the speed limit, she might never have been caught."

I said, "She loved driving fast."

"Her list of speeding tickets certainly attests to that. And she almost never paid them, so the guys on patrol definitely kept an eye out for her." She smiled briefly before turning serious again. "It all went sideways for her when she was making a delivery with two of the other gang members. They got into some kind of dispute, and one of them shot a competitor and killed him."

I couldn't keep quiet. "She witnessed a murder?"

"Yes, and when she freaked out, as anyone would, the guy who had killed the man threatened to do the same to Nicky and her family if she talked. I'll say this for her. She's made some very bad life choices, but she's a smart woman, and she knew she had to keep a level head if she wanted to survive."

"Wow." Part of me was appalled at how little I knew about my former girlfriend, but another part was impressed by her strength.

"Wow, indeed," Raymond said. "She stayed calm, went back to work with the gang, and made like everything was normal. They apparently kept a close eye on her until they thought she was back in line, and then she was out making solo deliveries again. That's when she called the bureau for help. Once Detective Nelson learned more about her situation and the extent of the gang's activities, he contacted the DEA."

"But you're not DEA agents." Patrick said to the marshals.

"We're getting to that," Raymond said. She turned to the agents. "Go ahead."

The man introduced as Christopher Jones leaned forward in his chair. Even though he opened a file folder, he didn't look at its contents.

"Mr. Wyatt, Miss Velasquez, Detectives, what I'm about to tell you must not leave this room. I've been authorized to disclose certain information to you. Of necessity, it is incomplete, but I understand why you need to know it. Do you agree to keep what I tell you confidential?"

I glanced at Patrick, and he gave me a warning shake of his head. "We can't agree without some idea of the subject matter of your disclosures. Can you give us a nonconfidential description? Some idea of what you're talking about?"

Marshal Jones conferred in low tones with the Marshal Barker, who was seated next to him.

"Yes, we can do that," Barker said. "I'm sure you realize this information concerns Nicole Fleming."

I couldn't help myself. "Do you know where she is? I went to see her at the hospital, and she had been discharged."

"Yes, we know where she is," Barker said. "But first, do you agree to keep the particulars confidential? Given what Detectives O'Brien and Raymond told us, it's only fair for us to give you this information."

Patrick and I exchanged glances, and he spoke for both of us. "Yes, we agree."

She handed us two sheets of paper. "Please sign these."

Patrick read through the confidentiality agreements and nodded his approval. We signed them, and she tucked them neatly into her briefcase.

Marshal Jones said, "Nicole Fleming is safe and sound and under medical care. We are not at liberty to tell you where she is."

"Is she under arrest?" Patrick asked.

"No. But rest assured she's quite safe and doing well. The surgeons here in Portland took excellent care of her, and we expect her to recover fully." He paused, thinking before meeting our eyes. "As Detective Raymond has said, federal agents became aware of Miss Fleming almost two years ago due to her involvement with a local gang. As the detective explained, her role was minor, making deliveries in small quantities. She also bought or stole the chemicals needed for meth production.

"Once she escaped, the Portland police called the DEA, but they were already aware of the gang she was with. They were making and selling a variety of drugs, mostly methamphetamine, but other drugs as well. The DEA had been monitoring the gang for some time because its members were known to be violent, and the gang had aspirations to expand into other territories."

"How did they know that?" Patrick asked.

"They were close-mouthed about it, but I suspect they have an agent in the gang or somehow closely related to it," Marshal Jones said. "I think that's how they learned about Miss Fleming, though, honestly, I'm speculating."

"Detective Raymond is right," Marshal Barker said. "Miss Fleming has made some terrible choices, but she's smart. Purely coincidentally, her escape from the gang and our involvement all happened about same the time as the fire at your dad's bike shop. We took her in immediately, and she's been in witness protection ever since. We will, of course, not tell you where."

"But she came back," I said.

Marshal Jones had a rueful expression on his face. "Yeah, she's smart, but she's also damn stubborn. I don't know how, but she learned her mom was ill, so she took off. Fact of the matter is, people under protection aren't prisoners. They can leave whenever they want, though it's seldom a good idea. If the gang sees her, they will want to silence her, but she was determined to see her mother. The rest you know."

"So now she's back with you?"

"Yes, and again, I won't tell you where. It's critically important you keep this to yourselves. They gang may be local, but make no mistake, they are hard core. Even what little you know could be dangerous to you if they get wind of it. I know you'll want to share this information with family and friends, but you must keep it confidential. I can't emphasize that enough."

"Will I see her again?"

His smile reappeared. "You shouldn't, but who knows?"

The marshals stood and collected their belongings. We shook hands, and after Patrick and I thanked them for the information and repeated our promises of confidentiality, they left.

I dropped back into my chair. "Holy shit. I never would have guessed." I turned to Beth. "Did you have any idea?"

"No, I was almost as shocked as you are." She went to a small refrigerator I hadn't noticed and brought us all bottles of water. When she'd resumed her seat, she said, "Two more matters and we're finished. First, I think it's obvious by now, but you're no longer a person of interest in the homicide of Nicole Fleming. She is definitely alive, despite what your mother tried to do. The case is closed."

Of course Patrick had to throw a wet towel on it. "What about the woman in the alleyway? The one who had Nicky's belongings with her?"

"That case is open, but we've found no evidence connecting Annie to it. We still haven't been able to identify her, but we're trying something new. I've gotten approval to contract with an expert in genetic genealogy. Maybe you've seen news articles where cold cases have been solved using it, so maybe we can learn who she was. She must have family and friends who miss her." She peered at me, concerned. "Annie, are you okay? Isn't this good news?"

I could finally take a breath. "Of course, it is. It's the best news. I've gotten so used to being under the microscope, I'm not sure how to feel."

I'd hoped it would happen, but hearing the words, getting it directly from the detective who'd been in charge of the investigation, was a relief I felt down to the atoms in my body. Even my subatomic particles were happier.

"Now for the less-cheerful news." She must have seen an alarmed look on my face. "Not *bad* for you, but we need to talk about it."

"Okay." I drew the word out, unsure of her meaning.

"Laura Lindberg is being held here in the jail. While you were in the hospital, she was arraigned on multiple charges, including kidnapping, arson, and two charges of attempted murder for what she did at the bike shop. She was charged with arson and murder for the original fire and your dad's death and also for the murder of Brittany Tucker." She sipped her water. "When we searched the apartment she rented, we found two more guns and a supply of ammunition. We also found several half-empty spray paint cans. Didn't you say your shop had been vandalized with spray paint a couple of times?"

I nodded. "It was before we got the security cameras up, so we couldn't prove who did it. And at that point, we thought Mandy Tucker was the most likely suspect."

"Did anything else happen at the property? I'm asking, because they found a weird assortment of what looked like carpenter tools in her apartment. If I remember right, there was a box of nails, two or three large tape measures, and some random metal pieces that looked as if they belonged to some kind of tool. Does that make sense to you?"

"It makes perfect sense. Our general contractor, Brad Baumeister, told us stuff had gone missing, and you just described it."

"Do you think he'd want to press charges?"

"We can ask him. He was pretty frustrated that he was losing things. He said the individual value was low, but the costs added up fast when he had to replace them. He's likely to want everything back."

"Well, now it makes sense," she said. "So at the arraignment, her request for bail was denied."

"Does she have an attorney?" Patrick asked.

"Yes, a public defender was appointed for her." At Patrick's expression, she continued. "Don't worry. I know him. He's an excellent lawyer. He's been with the public defender's office for many years. She'll get a solid defense. I'm not at all concerned about her avoiding conviction because of an overworked attorney or any kind of procedural mistake." She gave Patrick his name, which he jotted down.

I said, "I'm absolutely willing to testify."

"I'm sure her attorney will be in touch with you. If she's smart, she'll agree to a plea bargain, if she's offered one, and avoid going to trial. Even so, she's facing many years in prison, perhaps even for the rest of her life. And a trial with this array of charges is almost sure to draw the attention of local media. Since she's your mother, if there is a trial, the story will come out."

"It will? Does it have to?" I was dismayed at the idea of my life being publicized yet again.

"The judge and the jury, if there is a trial, will need context. There's no way to avoid revealing that the defendant was the wife of her first victim and is the mother of one of the current victims. They'll need to know the whole story, about your parents' marriage, why you never knew your mother, why she wasn't part of your life growing up, all of it. Your grandmother will also have to testify. Is she aware of what's happened?"

"I don't know. We've tried to reach her, but she's not answering our calls or emails."

"The story's already been in the local news, so maybe she's seen it and doesn't want to talk about it, or maybe she can't face it yet." She tapped her pen again. "There's more. Laura has been asking to see you."

"No." I was adamant. "Not happening. Seriously, what purpose could it possibly serve?"

"You don't have to talk with her if you don't want to."

"Which I don't."

"But if there's any chance at all she might say something we can use…" She left the rest unsaid. "Please think about it. That's all I'm asking. She's not going anywhere any time soon, so if you change your mind, let me know."

"I'll think about it, but don't expect a different answer."

"I understand. Okay, hold on." She turned to Detectives Winston and Grant. "Your turn."

Each of them spent a minute or two apologizing for putting the tracker on my car. I let them speak and thanked them. They left the room.

"That's it?" Patrick sounded skeptical.

"Not at all," Beth said. "They've both received written reprimands and demotions, including pay cuts and have been reassigned to misdemeanor cases. I can't divulge details, but your trouble with them is not the first time there have been issues. One more transgression, and their careers with the Portland Police Bureau are over."

"Good enough for me," I said. "I hope they had fun putting the tracker back together."

Beth laughed. "I heard it turned into a group project with four or five guys from another division. I still can't believe you took the damn thing apart."

"It wasn't easy, but it was worth every minute."

We shook hands all around and went to the door.

Beth asked, "What will you do now that you're a free woman?"

"I'm not sure, except for one very important thing I have to do today, taking Rachel's dog to the park. After that, who knows?"

"What do you want to do? Celebrate?" Patrick started his car, waiting for me to respond. "We could go get a beer if you want to."

"Let's go to Grandma Natalie's house first. There must be a reason she's ignoring our messages. She asked me so many times to talk. For her to go silent now is starting to worry me."

As Patrick drove, I pondered how to approach my grandmother. Joe had left messages for her, as had the rest of us, so she had to know her own daughter was in jail, that she'd attacked me and tried to kill Nicky.

A sudden thought struck me, and I grabbed Patrick's arm. "Drive faster. Maybe she's not answering because she can't, not because she doesn't want to."

"I'm an idiot." He sounded horrified. "Why didn't I think of that before?"

"All of us should have."

He stepped on the gas, and we sped along the streets, arriving at the house in record time.

I jumped out of his car before it had fully stopped and ran to the garage door. I used the keypad to open it, but with worry propelling me, I didn't wait for it to fully retract and ducked under it into the garage.

What I saw—or didn't see—stopped me in my tracks.

"What is it?" Patrick came into the garage once the door was fully open.

"Her Harley is gone. She's not here." Relieved, I blew out a breath. "At least we don't have to worry about finding her lying at the bottom of the stairs."

We went through the garage and into the house. All of the blinds were down, and the curtains were drawn. The air was musty. The air conditioning was off.

I went into the kitchen. The faint smell of spoiled food permeated the room. No way was I going to open the refrigerator until I had to.

We went up the stairs to her bedroom. Her suitcase was gone. Her closet was emptier than usual, and her dresser drawers had been emptied. Her toiletries were absent from the attached bathroom.

Patrick said, "The towels and shower are dry. It's been some time since she's been here."

"You should be a detective," I murmured, but my mind wasn't on my feeble attempt at a joke.

We went back down to the kitchen. I opened the windows and turned on the ceiling fan in the living room, trying to dispel the smell and get some fresh air into the house.

Patrick took his phone from his pocket. "I'll try calling her again. He pressed buttons on his phone, held it to his ear, and waited.

Our eyes met when the familiar sound of her phone's ring tone reached our ears. We followed the sound into the living room, with Patrick holding his phone carefully to keep the line open.

Then he shut it off.

Grandma Natalie's cell phone rested on the table where she'd arranged some family photos. She'd left it next to the only picture of my mother I'd ever seen, taken when I was a toddler.

"Why would she leave without her phone?"

Patrick reached down and picked up a piece of paper I hadn't noticed.

"Did she leave us a note?"

He didn't speak.

"What is it?"

He turned it so I could read it. It wasn't a note, at least not one she'd written, but it was a message.

It was a certificate, attesting to the marriage in the great state of Oregon between Natalie Lindberg and Edward Bailey.

"No, she wouldn't do that! Patrick, something's not right here."

He looked as stunned as I felt. "I agree, but it appears she packed a bag and left on her Harley." He sat on the couch and stared at me. "She is an adult, Annie. She can do whatever she wants. But you're right. It's definitely out of character."

"She's only known him for a couple of months. I can't see her doing this."

He shook his head. "Me, neither, but I doubt we can do anything about it." He scanned the room. "She didn't take all of her stuff, so she must be planning to come back. All we can do is wait."

Three days later, I stood in the parking lot of our bike shop with Rachel, admiring the little building as it glowed in the September sunlight. I most enjoyed the sight of people going into the shop and emerging carrying their purchases, or even better, wheeling a new bicycle. A brightly-colored banner proclaiming Velasquez Cycles to be open for business snapped in the breeze.

"I wondered if you'd ever get this far." Rachel stood next to me holding Harvey's leash.

"I did, too, a lot of times. But here we are, finally. It almost doesn't seem real."

"Hey, Annie," Joe called from inside the shop. "This young lady wants to test ride a bike. Will you help her? She's good to go."

The woman who came outside with a shining blue bicycle was at least my grandmother's age. "He's a clown, calling me a young lady."

"Trust me, I'm aware. He's my brother, so you can imagine what I have to put up with." I made sure her helmet was on correctly. Joe had adjusted the seat height for her. "Do you ride much?"

"I love to ride, but my bike is as old as I am. It's time to upgrade. Old Sadie will understand."

She took a spin around the edge of our parking lot and then went down the street. I watched for a few moments, but when I saw she was as skillful a rider as her comments had seemed to indicate, I went back to where Rachel was waiting.

"She's a better rider than I am," I said.

As the day wore on, the crowds didn't diminish, much to our delight. Joe had predicted we'd start off with a bang, but he told me not to expect that level of excitement to continue. Business would most likely decrease to a more normal level after we'd been open for a time. Still, it was gratifying to see how happy the people were about the shop being opened at last.

"Hi, Annie." I heard a familiar voice and turned to find the couple with the baby standing there. The N Plus One family.

"I was hoping we'd see you again," I said, shaking their hands. "Welcome to our grand opening."

"It's going gangbusters, isn't it?"

"Yeah, so far, so good. My brother is inside, if you want to talk about new bikes and a trailer for your baby. He's in a wheelchair with his leg in a cast, but it's not slowing him down a bit."

They waved and headed into the crowd.

Theirs weren't the only familiar faces I saw. Many of the people who had stopped by during construction came back when they saw the banner across the front of the store. I hadn't considered I was doing customer relations while I collected discarded plywood and used paint stirring sticks, but evidently I had.

Without warning, someone picked me up from behind and whirled me around. When I was back on my feet, I turned to find Carlos laughing at me. I gave him a playful slap on the shoulder.

"You scared me, you idiot," I said, and then I hugged him. "You've been taking lessons from Joe. At least you're not in uniform. You would have scared the rest of the customers away."

"Not a chance. Look at this. They love it."

"Joe's inside, regaling everyone with heroic tales of how he broke his leg."

"All entirely fictional, I imagine."

"You do know my brother."

Carlos gave me his trademark "adios" and went into the shop. Rachel nudged me with her elbow.

"You know they're not just friends, right?"

"Yeah, I've suspected for a while. I'm definitely going to talk with my jerk of a brother about keeping secrets from me." Despite my words, I was happy for him and Carlos. Joe deserved someone to love him.

As the day progressed, more of my friends and acquaintances joined the crowd. Sally got off her shift at the fire station in the midafternoon. Freddy and Mo drove in from Charbonneau with food, of course. More people I recognized from their visits to the construction site showed up. Brad and most of his crew also stopped by.

The more I was surrounded by friends and well-wishers, the more deeply I missed my grandmother. I loved how so many people had come out to see the new shop and I thoroughly enjoyed talking with all of them, but I felt a sense of loss, despite it all.

"She should be here." Rachel spoke quietly, evidently reading my mind.

"I know." I took a deep breath and let it out slowly. "But she's choosing to stay away. Maybe she's having the world's best honeymoon. At least I hope so."

As if sensing my lowered mood, Harvey jumped up and licked my face.

"Am I going to have to give you my dog?" Rachel loved to tease me about how much Harvey liked me.

"No. At least not until I move out." I smiled to let her know I was joking. "I'm thinking I should move back into Grandma Natalie's house. I can't impose on you forever."

"Do you want to be there when she comes back?"

"I don't know." We had so much to work through, so much damage to repair.

"Stay with me. It'll make Harvey happy."

I put an arm around her shoulder and squeezed. "Be careful what you ask for."

Over the next hour, I helped four more people take test rides. Two of them, including the woman Joe called "young lady," purchased the bikes they rode, and the other two promised to come back.

Later in the afternoon, the crowd thinned. I went inside, accompanied by my friends. We helped a few customers pick out helmets and shoes, and we sold several frame bottles emblazoned with the Velasquez Cycles name.

"Look at this." Joe handed me a sheet of paper. Almost every line was filled with the name and email address of a customer who wanted to attend maintenance classes. "See, I told you it was a good idea."

"And I always agreed with you. Just don't get used to it."

Minutes before closing, Joe called my name. "You have company." He pointed toward the door.

Beth O'Brien stood in the opening.

"Hey," I said. "Welcome to our little shop. We're finally up and running."

She looked around admiringly. "It's perfect."

I had to agree. The color scheme had earned us a few compliments. Even better, we'd sold several bicycles and heard from many people how happy they were that we were open.

"It was a long journey. But we finally did it."

"Your dad would have been proud."

"Would you like the nickel tour?"

"Sure."

The tour was overpriced at a nickel since it was possible to see almost the entire shop from the front door. Still, I wasn't one to pass up an opportunity to spend time with her. I showed her the checkout stand, salvaged from the original shop, and the snack bar, already in need of restocking. She learned more than she probably ever wanted to about helmets and pedals and inner tubes, but she asked questions and didn't seem at all impatient or bored.

I took her to the stockroom, stopping at the door. I still found it difficult to go inside.

"Was this where it happened?" Beth put her hand softly on my shoulder.

I nodded and swallowed. "Yes. I know it's silly, but when I come in here, I still see her pointing a gun at us, shooting Nicky, and being happy my dad is dead." I looked into her eyes. "She was dancing, she was so happy. How do I get past that?"

"I don't know. Counseling might help. Or…" she sounded reluctant to continue.

"Or what?"

"Testify. Do whatever you can to make sure she never walks the streets again."

"All I need to know is when and where."

We went back out into the main room of the shop. Joe was gently encouraging everyone to leave. Everyone except Carlos. He was staying.

"Time for us to close, folks," Joe said. "We'll open at ten tomorrow morning."

I walked outside with Beth. She unlocked her car door, but instead of opening it, she turned to me and took my hand. "There is one other thing you can do, you know, to move on with your life."

"Oh?" I hoped she couldn't feel my pulse or hear my heart pounding.

"Yes, it's the perfect antidote." She leaned in and kissed me lightly on the lips, just a fleeting touch. When she spoke, her voice was breathy. "You can let me take you to dinner."

The End.

To be continued in
Aftermath

Book Three of the
Annie Velasquez Mystery Series

In the three months since Annie and her brother, Joe, opened their bicycle shop, Annie's life has been more stressful than ever.

Grandma Natalie hasn't returned home after unexpectedly marrying a man she'd only known for a short time. The only communications Annie and Joe have received are a series of postcards purporting to show where the newlyweds have traveled.

In addition to Annie's long-lost mother being in jail, charged with multiple felonies, Annie's recent breakup with Beth O'Brien has broken her heart.

Deciding to pour her energy into looking for Grandma Natalie, Annie recruits Joe and her friends, and they go to work.

Aftermath follows Annie's efforts to navigate the maze of problems she faces and come out whole on the other side.

Acknowledgments

Heartfelt thanks to the ladies of the Portland Lesbian Writers Group for their enduring patience and encouragement while I took entirely too long to write Family Secrets. The Polliwogs are already urging me to write the third book in the series, so I will.

I want to thank Jane Cuthbertson, who read the first draft and told me exactly what she thought. And thanks also to Lori L. Lake, who tolerated the approximately three thousand questions I asked along the way with endless patience and more writing resources than any one person should have at her fingertips. The final product is much improved thanks to both of you.

Thanks also to Jesse Fairbank and Brice Stivers of River City Bicycles, Portland, Oregon, who generously answered my questions about the inner workings of a bicycle shop. If any of you are in Portland and interested in bicycles, be sure to visit River City Bicycles.

And finally, thank you to Jodi and Peggy Zeramby, new owners of Launch Point Press, for taking a chance on my writing. I may complain a lot, but I am grateful.

About the Author

E.J. Kindred is a retired Oregon attorney who is delighted to have substituted writing mysteries for writing contracts. She's always loved to write, and in her youth spent more hours than she'll admit writing "Star Trek" scripts and bad wild horse stories. *In Harm's Way* (2019) was her first published novel, though her short story "The Other Marie" appeared in *Time's Rainbow: Writing Ourselves Back into American History* (2017). The "other Marie" was Marie Equi, one of Oregon's first women doctors, a crusader for humane working conditions, an anti-war activist who spent time in San Quentin for sedition, and an unabashed lesbian at the turn of the 20th century. *Family Secrets* is the sequel to *In Harm's Way,* which again features intrepid sleuth Annie Velasquez and her indomitable Grandma Natalie.

When she's not writing, E.J. spends time with friends and takes care of her cats, who take care of her in return. In addition, E.J. loves old movies, jigsaw puzzles, and making quilts, some of which she donates to local cat rescue groups for fundraising. With the pandemic behind her, she plans to start traveling again, provided the cats agree.

Note to Readers

Thank you for reading a book from Launch Point Press. We have made every effort to edit this book. However, typos do slip in. If you find an error in the text, please email publisher@launchpointpress.com so the issue can be corrected.

We appreciate you as a reader and want to ensure you enjoy the reading process. We would like you to consider posting a review on your preferred media sites and/or your blog or website.

For more information on upcoming releases, author interviews, contests, giveaways and more, please sign up for our newsletter and visit us as at Launch Point Press: www.launchpointpress.com and "Like" us on Facebook: Launch Point Press.

Bright Blessings

www.ingramcontent.com/pod-product-compliance
Lightning Source LLC
Chambersburg PA
CBHW070520100726
47907CB00004B/920